FOUNTAIN OF FLAMES

VANESSA MILANO

This book is a work of fiction. Names, characters, places, and incidents are the product of the author's imagination or are used fictitiously. Any resemblance to actual locales, events, or persons, living or dead, is entirely coincidental.

Book design by Patricia Pria
Map by Chris Stanzione

To my best friend, Rachel, who asked me the question, "Have you ever thought of writing a book?"

PRONUNCIATION GUIDE

CHARACTERS

Echethier: Eh-cheh-thee-air

Nimreth: Nim-rehth

Kynra: Kin-ruh

Halline: Huhl-een

Allania: Uh-lawn-yuh

Nillipa: Nil-ih-puh

Euthemio: Yoo-thehm-yoh

Fenric: Fen-rick

PLACES

Grigaros: Grih-gar-ohs

Brittelia: Brih-tell-ee-uh

Iavothae: Ee-ay-voh-thay

OTHER

Breoslies: Bree-oh-slees

Ilaidae: Ill-uh-day

Xefta: Zehf-tuh

Solrac: Soul-rack

Luhaeva
Iavothae
Adayfian
Sea
Grigaros
Druharen
Sea
N
W
E
S

CHAPTER 1

It was only 9 am, and Lillian Echethier was already in a panicked frenzy.

Her generally nice and orderly little room looked like a pack of wild animals had decided to make it their home as she continued to rifle through it. Her room—consisting of only a broken dresser, a nightstand, and a bed that sat up against her window—was fairly small, allowing for any amount of mess to make it look cluttered. She had been rummaging through every inch of her room for some long minutes now resulting in numerous mounds of clothing to be littering the once empty floors.

Sighing in frustration, she checked her closet for what felt like the thousandth time, still unable to find what she was looking for.

On frantic feet, she bolted out of her room to find her mother, Halline, and younger sister, Nimreth, already in the kitchen preparing for lunch.

"Have either of you seen my brown boots?" Lillian yelled as

she began running through the kitchen, spiced meat drifting up her nose and floorboards creaking as she hurtled past. "I can't be late again, or they'll leave without me!"

Her mother was the first to respond to her outburst, halting her chopping of parsley as she placed two hands on her hips. "I really don't know why you must bother with such *beastly* activities. You really should be more inclined to helping out your sister and I."

Lillian rolled her eyes, already knowing where this conversation was heading. "As I've said *many* times, hunting is a perfectly respectable activity for any person to partake in, *mother*."

"I just wish you were a little more lady like is all," she said in a defeated sigh. "Your sisters Nimreth and Kynra don't feel the need to indulge in this *hunting*." She added emphasis on the last word as if merely saying it disgusted her.

"Well, you must already have your hands full with two such lovely daughters that I would just be taking up more of your precious time."

There might have been a glimmer of a snap to her tone, but Lillian had no time to spare for that ridiculous conversation and instead ran into her older sister Kynra's room, not waiting on her mother's response. "Aha!" she exclaimed as she saw her brown leather boots by the dresser.

Lillian's eyes rolled with annoyance. Her sister always had a tendency of borrowing her things coupled with a lack in ability to return them; but the roll of her eyes at the notion wasn't entirely justified seeing as Lillian much did the same to her.

Throwing on her shoes, laces flying as she haphazardly knotted each boot, she scurried out the door to find her brother and father setting up their gear.

"About time," groaned her older brother Maxith. "We were beginning to think you wouldn't show."

Lillian gave herself a minute to catch her breath before uttering a reply, the steadying of her breathing allowing just enough time to dredge up a rather unpleasant memory as she glared up at him. "I would hate for you to leave without me like *last time*."

Punctuality was never a strength of hers but such a dire punishment was unwarranted. She had shown up not even ten minutes late and they had left her to the mercy of her mother and her incessant prattling of how cooking was the most important skill a young lady could learn. She seethed, not having quite yet forgiven her father and brother for that offense.

Maxith stared at her, a smile curling on his lip from where he knew her mind went, and clapped his hands. "Well, don't just stand there. Get your stuff ready and let's head out."

Forcing herself to snap out of that bothersome memory, she sauntered over towards her favorite bow, her fingers working in schooled practice as she slung a quiver full of arrows across her back and strapped a dagger to her thigh. The obvious lack of weight on her hips caused her eyes to roam to a long blade propped up against her house—she much preferred a nice sword as opposed to a bow, but unsurprisingly deer never cared for her to get too close.

But as she continued to stare at the blade, Lillian found her hands fastening it to her side as she decided on bringing it along anyway. Extra protection was never unnecessary, especially with Grigaros' grave past. A chill slithered down her spine at just the thought. It hadn't happened in several years, but the wicked Ilaidae, the fabled deadly and magical creatures, had been known to drift past the borders, attacking and kidnapping anyone unfortunate enough to stumble upon their wretched path.

Pressure built behind her eyes as a throbbing pain pounded in her chest. Her heart ached a little as she remembered Peter, the boy who had stolen her heart so long ago.

But she shook that thought away faster than it had appeared. Now was not the time to delve into old memories. She needed a clear mind, or she would be a lousy shot, and she would never hear the end of it from Maxith if she had a shoddy aim.

A faint whistling and shuffling of feet jerked Lillian from her own musings, the subtle sounds the only indication her father had given that it was time to go. He had begun walking away and Lillian and her brother followed as they padded down the familiar path to their favored hunting grounds. They had a preferred general area, just barely into the woods, that always proved to be bountiful with deer—they never dared venture too deep into the forest, the potential consequences and fear of the creatures that prowled the grounds a more than sufficient deterrent.

Sounds of soothing nature accompanied them as they went, their pounding feet on the earth, the snapping of twigs, and peaceful chitterings of birds a break from the world happening around them. On occasion, they'd walk the long wooden path in silence, the three of them content with the mesmerizing forest song, but today didn't seem to be one of those days.

They continued on their trek, the squabbling of her and Maxith's mutterings breaking the tranquil atmosphere. Her father, however, despite their chatter, never elected to speak, always claiming he needed to be quiet to still his mind, thus leading to the usual dynamic of Lillian and Maxith bickering back and forth on who the better shot was. She could admit that Maxith had always been more skilled with the bow, but when it came to swordplay, Lillian knew she would always have her brother beat—she was no master yet but knew enough to not be completely helpless.

But their never ending argument came to a pause as her father came to a sudden halt. His eyes narrowed as he took in their surroundings, the nod of his head concluding that this would be the day's favorable site.

Lillian couldn't help but copy his motions, mimic where his gaze had landed. She was starting to understand the importance of picking the right location. Her father had selected an area dense with trees that possessed a small stream running through it where the deer and other creatures liked to indulge in fresh water—a location typically bountiful with prey when it came to a hunt.

On most days when they settled into their spot, Lillian liked to take a moment to assess the area and reaquaint herself with the weapon slung across her back, but her attention was dragged elsewhere as Maxith began whispering in her ear. "I bet I'll get a rabbit before you do," he boasted.

A wide grin surfaced on her face at his bold claim. "You can keep your rabbit. I'm going for that deer."

Maxith whipped his head to where she stared and saw the beautiful deer drinking from the stream, unaware of the hunters surrounding her.

Lillian pulled her coppery hair into a bun, not needing her thick strands obstructing her line of sight. Picking up her bow, she eased an arrow from her quiver, making sure her mind was still as she drew back the string and lined up the shot.

Its spotted neck craned downwards as the pink tongue peeking from its mouth lapped up the slow flowing stream. There would be one shot, Lillian decided as she noticed the muscles lining the doe's body twitching as if anticipating the need to bolt. If she missed, the creature would be long gone before she even moved an inch to pull another arrow from her quiver.

Fingers aching, she held the shot firm, Lillian determined to make the first one count. The delicate deer in the distance had her full attention, her hand seconds from releasing the taut string, but her focus was interrupted as she felt a warm breath creep up her ear.

"Make sure you aim right above the shoulder, so you get the heart or the lung," uttered her brother.

A rather obvious statement, one she had learned many months ago. She ignored Maxith's comment, already having known that and not in any need of a refresher.

Narrowing her gaze back into concentration, Lillian turned back to the doe but immediately rolled her eyes as she heard his irritating voice pester her once more.

"Don't forget to *really* line up the shot and draw back or your arrow won't go far enough."

Annoyed, she replied, "*I know.*"

Doing her best to ignore him, she refocused on the deer. But when her fingers at last loosened on the string, eager to take the shot, he interrupted her once more. "Now you want to make sure your elbow—"

"ENOUGH!" Lillian yelled as she released the string.

The arrow sailed past the deer's head, piercing a nearby tree instead and causing the frantic animal to dart into the woods.

"Now look what you made me do!"

"Me? I was just trying to give you some more pointers!"

Her father's pronounced voice ceased their arguing. "Enough, children," he bellowed. Both Lillian and Maxith turned to face him in silence. "There is no need for yelling over a deer. There will be plenty more along in a bit."

Lillian pinned her brother with a glare as she addressed the both of them. "Well, we wouldn't *need* to be arguing if he had simply shut up and let me be."

"Ah, well, when has your brother been one to keep that mouth of his shut?"

Maxith feigned offense as he spoke in a shriller voice. "Hey! I'm not that bad."

Both Lillian and her father couldn't help but burst into laughter as they took in his ridiculous statement. A world where Maxith was quiet simply did not exist.

"Okay, sure Max, you keep telling yourself that," she said, her chuckles echoing in the grand forest as she finally went back to the hunt.

Lillian's arms felt unbearably sore as she slid her bow across her back. Many hours had passed from the time they had gotten there to when they had finally decided to leave. Darkness had begun descending upon them, the setting sun nature's cue that it was time to return home.

In her eyes, today was a most successful hunt as she had managed to capture a deer and three rabbits; she smiled to herself in secret, pleased that Maxith had gotten significantly less. He had told Lillian not to brag too much, claiming that she had missed far too many easy shots—but Lillian knew her brother well enough to know he was just a sore loser and couldn't *stand* that his younger sister had bested him.

It was a struggle to contain her grin as they made their way back, but after a brisk walk, the constant need to stifle her chuckles a challenge when Maxith caught a glimpse of her glee, their little cottage came into view right as the sun began to inch beneath the horizon.

Lillian always loved this time of day, watching the sun set every night as it cast the skies in beautiful arrays of oranges and purples and magentas. She envied artists who could somehow masterfully capture the numerous hues that painted the horizons, forever able to gaze upon the view whenever they wished—that, however, never stopped her from admiring the enchanting sight. But Lillian woefully didn't get a chance to as her father ushered her through the door.

"We're home," he bellowed as they waltzed past the threshold.

Her mother dashed to the front door and greeted her father with a kiss, a custom whenever they arrived home. "Get anything good today?" she asked, a smile parting on her lips.

"It was alright," he answered. "We didn't get as much as I had hoped but enough to fill our bellies for a little while."

There was a gleam in her mother's eye as she turned her attention to Maxith. "And how did my darling young man do? One day you'll best your father in the amount you get us!"

Her father let out a low titter at the statement. "Well first, he's going to have to best Lillian over there before he can best me."

Lillian tried—she really did—but horribly failed at hiding the wide grin emerging on her face as Maxith glared daggers at her.

"She cheated," he barked as he continued to complain. "She *clearly* saw that I was aiming for the same deer but took the shot anyway."

"You were taking *forever,"* Lillian groaned. "The deer would've run off by the time you finally decided to take your shot."

Their father chuckled louder at their bickering but steered away from the conversation. A wise decision if he wished to avoid it turning into a screaming match. "Anyway, what did my lovely wife make us for dinner tonight?"

Her mother, clearly displeased with the previous interaction, wasted no time in allowing for the subject to change. "Nimreth and I made you all a delicious rabbit stew." Her nose scrunched as she noticed the dirt and grime that glazed them. "Now go and clean up so we can all sit down."

Lillian did *not* need to be told twice to walk away from that conversation. She was positive she would get an earful whenever she and her mother were alone again.

But hoping that wouldn't be anytime soon, Lillian dashed into the bathing chamber and stripped herself of the filthy clothes coating her body. She kept her copper hair up in a bun as she stepped into the tub her mother had prepared and submerged herself into the hot water.

A moan escaped her lips as the heat spread all over her body, goose bumps flecking her skin in its wake. There was nothing she wanted more than to stay in the warmth all night, the deliciously heated water easing the aches on her already sore muscles. Her mother, however, would not be pleased if she went hunting *and* skipped out on dinner as well.

A loud groan tumbled out of her as she finished washing and grabbed a towel to dry off as she stood. Lillian walked across the floor with careful steps as she made her way towards her pile of clothes—somehow turning the bathroom floor into a pool of water in the process—and threw on her clean clothes. Before leaving, she tried to soak up the flooded bathroom with her towel, not needing to give her mother any more ammunition to yell at her about. Lillian did more than enough for herself on that front.

The floor not as sopping wet, she exited the bathroom and found her way into the busy kitchen.

The Echethier house was no lavish castle, but it was the perfect fit for them. The house was large enough that it had rooms for each of them and also had one big open area in the center of the home. The room consisted of a decently sized kitchen, with just enough space for a table, and a little lounging area near a big fireplace.

Her brother was throwing another log onto the fire as she walked by, the embers crackling as if chirping in pleasure from being fed. Even though spring had finally graced them, a fire was still a necessity as the nights grew rather cold in Grigaros this time of year.

A sudden ravenous feeling overwhelmed her as the savory smell of roasted meat made it to her nose, and she rushed to the stove, inhaling more of the divine scent. Everyone was already sitting down and waiting as she poured herself some of the freshly made stew. A usual occurrence that she was the last to arrive.

Lillian's tongue swiped over her lips as she finished shoving a spoonful down her throat, her belly moaning with content as she consumed more of the delicious broth and sat down.

Her mother was a true talent in the kitchen, a useful trait that her younger sister, Nimreth, had inherited as well. But Lillian, to her despair, had not been so fortunate, and it was not for lack of trying.

She winced as she painfully recalled the dreadful occasion when she had tried her skills out in the kitchen. It was a wonder that she hadn't noticed or even had the faintest inkling that she had burned absolutely everything. Her family had tried to play it off to not hurt her feelings, actually possessing the immense courage to consume the wretched food, but it was Maxith, who could no longer bear taking another bite, who broke the news to her and cried out that it was atrocious.

A smile danced upon her face at the fond memory while she sat back eating her food, her mother and sisters recounting what they had done that day. She tried not to show too much relief on her face as she listened to their boring day of cooking and cleaning. But she *was* glad, however, that the conversation hadn't steered to her recent *un-lady like* actions.

As if willing it into existence, her mother's attention had then all at once fixed itself onto her as she had perhaps spoken too soon. Lillian tried avoiding her gaze, her eyes fixing on a truly fascinating crack on the table, as she presumed that she was about to get an extensive lecture on how she's been wasting her time with such horrid activities.

But right as her mother opened her mouth, her older sister, Kynra, began to speak of her upcoming nuptials to the blacksmith's son.

A gift from the gods. She'd have to thank her sister later for saving her from their mother's perpetual scolding.

The minutes then passed swiftly and after what felt like the *longest* discussion of her sister's marriage, Lillian excused herself from the table and went on to her room, finally turning in for the night.

Shutting the door behind her, she lit the candle at her bedside table and eased towards her closet, changing out of her regular clothes into a loose cotton shirt.

Lillian sighed as she slumped onto the bed and stared out into the dark empty space of her room. Her breaths came in slow and even, her thoughts picking apart what the day had brought and what the others would soon bring.

Another sigh. What she *wished* they would bring.

If she closed her eyes, she could almost imagine her life being something else.

It's not that she loathed the current life she was leading—she adored her family, no matter how infuriating they could be at times. She just felt as if there were something missing, as if there were a part of her that she could feel was out of place. Lillian didn't know what she wanted out of life, but she knew that what she had was not enough.

Her throat bobbed as she took in a slow breath—perhaps long ago it would have been. The control over her thoughts was lost as they drifted to a few years back, back to that boy who had made her heart skip a beat every time she saw him.

Peter.

He would have been enough. Maybe the emptiness she felt in her heart was the aching hole he had left.

Her mother's comments came flooding back to her of how she wasn't a traditional lady and that no man would want someone as boorish as her.

"Peter would have," she whispered.

Never *once* would Peter have dared to say she was anything other than absolutely perfect. She remembered the times that he would encourage her *questionable* interests and even taught her how to hold her own in a fight. She was never nearly as good as him—Peter being the son of a trained guard and having been sparring as soon as he could take a single step—but that never stopped him from teaching her.

So what started off as an innocent friendship between mere children blossomed into something more, and, as time went on, she eventually gave her heart and all of herself to him.

Sobs broke out of her as she tortured herself with the memories of him. She couldn't bear to recall the day that she lost him and willed herself to think of anything else.

Sniffling, Lillian forced her thoughts away from Peter and tried to ponder on her present life. There was no use in dwelling on the past when there was nothing she could change. Moving forward was the only option and that's what she would do—she knew that's what Peter would have wanted.

Lillian continued on with her previous musings, desperately needing to fill her head with something else.

Sighs escaped her at her current predicament. She loved her family and Grigaros was all she had known growing up, but she couldn't help to think that there was so much more out there—something that beckoned her forth. She had heard tales of places and cities past the forest and trees. A magical land known as Iavothae.

"Iavothae," she said out loud into the darkness. The wind howled and branches banged against her window as if simply speaking its name altered something in the atmosphere.

All she had gathered of that realm was that it held nothing but terror and death. The Ilaidae—who possessed untold powers—were known to live out there, and anyone who dared venture forth rarely ever made it back.

Lillian knew she would never be so bold as to go there, but she couldn't help but be curious as to what lay beyond those dreary woods—and after all, there was no harm in just using her imagination.

More than likely, she would either give into her mother's demands or be brave enough to travel the human world.

How she would do it? She hadn't the faintest clue. But Lillian couldn't bear the thought of never experiencing what the rest of the world had to offer. There was something out there for her, waiting; she could feel it. The truth in that vibrated her bones.

"No," Lillian declared to the room, a sudden sense of urgency possessing her. Not now and not ever would she give up. She would find that something, would spend her whole life searching for that piece her soul sung too.

The candle at her bedside flickered wildly as wind blew in from her cracked window, the raging breeze a sign that the world stirred at what she was about to declare.

That night she decided to make a promise to herself: Lillian Echethier would not settle for anything less than what she deserved. And Lillian knew that she did *not* deserve a life of being the meek little housewife that her mother *oh so* wanted her to be.

Lillian's head swirled with thoughts of the future until it was enough to drive her insane. There would be enough time to lay out her plans some other day, she decided. Right now, she was exhausted and getting a good night's sleep for the upcoming day was her current concern.

A faint smile curled on her lips as she blew out her candle, darkness flooding the room in the flame's absence.

The future was hers.

CHAPTER 2

"Lillian!" she heard her mother's distant yell from the kitchen.

Lillian groaned in annoyance. The sun had barely risen, and her mother was already calling her name. Maybe if she pretended that she hadn't heard her, she would leave her be and let her sleep in for a few more hours.

"Lillian!" her mother continued yelling. "You better not be ignoring me! That won't work on me anymore!"

Turning, she grumbled into her pillow. It was useless. Her mother knew her all too well as Lillian had always dreaded the thought of getting out of bed.

"What?" she yelled back.

No response from her mother.

"What!" she yelled louder, but still with no response from her mother.

Defeated and aggravated, Lillian shot out of bed and stormed into the kitchen. She knew her mother could hear her perfectly well but refused to respond in order to get her up and out of bed.

There was no winning at this game between the two of them. If she ignored her mother, Lillian would be in trouble, but if she responded and her mother did not answer, Lillian would still, again, be in trouble for not going out to find out what she wanted. It was a cruel trick she always played, and all the woman would do was feign innocence in that she hadn't heard her.

But Lillian knew that was such a lie. Anytime Maxith would try and sneak away in the middle of the night, their mother would somehow conveniently catch him even though her room was all the way across the cottage. Lillian thought that was rather suspicious but knew her mother would just deny it and blame it on her old age if she were ever to be questioned.

She found the devious individual humming to herself as she polished a glass. The cup already looked glossed and shiny but that didn't seem to matter to Halline who would not stop until it resembled a glittering star.

Glaring, Lillian said, "How could I *possibly* be of service to you, mother?"

Her mother turned to look at her, a brow raised in distaste. "Is that sarcasm I'm getting from you, Lillian Echethier?"

"Of course not, I'm positively *thrilled* to be up at this ungodly hour, eager to help you in whatever it is you need."

Voice turning a degree harsher, she gestured to the stool next to her. "Come sit, my darling. I want us to have a little chat."

Lillian's eyes widened as her brows shot upwards. "Are you

serious? You woke me up to have a *chat?*"

Irritation dripped off of her. "I ignored your tone the first time but that's twice now that you have addressed me with an attitude. I don't recommend a third. Now don't make me ask you again, Lillian. *Sit.*"

Grumbling, Lillian dragged herself over to the stool and, in an effort to keep things civil, used her calmest tone as she asked, "What would you like to discuss?"

Her mother ironed out the wrinkles in her apron as she settled down beside her. "As you may know, your sister has her marriage to that wonderful young man coming up and I couldn't help but think of you."

Oh gods, Lillian thought to herself. This was way worse than she had anticipated. She had believed this conversation was going to be about her mother's strong distaste of her preferred hobbies not about *marriage*.

Not noticing Lillian's dread to what her mother had casually laid out, she continued. "I know how you love to partake in those *interesting* pastimes of yours and that no ordinary man would put up with such things. However, I have marvelous news! I have found you a match!"

Nausea threatened to overtake her. She knew that her mother had planned on trying to marry her off eventually but thought she would have at *least* until after her sister's upcoming day. "What? Who?"

"Well, I know it's not your *ideal* choice, but you will just have to make do. Mr. Havernish has seemed to have taken an interest in you."

Now Lillian was sure she was going to ruin the kitchen's floor. "Mr. Havernish? The very *same* Mr. Havernish who used to take care of me when I was a child? The man who is more than *twice* my age!"

Her mother took a long pause before replying. "Yes, it is the same Mr. Havernish. But don't phrase it like that, Lillian. It's not the worst of situations, and you always claimed to have been so fond of him in the past."

"Yeah, when he would sneak me dessert when it was well past my bedtime—when I was *six.*"

Her mother let out a sigh. "Why must you make everything so hard, Lillian. I'm just trying to do what's best for you."

Footsteps made their way into the kitchen, and a familiar voice began to speak out. "I'm not interrupting anything important, am I?" uttered Kynra.

"No, not at all, darling. Your sister and I were just having a nice conversation about her potential suitors," replied her mother, the sentence sounding harmless and not like it made Lillian want to gouge her own eyes out.

"Well, by the look on Lily's face, I take that it's going *splendid*"

She waved a dismissive hand. "You know your sister. She's just a little difficult when it comes to this matter."

Kynra let out a soft chuckle. "Oh, please, mother, there is no need to bother her with this issue now. Lily will let us know when she's ready. You can busy your time with Nimreth in the meanwhile. I'm sure she would be more than thrilled for you to find her a willing suitor."

Their mother took a minute to think on what her sister proposed, a sigh huffing out of her as she surrendered. "I suppose you might be right. There's no sense in trying to tame a feral beast when you could play with a gentle rabbit."

It was impossible to hide her face of relief as she looked at her sister—she would have to remember to buy Kynra the most expensive wedding gift she could find for saving her yet again from that meddling.

Her mother stood and placed a few more dishes into the cupboard, the woman acting like she hadn't just insinuated the most preposterous idea to ever cross her mind, and retired into her bed chamber, leaving Lillian and Kynra alone in the kitchen.

"I can't thank you *nearly* enough for saving me from that mess."

Her sister laughed. "You know she means well. She's just worried that you're going to end up an old, miserable spinster."

"I'd *much* rather be a miserable spinster as opposed to being *Mrs. Havernish.*" Lillian shivered, barely able to get those words out of her mouth. She couldn't believe her mother thought for even a *second* that Mr. Havernish was a good match.

"Yes, I can agree with you on that. A marriage to Mr. Havernish does not seem... ideal. It was not one of our mother's finer ideas." Kynra's face suddenly switched to one that resembled excitement. "But let's not think on that right now—hurry up and get dressed."

"What for?" Lillian asked, intrigued at the abrupt shift in mood.

"There is still *so* much to do before the wedding and time seems to be catching up too fast."

The intrigue died in an instant, dread blossoming in its place. Her brain rifled for an excuse but came up with nothing, leaving her instead with the truth. "I truly wish I could help, but I do have imminent plans with my pillow that I really must attend to first."

"Don't be like that, Lily. It'll be fun, and I *really* need your help. I seem to be a little bit in over my head with all these last-minute details."

Spending all day planning her sister's wedding was not something she wanted to do, but, unfortunately for her, that would make her a very poor sibling if she abandoned Kynra when she was clearly stressed. And who could forget that fixing her family's problems was always Lillian's designated task.

"Ugh, fine," she groaned in defeat. "I guess I'll help. Just let me change, and I'll be right back."

"And make sure you do something about that hair as well," Kynra called out. "It looks like you were on the losing end of a battle with a rabid fox."

Lillian stuck her tongue out at her sister as she retreated into her chambers, nose scrunching as she stood before her mirror, Lillian realizing her sister's description of her locks was unfortunately accurate. Unwilling to brush through the knotty mess, she threw it up and decided to sport her usual attire consisting of a white tunic, with a brown leather corset fastened over it, and black pants. Ready, she waltzed back out into the kitchen, prepared to do whatever wedding task was delegated to her.

"Alright, what's first on the list?" she sighed.

Kynra scanned a piece of parchment as she fiddled with a strand of hair. "I've gotten most of everything finished but I still need help with the flower arrangements and picking out my gown."

Her eyes widened with shock. "You waited until weeks before the wedding to pick out a gown? That seems rather last-minute of you, Kyn."

"Well, I have it picked out," she whined in frustration. "But I've been haggling back and forth for over a month now with the seller." Kynra's nostril's flared, that short temper of hers seeping out. "But whenever I agree on a price and go to fetch the money, he raises it to something absurd. I was hoping you could come with me and maybe *persuade* him a little bit."

She smirked at her sister's request. It was no surprise to Lillian that her sister had asked her to try and sway the seller's price. Their father was far too calm to haggle with any buyer and everyone knew Maxith was the least intimidating man around—the seller would likely raise the price even more if the fool showed up.

"I see," she drawled with genuine glee. "This day might turn out to be fun after all."

Kynra let a big smile form at those words. "I told you today wouldn't be dreadful! I know how much you love making people un-comfortable." A determined look took over her face as she slung a cloak around her shoulders. "Now let's start walking over; I want to be the first one at the store when it opens."

Putting on her shoes, she slipped her favorite dagger into her boot—it never hurt to be prepared for anything unexpected—and Lillian and her sister journeyed on to the boutique.

The shop wasn't anything extravagant, but it had some nice gowns for special occasions and was the only place near them that had finer clothes for weddings and such events.

A bell sounded as they walked through the door, the gentle chime letting the owner know they'd arrived.

Fabrics of all shapes and colors were the first things that greeted her followed by the golden rimmed mirrors adorning the long walls. Varian's Variety. An unimpressive shop for what they claimed to be.

The store was just one large room with rows of clothes lining the walls and a curtained off dressing room in the back. The whole place was painted a stark white and had an emerald velvet couch in the middle to make the shop seem more elegant than it truly was.

A man who appeared to be in his mid-forties walked out from behind a desk and darted straight for Kynra, the fragrance he wore resembling that of a bonfire and causing Lillian to choke as he passed. "There's the lovely bride to be!" he beamed. "Come to finally buy that gorgeous dress you've been eyeing for some time now?"

"Good morning, Mr. Varian," Kynra delivered with forced lightness. "You know I've been wanting to buy that dress, but it's the price I'm not quite too keen on."

The man put on the most insincere frown she had ever seen. "Oh, how I hate to price the dress as such, but I can't afford to lower it. It would be an offense to the fine silks and time it took to make the exquisite gown. I'm afraid I will not budge on the set price." He released a lousy sigh, the sound as authentic as the silks he liked to boast. "You understand, don't you, Ms. Echethier?"

Lillian's lips pinched into a tight line. She didn't like the condescending way this man seemed to be talking as if understanding how running a business was too great a feat.

"Oh, please, Mr. Varian, that's just ridiculous," Lillian interjected chuckling. "How many times have you used that line on poor unsuspecting customers?"

Mr. Varian turned his attention to Lillian for the first time since entering, a sneer flashing for half a second before returning to that saccharine smile he kept plastered on. "And you must be the lovely Lillian. I haven't had the pleasure of meeting you but have heard such wonderful things!"

It was an effort to rein in her snort. She delighted in how business owners couldn't speak their minds in fear of offending their customers. Lillian knew that not a single soul would describe her demeanor as wonderful or lovely, but Mr. Varian had to, despite what he actually felt.

"I'm sure you've heard *many* great things about me. I, however, can't seem to say the same of you."

Mr. Varian blinked, looking offended and confused at her comment. "I beg your pardon, miss. Whatever do you mean?"

"Oh, nothing too serious," she crooned as she ran her fingers over one of the gowns he had hung up, her face looking utterly unimpressed at the quality as she moved on to another. "It's just that I've heard a few things here and there regarding the *exquisite* gowns you sell. Especially concerning those fine silks you go on and on about."

His mannerisms seemed to switch in the slightest as he cleared his throat. "Wh—what about the silks we use?"

Lillian could tell she had hit her mark. She wasn't the best at reading people, but it was rather easy to tell that he had grown increasingly nervous; Mr. Varian had the smallest bead of sweat on his temple and cleared his throat far too often to be coincidental.

"I know you claim to use the finest silks imported all the way from lands across the sea, but we both know that's obviously a lie, don't we, Mr. Varian?" Her nose wrinkled in distaste as she moved on from a satin shift, Lillian enjoying herself far too much. "But luckily for you, my sister and I tend to be *very* forgetful young ladies. In fact, I'm almost positive once we leave with that gown, this little conversation will have slipped our minds."

Mr. Varian bit his lip as he narrowed his eyes. Lillian knew she had struck true with the silks, but he still seemed to be hesitant. Perhaps a smidgen more of encouragment was needed. And Lillian was more than happy to comply.

"But who knows," she continued on, her tone sweet as she sifted through more dresses. "If we happen to leave empty handed, I could see my sister and I stopping by the market. Oh, how chatty we get while perusing the wares."

The set jaw of his was enough to force Lillian to subdue her grin. "Very well, *Ms. Echethier*," he hissed through clenched teeth. "You drive a hard bargain, but the dress is yours."

Kynra could hardly contain her squeals of excitement as she handed Mr. Varian the money for the gown.

With the dress freshly in hand, they began walking out of the store, Lillian unable to help herself as the words flowed out of her mouth. "Have a splendid rest of your day, Mr. Varian. It was *exquisite* meeting you."

The second they stepped out of the boutique, Kynra threw her arms around her while letting out the loudest shriek. "That was incredible, Lily! Thank you so much—you truly are the most magnificent sister ever! How did you even know about the silks?"

"Funny enough, I had no idea that he had lied about them. Once he brought them up, I just went off that, and he seemed to get a *tiny* bit nervous."

Kynra shook her head and grinned. "You certainly are the most devious woman I've ever met. Now let's hurry home lest he change his mind and come chasing us down."

They both rushed home, laughing the whole way as they recalled Mr. Varian's face of disdain, and Lillian was out of breath by the time they made it to the door. Kynra, however, didn't seemed to be fazed as she barreled straight inside, bursting with joy to show off her new gown.

Not one to waste a gifted opportunity, Lillian snuck into her room, collapsing onto the bed instantly. It was obvious that she was exhausted because simply the act of laying on the soft mattress was lulling her to sleep.

A yawn trickled from her mouth as she curled onto her side.

Surely her sister could pick out the flowers on her own or employ the help of Nimreth. A little nap was all she needed before running around town searching for the perfect bouquet.

Or at least that's what she told herself as her eyes fluttered shut and she began drifting off into a quiet slumber.

A rapping at her door jolted her awake.

Slowly, she cracked open her lids, widening them as she realized that it was completely dark. Had she really slept all the way into the night?

There was another knock at the door accompanied by Nimreth's soft voice alerting her that dinner was ready.

Lillian jumped out of bed, still clad in the same clothes she wore out earlier, and dashed into the kitchen.

Maxith was the first to look at her. "There she is. What a vision she always is when first awakening."

Not having the energy to respond, she gave him a vulgar gesture with her hand. Maxith always thought he was rather humorous and as his sister it was her sworn duty to remind him he most certainly was not.

The lovely action ushered a chuckle from him as he motioned for her to sit next to him.

Lillian dragged her groggy limbs over just as their father finished cutting up the deer being served for dinner. Roasted venison never dissapointed and Lillian shoved a mouthful down her throat the second a plate was set in front of her.

Only half awake as they ate, she chewed, content with being silent, but her mother's statement woke her up lightning fast.

"I heard you had an eventful day at Mr. Varian's shop earlier today," she commented.

Her thoughts shifted to earlier and how in *some* people's eyes it could have been construed that she had blackmailed the owner. There was no way Kynra would've told on her, especially after helping her get the dress, so she had to assume this truly was innocent.

"Indeed, we did. I got to practice my haggling skills on Mr. Varian himself," she said as she swallowed another chunk of meat.

Her mother looked impressed with her statement. "You *must* teach me your ways, Lillian. Anytime I try and get a dress's price lowered the man becomes insufferable."

Lillian chuckled, coughing quickly to mask the amusement. Her mother would undoubtedly never utilize the *particular* skills she had used on Mr. Varian earlier that day, but she had to say something, or she would start to suspect that she hadn't been a proper lady. And to not be a proper lady would be entirely too absurd.

"It was nothing special really," she began. "I can— "

The words came to a crashing halt on her tongue as a piercing scream interrupted her sentence.

All their attention turned to more shrieks from outside as a voice rang out in the night. "They took him!"

CHAPTER
3

T*he screams wouldn't stop rolling off her lips as Lillian stared at the horrifying creature.*

"Get that slimy thing away from me!" she shrieked.

"Oh, come on, Lil—It's just a little frog," chuckled Peter.

"Then it can be 'just a little frog' over there—far away from me. Look at it. It's all green and slippery and disgusting. How can you stand to even pick it up?"

Peter tried to walk closer to her, but she backed away. "You are not *allowed near me with that grotesque thing."*

Lillian didn't know why she hated frogs so much; there was just something about them that didn't sit well with her. They were always secreting mucus, and they could breathe on land and *in the water—that just didn't seem natural.*

"Fine, fine. Stop your screeching. I'll put him down." He walked over to the edge of the forest and looked back at her, a mocking

curl parting his face. "Is this far enough to your liking, my lady?"

Satisfied with the distance between her and that wretched creature, she nodded her head, giving the okay to put the beast down.

Peter let the frog hop out of his hands and sauntered back to her, sniggering. "Of all the things to hate, you chose that tiny little thing to get you all worked up?"

She could tell Peter was teasing her. "Don't act all levelheaded and mature now. I seem to recall a certain someone flailing and running away from a chicken not too long ago."

He swapped his grin for a stern expression. "That's different. Chickens are vicious creatures that will sink their little claws into you and peck you to death." He shuddered. "I'm convinced those things don't have souls."

Lillian couldn't help but huff out a laugh; picturing Peter running from a chicken always put the biggest of smiles on her face.

But those humorous thoughts became interrupted as Peter grasped her by the hand and led her over to an area hidden behind a rock. "Now I know you told me you didn't want anything and that you hate people acknowledging it's your birthday, but I just couldn't help myself."

Laid out in the grass was the most thoughtful thing anyone had ever done for her. Peter had set up a wool blanket over the soft blades and lit dozens of candles all around them, the flickering lights like dozens of fireflies. A wicker basket sat in the center, a bottle of wine and flowers sticking out from its top.

Her eyes had started to gloss and fill with tears at what she beheld. And they only welled up more as Peter came up, hugging her from behind, and whispered in her ear. "Don't you even think for a second that you don't deserve this. I know how that mind of yours works."

Peter did know her all too well; the thought had indeed crossed her mind that she was not worthy of all this admiration.

Lillian blinked back the tears and cleared her throat. "Peter. This is too much. It's all so perfect, but it's wasted on me."

His voice came out softer. "That's where you're wrong, Lil. Anything I do for you will never be enough." As a droplet slid down her face, Peter turned to look at her, cupping her cheek in his hand, and wiped away the single drop. "Happy birthday, Lil. I'll never stop trying to prove to you how deserving you are."

Grabbing her by the hand again, he sat her down on the blanket. "No more tears. Today is meant to be a happy day—it's my favorite actually. The day the most wonderful person was brought into this world."

A warmth bloomed in her cheeks. "Thank you." It was all Lillian could manage to say without flooding the entire forest.

Peter could tell she was on the brink of sobbing, her eyes shining and lack of speech making it embarrassingly obvious. She wasn't the most graceful of criers, but Peter gazed at her as if she were more breathtaking than a setting sun as he leaned in to press a gentle kiss on her lips.

Blushing furiously, she asked, "When did you even find the time to arrange all of this?"

His eyes sparkled with mischief. "While I am *known for being a notoriously good multitasker, I did, however, have a little help from two people you may know."*

It all made sense now—no wonder Nimreth and Kynra had been acting so odd earlier. She had thought it strange that they hadn't even invited her to go to the market when they made it a point to always go together.

"I would except nothing less from those traitorous sisters of mine."

Peter chuckled. "You make it seem as if they'd done some horrible wrong, when in truth they only helped me try and show you how special you are." Reaching over for the wine, he popped open the top and poured two full glasses of the rich colored liquid. He handed one over to Lillian and raised his glass. "To seventeen incredible years and to all those we shall celebrate together."

Lillian raised her glass and echoed the sentiment. "For all those to come."

They both gulped down a sip and Peter set his wine to the side as he dragged the basket over to him. Opening the lid, he produced a singular muffin.

Lillian sighed. "You're unbelievable." Not only had he known her favorite flavor but there was a candle sticking out from its top.

Peter reached over to one of the lit candles surrounding them and pressed the wicks together, lighting the one on her small cake. "Make a wish, Lil. Better make it a good one—you only get one shot."

What more could she possibly wish for? This was all she had ever wanted and more. But she still closed her eyes anyway and blew out the tiny flame as she made her wish.

"What'd you wish for?" he asked almost immediately.

Lillian shook her head at his question. "Now you know I can't tell you or else it may not come true."

"I suppose that's fair," he said in an exhale. "But I bet you wished for a better dance partner."

Her head jolted back at his absurd statement. "Don't be silly—you're a perfectly good dancer."

"Now that's being generous, Lil. I can maybe keep up with you on a good day."

Standing up, she held out her hand. "That's only because I've been dancing since I could walk." Lillian refused to let him continue with his foolish thoughts. "Take my hand. I'll show you how good you can be."

Peter locked his fingers with hers as he hoisted himself up. "I know I might regret this, but I could never pass up seeing your hips sway against mine."

Face burning red, Lillian pulled Peter in close until their chests were almost touching. There was no music playing, but she didn't need it to be whisked away into motion. And like Peter had claimed, he was no magnificent dancer, but he was skilled enough to follow her steps and twirl her when need be.

A smile widened onto her face the second they moved. Dancing would forever be a feeling of pure bliss. A world where she couldn't lose herself in the steps, where a simple twirl couldn't make her blood sing, was one she couldn't even begin to fathom. And with Peter—her heart glowed—that's who she planned on sharing it with even when her bones groaned with age.

He spun her, Lillian beaming as she whirled. She could stay like this forever in their own little world. Just the two of them as they had always planned. A more perfect life couldn't exist.

Dappled light skirted across them as the sun began to set, the fading shine painting the sky in a beautiful mirage of pink and orange. An enchanting scenery as if the gods themselves smiled down on them.

Peter came to a halt and looked into her eyes. She was mesmerized by the way the sun's rays reflected on his golden-brown hair and made his irises look like warm pools of amber.

"Dance for me," he whispered.

Slightly confused, she said, "Is that not what we've been doing?"

"No. Well… yes, but I want to watch how you blend in with that melody playing in your head. Want to see how you move when you forget everything around you."

A blush crept onto her. "You make it sound as if what I'm doing is akin to something heavenly."

"No, not akin to. You are heavenly."

Her cheeks turned even brighter at his compliment. She had danced in front of others before, but never like this. Practicing around her family and out in the town square was one thing, but this was entirely different. Never had anyone's sole attention been strictly on her and her alone.

A sudden pang of insecurity flitted through her at the thought, but she chased that absurdity away. Lillian knew being insecure around Peter was a ridiculous notion. She could do absolutely anything, and he'd think it was the most breathtaking thing of all. He made her feel perfect in a way no one ever had. Love was too little of a word to describe what she felt for him.

At last, not knowing what else to say, she broke into dance.

And much like Peter had said, the world around her disappeared. She thought of nothing else but the way her body guided her into steps, each movement making her sway like a flame flickering wildly in the wind.

Her hair had become loose as she glided into a pirouette, the copper strands now moving in tandem with her as if an orchestrated addition to her entrancing symphony. There was a pounding in her chest, her heart singing with joy and exhilaration. Gods, she'd never grow old of this. How people could go their whole lives without something like it, without feeling truly alive, *would forever baffle her.*

A tingling crept over her skin as she glided, the sensation a faint feeling that Peter had called her name, but she kept on twirling to her own beat, oblivious to her surroundings. This time however, she could not ignore what sounded like screams of agony.

Lillian whipped her head around and almost thought she had gone mad. Her eyes threatened to burst from her skull at what they beheld.

Where Peter had been watching... stood a thing of nightmares.

The creature was as pale as the moon with leather-like skin barely thick enough to stretch over its bones. Stringy dark hair sprouted from the top of its head, the color a perfect match to the black gaping holes where its eyes should have been. Her gaze caught on the thing's face as it grinned, the horrifying smile unveiling teeth that ended in unnatural points.

Bile inched up her throat as she stared. This couldn't be happening. This...this couldn't be real.

Time had ceased to exist, the seconds dragging on for hours from what her brain failed to accept.

Because under one of its long spindly arms, bony twigs that ended in flesh shredding talons—was Peter.

Her heart stopped. Lillian had never known such fear. She had heard tales and fables of horrifying things, creatures that liked to lurk in the darkness, but she had assumed most of it was something to scare children into behaving.

This, however, was very much real.

There was blood dripping from those curved talons and a slash that corresponded on Peter's chest. Lillian's face paled; she had never seen so much blood pour out of a person before.

Peter. Her lip quivered. The boy she loved. It didn't feel like she was breathing, didn't feel like her heart beat.

The beast shuffled to the side, Peter's head lolling as it moved.

Choking down a sob, she willed herself to calm. Peter... Peter needed *her.*

Her eyes narrowed as she flew through her options. She had to act fast, and she had to act now.

To her great disadvantage, Lillian had never had the opportunity to be in an actual fight for survival. She had to hope instinct would take over and all the memory of previous practices would come flooding in. The shaking of her limbs, however, didn't reassure her too much in that respect. But that didn't matter. Peter was the only thing that did.

Using small movements, she pulled the dagger out from where she kept hidden in her boot.

The creature, taking notice of her unsheathed blade as it glinted in the fading sun, dropped Peter from its arms. A loud thump sounded when he fell, Peter already unconscious from the loss of blood.

It was torture not to run up to him, to not shriek in despair, but Lillian forced herself to remain focused as she brandished her weapon.

The beast inched towards her with a menacing slowness, its right leg dragging behind it. The thing was already very injured; she could tell that much from the way it limped and bled.

Oh gods.

An intense feeling of guilt swarmed her. Peter should have been able to kill it. She choked down a sob. He had been distracted—had been distracted because of her*.*

Lillian tried willing away the powerful emotion. She had to save Peter. She had *to.*

The creature was a mere foot away from her when she decided to pounce, but the vile thing was impossibly fast. Even with the injuries it had sustained, it dodged her and lashed out its talons to strike, but it fell short, swaying, as it placed weight on its broken leg.

Utilizing the mistake to her advantage, she swiped her dagger, ripping a gash in the creature's side.

The beast cried out in rage, an ear-piercing shriek that reverberated through the whole forest. Snarling, it grabbed her with an unnatural speed as it slammed her against a tree by her throat.

Tears streamed down her face as she gasped for air, Lillian writhing as it pressed its icy skin against her.

Her blood went cold as a vicious smile parted on its lips, the revolting expression revealing a lengthy black tongue. Utter disgust filled her as the inky tongue swirled across her cheeks, swiping with glee as it licked away the evidence of her sobs.

Lillian thrashed against the thing's considerable strength and with a stroke of luck managed to kick it in its mangled leg. The monster dropped her, and, with the momentum of her fall, she brought down her blade on its neck, black blood spraying as the creature wailed and clutched at its gushing wound.

The nightmarish thing locked eyes with her, dark liquid leaking from its fingers as the creature shook from the strength it took to remain standing.

It was weak. Lillian blinked as she shuffled to her feet. It was almost dead. The monster was weak and she could end it.

But the creature must have been intelligent enough to realize it. Today it seemed would not be the day it ceased to exist, not by her doing at least.

The beast walked backwards, those haunting black holes holding her stare as it retreated into the night.

Lillian waited no more than a full minute to see if it returned, and, after what felt like the most agonizing seconds of her existence, she was unable to hold out any longer.

Crashing to her knees at Peter's side, she put her hands to his wounds, staining them a bright crimson as blood continued to rush out.

Peter had never looked so ghostly.

Was he breathing? She couldn't tell if his chest was moving up and down. "No, no. Come on, Peter. Don't do this to me."

His heart—his heart must not be beating. There had to be a way for it to start pumping again.

Lillian placed her hands onto his sternum and began pressing her palms down into his heart. She'd pushed on his chest until her arms felt numb, but still there was no response.

"Just one breath, Peter," she pleaded. "Come on. Talk to me. I can't lose you—not you. Please—just let me hear your voice."

But the only voice she heard was the one in the back of her mind whispering that he was gone.

She ignored it, not willing to accept that. Lillian pounded her fists on his chest, screaming his name as she cried hysterically. A bone cracked from the force with which she brought them down, and her hands trembled as she removed them from his broken abdomen.

He was gone.

This was real.

She was here but Peter was not. How could that make any sense? She refused to fathom a world where he was not breathing. Lillian held Peter in her arms not entirely processing what had just occurred.

The meaning of time was lost on her, minutes no longer a thing that mattered or passed, but after what felt like an eternity, her weeping came to a stop, Lillian physically unable to produce more tears.

Oh gods—Lillian brought her hands to her open mouth, smearing blood all over herself—what was she supposed to do? She tried picking up his lifeless body but didn't have the strength to haul him back. She hated the idea of leaving him lying there for any creature to devour, but she had to find someone to help.

"I'll be right back, Peter. I promise." She half expected a response from him, but her heart splintered even more as she realized one would never come. Not now. Not ever.

Lillian broke into a run, sprinting as fast as her legs could take her. She tore in through the threshold of her home sobbing and yelling in incoherent sentences.

Her mother burst out of her room, and Lillian couldn't even imagine what she thought upon seeing her—she was covered in blood from head to toe and looked like death had tried taking her. A part of her wished that it had.

Lillian didn't know exactly what she had told her mother but remembered speaking the words—Peter and woods—aloud in between sobs.

A clinking against a far wall got her attention, and she saw her father pick up a sword and step out into the night. Lillian rushed to follow, screaming that Peter needed her, but her mother held on to her tight. "PETER NEEDS ME!" she wailed, thrashing with such dire desperation, but she was unable to break from her iron grasp. Eventually, Lillian gave up on struggling against her mother's grip, and they both sank onto the floor, hugging each other fiercely.

It felt like there was a hole in her chest, the blackness growing until it consumed everything inside. Never had she felt such pain before.

Peter...

She would never once again see that boy who she loved so deeply. Never hear him laugh hard enough to the point where he couldn't breathe. She would never feel the brush of his lips or the touch of his palm as it interlocked with hers. But what hurt most of all was that she would never feel his arms wrapped around her as they talked endlessly into the night of the future they would share.

Lillian recalled the birthday wish she had made with him earlier that night, back when everything had been so right. An overwhelming dead weight in her heart threatened to swallow her whole.

A despair-filled laugh slid past her lips. Gods, she was so stu-

pid. Her wish—her stupid, useless wish—had been for nothing to change because her life had already been perfect.

She had been so foolish to think that it would actually come true.

CHAPTER 4

It was a curse that every scream she heard took her back to that wretched day.

Her father abruptly stood, snapping her out of her daze. "Everyone into the back room. *Now*."

They had a little room at the far end of the cottage where they kept extra food and supplies. It made sense why her father was ushering them there. Theoretically, it was the safest place in the house, being windowless and far from the commotion outside.

But while her father and brother were situating her mother and sisters, Lillian made her way to the entrance and grabbed her father's sword. With all the chaos, Lillian was able to slip out through the door unnoticed.

She had made it all of two steps when a woman ran up to her. Fear, sharp and jolting, had clearly stricken her as she shook Lillian by the shoulders. "You have to help him, *please*! I'm terrified of what they'll do to my poor boy!"

The woman's words came out frantic and hysterical, and Lillian quickly realized she would be of no assistance in retrieving the boy.

Her pulse hastened as she took in a deep breath. That meant... that meant she would have to go alone.

Using her most soothing of tones, she asked the woman to try and remember anything about where her son was taken. *What* had taken him was of no concern. It was an Ilaidae. The horror in her eyes suggested nothing other.

The mother trembled so much that her words came out in stutters but the trail of blood she pointed to, dark crimson drops that led into the forest, would have to be enough.

Only terror awaited in the dense thicket, but Lillian couldn't abandon the child even if it did mean walking into woods that reeked of death. She didn't know these people, but she knew herself—she couldn't leave that boy in the hands of whatever horrifying beast had taken him.

Lillian lifted her sword and proceeded to the edge of the clearing. No one else would have the nerve to go in. It had to be her.

One last look behind her revealed the silhouette of her father standing at the threshold of her home, far off into the distance. She burned that image into her head as she ventured into the forestland.

Branches snapped and icy leaves brushed against her skin as she went, the dread and cold leaving goosebumps flecking her skin. *You've walked these woods a thousand times,* Lillian reminded herself. She knew the lay of the land, knew what was masked by shadows. But when the sun faded and night leaked forth in its stead, everything changed. This was no longer the woods that lined Grigaros, no longer the woods she traversed to go hunting. This was a living nightmare and to enter would be to sentence yourself to death.

A sentence Lillian had just accepted.

Iron tainted her senses, the scent of blood a heavy presence looming in the air. The deeper she went into the darkness, the harder the stream of blood had become to see. But the amount of light didn't seem to be the problem anymore.

The maroon stained dirt led her farther into the woods until it suddenly came to a stop. Lillian turned around to rule out that the trail hadn't forked off in another direction, but as she went to peer at the ground, she noticed that the trail of blood had disappeared, vanished completely as if it had never been.

Blinking a few times, she wondered if her eyes were playing tricks on her but the two fingers she pressed to the dry soil told her they weren't.

Baffled, she stood up and tried to discern her surroundings—there was nothing other than the vague outline of trees and gloom in every direction she turned.

Lillian wanted to scream.

It was utterly pathetic and useless that her only option was to trudge aimlessly through the dark.

Defeated, she trotted along the same path the blood had been leading, freezing when she heard a clamorous rustling behind her. Lillian spun herself around and brandished out her sword, pounding steps growing louder in the opposite direction. She twirled to face the new noise, the handle of her sword gripped tight.

Laughs and snickers echoed all around her, but she couldn't distinguish where they were coming from, the noises bouncing all around her in the night.

Her head twisted in every direction as she tried pinpointing where the strange sounds originated but before she even had the chance to process any of it, an abrupt flash of light illuminated the clearing.

Lillian's eyes stung as they adjusted to the unexpected brightness. She tried to look out in front of her—blinking away the spots in her vision—and no more than thirty feet away sat a frail looking boy with knees tucked into his chest.

The boy. He was alive. She almost wept with relief but remained focused, Lillian hurtling after him. Her legs sliced through the forest, each step propelling her further. She was so close now, only a few feet away.

But just when she was mere inches from the boy, seconds from hauling him into her arms, the sudden blaze turned back to night.

Lillian dug her heels into the dirt and raised her sword, expecting a figure to come and surprise her in the inky blackness. Her pulse skittered as nothing came.

She waved her arms out in front of her, at the place where the boy should have been—where he *had* been. Empty—as if he'd vanished into thin air.

Standing up straight, she clutched her blade hard enough for her knuckles to ache. There was nothing. Nothing she could see, nothing she could hear. Even the crickets that sung and frogs that croaked had gone silent. The hairs on her nape pricked at the gloomy quiet.

He was here. He was alive. She just had to find him. If her eyes were of no use, then her ears had to be able to pick something up. But the same unsettling silence remained, Lillian's ragged breaths the only thing breaking it.

After too long of the eerie calm, she began feeling restless, but the emotion was chased away as the powerful gleam returned, her eyes searing once more. Tears blurred her vision as she commanded them to remain open.

Her head whipped back to where the boy should have been, but instead of being right behind her, he was now thirty feet in the opposite direction.

Her legs tore into a run, and this time she had made it three feet from the boy when the darkness returned.

Lillian roared in frustration. "Enough pointless illusions! Show yourself, you coward!"

A low, disembodied voice echoed out into the night. "That's a *very* nice sword you've got there. Didn't anyone tell you it was dangerous to run with something so sharp?"

Each word sounded like it was heard in the opposite direction of the previous, making it impossible for her to discern where it was coming from. Lillian stared out into the night, not sure if she was feeling brave or mindless as she spoke. "Give me the boy, and I will allow you to leave with your life. Stay, and I will make certain you regret it."

The creature let out a low, guttural laugh. "You give me the freedom of choice?" The demon pondered her statement. "I can either end my enjoyment and relinquish the boy, or I can take my chances with you?" The monster let out a chuckle that made a chill crawl down her spine. "I think I would *much* rather amuse myself with the both of you."

The voice vanished and Lillian held out her blade just as a

swift gust of wind swept past her cheek, her sword swinging towards the movement. The blade sliced through air as something yanked her hair from behind, the sharp motion causing her balance to waver. Startled, she cleaved her weapon again but met nothing as whispers of giggles breezed past.

Lillian tried relying on her eyes to make out even the smallest glimmer as to where the thing stood, but only black swarmed her vision.

This has to be an illusion, some trick of the mind, she thought to herself.

Clamping her lids, she desperately tried listening for anything of use, the never-ending taunts and laughter the monster threw out making it infinitely harder. But even with the raucous titters, she was able to make out the faintest sounds of footsteps to her right, roughly twenty feet away if she had to guess.

Kneeling down, she grabbed the dagger from her boot and stood back up, holding the blade by its edge. Praying to all the gods she knew that the creature was humanoid size, she aimed for where she believed the throat would be. She feigned as if she were going to throw the dagger out in front of her, towards a string of mocking laughter, but right as she would have let go, she hurled it towards where she had perceived those muffled steps.

A distinct gurgling, choking sound replaced the chatter as the darkness began to let up a little.

Moonlight glistened through the forest, illuminating the scared little boy curled up into a ball. She raced to where he lay and scooped him up in her arms. Blood leaked from a gash along his back, but he was mercifully still conscious.

Lillian flew through the forest, not waiting to see if her blow to the creature had been fatal. It took longer than she would have liked to exit, Lillian not having noticed just how deep inside she'd truly been, but a sigh of relief huffed out her as they finally made it to the thicket's edge.

The boy trembled in her arms as she set him on his feet, and Lillian grabbed him by the hand as she walked him to where his mother stood.

The mother sprinted to her son, screaming his name, and whisked him into her arms. They both sobbed into each other and after a few minutes, the woman turned her tear-stained eyes to Lillian. "I can never repay you for this. What you did" —the woman choked on a sob— "We haven't much but name anything and it shall be yours. I am forever in your debt."

Lillian gave the stranger a soft smile. "There is no debt needing to be paid. I only wish for this night to not haunt the rest of your family's days." She could never accept a reward for doing what she deemed as only right.

The woman was sobbing on her knees as she held her boy. "You must be an angel sent from the gods—not many encounter the terrors of the night and live to tell of it. May the gods bless you more than they already have."

Blessed by the gods. Lillian wouldn't exactly describe her life as such, but simply nodded her thanks.

She watched as the boy and mother walked the path back to town, seemingly safe as more townsfolk huddled around them. Only then did Lillian realize how terrified she'd been. Her entire body began to tremble as she sank to her knees.

The boy. The woods. She'd done that. She'd gone in there and rescued him. Lillian didn't know what bravery had possessed her in that moment. Twice now she had encountered an Ilaidae and survived. There was a sharp jab in her heart at the memory, but she ignored it, willing her focus on what had just occurred.

Lillian could've died—should have really for saying such foolish things to a monster. But despite everything, despite the fear that still churned raging and fierce, she knew she didn't regret it, would have done the same if given the chance.

Brushing the dirt from off her knees, she stood on shaking feet. Home. She didn't want to stay here for another second.

Lillian walked the whole way back, giving her mind and body time to process what she'd done and her nerves a moment to settle. It didn't take long for her to reach the little cottage, and as she swung open the door, she saw her family all gathered at the table.

Their attention landed on her as she placed her father's sword against the wall with an audible clink, their red, puffy eyes evidence enough of their distress. Her heart beat a little faster. She hadn't thought about how they'd feel to find her missing.

Her father stood from his chair, a silent fury on his face as he stared her down. "*What* in the gods names were you thinking, Lillian Echethier? I know I raised you better than to be an empty-headed idiot."

Outrage, however, was not what she'd been expecting. Never had Lillian been the direct subject of her father's anger, and she gaped at him, words failing to find their way to her mouth.

"Nothing to say? We've been sitting here, terrified, believing the worst had befallen you."

Lillian finally mustered words, surprised by what came out. "What would you have had me do? Leave the boy to the mercy of that creature? Of—of that monster?"

"That child was no concern of yours. You had not even the smallest *inkling* that he still lived after being taken."

"I had no reason to believe otherwise," she snapped back.

She began to stomp away from her father, not wanting or sound enough to hear more, but he blocked her way. "We are not done talking until I *say* we are done."

"I have nothing more to say. I will not *stand* here and justify my actions when all you did was cower in the safety of your home." Lillian no longer cared if her father was outraged. She knew what she had done was nothing short of valiant and would not have anyone convince her otherwise.

"Cowered?" he said with a heavy chuckle. "Is that what you believed me to do? I went all the way to the edge of the forest and screamed your name until my lungs burned. But no matter how much it pained me, I couldn't afford to venture forth and leave the rest of my family defenseless. I know my place. It's time you learned yours."

Her eyes went wide, shocked with how he had spoken to her. Lillian shoved him aside and stormed past him into her room, slamming the door behind her.

Roaring into a pillow, she sunk to the floor, knees tucked into her chest as she bawled into the cushion in her arms.

That boy was alive because of her. That family did not have to suffer—did not have to mourn the loss of a son. Lillian had gotten there in time. She had gotten there. He was alive.

Alive... Alive... Alive...

She repeated the word like a prayer.

Five minutes or twenty could have passed when she heard the door creak open.

Lillian lifted her tear drenched eyes, ready to send away whoever had dared to enter. She was in no mood to be called an idiot or a fool, not when her lip quivered and body quaked.

It was her father who emerged from the opening, concern washing all over his features.

She stared at him, her lids feeling tired and heavy as she blinked. The adrenaline of the night had long since worn off and she found herself no longer possessing the energy to bid him away. Lillian sunk her head back down into the pillow, not wanting to see anything but darkness.

The closing of the door wasn't enough to pique her interest, and she didn't even bother lifting her head again as she heard her father light a candle and lower himself next to her.

But the steady quiet she cherished broke as he spoke in a low voice. "No one is claiming you weren't astoundingly brave today. You did, however, take many unnecessary risks in our eyes."

Lillian said nothing.

"There are things and creatures out there we know nothing about. All we know is that they are dangerous and more powerful than we could possibly imagine."

Lifting her head, she murmured, "I couldn't live with myself if I left him to die."

His eyes softened as he looked at her. "You have an extraordinary soul, my Lily, but that shouldn't be your burden to bear. Terrible things happen every day and people get hurt. It's the way this world has always been."

Lillian took a second to think before replying, trying to find the best way to convey herself. She found that her answer was simple. "If I don't fight, then who will?"

A look of resignation clouded his eyes, and he gave no response, the silence long and sullen. "Very well, my brave girl," he said at last. "If I cannot sway your decision, then I would be remiss to stand in your way." He sighed but his tone turned light in a way she hadn't been expecting. "But I suppose the very least I can do for you then is give you nothing other than your best chance at survival."

Lillian looked at him with utter shock. That had not at all been the response she'd expected.

"If you plan to use my sword, then you will do so correctly. I will not put up with seeing you swing it in whatever direction you so please. I know you think you can fight, but a true warrior must practice their skills everyday if they are to hone their abilities."

Now it was Lillian who was stuck for words. All she could think to do was throw her arms around her father and squeeze him tight.

He chuckled as he fell over from the force in which she launched herself. "Now don't go thinking this is going to be easy. I want to see you outside and ready as soon as the sun rises each morning."

Lillian could hardly contain her squeals of excitement but put on the most serious tone she could muster. "Yes, sir. I will be there without fail."

Her father smiled as he got up. "Good. I expect nothing less from my most ferocious soldier. Now get a good night's sleep. We begin tomorrow."

With that he gave her one last kiss on the forehead and closed the door behind him as he exited.

It was impossible to wipe the big smile off her face. How was she expected to sleep now with all the anticipation tomorrow held? Lillian screeched into her pillow, glee coursing through her veins, but frowned as she came up, noticing the white cloth covered in grime.

Gods, she wasn't even sure she wanted to know what she looked like.

Sauntering over to the tall oval mirror leaning up against her wall, she winced at the sight of herself. Her rust-colored hair hung half out of her bun, and she was covered with dirt and sweat. Her emerald eyes were all pink and swollen from her most recent sobbing episode and the plain shirt and pants she favored were ruffled and out of place; they would have been rather clean except that they had been thoroughly coated in dried blood.

It would be a mistake she would certainly regret in the morning if she chose to give in to the temptations of the soft, cushioned bed before her. With a loud groan, she tore her eyes from the mattress and scurried off to the bathing chamber.

Lillian crossed her fingers as she approached the door, hoping that her mother had drawn her a nice, hot bath once she had seen the state of disarray she'd come home in.

Turning the knob, she smiled as she had indeed wagered correctly. The massive tub was filled with scalding hot water and had puffs of steam curling off of it, indicating that the water's temperature must feel divine.

Lillian stripped herself of her soiled clothing and let down her hair as she sunk into the welcoming tub. An intense wave of pleasure undulated through her as the water reached out and touched every part of her skin, the bath a scorching flame pulling her into a much needed hug. A sigh slipped past her tongue. This had been *exactly* what she'd needed to end her day.

Her fingers ached as she scrubbed away the dirt and blood from her body, but she didn't mind as she took joy in the warmth singeing her flesh. She even didn't mind the effort it took to work out all the knots in her long red hair. All she wanted to do was soak in the blissful heat as long as possible, Lillian more than content to take her time with the task of cleansing herself.

But even once she was finished, Lillian unable to pretend there was something else that needed washing, she couldn't help but wish to linger in the heat a little while longer.

The second she laid her head on the rim, her tired eyes flitted shut, Lillian not caring in the slightest that she drifted off.

CHAPTER 5

Lillian dreamt that she was out in the middle of the sea, floating carelessly with no land in sight. The sun's rays shone down on her, glistening off the waves as they carried her farther and farther away from the dingy little boat that bobbed alongside her. Lillian had never even seen the ocean but none of that mattered in the deepest realms of her mind.

Sweat glimmered on her brow, the blaring sunlight leaving beads dripping down her face. She sighed as she dragged her fingertips across the ocean's top, the water feeling divine as it grazed her flushed skin. Whether it was the heat's doing or the sea's beckoning, a sudden urge to dive in possessed her, and Lillian smiled wide as she submerged herself under the indigo ripples.

A refreshing strength coursed through her the second her head sunk beneath the surface. She hadn't realized how powerful the sweltering heat had been until the cold water wrapped around her like tendrils of ice, the contrast so jolting it caused blissful shivers to slide past her skin.

Wonder coursed through her as a school of fish swam past, their scales shimmering in different shades of mesmerizing. There was so much beauty in the sea she had known nothing about. Corals and plants that thrived in the salty blue, creatures with fins and tentacles she'd only ever heard of in stories. All here. All enchanting. How had she not ventured here sooner?

Bubbles burst from her mouth as she glided over a patch of algae, the green slimy feel causing giggles to escape through her lips. Salt kissed her tongue as she waded past, Lillian reveling in every part the ocean had to offer. So much peace. So much tranquility. She could spend an eternity here.

There was a jabbing in her chest as she floated on, her lungs starting to feel tight, and Lillian swam towards the surface, hungry for a nice breath of fresh air before diving back down. The edge of the water was so close that she could almost feel the balmy breeze that would caress her face as she emerged.

Her fingers skimmed the open air, the warm sun sweeping over her hands as she surfaced. Lillian smiled as the top of her head peeked out, but seconds from emerging entirely, something rough clawed at her ankle. A frantic glance down revealed a taloned hand wrapping around her leg, yanking her farther below the surface.

The ocean turned into an endless abyss of pitch black, erasing that scene of wonder and making it impossible to see what manner of beast had its hold on her. Lillian thrashed against its grip as she battled the ache in her lungs, but the unseen monster only pulled her deeper and deeper to the ocean floor.

The more she fought the more her lungs felt like they would implode, the sensation so agonizing it felt like the beast's taloned hands were raking down them.

Time was running out and, if she didn't do something soon, the ocean water would charge down her throat, Lillian unable to do anything but swallow the churning current.

She contorted her body, striving to break free of the creature's weighty grip on her leg, but her struggling was futile against its steel clasp. Her mouth opened to scream but her body—not being able to hold out any longer—gave in and began devouring the salt filled water.

Dreaming of choking down the ocean, Lillian jolted awake from the tub, retching her guts all over the tile floor. She coughed up half her bathing water and gasped for air as she lay naked on the cold ground.

Lillian muttered a curse to herself. She must have fallen asleep and slipped under the water at some point in the night.

A faint trickle of light snuck in through the curtained window, Lillian squinting her eyes as she peered at the glass. It was a small mercy that the sun had just barely begun to rise. Simply knowing she'd let this happen was embarrassment enough. She certainly did not need her family witnessing it as well.

On careful limbs, she rose from the freezing, soaked tiles, wrapping a warm towel around herself as she stood. She began wringing out her drenched hair—her hands and feet covered in wrinkles from the prolonged soak—and used the towel to dry off her body, skin pricking from the unintentional lengthy contact with the cool tub.

Lillian held the towel tightly across her chest as she made a swift dash to her room, praying that the loud creaking of the wooden planks wouldn't alert anyone that she had stirred. Her face cringed as the old hinges on her door screeched as they shut.

Sighing, she plopped down onto her soft, cushy bed, relishing the feel of her bare skin against the smoothness of her sheets. Lillian wrapped herself in the fur-lined covers, ready to doze off into a relaxed slumber but froze as she recalled her father's command: she had to be up and ready to train by the time the sun had fully risen.

Lillian groaned into her pillow, tossing it aside as she rose. Dragging herself over to her dresser, she pulled out a fresh pair of clothes and slipped on a simple tunic and pants that would allow her to move easily through the day's exercises. She then went over to her mirror, yawning as she began brushing through her tangled wet hair.

Moments from throwing it in a braid, a rapping came at her door accompanied by her father's voice. "I was hoping you wouldn't miss your first day of lessons. That would make you a *very* poor student," he teased.

Sauntering over, she pulled open the door. "Oh, stop your useless chatter. As you can see, I'm already awake and *ready to embrace the day*." She left her door ajar and walked back over to her mirror.

"Well, consider me impressed, Lillian. I thought it would be a much harder task to awaken you. I'll be waiting for you outside whenever you finish with your hair."

With that he walked away, leaving her to tend to her plaiting. Lillian shook her head—so rude of him to not have any faith in her—but a curve still parted on her lips at the well-earned assumption. Her father hadn't been wrong in that it should have been more difficult to rouse her, but he hadn't known that drowning in the tub was what had her feeling so lively this morning.

The dream. Her mind drifted back to it.

So odd that her subconscious had chosen to conjure up the ocean. The region of Grigaros she lived in was nowhere near the coast, so she had never been able to venture towards the sea—not that she ever wanted to.

It was a rather silly fear now that she thought of it, but the idea of even being in a body of water where she could not see or feel the floor made her blood run cold. She had swum in lakes and streams years before, but, anytime she made it past the bank, her legs would stiffen up, and she would sink to the bottom like a stone. After having far too many near death experiences, she began to avoid areas with water all together—save for the bath, but now it seemed she could add that to her extensive list of close drowning encounters.

Shaking her head at the embarrassing thought, she walked out into the front yard of her home and saw her father going through an array of exercises, cleaving his sword through the air in practiced slices.

Lillian sighed. How she wished she could do that. No, not wish. She *would* do that—no matter how long it took.

Mesmerized by his moves, she waited in approaching her father until he stabbed his sword into the grass, coming to a stop. "Come simply to watch or are you here to learn?" he asked.

Lillian was eager to begin. "Hand me a sword and let's get going."

Her father chuckled. "Someone seems to be getting ahead of themselves this morning. No swords—not yet at least."

Disappointment crept onto her face, the turn in her features rather noticeable.

"Did you not wish to learn how to properly spar? If not, let me know now and we can save each other lots of time."

"No, no. It's not that. I just assumed that we would already start with swords since I'm not a true beginner."

"Beginner or not, having the correct footwork is just as important as wielding the blade."

Lillian let out a loud exhale but gave into his requests. There was no use in arguing with him. He *was* the teacher after all. "Very well then," she said gesturing to him. "Show me how it's done."

Satisfied with her response, he began his lesson. "The art of fighting is similar to a dance; each step is purposefully placed in order for you to evade or strike your opponent. You, having a background in dancing should help tremendously in getting the perfect moves. Now," he said clapping his hands together. "Let us commence."

The entire morning was spent with her father showing her the proper positionings and Lillian spending hours on end going through different series of attacks until her feet ached from the constant motion. Anytime she made the smallest mistake, he made her start the whole sequence from the beginning, not even caring if she quickly corrected it. She realized rather fast he was a most obnoxious instructor.

But mercifully, noon had soon come about, and her father decided that today's lesson had been a good start and was content with her progress.

"Now make sure you eat a hearty lunch," he instructed. "I want you to start building muscle in those thin limbs of yours so the sword doesn't even falter in the slightest when you raise it."

Lillian—too exhausted to reply—only nodded as she crawled up the steps of her home. She collapsed onto a chair in the kitchen immediately and closed her eyes as she rested her damp forehead on the table.

"Lillian! Don't put your sweaty hair all over the table!" her mother scolded. "We're about to set food on it!" Halline darted from cutting board to pots and pans as she prepared for lunch, but naturally even with her cooking frenzy, she still had time to notice Lillian's misdoings.

More than anything Lillian wanted to ignore her mother's nagging, but she raised her head, not wishing to be subject to more of her harping.

"I hope you're not too tired, darling," she said sweetly. "I need you to run to the market and buy us some spices that I plan on using for our meal." Halline wiped down the wood that had left an obvious imprint of Lillian's weariness on it and dashed back to the stove as she stirred a large pot.

"You can't be serious," Lillian whined. It was absurd that her mother would even *think* to ask her of this upon seeing how fatigued she was. "Why can't one of your other devoted offspring run to the market for you? I'm shocked Nimreth isn't already here *begging* to be of aid."

Her mother showed the smallest bit of displeasure at Lillian's jibe at her sister. "Because I asked *you*. You do not get an excuse to stop helping around the house solely due to your new pastimes. Now go before you make me upset, and I discuss with your father that this new practice of his is impeding with your ability to help."

Glaring at her mother, she snatched the list of spices from her hand and stomped out the door. The nerve on that woman, threatening her with what she'd worked so hard to get.

Angrily, she made her way to the town square where the daily market was being held. Noon was when it was at its peak and there would be dozens of individuals purchasing or selling their wares. Lillian hated coming at this time of day, having to shove her way through the big crowds, all packed in so tightly they might as well have been blades in a meadow.

Tipping her head back, she groaned. The town square had barely come into view, and she could already see the hordes of people gathering by the multitude of stalls. Lillian braced herself for the horrid stench of all the town's folks mingling aromas as she plunged herself into the chaos.

The square was generally pleasant to be in—with the exception of the hours the market took place. There was an extravagant abalone fountain in the middle of the square, glittering water pouring down its levels, surrounded by all manner of buildings, houses and shops alike. But at this dreadful hour, the usually vacant, cobblestone streets were filled with a variety of different stands, all aiming to entice you into purchasing their goods.

Lillian fought her way through the mobs of people, attempting to spot any semblance of a spice shop as her eyes stung from a scent she could only describe as body odor mixed in with onion and dirt. Having not yet found the stand and eager to get away, she dashed over to an empty corner of the square and stood on the tips of her toes, hoping to catch a glimpse of anything useful.

She had been seconds from giving up when she caught sight of a lone elderly woman tending to a measly, little stand. Lillian sauntered over to the deserted stall, watching as the white-haired woman rifled and sorted through an assortment of different herbs.

Glancing through the list her mother had given her one last time, she approached the unfamiliar elder.

The woman stopped arranging her wares and put a smile on her face that showed off her stained and crooked teeth. "What can I help you with today, dear?" she croaked.

Already having forgotten half the items on the list, Lillian just handed her the crumpled piece of paper. "I was hoping you might have a few of these things or perhaps point me in the direction of someone who does?"

The woman squinted her weary eyes, the corners creasing with heavy wrinkles as she scanned the list. "Well, my dear, you appear to be in luck. I just so happen to have all the items you're looking for."

With an ecstatic smile, Lillian handed her a cloth bag to put the items in, overjoyed with not having to set foot in the throng of people again.

The lady began to sift through her wares, holding each different colored bottle up to her nose as she sniffed. A strange way to run a business when labels seemed easier, but who was she to judge. As long as Lillian didn't have to go back into the crowd, she could stick her fingers in them for all she cared.

After she inhaled a few more spices, placing them into a neat pile as she went, the woman let out a heavy sigh. "It's a real shame what'll happen to these townspeople. I'm only traveling through, but I've found myself enjoying the weeks I've spent here."

Unsure and perhaps the slightest bit intrigued as to what the old woman was referring to, Lillian said, "Whatever do you mean?"

"Oh, you haven't heard?" The woman rubbed at her fuzz covered chin as she mumbled, "I suppose word wouldn't have gotten here. It would make things more complicated." She then lifted her gaze back to Lillian, unconcerned that she had just been conversing with herself. "It's just that the Ilaidae are becoming rather impatient and planning something."

"Planning? Planning what?"

"Well, it must come as no surprise that the Ilaidae do not view mere mortals as a threat. They view them as… a sort of pest or vermin, and, to put it in simple terms, have come to exterminate them."

Not knowing what to say, Lillian stared at the woman. What a strange thing to tell her. She had absolutely no faith in what the old lady had so plainly uttered. How could she possibly know what those horrid creatures had planned? But Lillian decided to humor her anyway by saying, "And why have they *suddenly* decided to plan this attack now when they could have easily done so decades ago?"

"Let's just say there's been a shift in power in these recent years, and the Ilaidae have determined that the time to strike will now be sooner as opposed to later."

Lillian handed the woman coins in exchange for the bag full of spices, her tone light as she took what she uttered to be the machinations of a lonely person in search of some attention. "Then I guess the best we can do is hope the Ilaidae end up deciding that later is indeed better than sooner."

About to leave, she turned her back on the crazed elder but felt a bony hand snatch her wrist. The older woman gripped her wrist hard as she pulled her in and whispered sternly in her ear. "You listen to me now and you listen to me well, girl. This is real and what I say will undoubtedly take place and it will not be a simple battle. Believe me when I say it will be a bloody massacre."

Lillian stared down at her with wide eyes as she continued on, her voice grating like sandpaper. "If you refuse to take my word for it, then know this. The animals will be the first to become restless and these little attacks that have been happening will only keep on occurring more and more frequently." The lady clasped onto her arm tighter as if trying to convey her seriousness with her grip. "Next, you must beware of those who claim they speak for the gods for they will find themselves closer to them than they ever imagined." Nails dug into her skin as the woman held her with a startling strength. "Now, if you see all these signs and still choose to believe them all coincidence, then there is one sign you cannot ignore." The buzz of the market had gone silent as if her senses knew that all the attention had to be here. As if this moment were important. As if it meant something she'd yet to realize. "When the sun chooses to abandon you and the darkness swallows the light then you shall know what I speak is true."

The woman let go of her wrist and Lillian stumbled back a few steps.

Shaking the slightest, she turned to go as she heard the woman call out one last time. "But there is a way to save your little village. Once you know what I speak is true, come find me, Lillian, and I will spill the rest of my secrets."

Lillian didn't linger a second longer and ran home, not wanting to hear any more of the eerie ramblings of the creepy woman. What she spoke of had to be false. How could she possibly have come by all this information, and why would she be giving it out so freely? A leeching cold crept past her nape. Even though she was clearly deranged, there was something about that conversation that stuck with her, and Lillian couldn't help feeling that she was fated to have met the strange elder.

But despite the urgency with which she spoke, she didn't trust a single word of what she had said. Lillian refused to believe in her words, not only because they were insane, but because if they were true…that meant all those she loved would be slaughtered.

No. Lillian shook her head. It wasn't real. It just couldn't be.

Her mind thought back on all the ominous prophecies the woman had spoken, and she had forgotten one detail of the discussion that suddenly terrified her to her core.

Not once in the entire encounter had Lillian mentioned her name.

CHAPTER 6

Weeks had gone by, and Lillian's training had started to become more evident in her appearance; she had built up some muscle in her arms and could now hold the sword upright with little to no effort.

Her father had been right in the importance of learning the footwork first. Once he'd allowed her to add the sword into her routine, everything else seemed to flow together naturally.

Bending over, she placed two hands to her knees as she took in labored breaths. She wished she could say it'd gotten easier, but each time Lillian felt like she'd gotten the hang of something, her father took that as meaning she was ready for another challenge. He claimed that it would all be worthwhile and came from the goodness of his heart but the chuckle he hid when he caught her wheezing made her doubt his supposedly good intentions.

Already aching and drained from the day's torture, Lillian hobbled to her room, her tired limbs thrilled to have finished sooner than normal. On a typical day, she trained for much longer, but her lessons that morning had been cut short in accordance with her sister's impending nuptials, the 'merry' event taking place later that evening.

Visions of weeks prior resurfaced in her mind, a bitter taste emerging in her mouth at the memories. Lillian was *more* than ready to get the whole ordeal over and done with.

Kynra had been fretting months now over her wedding day, the last minute details causing her to become more easily agitated than usual. When one got married Lillian had assumed the bride would be living in bliss, happily floating through life as she planned her big day.

How wrong she'd been.

It might appear that way when they walked down the aisle, all lovely and smiling with newlywed glee, but up until that joyous occasion, they were demons capable of much worse than Lillian had ever anticipated—and Kynra, as regal and kempt as she might seem, was no exception to the hellish possession.

But perhaps she couldn't entirely blame her; Grigaros' recent developments hadn't helped her crazed state in the slightest.

The ambushes had gone from occurring every two years to once a week in the span of a month. The town naturally had turned anxious, Grigaros buzzing with fear from the Ilaidae that snuck in through the twisted dark forest.

Shivers fluttered down her spine as her thoughts drifted to that strange day in the market. With reluctance, she recalled those ominous words and was unable to deny that perhaps some of what the elderly lady had prophesized had proven to be true.

Only two of the signs she'd warned Lillian against had come to pass—the attacks had indeed started to become a reoccurring event, and the animals had begun acting uneasy.

No one thought it strange that their cattle or pets had become nervous, the reactions expected due to the attacks, but Lillian knew—had even noticed the change days before the first assault.

She tried not to read too much into the babbling of a clearly deranged individual, but a small part of her couldn't help but wonder if it all might be real.

That, however, would be something she thought on later as her musings became interrupted by a pounding at her door.

Nimreth's honeyed voice came from the other side of the entry. "Are you in there, Lily? I think I may be of need of your assistance… It's Kynra."

Of course, she groaned internally. Who knew what it could be this time. Lillian knew Kynra well enough to glean that she must have been in an unending state of panic—even more so than usual—today needing to be the most perfect wedding day of all. She let out a loud exhale—mentally preparing herself for the hysteria her older sister was undoubtedly in.

Springing out of bed, she bounded towards her sister at the door. "Let's go see what that lunatic is twaddling on about this time," she sighed.

They went over to Kynra's room and found her pacing back and forth in apparent distress.

Nimreth inched up to their sister, her movements gentle as if she were a wild mare about to buck, and put a hand to her back, guiding her to sit on the bed.

Lillian could scarcely make out any of the words her older sister was rambling on about as Nimreth soothed her with soft tones. "What's gotten you in such a worry?" her youngest sister asked.

Kynra looked like she was on the verge of sobbing. "Everything is going wrong. Today was supposed to be a marvelous and absolutely flawless day but that could not be farther from the truth."

It was Lillian who answered this time. "Oh, you make everything always seem worse than it truly is. What could *possibly* be so horrible that it's got you on the brink of tears?"

One of Kynra's eyes twitched as she lifted her gaze to Lillian—perhaps she could've used kinder language, but it was far too late now. "You think I'm merely being dramatic, is that it?" A crazed chuckle fell loose from her mouth, the sound making Lillian pinch her lips into a tight line so she didn't laugh. "Well, let me tell you what has happened, and you try and tell me that this day isn't already ruined. The pastor who was meant to marry us got an unexpected ailment and cannot bear to be out of his chambers, the food we were supposed to serve accidentally contained a spoiled ingredient and made the cook violently ill, and the doves we were meant to release have become deranged and broke free of their cages." Kynra cocked her head to the side and gave her a terrifying smile. "Tell me, is that me being dramatic, Lillian?"

It was true that what her sister spoke of was not necessarily the *ideal* wedding day. But even though her sister had not been the most... pleasant person to be around at times, she still deserved to have the wedding she'd dreamed of.

"I suppose you're not being *too* dramatic but worry no further." Lillian placed a hand to her chest and raised her other in a vow. "I will make it my personal mission to make sure that everything goes as planned."

Her sister looked doubtful of her as she cut a glare in her direction. "And how exactly do you plan on accomplishing that?"

"That, my dear sister, is no concern of yours. You just worry about putting on the pretty white gown and leave the rest to m—"

Kynra threw herself around Lillian before she could even finish her sentence. "Oh, thank you so much, Lily! I should have known you'd be the answer to all my problems."

"I'm offended you even doubted me for a second," Lillian said chuckling as she pried herself out of her sister's arms. "But now seeing as I have a *very* busy day ahead of me, I should really be on my way."

Giving her sister one last big hug, she left her in the tender care of Nimreth and exited the room. Now all Lillian had to do was save this sinking ship of a wedding.

Oh gods, what had she gotten herself into?

She hadn't the faintest idea on how to fix this mess, but Lillian couldn't help saying the words that would ease her sister's affliction. She didn't know exactly why but she felt a certain sense of responsibility over her family. If Nimreth was a carbon copy of their mother, then she supposed she was one of their father's. He was the problem solver, the one that helped them in any way, and the steadying presence that made them all feel at ease. Lillian always put their needs before her own and that's just the way it had always been. She would not hesitate in doing whatever was necessary for her family. So, indeed, it did look like she would be the one to fix Kynra's day.

There were only a few hours left, but even with the strict

timeline, she would not allow herself to be intimidated by three simple tasks—after all, how hard could they truly be?

Pacing back and forth in the kitchen, she weighed her options and decided that finding a new pastor was the simplest and most important of the three tasks. She would get it out of the way quickly and then give her full attention to the other two minor wedding mishaps.

As she hurried out the door, cloak flying around her shoulders, Lillian concluded that the best place to begin her hunt for a new pastor would be at the church and began the ascent to her town's beloved holy place.

Her breathing had turned ragged not even ten minutes into the climb, her sore limbs aching with renewed fervor. How people made this trek once a week, sometimes even more, was bizarre to her. Years and years before when she'd been much younger, she'd accompanied her family to the weekly mass, but the older she got, the less she went until eventually not at all. Another quirk her mother had not approved of, but Lillian didn't much care especially since gods had always been a peculiar topic to her.

Long ago there had been deities that were worshipped, revered and honored throughout the lands, but somewhere along the way, through the cracks of time, scriptures had gotten lost and all record of the holy beings had disappeared. All that was left were a people that no longer remembered. But despite the immense lack of knowledge, they still worshipped, still carried on with churches and traditions. They knew there was a glorious heaven and a fiery hell and that was enough to still praise the nameless gods.

Lillian, however, didn't know what to make of them. Something about it just didn't sit right with her. How could she worship gods who created the Ilaidae? How could the supposedly benevolent and caring beings of power have created such a hateful and malicious race? And if those were truly the gods that formed this universe, did that mean the Ilaidae worshipped them as well? The taste in her mouth soured at the idea. She would not worship a god that had such wretched disciples.

A sigh found its way past her lips. But yet it seemed today she would be as she peered up at the supposed house of love and glory.

It only took half an hour to get to there, Lillian's musings allowing for the minutes to pass swiftly, and she was out of breath by the time she made it to the ornate building sitting atop a grassy hill.

It'd been forever since she'd last been there, but nothing had changed. The building was simple but breathtaking, completely made of different colored, mismatched stones save for the numerous stained-glass windows lining its walls.

She stood at the tall wooden door, staring at the impressive looking silver bell swinging high above as she contemplated on what she would say. Lillian grasped the cross shaped clapper and struck it against the oak door a sufficient number of times. Two minutes had passed when she reached for the metal clapper once more, but she didn't get the chance to pound it as it slipped from her fingers.

A boy no more than ten looked up at her from the open door. "Can I help you?" he asked.

Lillian took a second to respond, not having been expecting a small child to be the one to answer her knocking. "I was hoping I could speak to someone who could help me find a pastor to officiate my sister's wedding?"

"Ah, you must be part of the Echethier family; I can see the resemblance. But like I told your sister, my daddy hasn't been feeling too good as of late and won't be up for performing any ceremonies."

"There has to be *someone* around town who can marry my sister. Who was the pastor before your father took over?"

"That would be Father O'Hare. But good luck getting him to help you; he is as mean as they come. Not sure if it'll do much, but I can point you in the direction he lives in if you'd like?"

"That would be splendid! I appreciate your assistance in this matter." She spoke to him in a slightly teasing tone, amused with the young child's gentleman-like demeanor.

"The least I could do, ma'am. No bride should have to postpone her happy day."

The charmingly polite little boy told her that Father O'Hare lived all the way across town. Lillian had to force back her groan when she'd heard that delightful fact. She was *thrilled* with having to waste so much time on simply getting to the old pastor's home. And in addition to that, she still had to convince the evidently ill-tempered Father to even officiate the ceremony.

Pondering over why she'd agreed to fix all this in the first place, she followed the young child's fairly simple directions and made it to the O'Hare's family home. The small cottage was a rather pretty house, the yellow paint and stone path making it seem adorably quaint, and had a beautiful garden filled with all kinds of dazzling, colorful flowers.

There was an older man outside, Lillian noticed as she neared the home, a straw hat atop his head and a bushy white beard bracketing his kind smile. He had a watering can in his right hand and appeared to be the one tending to the lovely garden.

Mumbling greeted her ears as Lillian approached, and she swore it was the man speaking even though he was the only one around. As she got closer, she realized that he was in fact speaking, not to a person, but to the flowers he was watering. The man was going on about how vibrant his tulips had been this season when Lillian interrupted.

"Are you Father O'Hare?" she asked.

He stopped his chatter, that warm smile vanishing and his voice turning a degree harsher. "Who's asking?"

"My name's Lillian Echethier, and my sister is getting married later today. I was wondering—"

The man cut her off. "Nope, no Father O'Hare here. He's away on business."

Her eyes narrowed into slits. It was entirely too obvious that the man was blatantly lying to her. "Oh, come on. It's very clear to me that *you* are Father O'Hare."

The man turned his stern face to her. "There is no Father O'Hare here, girl. He's been gone for years. Only a Mr. O'Hare remains."

Lillian rolled her eyes. She was on a time crunch and did not have time to hear about his surely tragic back story of how the church had done him wrong.

"Listen *Mr*. O'Hare," she said with a snap. "I only require your services for the evening and then you can go back to your life of avoiding the church or whatever it is you're doing."

The man formerly known as Father O'Hare did not look very pleased with her response. Lillian never claimed she was a diplomatic woman—she just knew how to get results.

"Did you not hear what I said, girl? No means no. Now leave me to my gardening in peace."

Resuming his task of watering the rest of his flowers, he turned his back, ignoring her as if she had never even spoken.

Lillian rubbed her palms over her face. There was no time to delve into his issues and solve whatever inner turmoil he had with the church. She needed a pastor today.

Trying to figure out a solution, Lillian watched the annoying individual as he whistled to himself, pretending that she simply did not exist. It was an effort to mask her glare and stop herself from saying something rash. Being ignored was not something she took well, but she was wise enough to know that a bad attitude would get her nowhere with this stubborn man.

Lillian opened her mouth to reason, beg, whine if she had to—but swallowed down the words as the Father stopped in front of his petunias. His feigned tranquility faltered as he flinched, his face showing the slightest bit of displeasure as to how they were faring—compared to all the other flowers, the petunias did look a bit dreary.

Almost immediately did Lillian notice the issue. With the way the garden was situated, the petunias had no access to direct sunlight, and they needed as much as they could get to have a livelier bloom.

An idea struck in her head as she walked up behind him, a swagger in her step as she smirked. She hated that the countless hours of gardening her mother had ingrained in her had actually proven to be useful, but who was she to waste such a perfect opportunity?

With a coy twitch decorating her lips she said, "It doesn't look like those petunias of yours will be able to hold out much longer in the conditions they're in."

Father O'Hare turned to look at her, suddenly inclined to acknowledge her existence. "And what would you know of maintaining a garden?"

"Well, my mother just so happens to be a very talented gardener herself and taught me everything she knows."

She knew she had his attention when he asked, "Then let it out, girl. How do you suppose my petunias should be?"

"I'm afraid my knowledge will come at a price," she said sucking her teeth. "But I'm positive you can afford to pay it—*Father* O'Hare."

Oh, he looked seriously irritated now. "You truly are an infuriating young lady," he grumbled. The Father glared at her, debating what she suggested before eventually groaning. "Very well... I'll do your sister's wedding."

A big smile bloomed across her face. "Perfect! Be at the church no later than 1 pm."

The man called out to her as she began to walk away. "But wait! What of my petunias?"

Still walking forward, she yelled, "They have access to too much shade. You need to move them to a place where they can have more sunlight."

A huge grin was plastered on her the entire way home, but her amusement was cut short as she checked the time. It was noon by the time she arrived, which meant she had less than an hour to find a new cook *and* fix the missing dove problem.

She had planned on running straight into Kynra's room, eager to deliver the good news but slowed when she spotted her mother in the kitchen cooking up a storm. Lillian stood by the table, gesturing to the mayhem around her. "What's... what's with all this?"

Her mother looked higher strung than usual and kept on going about her task as she answered. "Kynra needed a new cook, didn't she? Well, now she's got one right here. If you find Nimreth, *please* tell her I could use some assistance in the kitchen."

Leaving her distressed mother to her cooking, impressed that she could chop and stir at the same time, she waltzed over to her older sister's room. She felt a twinge of guilt about leaving her alone to whip up an entire feast, but it's not like Lillian would be of much assistance in the matter. The great news regarding that, however, was that she no longer had to find a caterer for the wedding. That meant the only thing left was finding a few doves and shoving them all into a cage. Had to be easy enough.

Swinging Kynra's door open, she found Nimreth finishing up her sister's hair—half of her dark mahogany locks were pulled up and braided into a crown while the other half fell loose with curls.

"You look absolutely gorgeous, Kyn," Lillian observed in awe.

Kynra's cheeks had begun to stain red. "Oh, stop, you're only saying that so you can get out of more last-minute errands."

"Believe me, if I had known that was an option, I would have started months ago." Not able to keep it in any longer, she blurted out the exciting news. "Father O'Hare agreed to do your ceremony!"

An earth-shattering squeal burst past her tongue. "That's amazing, Lily! How did you manage that? I heard he was a *sour* old man to put it mildly."

"Oh, you know me—I can woo over anyone with my award-winning smile." Lillian beamed as she flashed the choice feature.

"Hmm, I'm sure that was it," she said, her tone leaking with doubt of Lillian's diplomatic skills. "But I don't care how you did it!" Kynra let out another ear-piercing shriek. "It's really happening! I'm getting married!"

Recalling there was one more thing she had to do, Lillian was unable to share her sister's enthusiasm. With a sigh she said, "Now about those doves…."

"Oh, don't worry about those silly birds. My main concerns were the food and the officiant and now we have both!"

A sudden wave of relief fell over her. She had been sure she was going to have to convince Maxith to paint a dozen crows white.

Thrilled that she was done, she informed Nimreth of their mother's request in the kitchen and scurried into her own chambers, needing to change into her own wedding attire.

With haste, she threw on a long, emerald gown made of a flowy chiffon material that cinched snuggly at her waist, its sleeves resting off her shoulders, tastefully rolling all the way down to her wrists. Her silver bangles clinked as she undid the braid in her russet colored hair, the plaits having left loose curls trickling down her back as she untwisted them with speed. Once she slipped on her simple brown sandals—not in any mood to torture herself with heels—she sprinted out of her chambers to find her family ready and waiting on her to leave for the church.

Luckily for them, it didn't take too long to make it up the steep hill, and they hurried in through the grand entrance, the church elegantly decorated inside. Flowers, arrangements of lavenders and baby's breaths, hung from the ceiling's wooden beams and long white ribbons dangled from the edges of the pews, making a walkway for the bride along with the dozens of white roses littering the ground.

Dashing past the rows of guests, the colorful light sprinkling down on them from the stained windows, they made it to the front of the church where a pew had been reserved. Sitting down, they turned their attention to the front where Father O'Hare and her sister's husband to be stood at the altar.

In a manner of minutes, a violin's rich melody began to fill the hall, and the room quieted down, everyone turning to the back of the church as Kynra appeared in the doorway with the most beautiful smile on her face.

Lillian sucked in a breath. She looked absolutely radiant.

Her sister wore a lace and bead encrusted gown that had a sheer train trailing behind, numerous roses embroidered into the flowing thin fabric. Not a single eye wasn't on her.

Kynra had always been stunning, her striking cheekbones, full lips, and deep brown eyes having made her a prize to be sought after, but now she glowed—glowed with such a beauty that only a woman who was truly in love could possess.

Beaming with pure joy, she began making her way down the aisle, her fiancé watching with a profound amount of passion as she walked past the pews.

That.

Lillian wanted that.

She wanted someone who could just look at her and cause the entire world around them to dissappear. Wanted to have that one person who was her perfect match. The moon to her sun. The dark to her flame.

Her heart beat stronger as she watched the love they had for one another shine in their eyes. Lillian had to hope that kind of love was out there waiting for her, because a world without it would not be worth living. It was hard to force her mind away from where it wanted to drift but today was a happy day, her sorrow had no place.

Kynra glided to the end of the aisle and took her husband to be's hands in hers as Father O'Hare began to speak, the crowd watching in silence as he commenced.

Beautiful was the only thing she could think of to describe the ceremony. Despite the few minor hiccups, it had been so perfect. The Father performed a truly heart-warming ceremony that had even managed to make Lillian tear up when she'd heard the exchange of vows.

But now it was all coming to a swift end, and Lillian was more than ready for the couple to be declared wed so the festivities could finally begin.

Father O'Hare was in the process of pronouncing them husband and wife, the couple smiling as they both blinked back tears of joy, when the pastor suddenly doubled over, stricken with a violent coughing attack.

Clearing his throat, he recovered swiftly from his weakened state and carried on with his words. "My apologies ladies and gentlemen, where was I? I now pronounce you husband and wife. You may—"

His sentence was cut off again as the Father bent over in agony, another intense hacking fit ailing him. But this time when he got back up, red stained his robes from where he had coughed up blood.

All everybody could do was stare—not a soul knowing what to do as blood began streaming down from the pastor's eyes.

Lillian and her father rushed to catch the old man as he began to sway and laid him on his side as he continued to thrash and pour out blood from every orifice in his body.

Horror clouded her vision as the pastor continued to writhe, screaming in pain until he came to an immediate stop. His eyes were glossed over and empty, and Lillian knew then that he was gone.

The room went silent, shocked with what had just occurred. But the eerie calm only lasted for a mere second before everyone started going into a panic, not knowing what killed Father O'Hare and scared that it would happen to them as well.

Yelling at the top of her lungs as everyone ran in alarm, Lillian told them to all remain calm and that there was surely an explanation for what had transpired.

The guests quieted down some, but the reprieve had been extremely short lived.

A sudden darkness began to sweep over the church as if a massive storm cloud were passing over them.

Everyone stared at the windows as the daylight began to slowly disappear—until nothing but complete and utter darkness remained.

CHAPTER 7

Lillian stared out in a stupor at the pitch black surrounding her.

Her lashes fluttered as she blinked, her brain refusing to believe there was truly nothing. But it was true. No matter how many times her lids beat, it didn't change the reality.

Where light had once been, where color and life had shone so brightly...was now gone. The dullness, the terrifying black void, was what she imagined the world appeared like long before. Just a frigid and empty cold space.

Fingers shaking, she raised her hand up in front of her. She couldn't see it. It... it should've been impossible. Even in the darkest hours of the day, she'd been able to see something. A silhouette, a frantic wave of the hand. *Something*.

But this... it would be entirely misleading to say this was night. At night, you had the stars illuminating and the moonlight shining down on you, but here—there was nothing. Every fiber of her screamed that this wasn't normal, that this wasn't natural.

And it wasn't; she knew that. The people that shoved by her knew that, all screaming and wailing as they tried fleeing the church.

Havoc jerked her out of her daze, and she called out to her family, hoping at least one of them could hear her over the deafening shrieks. Nimreth's voice was the only she heard, the shaky squeak coming from a corner behind the altar.

Blindly, she made her way over to where she'd heard her sister and called out her name a second time. It came from a few feet beside her, and Lillian flailed out her arms to grab her. After only catching air, she realized that Nimreth was on the ground, curled up into a fetal position by her feet.

Lillian lowered herself and placed a hand on her shoulder. "Grab on. I'm finding the rest of our family and getting us out of here."

With trembling feet, Nimreth rose, locking her fingers with Lillian's. They had made it only a couple of steps from the altar when someone began lighting the church's candles.

The dim flickering illuminating the room, she was able to make out where the rest of her family stood as she darted over to them.

Her mother had tears in her eyes as she ran to pull Nimreth and Lillian into a big embrace. "Thank the gods you two are okay."

Lillian squeezed her tight, trying to ease her mother's nerves. She hated to see her family so upset.

And evidently, so did Maxith.

Whenever situations became too intense or serious, her older brother always tried to use humor to ease their growing anxiety. "I didn't see you *nearly* as emotional when you found me," scoffed her brother.

Their mother let out a small laugh. "That's because I knew if any manner of beast captured you, they'd quickly grow tired and give you right back."

Lillian and Nimreth let out a snicker as Maxith put on a face of pretend outrage. But they were snapped out of their momentary glee as their father motioned for them to exit the church, leaving Kynra in the care of her new husband.

As they walked home, Lillian recognized what this all meant... She couldn't pretend it wasn't real any longer.

The old woman had been right in her cautions.

All the signs she had prophesized occurred just like she had promised. And if this had all come to pass.... she knew what would come next. Lillian clenched her teeth as her blood churned with icy fear. She had to find the elderly woman. That bloodbath could not take place.

Looking out around her, Lillian prayed that the current darkness was not a permanent one. Wandering through perpetual gloom would make the task of finding the old woman all the more grueling. But at the very least she could be thankful it wasn't completely black as the townspeople had already begun lighting candles all around their houses, and as soon as they arrived home, her family too began lighting candles of their own to brighten the inky surroundings.

She left them all to their own devices and went to her room to change out of her dirty dress. Lillian really had to quit making it a habit of soaking her clothes with the blood of others.

Shimmying out of her filthy, red-crusted gown, she put on her usual tunic and pants. But just as Lillian began fitting her leather corset over her shirt, a sudden blinding light appeared, driving away the shadowy dark. Lillian let out the panicked sigh she'd been holding in and thanked the gods that the darkness hadn't been an eternal one.

Not willing to waste even a sliver of daylight, she flung on her brown leather boots and slipped out the back door. Lillian figured the best place to start her search for the old woman was where she had seen her last, but still she cursed herself for not inquiring more when she'd had the chance. Lillian had just assumed that the woman had gone stark raving mad and was spewing nonsense to anyone who came her way. How was she supposed to know she was being truthful?

Thoughts of what the woman had said swirled in her mind as Lillian walked the barren cobblestone streets of the town's square.

Never had she seen them look so desolate.

Usually, she reveled in walking the empty paths, but it felt so wrong to not see a soul in sight.

Unsure of what she was looking for, she surveyed the deserted street, a movement catching her eye in the distance. Lillian eased towards the abandoned alleyway where she had caught the glimmer of motion and saw a shadowy figure rounding a corner. Lillian moved faster now, wanting to catch whatever creature was evading her. She drew her dagger from her boot and trailed the mysterious individual until they both reached a dead end.

With nowhere left to turn, the hooded figure came to a halt, whirling around. "Put that dagger away, Lillian," a scratchy voice croaked. "Unless you're planning on using it on a poor, defenseless woman." The individual pulled down their hood, revealing themselves to be the very same elderly woman from the market.

Lillian let out a breath as she sheathed her blade. She didn't have time to care why the woman had been darting away from her and was sure the woman would have some strange reason that was of no interest to her right now. “You were right,” she admitted. “Everything you said would happen came true.”

The woman smirked at her, those stained teeth glinting in the newfound light. “I did warn you, child, did I not? Now ask what you truly came to me about.”

“You said there was a way to prevent the massacre—how?”

The older lady thought on her words as she picked at her broken and cracked nails. “There is a rumor from long ago that if you travel far into the lands of Iavothae and compete in the infamous Trial of the Flame, then the ruler will grant you a single wish.”

Trial—wish? She had never heard of such a thing occurring in their lands. But then again, she didn’t know much at all regarding the Ilaidae. “What’s the Trial of the Flame?” she asked.

“That, my sweet Lillian, you will have to figure out on your own.”

“Why have I never heard of this? Shouldn’t this be well known if the reward is so grand?”

“Make no mistake. It is no easy task being the Champion of the Flame. You will have to face many hardships once you enter the lands of Iavothae along with the dark forest you must cross. It will take a brave and skilled warrior to venture forth into the lands of the Ilaidae and live.”

Lillian turned around, pacing as she tried to process all the information she’d just been given. “Then why tell me this? How am I supposed to find this *champion* and convince them of what I say is true?”

She waited on a response from the old woman but when she

turned back to face her, the woman had vanished.

Great, she thought to herself. She despised when people spoke in riddles. And the woman had the *nerve* to evaporate into thin air without even bothering to explain all she had just professed. How was Lillian meant to find this champion or even convince them to journey forth into Iavothae?

Lillian groaned. She knew this was going to be a challenge and that everyone she approached would assume she had gone insane, but she had to try. She had to for Grigaros.

With a heavy sigh and low spirits, she began her quest to find the Champion of the Flame and started knocking on every door she came across.

The hours passed by, and Lillian had already lost track of how many doors got slammed in her face.

The people in Grigaros were unbelievable.

Lillian pleaded her case in every way imaginable and *still* managed to get the same results. She also couldn't forget the plenty of fun names she got called along the way, ranging from demented to downright certifiable.

Overwhelmed with the crushing defeat of her evening, Lillian marched on home, unsure of what to do next. She refused to bring up the matter to her family in fear that they too would come to the same conclusion that she had become unhinged. No, there had to be some other solution. One she hadn't thought of yet.

Tired and not wanting to think on the matter for the remainder of the night, she walked in through the threshold of her home and planned to take a long, relaxing bath.

She had almost made it to the bathing chamber when her mother stopped her. "Do you care to explain yourself, young lady?"

Lillian winced; she had forgotten the small detail of not mentioning to her family that she had momentarily stepped out. "Can a grown woman not go out for a walk on the town?" she responded.

Her mother's voice turned shriller in a way that made Lillian's ears hurt. "You may believe that you are a grown woman, but you are still my daughter. You live under my roof and therefore are subject to *my* rules."

"I wasn't under the impression that I lived in a prison. I'll be sure to report to the warden the next time I wish to request for time outside my cell."

The beginnings of tears started to form in her mother's eyes, and Lillian instantly regretted her sneering tone. "Please, Lillian, why must you make this so difficult? After all that occurred today, it's like you don't even *think* on how your actions can affect others."

Taking her mother into her arms, she spoke in a gentle voice. "I'm sorry, mother. I know I should have at least mentioned to you that I was going out—especially with all that happened."

Her mother was bawling in her arms now. "I worry for you. I know you think that I am a nuisance and live to make your life as horrendous as I can, but all I want for you is to be safe and happy."

Lillian blinked away the tears that threatened to drop. "I know, and I do love you very much—even though at times it might not seem like it."

They stood there for a few minutes, holding one another in a calming silence until her mother stood up, straightening the wrinkles out of her dress. She cleared her throat and wiped a few stray tears from her eyes. "That's enough of that now, don't you think. But please, at least tell me next time you step out." She gave Lillian one last big hug and a kiss on the cheek before retreating into her bed chambers.

Gods, she was awful. Lillian hated making her family feel like they didn't matter. They were the *only* thing that mattered. She had been so caught up in her own thoughts that she had forgotten how her family would react to finding her missing. Lillian hadn't deserved to get off so easily, and she knew she only had because her mother didn't wish to bawl in front of her any longer.

With shame flowing in her veins, she trudged over to the fireplace and began heating up pots of water to pour into her bath. She felt even worse as she filled up the tub, thinking back on all the times she took for granted of when her mother would draw her nightly bath.

After dumping the last pot into her bath, she undid the strings of her corset and slipped out of her tunic and pants. Lillian touched the water with the tip of her finger, finding it to be just the right amount of scorching hot, and sunk into the tub, savoring the feeling of warmth spreading over every inch of her body.

Lillian wished the blazing heat of the water would melt all her troubles away but found the water unable to do what she wished. Instead, she distracted herself with the cleansing of her hair and body, but she was only able to lather herself so many times until the words of the old woman invaded her thoughts.

What an impossible task finding this Champion of Flames

turned out to be. It made absolute sense that the woman had been so eager to pass the duty on to her.

Now Lillian had to scour the lands in search of someone to compete in whatever the Trial of the Flame was—but would anyone willingly volunteer? She had to assume that everywhere she pleaded would treat her the same as they had here, and Lillian was in no mood to be regarded as the town's madwoman all throughout Grigaros.

Lillian sunk her head beneath the surface as she tried drowning the problems in her head. She hadn't the faintest idea on how much longer the Ilaidae would hold off on their annihilation, so, she had to find a champion—*now*.

A wave of realization crashed into her as she sat up. Thinking back on Peter, her family, and on all those who had been victims to the Ilaidae's attacks made the decision that came next rather simple.

She had to be the Champion of the Flame.

CHAPTER 8

Lillian awoke the next morning, feeling confident in the decision she'd made.

Yawning, she hopped off the bed, her feet pressing into the cold wooden boards as she drank in the steadying dark of the room. The sun had yet to appear on the horizon, stars and moonlight still gleaming as she had risen early to gather all the necessary supplies. For now, she wished to keep her choice a secret.

With that in mind, she tip-toed into the kitchen and began putting together provisions for her trek to Iavothae. An abundance of food lay strewn all around the room from the after-wedding festivities that never took place, and she silently thanked her mother as she crammed a ridiculous amount of food into a bag, unsure of how long the trip would be. She then packed some extra sets of clothes, a canteen of water, and a few other supplies she felt would be useful to have. Her father's sword and her bow would be something she'd grab on the way out seeing as opening the door would undoubtedly alert her mother of her presence.

On quiet feet, Lillian headed to her room, setting the pack under her bed and grabbing a quill and paper to write her goodbyes for when her absence was inevitably noticed. Her quill glided along the pages as she wrote of her mission to save her people and of how she knew it all sounded nonsensical but could not sit back and watch Grigaros suffer. Lillian *explicitly* wrote not to come looking for her because she either came back and succeeded—or would die trying to do the right thing. Tears slid down her cheeks as she finished sealing the letter and set it on her dresser.

Reaching for the quill and paper once more, she began to write a second note stating that she would be out for the day and would return by nightfall. A lie but a necessary one. She had to slip out before anyone awoke because if she saw her family one last time, she knew she would break down and tell them everything. She couldn't have them convince her to stay. Or worse. Try coming with her.

After putting on her regular corseted tunic and pants ensemble, she walked out of her bedroom door, placed her pack by the entryway, and strolled into the kitchen. Lillian sunk down into a chair and cradled her face in her palms.

This was insane. This was all too insane. Was she actually about to do this? Was this all a huge mistake? Her heart hammered in her chest.

No. She knew it wasn't. She'd tossed and turned with everything she'd seen and heard the entire night. Lillian knew this was what she had to do. All that had happened...it wasn't just coincidental. It was real. That crone had found *her* for some bizarre reason, and if no one else would go, then that meant it had to be her. This would work.

It had to.

Feeling like a thousand dragonflies fluttered beneath her skin, she stood, depositing the second letter on the kitchen table. That was it. That was the last thing on her list. Now all that was left was lea—

Her head whipped as she heard the turning of a latch followed by delicate footsteps.

Nimreth waltzed into the kitchen, jolting back with surprise. "My goodness, you scared me, Lily. What are you doing up at this hour?"

Not having anticipated the need to provide an explanation, she parroted her question right back. "What are *you* doing up at this hour?"

"I'm getting a glass of water. Why are you wearing attire as if you went somewhere?" Nimreth gasped and whispered, "Were you sneaking back in? How did you manage to get past mother? The woman has ears of a bat."

Lillian hushed her loud muttering. "Calm yourself, Nimreth. I'm not doing anything. I left a note saying that I'd be out for the evening and would return by dark."

Nimreth was too groggy to notice that she hadn't specified exactly where she was going and nodded as she poured herself a glass.

But as her sister turned to walk back into her chambers, Lillian threw her arms around her, pulling her into a strong embrace. "Never forget how much I love you and this family—promise me that."

A confused Nimreth hugged her back. "Okay, you lunatic, I promise. I love you too."

Letting go of her and needing to leave before she said too much, Lillian ambled over to the door and grabbed her pack as Nimreth called out one last time. "Be safe. I'll see you later tonight."

The only thing she could do was nod, Lillian unable to make that false promise.

And for perhaps the last time... she crossed the threshold of her home.

Blinking back the dampness that clung to her eyes, she equipped herself with various weapons, wanting to be prepared for anything that came her way. But needing to travel relatively light, she settled on two daggers, her father's sword, and a bow and quiver filled with arrows. She strapped the sword and dagger to either side of her and slipped the remaining dagger into her boot. The bow and quiver would be inconvenient to travel with, but she would rather bring them and not need them than have it be the other way around.

Lillian made it to the edge of the property and looked back at her family's cottage. She seared the image of them all gathered outside her beautiful home, not wanting to ever forget, before finally turning towards the forest in the distance.

"It's now or never," she murmured as she marched her way into the terror-filled woodland of Brittelia.

Walking had become her least favorite thing.

In the not so distant past, she used to love taking leisurely strolls or meandering through the town's cobbled paths, but she'd come to dislike it rather fast when she found it was the only thing to do.

Already sweaty and tired, she had been traipsing through the wide expanse of trees for half an hour when the sun at last fully rose. Lillian felt drastically more at ease with the forest now filled with bright glinting rays. Though she knew the creatures still prowled during the day, she would at least have a better chance of defending herself when she could actually *see* her foes.

There was a jolt of panic in her blood at that notion. She'd yet to really process where she was and what exactly she was doing. It was like her body was in control and her brain had yet to catch up, like she was working off pure instinct. It reminded her of when birds flew south each winter; that it wasn't something they thought about but just did. However, if Lillian were the bird, she felt like her wings were about to fall off and cause her to crash at any second.

Hauling one leg at a time, unable to shake away that horrid visual, a small demeaning part of Lillian was almost hoping for this to be a one-way trip. The way there would be long and punishing, and she couldn't even fathom what state she'd be in for the trek back. If she managed to make it that far, that is.

Gods, she wanted to slap herself for thinking that way. Even though they weren't sincere, she banished away those thoughts, not wanting to manifest a certainly gruesome demise. Her mind could think all day on the hundreds of nightmarish ways this forest could put an end to her existence. It was funny like that.

Instead, Lillian focused on her steps; a broken leg or ankle would be an entirely too humiliating way for her to meet her end. So the hours went by trudging beneath the dense canopy of curving branches and making certain to mind her footing.

Thick smells of bark and moss journeyed alongside her, the crisp breeze whisking it past her nose. She inhaled deeper, sighing as she welcomed more of the heavenly aroma. Was it strange to love that earthy scent?

There was so much about the forest she adored. Its inherent beauty, the serenity and peace it offered. In fact, if she didn't know of the dangers these lands possessed, she would've felt utterly at ease. But Lillian knew what this place was. The horrors she'd witnessed would be forever branded to the inside of her skull.

However, she did find it strange that she had yet to encounter one of those foul beings—not that she was complaining. Perhaps she had been right in her earlier musings in that the creatures truly did slumber throughout the day. But it was unsettling that she hadn't even seen a glimmer of movement from any beasts lurking about, and she couldn't help but feel that something was coming. That this was the calm before the storm.

But for now, to her immense content, her only company were the unending plague of insects that buzzed by her ears, pestering her nonstop. As annoying as they were, she had grown accustomed to her aggravating buzzing companions, but was forced with silence when they all at once disappeared. The immediate stillness of the forest made her tense, and she had the sudden urge to lie low and get out of sight.

Choosing to trust her instincts, she took cover between two large rocks, waiting for something to take place. She removed her dagger from her boot and held it at the ready, priming herself for a fight—but her attention turned elsewhere as a rustling of bushes drew her attention.

Lillian held her breath, bracing herself for whatever manner of death prowled beyond those leaves. Her heart raced a million beats a second as the noise grew louder.

Through half-lidded eyes, she watched, knowing whatever

creature emerged would be horrific. Her fingers started shaking as she stared, and she clutched the dagger tighter.

She knew this would happen. She knew that she would eventually come across these demons. Lillian knew how to fight, she'd trained for this, she'd clashed with them before. Today would be no different. Today she would get past whatever creature this was. She couldn't die this quickly, could she?

The clamor of shaking leaves intensified, Lillian holding her panicked breaths as the monstrous beast stalked out of the bushes, revealing itself to be….

Gods, she couldn't breathe. It was too much. It was too horrible. It was...

A darling little deer?

A deer. She exhaled shakily. It was a deer.

Lillian had almost burst out in laughter when the animal popped out from behind the thick shrubs. This adorable little fawn with its soft, tan hide and white speckles had her in such an intense state of panic that she had sworn she was going to pass out from how fast her heart galloped.

Seconds from rising from her concealed space, smiling to herself for the overreaction, a flash of black darted past her, snatching the doe right before her eyes.

Lillian's face turned ashen as the sounds of claws ripping into flesh and whelps of agony filled the hollow forest. She sat in her tucked away spot, paralyzed with fear of the creature that could so easily tear apart the innocent animal.

It was a never-ending nightmare, sitting hidden, forced to hear the beast growling and gorging itself on the torn flesh. Her terror was so strong that even her hands had begun to cramp from how tightly she gripped her dagger, expecting at any second for the creature to turn its claws onto her.

The unknown beast let out a guttural snarl as if declaring satisfaction with its meal.

That unnatural noise, the way it had snapped its bones with such a vicious crack, had startled Lillian, causing her to drop the dagger into the fallen leaves around her. Instantly, she felt the creature freeze. She didn't dare move a muscle, fearful that the thing could even hear the loud thumping inside her chest.

The creature's heavy breathing grew wilder as it approached the two boulders, as if each whiff of her scent was sending it into a frenzy.

Lillian prayed to any of the gods that would listen to ward off the monster into any direction but her own, but the beast inched closer, seconds from uncovering her and ripping her apart just as it had done the deer. She squeezed her eyes shut in a fool's attempt to make herself invisible.

However, it seemed she didn't need shrouding as a crackling of fallen twigs sounded in the complete opposite direction. It appeared as if the gods had indeed answered her prayers as the beast turned its attention to the sudden noise and chased whatever animal now ran for its life.

The pounding of the creature's powerful limbs on the earth disappeared, and she sunk back against the rock, finally able to breathe as she picked up her fallen blade. She'd never been the religious type, but that didn't stop her from getting on her knees and thanking whatever god had been looking over her.

That had been way too close, Lillian thought to herself.

Even with the terror she felt, she only stayed in between the boulders for half an hour longer, not willing to waste any more time. The incessant buzzing returned all around her, and she felt confident that the thing was long gone; never had she thought one could be so overjoyed to hear the bothersome chatter of an insect.

And with that, that horrific experience that still made her mind feel numb and limbs feel like mush, Lillian began her trek through the woods once more. Iavothae was still a long way away, and she needed to cover as much ground as possible before it got dark; it would only get worse once the shadows descended. Getting caught in the open once the sun vanished was *not* something she wanted to do, but she still had a while to go before she scouted out refuge for the night.

Lillian sighed as she passed another too similar rock. Gods, she hoped she was going in the right direction. No one really talked about it—everyone being equally terrified of anything to do with the Ilaidae—but she had a vague idea where the lands of Iavothae laid. So hoping she was heading the right way, the day went by with a punishing slowness, the routine of passing the same tired trees and wiping the sweat off her brows already growing old. Lillian felt as if her legs were going to fall off, but thankfully the sun had begun to set, allowing her to stop and find a decent place to lie low and rest.

She walked for a few more minutes, looking for some place suitable, until stumbling upon an empty, hollowed out oak tree, large enough for her to squeeze into. It seemed like the best chance of staying out of the clearing and she chose not to linger any longer as she crawled right in. Lillian unwrapped a few of her rations and wolfed them down, not wishing to attract anything with the smell of food.

This was all too absurd; even eating was far too dangerous. Everything about this was ridiculous. Being here, doing this, having to waste so much time staying hidden. The less she sat around, the closer she could get to Iavothae and out of these vicious woodlands. She almost laughed at the sentence. What a mistake that would be. Thankfully, Lillian was smarter than that and actually valued her life, so if she had to wait for a few hours until the sun rose, then that's what she would do.

Total darkness began veiling the forest at that precise thought, the full lack of sun seeming beckoned by her musings; it appeared she'd chosen just the right time to find shelter. She sat in silence for a long time, tucked away, the occasional rustling of leaves startling her, but luckily with nothing too sinister sounding coming her way. A mercy that she had chosen a good hiding spot.

Leaning her head against the inner trunk, the thought of sleep no longer seemed like such a risky idea anymore as Lillian found her eyes feeling heavy. She sat upright against the tree, barely noticing that her lids were now fully shut.

It was the middle of the night when Lillian jerked herself awake. She didn't know how long she'd slept but was glad to at least have gotten some rest.

Stretching out her legs, she shook off the drowsiness. It was all still quiet, the forest calm and steady, but something... something felt off. Lillian was never the type to stir in the midst of slumber, so it was odd for her to have done so—but it would make sense if it were due to her precarious surroundings.

But—Lillian squinted her eyes at the shadowy opening—she couldn't shake the growing feeling that her senses had roused her for a reason. She could very well just be overthinking things—per usual—but, as she leaned against the hollowed-out tree, there was a tingle crawling over her skin telling her that something was out there. That something... something was watching her. Her senses had never failed her before, so she became as still as possible while waiting for whatever she perceived to present itself.

For a few minutes nothing happened, and she had started to think that she was being irrationally paranoid when something wet hit her cheek. She brought her fingertips to her face and wiped off the drop just as another fell. The oak she had taken refuge in had an opening at the top, so it wouldn't be the ideal choice for rain, but the day had been completely clear without a cloud in sight.

Another droplet splashed her cheek.

Dragging her eyes up, she decided to glance upwards to see if there was any semblance of rain coming, but it wasn't storm clouds that greeted her.

A gray leathery face and mouth full of jagged teeth smiled down at her.

Lillian's eyes flicked to the corner of its open jaw where she could see dribbles of liquid forming. Her blood went cold as she realized that the drops of water on her face had been the drool that trickled from the creature's massive maw.

The thing stared at her as it licked its lips with its enormous tongue.

That was enough to send Lillian darting out of the hollow tree, running as fast as she could through the night. She didn't dare look back in fear of what the creature chasing her turned out to be.

Lillian flew through the woods, breaking and snapping branches as she went, most certainly alerting all the other beings in her vicinity of her presence. The thought of having an army of creatures hunting her down for their next meal terrified her, fueling her limbs to go even faster.

Lillian didn't know how much longer she could keep up the pace and veered right, thorns and branches tearing into her cheeks, leaving beads of blood in their wake.

A light glowed out in the distance, and she hurtled towards it at full speed. Her lungs burned as she neared the source, and she could see that it belonged to a lone little cottage. Lillian sprinted towards the home, hoping for any sort of protection that the people or house could offer.

No sooner did she make it to the front, and she pounded on the wood with all her strength.

A middle-aged women opened the door, and Lillian didn't have time to ask for permission as she shoved her way in, slamming the door shut behind her. She took out her sword and stood by the entry, waiting for the wretched beast to break in.

But as she remained by the threshold, anticipating the creature to barrel in, the attack strangely never came.

CHAPTER 9

After Lillian felt that she was relatively safe for the time being, she remembered that she had barged into this poor woman's home—she must have not known what to think upon seeing Lillian charge her way inside.

Turning her attention to the matron of the home, she sheathed her blade, not wanting to spook her any further.

The woman stood motionless, her jaw hung wide open. "Pl-please, take whatever you want—just don't hurt me. I beg of you."

Lillian inched towards her, using calm tones. "I mean you no harm. I was only trying to find a place to fend off the creature that was chasing me. I apologize for any distress I may have caused."

The woman blinked, processing what Lillian had said before realizing what she spoke was sincere. "Then I am happy to act as your haven for the night if need be. My name is Irene."

It was a bit odd how easily this stranger had decided to trust her, but she chose not to question it any further. "You have no idea what a pleasure it is to make your acquaintance, Irene. My name is Lillian."

And at last able to relax some, she took a look at her surroundings for the first time since barreling in.

Irene's cottage was a humble one—having no elaborate decorations but still tastefully adorned. From what she could see, it was mostly one big room that contained a kitchen and lounging space and a door in the back which she suspected led into a bedroom.

Lillian had no idea what a woman would be doing out here on her own, so she asked the question in her mind. "Do you live here all by yourself?"

"Oh no, it's far too dangerous to be out here all on my lonesome. My grandfather built this home long ago, and I come here once a year with my husband and son."

"I couldn't imagine braving these savage forests every year."

"It's not so bad once you understand the lay of the land and know which areas to avoid."

"To each their own I suppose," Lillian said, shrugging her shoulders. "But you mentioned your husband and son joined you—where have they gone?"

"They like to go on a hunting expedition when they come out here, so they'll be gone for a few more days." The woman's eyes beamed as if she had just thought of the most marvelous idea. "But I would love it if you'd join me and keep me company!"

She did in fact need somewhere to hide out until the sun rose, so she chose to accept Irene's kind offer. "That would be perfect actually."

The woman rubbed her hands together in glee. "Oh, this will be great! I hate having to spend too much time alone. Are you hungry? We have plenty of food to spare if you'd like."

Lillian was never one to reject a generous home-cooked meal and nodded her head. "Something to eat would be lovely."

Irene smiled widely. "Excellent! I made a delicious stew earlier that I can have warmed up in a few minutes. Come sit while I heat it up."

Sauntering over to the small dinner table, she pulled up a wobbly chair and set her belongings on the floor by her feet—it was a wonder she had remembered to snatch them up with the chaos that was her night.

She watched as the kind stranger poured the stew into a pot, hung it over the fire, and gave it a few stirs with a wooden spoon before leaving it to come sit by Lillian. "Now tell me, what brings you to these woods so late at night?"

Lillian wondered how she would answer that question. She was in no mood to be called crazed or demented, so she came up with a lie. "I don't have much going for me back in Grigaros, so I thought to venture out into the lands of Iavothae for something new."

A mixture of surprise and sadness emerged on her face. "Surely you have *something* of value back home for you. A young woman such as yourself shouldn't throw her life away to the Ilaidae roaming those lands."

"Nothing worthwhile. And I wouldn't be throwing my life away. I know how to fend for myself."

A corner of her lip twitched upwards. "You do seem capable of putting up a fight, but it would just be a pity to see such pretty skin shredded apart by undeserving creatures."

Lillian thought the comment of her skin was fairly odd but glazed over it. "If things go according to plan, then no creatures will get their claws on me."

A smile that she couldn't quite read parted on Irene's lips. "I suppose we will have to see what delicious schemes fate has in store for you then." The woman got up and began stirring the pot. "Would you like something to drink?"

The mention of refreshment made Lillian realize how parched her throat had become. "Yes, please," she replied.

Irene grabbed a cup from her cabinets and filled it up with a pitcher of water as she brought it over to the table.

Thanking her, she picked up the glass, eager to take a sip. But while she stared at it, she thought her eyes might be playing tricks on her as her vision changed. The former glass of water transformed into a dirty smudged one full of a dark murky liquid with dead, floating insects.

She blinked her eyes, readjusting her sight, and the glass once again appeared as if it were filled with fresh water. Clearing her throat, she set it on the table, no longer feeling like taking a sip.

Irene must have noticed something seemed off as she asked, "Is something the matter?"

Perhaps too quickly to seem normal, she shook her head. "N-no, I think I'm just a little tired from the night's events. Is there anywhere I could freshen up?"

"There's a connecting bathroom once you go in through the bedroom door. Help yourself to anything you need."

Lillian thanked the woman again and walked over to the bedroom, shutting the door behind her. She rubbed her eyes, thinking that she must have already been very sleep deprived if she was starting to have hallucinations so early on.

Needing to get her bearings together, Lillian sat on the bed. The woman had been generous enough to offer her home to a complete stranger; she couldn't start freaking her out.

Lillian stayed for a few minutes and after feeling relaxed and more composed, she got up, ready to go back out, but stopped as her vision seemed to alter once more.

The nice plain looking bedroom no longer appeared the same. It had transformed itself into an old, abandoned room with broken furniture strewn out around her. The bed she sat in was torn to shreds, covered with numerous stains and dirt, and the windows on the far wall were shattered, the broken shards littering the floors where the wooden planks had begun to rot.

But all that, being quite the unsettling sight on its own, was not the most abnormal thing in the room. The ceilings and corners were covered in thick strands of silky webbing and hanging all around her were cocooned figures that appeared to be of humanoid shape.

Lillian staggered back a step, knocking over an old lamp from a nightstand.

"Is everything alright in there?" Irene called out.

With the crashing sound and her already taking a while, she knew it was starting to be more than just a little suspicious, but she came up with an excuse. "I just have a bit of an upset stomach. I'll be out in a minute."

"Oh—okay, let me know if you need anything."

Technically she wasn't lying—she really did feel as if she were going to be sick.

Looking around, she weighed her options on what she could do.

This clearly had all been some cleverly conjured up façade that stopped working. Lillian thought of making a run for it and leaping out of the broken window, but she had stupidly left her things in the kitchen. She would have to go back out and get them because she wouldn't survive a day without them.

From what she could tell, Irene hadn't noticed that Lillian was no longer under the influence of whatever illusion she had created. Her best shot at survival would be to act as if nothing were amiss, grab her pack, and make a speedy exit out the door. Simple.

Lillian settled her churning stomach as she readied herself for whatever manner of beast awaited her and put on her most believable smile as she entered the room with Irene once more.

Her features immediately faltered as she took in the creature before her. The rest of the home looked as worn down as the bedroom but where Irene had been... stood a monster of horror.

The only similarity between the sweet woman and the beast before her was the face attached to the unnatural body. The top half of the woman, who had so kindly offered Lillian a place to stay, was now connected to a black, rounded abdomen that had four spindly legs sprouting from either side of it.

Irene's familiar looking eyes stared back at her as Lillian struggled to maintain her false smile. The fangs on her face clicked together as she hissed, "Do you find yourself well?"

Lillian's voice shook as she tried to speak, but she feigned needing to clear her throat and answered with a calmer, steadier voice. "Yes…my bowels didn't seem to agree with me, but I'm feeling much improved," she said with a hard swallow.

The creature, formerly sweet Irene, grinned with her pointed pincers. "I'm glad to hear it."

It was an effort to loosen her rigid posture, to make her steps not seem forced, but she was able to manage as she made her way closer to where she had set her pack.

Irene turned back to the stew, and with her distracted, Lillian picked up her belongings and began backing towards the door. Slowly, she inched farther and farther back, careful to keep her footsteps silent. Just...a... few... more...steps.

Her foot landed on a wobbly plank, the floor letting out a horrific creak at her misstep. Lillian froze. She lifted her terrified eyes but was able to suck down a breath as Irene continued to go about her task. Gods. The gods were looking out for her.

Seeming to have gone unnoticed, she reached the door and turned to twist the knob, desperate to leave the ruined home. But just as she grasped the cool metal, a net of sticky threads shot onto her hand.

Lillian's stomach dropped as she heard Irene speak in a voice dripping with venom. "Now that is no way to treat a hostess who has so willingly offered you her home, is it?"

Lillian yanked on the door with all her might, but it wouldn't budge as if the edges had been bolted shut. Her eyes shot around the room with a wild panic as she assessed her remaining courses of action. How had she not noticed that there were no windows throughout the entirety of the room?

If the door was locked, then that meant her only viable option would be to make it to the bedroom and jump out of the smashed window. But there was one small issue—Irene and her humongous spider-like body were blocking the way.

The atrocious thing smiled at her as if it knew just how much of a problem she had become. "Planning on going somewhere?" she crooned.

It truly was getting quite hypocritical of her as to how many times Lillian had beseeched the help of the gods, but she couldn't help herself as she muttered another quick prayer and pulled out her dagger.

Irene's pincers clicked together as she let out a throaty laugh. "Really? You think that little thing is going to stop me?"

Lillian adjusted her grip on the blade as she braced herself. To a more seasoned fighter it might not seem like the best tactic—likely because it wasn't—but Lillian broke out into a run as she charged the odious monster. However, instead of trying to stab her way through, at the last second—using the momentum of her speed—she dropped to the floor and skidded under the beast with her blade held high, slicing into the creature's abdomen.

A green ooze dripped off her dagger as she got to her feet and slammed the door of the bedroom she'd slid into shut. She threw as much of the broken furniture as she could in front of the door as the monster's cries of rage rumbled the home.

Barricaded as much as she could, Lillian rushed to the broken window and leapt out of it, careful not to cut herself on the jagged shards still on the frame. Her legs wasted no time in tearing through the open forest.

As the wind cut by her cheeks, Lillian noticed that she had gotten rather decent at this whole running from terrible monster's thing. Now whether that was a skill she was glad to have practiced so many times, she didn't know. But she thought her odds of survival to be more realistic if she fled as opposed to if she stayed back and fought.

So Lillian Echethier did what she did best and raced through the woods from another horrifying foe. There weren't any noises that indicated the creature was on her trail, but she ran for as long as she could until unable to hold out any longer. If the insect-like woman was anything like other spiders, she gathered that it wouldn't take to venturing far out from its web.

Gambling on that, she stopped and pulled out her canteen of water, chugging down as much as she could until it felt like she would throw up from how much water sloshed inside her. She would definitely need to stop by a stream.

Antsy at being exposed in the dark, she began trekking through the forest anew, not wishing to linger any longer. But as she searched for a place to stay out of sight, the sun appeared on the horizon, dusting the skies in warm hues of orange.

She must have taken a much longer nap than she had originally thought or perhaps her stay in the spider woman's cabin had altered the passing of time.

A shiver crawled down her neck as she thought back to that demon. It had been a full day since she'd left, and already she'd encountered three monsters while barely managing to escape with her life. She would hate to think of what would have happened if she hadn't been able to get away. Lillian's low confidence in her ability to make it through the Forest of Brittelia significantly plummeted at the glim thought. If she wanted to make it the rest of the way through this forest, she would have to be far more clever because she was positive she wouldn't be able to cheat death much longer.

Lillian readjusted the pack on her back and shook the canteen of water. There wasn't a lot left, so she concluded that her first order of business would be to find a nearby source.

Stuffing the canteen in her bag, Lillian continued on her journey, feeling entirely unprepared for any more threats that came her way.

CHAPTER 10

Finding water was Lillian's main task for the day—with the obvious exception of remaining alive.

Scouring her mind, she thought back to what she knew of locating a body of water in the wilderness—thankfully she wasn't completely helpless when it came to that matter. Ever since she was a child, her father had made sure that Lillian could be prepared to survive in any situation. She had thought it rather silly back then but was glad for it now.

The first thing her father had said to do was listen; even if a stream was far off into the distance, there was always a good chance you might be able to hear it.

Lillian closed her eyes, silencing her thoughts as she concentrated on the forest's sounds. It wasn't clear, but she thought she heard water flowing but wasn't entirely confident in her efforts.

The next thing her father told her to do was look for animal tracks as they would likely lead her towards a source. She fixed her gaze on the earthen floor and found the tracks of a small animal, perhaps a rabbit, leading in the direction she had faintly heard the stream.

With those two tactics in mind, she deduced that was her best path and began following the footprints, hoping that the tracks weren't leading her to a lake. She did *not* want to drink from the stagnant water where all manner of insects and parasites festered in the still waters. Getting sick on her ongoing travels was not on the agenda.

As Lillian kept to the tracks, she thought back to when her father had taught her all these, now necessary, skills. Gods, it felt like a lifetime ago.

She had been maybe six or seven when her father used to have her and her siblings all camp outside in the backyard of their home. A small chuckle trickled out of her as she remembered how they had to pitch their own tent each year. And since it was an annual thing, they always forgot how to do it, causing the whole thing to end in a screaming match on who was doing it right.

Her mother hated the outdoors, so she always opted out of the family tradition, which in turn made Nimreth not want to be a part of it either. But their father forced all of them to stay and learn the basic survival skills he felt so passionate about.

While her father went on and on about his lectures of the outdoors, Maxith would always be too impatient to pay attention and would mess around or try and frighten them all. Kynra pretended to listen, but it was obvious that the topic was of no importance to her.

So it was always just Lillian, clinging to every word her father said. She had never dreamed she would use any of the skills he taught her but was fascinated by everything he showed her. That was where her intrigue for hunting had first blossomed, and, after a few years of participating in the annual event, she demanded to learn how to use a bow and arrow.

And now here she was, putting all those skills to the test. She wondered what that young girl would think if she knew that one day she would be running through the very same forest she had feared with such an intensity.

Had feared was perhaps not the correct term seeing she was just as terrified of these woods as she had always been. The difference she supposed was that she was braver than her past self. Lillian snorted—more stupid was the likelier option. But she chose to have a positive outlook on her current situation and settled on brave.

Lillian let her mind wander back to that fond memory—remembering those cool summer nights with her family just staring up at the stars. As they got older, they stopped having those yearly nights in the outdoors—her siblings no longer interested in sleeping out in the dirt and elements.

A sigh escaped her; she would give anything to relive those nights of joy and laughter. But she couldn't, no matter how much she yearned for it.

Exhaling, she snapped herself back into reality as the somber thought set in. It wouldn't do her any good to reminisce on the past and forget where she was and what she was doing. She was no longer in the safe comforts of her home. She was in the deadly Forest of Brittelia on her way to Iavothae where the murderous Ilaidae dwelled. And she wasn't learning how to make a fire or pitch a tent. But instead, was going to enlist herself in the supposedly famed Trial of the Flame—which she of course still had not an inkling of what it entailed.

Was she supposed to fight another champion or perhaps complete some sort of obstacle or puzzle? If any of what that ominous lady had spoken was true, then she at least knew it wasn't going to be a simple task. The woman had all but implied that not many—if anyone at all—had survived the Trial of the Flame. How exciting for her.

But she had already known the risks that becoming the Champion of the Flame warranted. Lillian knew that she had essentially sentenced herself to a gruesome death by accepting the role.

Imagining the numerous ways that the Ilaidae could end her life made her feel queasy, but the thought of sitting back and doing nothing made her feel sick to her stomach. Even fathoming relaxing and delighting in the comforts of her home, while she knew there was even the *smallest* chance that there was going to be a mass slaughter, made her food threaten to claw its way back up her throat.

And that was why Lillian had made the choices she had made. There was no point in fiddling with the subject any longer.

Shoving past those thoughts, she took a moment to look around as she took a swig of her water. The woods were incredibly beautiful—if she ignored all the murderous creatures that hid in between the trees. There was something soothing about how the sunlight filtered in between the far off branches and how the whispers of a gentle breeze rustled the leaves. Lillian could see how the tranquil ambiance of the forest could further distract any prey and give an even better advantage to whatever monsters lurked in the shadows. If Lillian weren't so worried about being killed every second of the day, she could find herself truly reveling in the enchanting forestland around her. But for now, she had to keep her guard up.

Stuffing her canteen back into her pack, she continued on to where she thought a stream might be. And as the time went by, she made her way closer and closer, the sounds of running water became more apparent.

Now confident in the direction she was heading, Lillian journeyed forth towards the stream, using her sense of hearing as the rushing water became unmistakable. She could feel as if she were going to near it any moment—and after a few more minutes of walking, she could make out the stream in the near distance. It wasn't anything humongous but wide enough for her to not be able to jump over it.

Lillian ran towards it, throwing her pack onto the ground as she crashed to her knees by the bank. Rifling through her pack, she pulled out her container and leaned over the water, filling up her canteen as much as she could without having the water spill out.

Feelings of thirst overwhelmed her as she gazed at the glistening current, causing Lillian to indulge herself with a huge gulp. An icy sensation slid down her dry throat as she cupped more of the stream into her mouth.

With her thirst freshly quenched and having put everything away, she took a moment to just sit in silence and look at her reflection in the running stream.

Gods, she looked like a wreck.

Her hair was a frizzy mess and strands had been plastered to her forehead from the absurd amount of sweat she had been producing. A fine layer of dirt now coated her face, and she could spot a few small tears in her tunic and pants from where she had slid on the rotten floorboards of Irene's cottage. Needless to say, she was not looking her most *presentable* self at the moment.

She may have to find a way to freshen up before meeting the Ilaidae if she wanted them to take her seriously—an issue to be dealt with at a later time.

Trying to at least clear away some of the smudges and grime coating her, Lillian dipped her hands in the water and ran them over her face. She scrubbed at her filth encrusted face as best she could and then sat back, staring at her sopping wet face. All she saw when she looked back at the mirror image was an ordinary mortal girl.

Gods, was she being a complete and utter fool for even *attempting* to go to Iavothae? As of right now, she had encountered all manner of beasts and *barely* managed to live. And these monsters were just the opening act—she knew that the worst was most definitely yet to come.

A chill went through her; the thought of facing the Ilaidae and venturing into Iavothae scared the living breath out of her. It should've been someone else. She still couldn't shake the feeling that some other person would have been better suited for being the Champion of the Flame. A more skilled fighter or knight would certainly not have been as afraid or let a few vicious creatures unnerve them from their duty.

As soon as those thoughts had entered her mind, she remembered something her father always used to say. Whenever Lillian was younger, she had always been in awe of how fearless her father had seemed, venturing out into the woods to hunt or always ready to defend their family at a moment's notice. And like any curious child, she had asked her father one day how he had come to be so brave and unafraid so she too could one day become a ferocious warrior like him.

He had answered her by saying that anyone who claims that they are fearless are either liars or utter fools. Being fearless is not what makes you a great fighter—the ability to overcome that fear and do what's right is what makes you a brilliant warrior.

Lillian clung to her father's words as she sat at the edge of the water. She could acknowledge that she was *very* afraid, but she wouldn't let that terror hold her back from finishing what she had set out to do.

A groan escaped her lips; it appeared that she was still stuck with the whole Champion of the Flame burden and would be seeing it through to the end. Hooray.

Feeling the smallest bit more confident, Lillian stood up from the bank and took a glance at her reflection one last time. She was about to turn and leave when she noticed something seemed off with the image in the water.

Getting closer, Lillian studied her figure in the stream. She held up one hand, waving it in the air, and then did the same with the other. She then proceeded to make a series of different expressions with her face and immediately took a step back, not knowing what to think.

The picture in the water looked like her in all aspects but there was something wrong—it was almost as if the reflection was on a slight lag.

Lillian approached the water once more, finding the features of the stream intriguing as she moved her fingers at her mirror image. She laughed as she made her movements even faster causing the magic of the stream to delay even more as it tried to keep up.

But her wide grin dropped as realization dawned on her. The figure in the water was not her. Something that looked a *lot* like her was observing her every move to then be able to copy it, causing there to be a slight falter in her reflection.

Whatever thing was watching her seemed to have noticed she had caught on as her duplicate in the water halted its mimicking. The creature stared at her, a devilish smile surfacing onto its face, as it launched itself out of the stream and pulled her under.

CHAPTER 11

Choking on water, Lillian thrashed as something held her beneath the surface. She desperately reached for her dagger and swiped it out in front of her, trying to wound whatever creature had its hold on her.

As she blindly sliced through the water again and again, she felt the blade make contact with something and whatever had been holding onto her, let go, allowing her to scramble to her feet; mercifully, the stream wasn't very deep, and the water only came up to her hip when she was fully submerged.

On shaking feet, she stood, coughing up the stream's water and gasping for air as she tried holding her dagger in any semblance of protection.

A voice tinged with annoyance came out from behind her. "Did you really just stab me?"

Lillian twirled in the direction of the noise and fumbled for words as she stared in awe at the Ilaidae who had spoken.

A creature with pale blue skin and long white hair stood before her. He wore no clothes, but by some unknown magic, the water from the stream fell over his lower torso, flowing like a waterfall to form a skirt. The humanoid looking creature gazed at her with its piercing sapphire eyes as it ran webbed hands over a slice in its glistening skin.

Struggling to keep her jaw closed, she took in the rather majestic looking monster, trying to instill intimidation into her words as she spoke. "Stay back—or I'll do it again."

The monster looked irritated as it rolled its eyes. "You mortals are such a bore. Does humor not exist in the lands you call home?"

Her fear of the beast before her got washed away with a newfound anger; did it think shoving her under the water to be a joke? "We don't find nearly drowning people to their *deaths* to be rather humorous."

"Oh, come on, you guys really don't play tricks on each other? And you make it sound worse than it was—I wasn't *actually* going to let you die."

Lillian gritted her teeth at what the thing uttered. This was a joke, all some game it found to be amusing. "Well, how could I have *possibly* known that?"

The creature looked at her as if the answer was obvious. "You wouldn't… That's what makes it funny."

She stared at the creature, baffled with what it said. "Just let me go and I won't cause you any trouble."

The thing looked at her eyes, a smile creeping on its lips. "Hmm, I *could* do that, but I'm also quite curious to see what sort of trouble you could cause." Lillian pulled out her sword, ready for the creature to pounce, but it only exhaled as it said, "Calm down already. I was merely kidding. It's far too early in the day to be dueling to the death."

Lillian kept her gaze on the creature, not uttering a word, and the thing—realizing she wasn't going to respond—continued talking. "Tell you what, I'll make you a deal. Simply stay for a while and chat with me, and I'll let you go on your way unharmed."

Not trusting in what the Ilaidae offered, she asked, "And what would you gain from conversing with me?"

"It gets *so* very lonely out here in these woods, and there aren't many intelligent folk to talk with now a days that don't want to dig their claws into you." The creature's tone turned excited in a way that made Lillian feel more nervous. "Does that mean you accept?"

"Seeing that it's basically my only option at the moment—Yes, I suppose I accept."

"Excellent! Now put that ridiculous blade away—it's as if you don't trust my word."

She scoffed at his request. "I bet you'd like that, wouldn't you? And the second I sheathe it, you come and kill me where I'm standing. Yeah. I don't think so."

The creature looked the mildest bit offended but couldn't keep the small grin off his face. "Have it your way then. I guess I can't blame you for being cautious." He rubbed his hands together like a child eager to play with a new toy. "Now, where to begin? Ah, names. Mine is Euthemio—and you are?"

"Lillian."

"A beautiful name for a beautiful woman." He gave her a quick roam with his eyes. "Well, maybe not right now but I bet underneath that sweat and grime is a true enchantress. What brings the lovely Lillian to the Forest of Brittelia?"

Lillian took a second to think of an answer, knowing she shouldn't say her true reason. "I just came to enjo—"

"Now no lying either. I want to have an *honest* conversation. And I'll know if you're being dishonest."

Not wanting to explain how she wasn't insane for the *thousandth* time, she huffed out a loud exhale. But perhaps this creature—Euthemio—could be of some assistance and know a little more about the Trial of the Flame. "I'm trying to cross through the Forest of Brittelia to get to Iavothae."

Euthemio stared at her, nodding his head and motioning with his hands for her to continue. "And? Go on."

"I'm going to Iavothae to..." She paused not wanting to say it out loud to this thing that would likely ridicule her and call her stupid.

He gaped at her with wide eyes. "You can't just stop now. The suspense is practically killing me."

Taking a deep breath in, she blurted it out. "I want to be the Champion of the Flame."

For a second all he did was blink as if not processing what she had said. "Surely you *must* be joking," he finally mustered. "I must have misjudged the mortals—it seems like you do have some humor. Now tell me the real reason because that cannot seriously be it."

Heat crept up into her cheeks as a mixture of anger and embarrassment shrouded her.

"Dear gods, you're being sincere. Why would you want to sentence yourself to such a horrible death?"

"I—I have no other choice. The Ilaidae are planning a massacre on all the mortals. I tried getting someone more suited to survive, but no one dared to go."

Euthemio rubbed his chin as he spoke. "I did hear murmurs that Iavothae was planning some schemes over in Grigaros, but I had no idea the extent. And I take it they all called you deranged or mad when you brought this all up?"

Lillian only nodded.

It looked as if he were sucked into deep thought as he pondered over her words. "I'd expect nothing less. The mortals of Grigaros—no offense—are very ignorant when it comes to anything with the Ilaidae. So I assume you plan on participating in the Trial of the Flame and using your single wish to save all of Grigaros?"

Biting her lip, she gave another nod.

"How very noble of you indeed. And would I be assuming correctly that you know nothing of what being the Champion of the Flame entails?"

"The woman who told me of it said I would have to see for myself. *But* I was hoping you could shed some light on the whole mystery."

The Ilaidae shook his head in what looked like lament. "I sincerely wish I could, but there is a strict rule—law really—among the Ilaidae that we must not discuss what the trial consists of. I believe it has something to do with that if the mortals knew, they wouldn't dare participate."

Well, that *definitely* didn't make Lillian feel better. Her mind swirled with all the horrible things that the trial could be, shivering as she thought of how they had to put a law in place in case the mortals decided that the trial was too much. "And you can't tell me anything at all?"

Once again, he shook his head no. "All I can say is that it will be the most difficult thing you will face. Many have tried, and all have failed. Are you sure this is what you want to do?"

"I've made up my mind. There's no turning back now."

Euthemio stared at her, a gleam in his blue eyes. "Not many would have the courage to do what you have and will do. I commend you for your bravery. I'm not sure even I would do such a thing."

She didn't know how to respond to that, but she didn't have to as Euthemio went on. "But the least I can do for you is show you a shortcut to Iavothae."

Her head recoiled, shocked in what he had offered. "Why would you even want to help me?"

A look of shame and sadness fell over his features. "Let's just say I had a chance to make a difference long ago, and I chose to sit back on the sidelines. I would like to help this time."

Even though his words sounded sincere, she had just met this creature and knew what the Ilaidae truly were. "How do I know you're not sending me somewhere to my death?"

Euthemio's face went blank with seriousness as he said, "I wouldn't need to send you anywhere other than where you are going to do that."

Her stomach dropped as she realized the truth in his statement. "Very well," she said with a swallow. "I will accept your help."

Lillian listened as Euthemio gave her the more favorable way to Iavothae, mentally noting each twist and turn he mentioned. It wasn't too confusing and, after he finished going over the better path, Lillian felt like it was time to take her leave. She had already wasted enough time on this little detour, but hopefully the shortcut would help her make up for lost time.

Bending down, she slung her pack over her shoulder before turning to Euthemio for the last time. "I really think I need to be on my way if I want to make good time before dark."

"Yes, I do believe you are right. I cannot hold you back any longer."

"So you'll allow me to leave in peace?"

"Of course, Lillian, you held up your end of the bargain, so it's only right that I do the same. But I really do hope our paths cross again someday in the future."

Lillian snorted. "I have to survive being the champion first before making plans with possibly murderous acquaintances."

He huffed out a throaty laugh, and she found herself letting a chuckle slip through her lips before starting to walk away. She made it a few feet when she heard Euthemio call out, "Please do try your best not to die a hideous death. It truly was an honor meeting you, Miss Lillian."

Smiling, she yelled back, "No promises." She took a pause and spoke in a low voice to herself. "Goodbye, Euthemio." She didn't look back again as she kept marching forward towards the trail Euthemio had gifted her.

Who knew she would meet a slightly likeable creature in these terrifying woods? But there was a lot of emphasis on the *slightly likeable* because she had not yet forgotten their first encounter of him drowning her in the stream.

Trudging along the path, she glanced at herself, clothes still damp from her unwanted swim. She was eternally grateful that the stream had only been a few feet deep. Because if not, she would have gone into a full-blown panic attack and sunk straight to the bottom. How embarrassing if she had managed to escape all kinds of terrifying beasts and what ended her was a little dip in the water.

She exhaled loudly at the thought; she really had to get over her irrational fear because one day swimming might mean the difference between life and death. But hopefully Iavothae wasn't known for its numerous bodies of water, and she wouldn't even have to worry in the slightest of her minor flaw.

As Lillian hopped over a tiny brook, she looked back on her interesting encounter with Euthemio—he hadn't seemed like all the other evil blood-hungry creatures she had previously met in the forest. He did however say that he was in no mood to kill so early in the day—did that mean his more savage tendencies became prominent at night? She found it hard to believe that such a well-spoken and polite individual could turn into a vicious killing machine at the flip of a coin, but she truly did not know enough about these creatures to know if all of them were murderous beasts.

Lillian decided the safe thing to do was to assume they were all trying to torture her in barbaric ways until shown otherwise. It had worked so far with Irene and the others, so there was no reason to switch up her strategy now. She had been so convinced that the sweet woman, Irene, was just a lonely wife, waiting for her husband to return, when in reality she was a monstrous spider-like demon trying to collect her for her next meal. Euthemio, on the other hand, was trying to drown her in a stream when they first met but turned out to be a civilized gentleman with an *interesting* sense of humor. There was no telling what the other beings she would meet along the way would act like, so she would treat them all as hostile enemies.

Lillian sighed—why must the Ilaidae all be so complicated?

But she relinquished that distracting thought and continued along, looking for the landmarks Euthemio had told her to watch out for.

He had said that the shortcut would be the same amount of dangerous as her original path save for one area—he had said to be extra cautious when she neared a cave she was meant to pass through. He hadn't given her exact details but said she should be alright if she were extremely quiet while going through. According to him, there was a monstrous being dwelling inside the cave that was very blind and relied on hearing and touch for its hunting.

Whatever lived inside the cave wasn't told to her, but Lillian wasn't sure she really wanted to know. All she needed to be informed on was that it was vital to be silent, however it unnerved her that Euthemio had visibly *cringed* when mentioning the pass.

Deciding to deal with that problem when she came to it, she moved her thoughts to concentrate on the dangers around her. She was still in the treacherous Forest of Brittelia and monsters could be lurking behind any tree; just because the sun was up did not mean she could let her guard down in the slightest. She recalled the unknown beast that had ripped that poor deer to shreds right before her in broad daylight.

The other monster that had greeted her flashed into her mind at the memory. Lillian would have to find a better shelter tonight seeing as her previous one hadn't been the most effective. There were caves lining the distance, but she wasn't mindless enough to presume they were empty. She would likely have to find a thick shrub or perhaps tie herself to the top of a very tall tree; sleeping up high wouldn't be the most comfortable, but it was far more preferable to being slaughtered.

Droplets of exhaustion slid down her face as she padded her way down the path. The remainder of the afternoon had mostly been uneventful after her interesting morning with Euthemio, but as Lillian continued, she found herself wishing she had someone to keep her company. Her first choice naturally wasn't Euthemio but even he might be better than nothing.

Lillian clung to that brief encounter, knowing that it might be the last nice interaction she would have before meeting her grim end.

CHAPTER 12

The sweltering heat of the day had been unbearable, and Lillian was glad that the sun had started setting so she could finally have some reprieve from the stifling weather.

Lifting up a hand, she wiped the beads of moisture dripping down her face. Lillian was amazed by the amount of sweat a mortal body could produce and was *more* than ready to let the night breeze drive away the sultry temperature and cool down her disgustingly drenched self.

The branches groaned as a gust of wind whisked by, leaving Lillian sighing as the cool air kissed her damp cheeks. But her sighs quickly turned to moans of annoyance as she looked around—she still had no idea where she would take shelter for the night. There weren't any hideouts that she could see, so sleeping in a tree was starting to look like her only option.

Lillian meandered through the woods and began assessing the trees, wondering which one would be most suitable for her weight. She had to choose a tree with a decent height but also one with thick branches that wouldn't snap in the middle of the night. It would be just her luck to be sleeping soundly to then suddenly plummet all the way to the cold, hard ground.

Wanting to be safely strapped up before dark, she halted her steps, scanning the perimeter. There were a copious number of trees that were befittingly tall, but once she glanced upwards, the branches near the top thinned out and would surely break under her ample pressure.

Not having yet found a suitable branch, Lillian kept strolling along, searching all over for the perfect place to rest.

She was beginning to give up on the notion of sleeping up high when she came across an enormous oak—never in her life had she *dreamed* a tree could be so massive. The colossal beast was exactly what she'd been looking for: it was tall enough for her to avoid any dangerous beings and had strong branches that would support her without a problem.

Now all she had to do was climb the damn thing.

There was no way she could scale it with the pack *and* her bow and quiver, so she would have to leave her trusty weapon at the bottom and retrieve it in the morning.

Wandering over to a dense looking bush, she shoved her bow and quiver inside, doing her best to bury it at the bottom with some dirt. She prayed no creature came by in the night and took her beloved weapon; she'd grown rather attached to the simple thing throughout the many years.

Lillian placed a few more twigs over the top of it and then sauntered back towards the tree, making sure her pack was strapped on tightly as she pulled out two daggers. She would use the branches to pull herself up but there were a few far apart areas where she would have to use her daggers to hoist herself up.

Beginning the ascent, she jammed one dagger into the thick trunk and bore her weight down on the hilt as she swung her leg out to the side. Once she felt her one leg securely wrapped around a branch, she used the momentum of the swing to bring the rest of her body onto it while tearing out the dagger.

Most of the branches seemed closer together now, so she sheathed her blades, relying on the strength of her arms to pull her way up. With a sigh, she reached for the branch above as she continued the climb.

Only once halfway up did she dare a glance down—what a mistake. She wouldn't consider herself to have a fear of heights because it wasn't being up high that bothered her, it was the plunging to your death part that freaked her out.

With a force of will, she tore her gaze from the faraway floor and took extra precautions to watch her footing as she climbed higher. At about two thirds of the way was when she decided she'd scaled enough and settled on a thick branch as she plopped down.

Thankfully the branch wasn't too wide, so wrapping a rope around it wouldn't prove to be very difficult. Carefully, she tied herself up, tight enough to keep herself from falling to her death in the night. She then looped part of the rope through one of the straps of her pack to ensure it didn't fall to the bottom if she did manage to doze off at some point.

Finishing the last knot securing her against the trunk, she rested her head against the rough bark. The forest had gone completely dark, and she sat in silence for a few minutes before she began fiddling with the twine around her. Lillian *really* hoped no monsters dared to come up this high because she would be absolutely screwed if that were to happen; she would either have to cut through the stiff rope or speedily untie the knot keeping her fastened.

The smallest bit paranoid, she ushered a quick positive thought out to the universe but rolled her eyes as she caught herself. There she went again, praying to the gods to keep her out of harm's way—they must certainly be fed up with hearing from her by now.

But her small prayer—hypocritical or not—caused her thoughts to drift to her mother and how she would pray each night for the wellbeing of her husband and children. Every evening after dinner, her mother would retreat to her chambers and utter a few words to the gods to look after her family. It didn't matter if she were feeling sick, sad, or even tired. Every night, without fail, Lillian would pass by her room and see her kneeling on the floor with her eyes closed and head held high towards the skies.

Time was a little hard to tell out in the woods, but Lillian supposed right about now would be when her mother would have her daily conversation with the gods.

A smile bloomed across her face at the thought of her family, and she wondered what they were doing right at this moment.

Feeling distraught would be the most probable answer.

It had been almost two full days since Lillian had left her family without even giving them a goodbye. Well, she sort of said her farewells to Nimreth, having been caught right as she was making her leave. She knew Nimreth had thought she'd sounded insane, and even called her a lunatic when she'd uttered how much she loved her and their family, but none of that mattered as long as she knew it to be true.

She wondered if they had found the letter she'd left in her room that explained why she had left and where she was going.

It also stated to not go looking for her, but she wasn't too confident that anyone would have gone after her anyway. Her father was the only one with the means to find her, and he had made it abundantly clear that he had a duty to the rest of his family and home, even if it meant leaving her unprotected.

As her ink had touched that parchment, she'd known that no one would be coming after her, but had written it down anyway, perhaps to ease her father's guilt. Deep down, she knew it was the right choice, but that didn't stop Lillian's heart from shattering a little at the thought of not being enough to brave the Forest of Brittelia.

Lillian shook her head, silencing that foolish thought. It was well known that all those who entered these treacherous woods were fated to die a horrible death. It would be unfair of her to be upset for her family doing the intelligent thing and staying far far away.

But fair or not, she still couldn't stop the deprecating feelings that came rushing in, telling her that she was unwanted. Lillian loved her family, but she had always felt a bit insecure in her whole family dynamic. Kynra was the first child and Nimreth was a carbon copy of her mother, so they were obviously in the running for their mother's favorite. And Maxith being the firstborn son *had* to be her father's first choice.

So all that was left was Lillian. Lillian, who was not very lady-like, who never did the right thing, and who apparently lived to make her family's life as complicated as she possibly could.

She got along perfectly well with her father, but she knew that she would never be Maxith, the humorous easy-going son or sweet Nimreth, the angel of the family. Lillian was just the rebellious leftover child who was more of a problem than anything else. And even if they were sad now to see that she had gone, they would soon think—if they haven't already—that their lives were far easier without her.

Tears slid down her cheeks as all the horrible thoughts swarmed her head. But loved or not, it didn't change the fact that she would do whatever it took to save her family. Lillian cried, low enough for only her to hear, as thoughts of her family continued to plague her mind.

A flood of tears was streaming down from her eyes when she heard a loud rustling come from the ground.

Instantly, she silenced herself, choking down her sobs as she strained her neck towards the base of the tree. For a few minutes, all she could hear were footsteps and the snapping of twigs, but Lillian wasn't naïve enough to think it was just an innocent rabbit or deer.

More muffled cracks echoed in the ill-lit night. Gods, the suspense of not knowing what was down there was killing her. Minutes had gone by, and she could still hear the footsteps but yet with a reveal; it felt like she would go mad if she didn't find out whatever thing was lurking down there.

Ready to give up and accept the fact that she would never know what creature roamed underneath her, she heard a voice speak out into the darkness. "There's nothing here. We've been walking around pointlessly for hours."

The voice sounded rather frustrated, and she was curious as to who he was talking to when she heard someone else speak out into the night. "Quit your whining and just keep looking."

The first voice let out an exaggerated groan. "For how long, Killian, just a few more minutes, a few hours, days? I'll become senile by the time we find the damned thing."

Lillian wondered as to what *thing* they could possibly be searching for this late at night.

"I'm in the same thing as you; don't take it out on me. I'm just as sick and tired of searching."

She looked down to her right where she suspected the voices were coming from and could make out two humanoid-like silhouettes in the dark. The voice who seemed annoyed at Killian, she presumed, spoke again. "We should just leave; there's clearly no one out here."

Killian scoffed at the other man's remark. "You go ahead and do that. I'll still be out here while you explain to our *gracious* ruler why you came up empty handed. I'll be sure they spread the tale of the courageous Malik who got too tired of walking and got his head chopped off."

"Screw you," spat Malik.

Killian huffed out a laugh. "Hey, I'm just trying to be realistic here. You'd be lucky if the worst that psycho witch did was cut off your head."

Malik seemed to calm down some but grumbled, "Yeah, I know. I'm just tired of being out here. We clearly got some bad information."

It was Killian who sounded bothered now. "I knew we shouldn't have trusted that spider whore to give us anything good. She swore up and down that she saw a mortal girl running in *this* direction."

Lillian stifled a gasp when she heard what the man had stated.

She didn't know how many *spider whores* were known to traverse these woods, but it had to be in reference to Irene. Confused as to why anyone would be looking for her, Lillian furrowed her brows. They clearly didn't seem to hold Irene in high regard, so it couldn't be to bring her back to that shamble of a home.

Thinking on what they'd said, she was amazed with how plainly and loudly they spoke, knowing the beasts that crept all around them in the night. Lillian shivered as she thought of what they could be to not even be the smallest bit afraid of the monsters in the dark.

Her attention turned back to the two men below her as Malik said, "We *have* to find her or Allania will gut us alive."

The other man sighed before responding. "Okay. Let's stop and think here for a second. Irene told us she was headed towards Iavothae for some bizarre reason. So what would be the easiest way there?"

They stood in silence, musing over that until one of them said, "Do you think she would know of the pass in the caves?"

Killian muttered a curse. "Of course that stupid girl would be senseless enough to go there."

The figures began moving past the tree, and Lillian shifted to hear them. But as she leaned over, her hand slipped against the bark, making a gash in her skin. The small cut caused her to wince in pain, and she bit her lip, silencing herself as she saw the two silhouettes turn in her direction. She muttered a series of curses in her head, praying that they hadn't heard her minor slip up.

The two men stalked towards the base of the tree, but one of them split off as something in the distance caught their eye.

Lillian watched as one of the two figures strolled over to the thick bush where she had stashed her belongings, her heart pounding as the man bent down and pulled out her bow—the things must have some sort of night vision to be able to spot anything at all in this pitch-black darkness.

It was Malik who had found her things as he said in a cocky voice, "Looky what I've got here."

Crossing over, Killian took the bow from his hands. "It seems to be in pretty good condition. If it had been here long it would have started to show some signs of wear." Killian flipped the bow in his hands. "Someone definitely hid it here not too long ago."

Lillian mentally kicked herself; she knew she should have found a better spot to conceal her weapon. She had to stop making stupid mistakes.

Her head whipped to the silhouettes as she heard Killian bark out an order. "Search the area, she might still be nearby. Don't leave any place unlooked."

They both walked off as they started poking around the area.

Her breaths began to quicken as Lillian did her best to calm herself—surely they wouldn't search a tree this high up, now would they? She steadied her hastened breathing, trying to convince herself that she was safe and that they would leave soon enough.

But while she continued failing to get a grip on herself, the moon began illuminating the forest, allowing light to trickle through the dense drapery of leaves.

Lillian looked down at the ground, somewhat able to make out Killian's face in the distance. He appeared rather normal, but the sight of him made her struggle even more in pulling herself together.

A cloud began to pass over the gleaming moon as she continued peering down at them, but just before it did, she saw Killian turn in her direction and lift his gaze.

She could've sworn they locked eyes as the woods darkened once more.

CHAPTER 13

Paralyzed, she pressed her entire body up against the trunk, trying to make herself as small as humanly possible.

She could feel Killian's eyes roaming over every single leaf as she heard his voice call out, "Do you think she would climb up a tree?"

Malik trotted up beside him. "I don't think a girl who came to Iavothae just for *fun* would be clever enough to take refuge in a tree."

Lillian glanced skywards, silently thanking the gods that she had told Irene a false reason for her comings to Iavothae.

"Yeah, I *guess* that makes sense. And I really don't feel like hauling my way up that massive thing." Malik began shaking down a shrub, but Killian stood there looking up and down the length of the thick trunk before muttering a curse and groaning. "We have to climb it, even if there's a small chance she's up there. Plus, it would make sense why she would stash her bow in the nearby bush."

"If you insist," he sighed. "But I'm staying down here. No

sense in both of us going up."

Wasting absolutely zero time, Killian crouched down and launched himself into the air, landing on a branch a few feet up off the ground. The crackling of twigs and rattling grew louder, signaling his coming closer.

Her eyes shut on instinct, thinking that it would make her disappear, but she made herself snap out of her panic and begin untying the knot keeping her fastened.

The snaps and shakings came nearer as Killian leapt from branch to branch. With ease he hopped as if it were no more arduous than a leisurely stroll down an open path; it seemed impossible how fast an Ilaidae could climb. When Lillian had made her ascent, she'd been out of breath after dragging herself up only a couple of the bark covered arms, but he kept on going, not seeming to be bothered in the slightest.

Killian was getting closer by the second, and she was nowhere near to undoing the thick knot. She cursed her quivering fingers as they fumbled with the simple tangle.

Running out of time, she unsheathed her dagger, ready to saw straight through, but halted as another voice yelled out from the bottom. "And what exactly are you two idiots doing?"

The voice didn't belong to Killian or Malik and as she shifted her eyes to the bottom, she could see another shape take form next to Malik's shadow.

Killian seemed to recognize who was at the base as he yelled back, "What? We thought the girl might have gone up the tree."

Lillian stilled at the sound of him; she hadn't realized how close he had come to finding her.

There was a snap in the unfamiliar voice. "If you had come to me *first* before taking matters into your own hands, you would have known I already searched this area. And now precious time's been wasted that could've been better used in tracking her down."

Lillian gleaned that this third person had come for the same reason as the other two, but she couldn't help but be drawn to the sound of him. Even though he was irritated, he had a gorgeous deep voice that made some primal part of her want to know who it belonged to.

She blinked a few times at her wandering thoughts. Was she attracted merely to the sound of someone's voice? That would be absurd to be enthralled simply by the way someone spoke. But for some strange reason, Lillian found herself yearning for the mysterious figure to speak again.

The leaves shuddered as Killian made his way back down. "Well, how were we supposed to know that?"

"You should have known. I was ahead of you. Did you really think I would have left something so obvious overlooked?"

Lillian couldn't get enough of hearing that figure speak. Each word that slid off those lips felt like a taunt filled with dark promises. And she wanted to find out what they were.

Her eyes went wide at her riotous thoughts. Lillian really needed to get a hold of herself. It had been a long time since she had felt the touch of anyone, and it seemed to be affecting her mind. These were bad people who wanted to capture and torture her in horrific ways. Lillian kept repeating those words in her head, but it only worked for so long until her mind wandered back to that melody.

Malik—now boring sounding—interrupted her foolish daydreaming. "You're right; we should have assumed you'd have looked here. We just didn't want to do the wrong thing and then have Allania be *upset*."

Allania.

From what Lillian had heard from the two Ilaidae, Allania was not a very fun person to make mad. She filed away that information, not quite sure what to do with it for now.

"Let's just get going," muttered Killian as two of the figures began slinking past the tall oak.

One stayed behind.

She had no way of knowing for sure, but she felt it in her bones that it was the man with the alluring voice.

The silhouette glanced ahead, perhaps seeing if the other two men had gone, and then dragged his gaze up the tree.

Lillian tensed as he scanned the branches and came to a stop, focusing on where she sat. The figure's stare bore into her—as if able to see precisely where she was in the darkness—and all she could do was look back at him, his gaze burning into every part of her being.

Surely, he couldn't see her *that* easily all the way up here. But Lillian was having a hard time believing herself as the mysterious form continued to lock eyes with her in the night.

Unease and dread began creeping into her when the silhouette suddenly tore his gaze away and glided towards where the other two Ilaidae had gone. She watched as the figure strode through the woods, getting out of sight and eventually blending into the gloom—only then did she let out a huge breath and begin thinking over all that occurred.

Everything was going absolutely *perfect*.

Not only did she still have to make it through the rest of the dangers of the forest but now she had people tracking her—this was all starting to be ridiculous. Why would anyone even be looking for her?

Now Lillian could really understand why no mortals lasted in these forests; they had to fight off all these terrible beasts *and* survive getting hunted down by these hateful folk. It had been an unfair playing field from the start but now the odds were really stacked up against her. She was, however, grateful at least *knowing* that someone was tracking her every move.

Taking a deep breath, Lillian went over everything she had learned. Irene, the spider whore, had clearly sold her out and pointed those nefarious individuals in her direction. Some woman named Allania, who they all feared, wanted her captured. And then.... there was that shadow with the irresistible voice.

The individual, who she still had no name to attach to, had claimed he had already searched the tree she was in. Lillian had already been here for quite some time and saw no one anywhere near the vicinity. Had he been there before she got there......or had he lied to the other two?

Lillian couldn't think of a reason as to why he would have lied to his other two companions, but she could have sworn he had been staring right at her. She had to assume it had just been coincidence or she would go mad coming up with reasons as to why he hadn't taken her prisoner.

But gods, that voice. Her grip on reality must've really been slipping as she couldn't stop thinking about that figure and how he had spoken, that voice of his a tempting caress in the darkness. Her cheeks burned red as she struggled to remember that he was an Ilaidae and would not waste a fraction of a second in killing her in a gruesome manner.

Pushing past those strange fantasies, she shifted her thinking to the other two men and how they had mentioned the cave pass. Amazing. How fortunate that they knew it. That meant she would have to be extremely careful as she made her way there.

Lillian stifled a groan. Why did things have to be so complicated? She still had to face whatever wretched creature was in the cave but now she also had to watch out for those three buffoons looking for her?

Absurd.

What was even the point of having her captured? Two of the three individuals clearly didn't want to be out there searching for her, so why were they doing it?

The name Allania popped into her head. It was obvious they were afraid of whoever this Allania was, and it seemed like she was the one ordering them around. Did that make Allania a queen of some sort? If so, she was *not* excited to meet her. From the sounds of it, she would be lucky if she were only murdered on the spot. Hopefully, the whole Champion of the Flame situation gave her some kind of immunity from being executed as soon as she showed her face, but the notion still caused Lillian to tremble.

She would never get used to anything in these lands. Every new thing she learned still terrified her to her core. But she had to get rid of those feelings now because they would certainly be of no use when she inevitably faced Iavothae's ruler.

Lillian tried to calm herself but was failing miserably at the task. She told herself that she had been doing good so far and had survived numerous dangerous foes, but, in truth, all she had managed to do was run and hide. If there were prizes given out for who was the best at evading their enemies, Lillian thought she could at the very least get herself a nice-looking ribbon.

Stop it, she yelled in her head. *You've done way more than most, and it's a miracle you haven't been driven insane yet.*

Hushing that cynical side of her mind, she forced herself to give a little credit as to how far she's gotten. If the directions Euthemio had given her proved to be true, then once she crossed the pass in the cave, she would be half a day's away from reaching the borders of Iavothae.

Now that would be impressive. Not many mortals could say they'd crossed through the perilous Forest of Brittelia *and* set foot on Iavothaen soil. All she had to do now was live to tell the tale.

Lillian scoffed. Easier said than done.

Too tired to think on that matter any longer, she scanned her surroundings as she stifled down a yawn; all she could see around her was darkness and, mercifully, no ominous shapes. She'd definitely had enough of that for one night.

Squinting her eyes, she glanced at the ground, searching for any trace of the bow they had inconveniently found. She really hoped they had left it there, not only because it was one of her weapons but also because it was one of the only reminders of home she had left. Anytime she picked up her bow, she thought of when her father had first helped her make it. Lillian tittered. 'Helped her' might be a stretch because he had been the one to do most of the work. Thanks to her father and Lillian's diligent supervision, the bow had proven to be quite durable, and she'd used it loyally all these years.

The only difference in her bow now and the one from her childhood was that Peter had helped her carve a few flowers into the delicate yew. He had chosen to etch in multiple clusters of lilies due to her namesake. A warm smile bloomed on her face at the memory; he had told her it was only fitting that such a breathtaking girl be named after an equally breathtaking flower.

Lillian sighed; she missed Peter—*especially* in these dark and lonely nights. As morbid as it may be, it brought her some level of peace knowing that if things went wrong, she might be able to see him again. But that wouldn't happen—hopefully, if Lillian had any say in the matter—for a very *very* long time.

Another yawn escaped her as she stared off into the pitch black. She still had quite a few hours before the sun returned, so it would be wise of her to try and get some sleep.

Lillian shifted, getting as comfortable as she could and closed her eyes, dreams of that mesmerizing voice plaguing her mind.

CHAPTER 14

A tingling flitted across the top of hand, and Lillian twitched her fingers in an effort to alleviate the annoying sensation.

Unable to wave off the feeling, she opened her eyes, squinting them as they got accustomed to the light shining all around her. Lillian was shocked that she had been able to sleep so soundly fastened upright to a tree.

The tickle danced upon her hand again, and she dragged her eyes towards it. A winged insect, about the size of her fist, lay latched against her skin.

In a panic, she flailed her arm around trying to get the disgusting critter to let go, but after seconds of squealing and waving her limbs, she came to her senses and used her other hand to slap the thing dead. An impressive amount of blood came out of the insect that couldn't have all possibly belonged to it.

Had that tingling sensation been the creature sucking out her blood? The thought of anything—even a smaller insect—siphoning out and drinking her blood made her queasy.

Lillian wiped off the insect's guts—and some of her blood, she supposed—onto her already dirty clothes; she really needed to find a shallow river where she could clean herself up a bit. All the sweat and dirt from the past few days was making her look and smell atrocious.

A vision of a pale blue Ilaidae flashed into her mind. When she did find a stream, she had to be sure no creature lurked in the waters. Lillian did not want to encounter another Euthemio, who could potentially be way less friendly. She would have to be careful getting herself washed up, but it would be worth it to get some of the grime off her body. She was also going through quite a bit of water, so it wouldn't hurt to fill up again.

Euthemio had mentioned that she would come across a few more streams and rivers as she made her way closer to the cave—hopefully that meant she would find a suitable one soon.

The sun already shining high and bright, Lillian began untying the knot around her, undoing it with care to not lose her balance so high up in the trees. Lillian scanned the area around her before unraveling the rope and dropping it to the ground below. She then slung her pack onto her back and began shimmying her way down, making sure to go at a slow pace to not lose her footing in the towering monster of a tree.

Gradually, she made it to the base of the large trunk and hopped off the final branch. Walking over, she stuffed the lengthy rope into her bag and examined the forest floor. Her eyes landed on her bow, and a wave of joy came over her as she ran over to her beloved weapon; she was so worried that those foul men had taken it.

Lillian then sauntered over to where she had stashed her quiver and heaved everything onto her back as she prepared herself to get moving. She only had a few things to keep in mind as she trudged along the forest—don't run into horrific creatures, stay away from those three imbeciles, and look for water.

Seemed easy enough.

But she supposed she would have to see just how far from easy and instead punishing it would most assuredly turn out to be.

Going on her way, she began hiking along the forest's ground. According to the directions Euthemio had gifted her, if she stuck to the path, she should come across a stream rather soon.

As she meandered through a glen of oaks, his directions made her recall a small bit of information he had mentioned—something along the lines of a flower's irresistible song?

Lillian hadn't the faintest idea on what he had meant, but all the Ilaidae seemed to delight in being mysterious and he probably had thought it funny to speak in riddles. She did know for certain that he had a particularly *interesting* sense of humor, so, it probably meant nothing, and he had merely mentioned it only to confuse her. It would've been too tempting for him to simply help her and not mess with her along the way.

The sun continued beaming down on her as she hiked, Lillian growing rather used to the routine of always having her guard up. She was glad that she could now do it unconsciously but was troubled that this was what her life had come to—to never feeling safe and always expecting something grave to befall her. She at least felt some comfort in the thought that this would only be a temporary situation. This would either end with her being tragically killed, or she would succeed and be able to return to her life.

Chastising herself, she shoved those darker thoughts from her mind and continued on her path, the loud running's of water becoming apparent in the near distance.

Hurriedly, she made her way to the source and was greeted with a large stream. It wasn't flowing too fast, so it would be hard for her to lose her balance and be swept off by the current. However, the part she was near looked deep, so she found a shallower area and ambled towards it.

Throwing her bag on the ground, she pulled out her canteen, draining the remaining water in the container before kneeling down to replenish her reserves. An air of seriousness glazed over her face as she studied her reflection, Lillian determined to make sure it was her staring back. Once satisfied with the water, she took a quick look around. Nothing seemed amiss, and all she heard were the incessant flies buzzing by her ears. As obnoxious as the chattering insects were, they did help in alerting her if any imminent danger was nearby.

Regardless of whether she was safe, she wanted to make her dip in the stream as swift as possible and began disrobing herself of her filthy clothes. Standing completely bare, she put all her belongings next to her in a neat pile. Well…almost all. Lillian wasn't trusting enough to go anywhere completely helpless, so she fastened one of her weapon's straps to her thigh, sliding her dagger into it before walking into the water.

Her issue with swimming still an embarrassing nuisance, she only went deep enough until the water reached her navel and then dunked her head underneath. She did her best to get rid of the sweat coating her, using her fingers to comb through her hair, and then proceeded to cleanse the rest of her body as she let the tranquil current wash away all the dirt and grime.

After a few minutes, Lillian felt infinitely cleaner and decided that she had spent long enough in the calming waters. She hurried out of the current and was about to throw on a fresh pair of clothes when a gleam caught her eye.

Her attention flicked towards the shimmering that revealed itself to be a beautiful flower. No. Beautiful was too little a word. Lillian had never seen such a mesmerizing array of colors come from any kind of flower before.

She wandered towards it, not being able to resist the urge to go over and inhale its certainly magnificent scent. The flower resembled a glistening star and was colored in a variety of fuchsia's save for the rich gold coating the petal's tips and pistil shooting out from its center.

As she neared the enchanting flower, the appearance that as if it were glowing grew more and more vibrant. Lillian didn't even care that she was naked—she just wanted to be as close to that flower as she could possibly be. She stared in awe at the radiant plant and bent over to take a big whiff.

Gods. Her eyes rolled into the back of her head. Lillian couldn't even begin to describe what it smelled like.

It was intoxicating in a good way and felt as if she were breathing in all things marvelous like love and laughter. It made her want to stay there forever, just taking in the deliciously wonderful scent.

While she continued inhaling the hypnotizing smell, she spotted another of the same flower in the distance. As if in a trance, she darted towards the other shimmering beauty and breathed in its succulent aroma.

More and more of the flowers appeared in her path, and she rushed towards each and every one of them, giggling with glee as they led her towards a wall of vines. Eagerly, she pushed past them, revealing a den full of the enthralling plants. The floor of the clearing was carpeted with the glistening stars as she twirled around in awe at the thousands of breathtaking flowers surrounding her.

There was a pang in her head, a small part of her mind warning her that something was terribly wrong, but she ignored that ridiculous voice as she spun around naked, dashing from flower to flower. Lillian wished for nothing more than to stay here, living out her days and tending to the mesmerizing garden.

Her thoughts immediately wandered to her mother and how Lillian had loathed all her lessons in gardening and killed any plant she touched. But she left that thought behind as if it were nothing and dreamed of how she would forever dance among the enchanting garden. The feelings of pure bliss wrapped around her even tighter as she twirled around with the marvelous flowers.

In the midst of taking another divine huff, a vision of a stunning night sky invaded her surroundings. Lillian knew very well that she was in the middle of the forest, but, in the vision before her, she seemed to be standing on a luxurious white balcony, looking out at a dazzling starry night.

A feeling of peace flooded her as she stared out into the quiet serenity. She had no recollection of what she was gazing at and knew she had never seen this view before, but something about it called to her.

Lillian shook her head a few times and braced her hands against the rim of the balcony, but her hands fell through as if nothing were truly there. It was as if someone had conjured up an illusion and willed her to see it through her eyes.

She wasn't upset at what she was seeing—it was in truth one of the most magnificent views she had ever laid eyes on—she was just confused as to where it had come from. She appeared to be high up in a castle, gazing out at the numerous stars shooting across the dark sky—each one a sliver of light illuminating the endless night. There was a forest far below the balcony, and she could make out a small river running through it, glittering in the darkness.

Lillian's mind shifted to Irene as she pondered the vision. The illusion before her was so different to her previous encounter in the spider cabin. In the cabin, Irene had *wanted* Lillian to believe that what she saw was real, but here, she knew that it was an illusion—it made her feel safe in a strange way.

Memories of where she was and what she was doing rushed through her as she stared at the conjured view. Utter shock crashed into her as she noticed that she was stark naked for anyone to see.

Her head pounded as she struggled to remember how she had gotten there. She had been getting out of the water and was seconds from getting dressed when... when she had seen that beautiful flower.

Lillian's stomach twisted as she realized what had occurred. Once she'd inhaled that scent, it had put her in some sort of trance.

Horror engulfed her as she realized that she would've stayed in that garden forever if the vision of the night sky hadn't invaded her surroundings.

At the mere mention of it, the illusion started to disappear, the enthralling garden beginning to appear around her once more.

No longer under the effects of whatever toxic aroma the flowers were secreting, Lillian held her breath as she ran back towards the river. She threw on her clothes and stood far away from the flower as she scoured the area.

As far as Lillian could see, nothing appeared to be out of place—the critters were still buzzing, and nothing had touched her belongings—but still she averted her eyes from where she had first caught a glimpse of that intoxicating plant, unsure if she could trust herself to even gaze at it in the slightest.

Lillian started along her path once more, anxious to get far away from the frighteningly divine garden. But despite how on edge she felt, embarrassment soon found her as she hiked through the woods. How stupid she must have looked twirling and prancing around naked.

An ember of that strange feeling remained with her—of wanting to stay there for an eternity, taking care of the enchanting garden. At the time it had seemed like an excellent idea, but now she was awake enough to see how ridiculous the notion had been. Sure, Lillian loved to look at flowers and admire their beauty, but she despised taking care of them.

Her mother had forced her to sit through hours and hours of her continuous lectures on how to tend to a garden. And Lillian, obviously uninterested, never paid mind to what her mother spoke of and always ended up killing any plant she cared for. It was truly commendable just how many plants she had managed to annihilate—as if her touch to any living greenery was lethal. She quaked at the thought of being stuck tending to a field full of them for the rest of her days—it was a miracle she had managed to escape and break free from the flower's spell.

The hairs on her nape pricked. But it wasn't a miracle, it was the vision of the bright starry night that had snapped her out of the intricate trance. Had her mind summoned the unfamiliar view in a desperate attempt to save her life...or had someone forced her to see it?

She hadn't felt the presence of anyone around her and was unsure as to who would care enough to save her in these treacherous woods. It had to have been her own mind rescuing her from that situation; she didn't even want to think on why anything would aid her in these woods. And it would be entirely too humiliating to know someone had been a witness to her dancing amongst the flowers utterly nude.

Perhaps all her praying to the gods had been paying off, and it had been divine intervention that stopped her from staying in that ridiculous state forever.

Shaking her head, she cursed out loud at Euthemio for not warning her better. All he had mentioned was to avoid the singing of the flowers. How was she supposed to know that simply being near them would make her want to forget everything and live in an eternal ignorant bliss?

Thankfully, it was all in the past now, but if she ever came across that water creature again, she would deliver him a mighty slap across the face. At the very least, Lillian found solace in that she was headed in the right direction. She still had a few hours until dark and wanted to reach the cave before night fell. The cave was already bad enough on its own, so she definitely did not want to pass through while the forest was dark.

Continuing on, nerves still jostled from whatever that whole situation had been, Lillian willed her mind to think on all that she had accomplished. She had gotten washed up, filled her canteen, and the greatest threat she had encountered today was a pretty flower—a pretty dangerous flower, but she chose to ignore that part for the time being.

And as Lillian calmed herself, only feeling slightly more at ease, she couldn't wait to see what terrifying thing came next.

CHAPTER 15

Lillian hiked through the woods up a small hill, her limbs feeling unbearably sore. If her legs had felt like they wanted to fall off before, she didn't know what this was. The past few days she hadn't ached nearly as much, but she supposed the constant motion had to catch up with her at some point.

Her face cringed as she thought of another reason as to why she might be hurting more today; she really had put on quite the show, prancing amongst the shimmering fucshia. She had been dancing nonstop and running back and forth as she inhaled the toxic aroma those flowers had been exuding. Her cheeks burned red as she thought of how ridiculous she must have looked twirling in that hidden glen.

Spinning without a care would have been bad enough, but what was even worse was having been nude while doing it. The only thing she had worn was a dagger strapped to her thigh, but that had done nothing to cover up the indecent areas on her body.

Lillian recalled how easily it had been for her to sashay around the garden and was surprised with how naturally it had all come back to her; it had been years since she'd even allowed herself to dance at all.

Her mind wandered back to the last time she had ever let herself get lost in such a powerful feeling and found her thoughts flooded with images of Peter.

An overwhelming sorrow surged through her as she thought back to that sunset by the forest's edge. Peter had given her the most thoughtful gift anyone had ever given her, and she had repaid him by letting him die.

It was her fault that he had been killed.

They never would have been out there if it weren't for her stupid birthday. She had been so foolish for allowing herself to get so distracted that close to the woods.

Somehow, Peter had convinced her to dance for him, and while she had been off spinning like an idiot, a demon was sinking its claws into him, slowly taking his life. If she hadn't been dancing like an insolent fool, Peter wouldn't have been caught off guard, and she could've been there to save him.

That was the last time Lillian had ever allowed herself to dance. After that wretched day, she had never felt the allure of dancing again and anytime it was brought up, it felt horribly wrong. Lillian knew it was silly of her and that Peter would strongly disagree, but it felt like the gravest insult to him if she ever even attempted the act again.

So she left that part of her life behind as if it had died out there in the woods with Peter. She had even convinced herself that if she ever tried to pick it up again, she would have forgotten everything she once knew so well. But that morning in the flowerily haven of death had proven her very wrong; it had all come back to her as if she'd never even gone a day without it. She had made an unconscious vow to never move in such a way again, and she hated that it had felt so good when she'd broken it.

As Lillian's sorrow threatened to overcome her, she remembered that she had also been bare while doing so and blamed the intoxicating scent on why she had felt that bizarre way while spinning. Because now when she thought of how she had been twirling and prancing, an intense guilt racked her, and she swore she could feel that aching hole in her heart.

Not wanting to burst into tears in these woods yet again, Lillian redirected her thoughts. She tried to think of anything else, but her mind kept coming up blank, and with nothing to drive away the constant torment, her thoughts had started drifting back to Peter until suddenly that strange vision came to mind.

The only thing that had managed to pull her out of the trance had been that magnificent view of the stars. The flowers had been beautiful in their own way, but the vision had been a different kind of enchanting.

It had felt so mystifying seeing the stars shooting past while being so high up on that elegant balcony. Lillian had no idea where her brain could have possibly conjured up such an illusion, but she was eternally grateful for it. It was the only thing that had been able to snap her out of the flower's trance. If it weren't for that, she might have still been there, spending the rest of her days tending to that horrible garden.

Lillian left the thought of those rotten plants behind as she mused over the beautiful view; she really hoped that was out there somewhere. It was highly improbable, considering her brain had likely made it up—but she would try her hardest to one day find that gorgeous view. A promise to be kept for another day seeing as she had more important matters to attend to, such as getting to that cave in one piece.

Focusing on the task ahead, she ventured forth to that mysterious cave, making sure to stay out of sight as much as possible. She didn't want to run into those three fools hunting her—well, two fools to be exact. She was still rather intrigued by the man with the seductive voice. Lillian knew that the three men were on a mission to capture and take her to that sadistic queen of theirs—for whatever reasons unbeknownst to her—but she couldn't help being curious as to what they looked like. Especially the one without a name.

If it came down to it, Lillian was positive that she would be able to put up a good fight against them. Now, would she win? She was less positive on that, but she would do what she always did and run as fast as her legs allowed her while praying that it would be enough.

Approaching a shady tree, she pulled out her canteen and took a swig as she assessed her progress. She should be nearing the cave soon enough if what Euthemio had told her was correct. So far, she had found his directions to be rather accurate but a bit vague at times. A sneer found its way onto her lip; she'd never forget how he had glossed over the whole deadly flower thing. Lillian would have to remember to reprimand him at a later time if fate ever allowed such a thing.

Setting her future plans aside, she went back to pondering over the directions. If those buffoons were speaking truthfully, then they would likely be waiting for her near the cave. She assumed they would be lurking by the entrance and not the other side because Euthemio had made it seem like there was something about going in that made everyone a little uneasy. No, not something. A monster. All he had said about that was to be quiet and not touch anything and she should be alright. That didn't make Lillian feel very confident or safe but when had she ever in these horrific woods.

Tucking that nervousness away, she began walking, not wanting to take too long of a rest or her legs would get sorer than they already were. Per the polite water creature's guiding, she should be nearing an unmistakable burned, lightning-struck tree and then make a sharp right. Once she made the turn and continued on for a few minutes, she should be able to see the lip of the cave in the distance. She carried on her given path and, sure enough, there was a tree a few feet ahead with jagged sharp gashes going down the sides of it.

Lillian was always fascinated by storms—intrigued by the flashes of lightning and booms of thunder that followed. She fondly remembered how she and Kynra would always sit on the porch, watching the rain pour down as it hit the roof like a steadying drumbeat. They both loved being near the storms, adored seeing how they could make even the largest of trees dance in the wind, and had always wanted to see the bright rays up close, but both knew better than to ever get too near.

This humongous thick tree had been hit by a single bolt of lightning and had been brutally scarred, the jagged wounds so viciously carved into its bark skin; she couldn't even imagine the damage it would do to a living person. She'd heard stories of people surviving, but she knew that if anyone got struck by the bolt that hit this very tree, they would certainly have died an instant, painful death.

Turning right at the struck tree, she began walking until she saw the beginnings of a rock formation in the distance. She was still a good bit away, but the wall of boulders ahead was impossible to miss, stretching on for what she could only assume was miles.

Lillian got closer to the rocks, a hole—wide enough to be an entrance—coming into view along with two figures. Her eyes went wide, and she dropped to the ground as she tried seeing what they were doing. Moving with the utmost caution, she began crawling her way towards them, but as she did, she noticed they had their focus on something else.

Their attention appeared to be on a tree that had something sticking out of its center. And as she made her way closer—it became evidently clear as to what they were doing.

Both of the humanoid-looking men held a few daggers in their hands as they stared at the oak. One man stepped the tiniest bit closer to it, holding up one of his blades by its tip as his eyes focused on the trunk's center with a serious sort of energy.

Following the man's gaze, she noticed that in the middle of the tree there was a dagger lodged in with a blue ribbon tied to its hilt.

The man took one last deep breath and let his dagger sail through the air towards the one with the ribbon. The blade landed decently close to the blue silk, but he let out a groan, unsatisfied with its position.

Disbelief rushed through her. She couldn't believe what she was seeing. If these two men were the ones trying to capture her, then they truly were imbeciles. They were supposed to be keeping a lookout for her but instead were playing what appeared to be a game of sorts—no wonder the third figure addressed them with such obvious irritation. Lillian would too be mad if her companions were as stupid and irresponsible as these fools. But she couldn't be too upset judging that this scenario would make sneaking into the cave a thousand times easier.

Silently, she got to her feet and began tiptoeing from tree to tree, staying far away from where they were playing their ridiculous little game.

The game itself didn't seem that bad—it was just absurd for them to be playing it when they were obviously meant to be on guard.

Lillian finally got close enough and was able to make out the conversation between the two, instantly recognizing that the two voices belonged to Killian and Malik.

The night she had first encountered the pair had been relatively dark, allowing her to only see their individual silhouettes. But now, she could see what they both looked like and was surprised to find that they appeared rather normal—to her standards that is.

They were leaner and taller than regular humans and both had very similar faces, enough so for her to think they might be brothers. The only real big difference was that one of the men had long blonde hair braided down his back and the other had hair of deep red that came down to his shoulders. She wasn't close enough to make out any distinct features but could see they both had ears that came to pointed ends instead of rounded ones like hers. She had heard that pointed ears were a trademark symbol of the Ilaidae but had never seen them so up close before.

As she continued creeping behind the trees, she discerned that the one with the deep red was Killian and the plaited blonde was Malik. They appeared to be in the midst's of an intense argument on whose dagger had gotten closest to the one with the ribbon. Lillian didn't have time to linger and listen to whatever foolish discussion they were having, but picked up bits and pieces as she snuck past.

Malik was claiming that Killian had cheated by being closer to the tree than they had originally agreed upon, and Killian had countered by saying that it wasn't his fault he had chosen to be farther away from the line they had drawn out in the dirt. They went back and forth like that for what felt like an eternity until they finally settled the debate by agreeing on a rematch.

They were getting ready to start throwing their daggers by the time Lillian reached the last tree separating her and the cave's entrance. A thirty-foot clearing stood between her hiding spot and the entryway, and the two Ilaidae men were roughly the same distance away, standing farther to the left. Lillian would have to either make a run for it and risk them hearing her…. or walk slowly and pray that they didn't turn around.

She thought of throwing a rock or branch in the far distance but decided against it as that would only alert them of an intruder and make it even harder for her to get past. Her best course of action would be to sneak her way into the cave. As nervous as she was, it didn't look like it would be too bad as that little game of theirs took longer than it should.

Rolling her eyes, she watched Malik shuffle his feet for the thousandth time; it would be so easy to win at their silly game but that wouldn't do much to help her out of her current predicament.

Taking one last deep breath, she thought of all things silent and took her first few steps into the wide empty field. Lillian placed her feet with care, making sure they didn't land onto anything that could snap or make a loud noise.

Her heart hammered in her chest as she went across. So far, she had made it a good twelve feet without either of the two noticing she was slipping by. Another three silent steps passed, and she couldn't believe her plan was actually working—only a few more feet separated her and that cave.

Ready to take another step, she lifted her foot when she heard Malik let out a yell. "You cheater! Your foot is so *clearly* over the line."

Killian groaned. "Oh, come on, it was the tip of my foot. I hadn't even noticed it'd gone over."

Lillian's heart had almost exploded from her chest at his outburst.

Her gaze flicked back and forth between them and the cave as she listened to the two bicker; she was so close now, only a couple more steps. She kept her eyes glued onto them as she began her creeping anew, easing her way towards the cave's entrance. It was a miracle that they still hadn't noticed her, but Lillian realized far too late that she had made a terrible mistake.

Too concentrated on their arguing, she had forgotten to keep watch on where her feet landed, and she had made the foolish error of stepping on a twig that snapped with a loud crack under her weight. She stood paralyzed with wide eyes as she stared in the two men's direction.

Slowly, they both turned their heads to where she had broken the branch. They locked eyes for only a fraction of a second before Malik tore into a run. "Don't let her get into that cave!"

Remembering she had legs, she ran towards the entrance as the two men hurtled after her. She sprinted as fast as she could, barely managing to enter without Malik and Killian catching up to her. The Ilaidae must be incredibly fast because they had been a decent twenty feet away and were able to graze her skin with their fingertips when the cave had been right in front of her.

Lillian barreled in and backed herself up against the rocky wall as she pulled out her two daggers. She didn't hear any footsteps coming in after her but instead the sounds of Malik and Killian yelling out a series of curses.

Killian was the first to yell out something that wasn't a string of vulgar words. "What in the gods are we meant to do now? We were supposed to catch her *before* she went into that damned cave."

Malik was laughing hysterically. "We're dead. We are *so* dead."

A sound of a hand hitting skin reverberated through the forest, and Lillian realized it must have been Killian slapping Malik when she heard what he spoke. "Get a hold of yourself. No one is dying anytime soon."

Malik didn't even seem to register the blow as he kept chuckling to himself. "Oh yeah? How? *Please* tell me how. If that queen of ours doesn't gut us first, I'm sure that equally perverted brother of hers would love to torment us in fun ways."

"That lap dog isn't going to touch us. We can still fix this."

"Then please oh knowledgeable one, how is this *fixable?* She already went in that stupid cave, and I am *not* going inside it. The only way is to go around it, and that'll take time that—guess what—*we don't have.*"

Killian paused, taking a second to think. "The best we can do is travel fast and hope that we can make it to the other side before she does."

A few more curses were muttered before she heard their running footsteps and voices fade into the distance.

Confident they were gone, Lillian let out a small sigh; she had made it into the cave *and* avoided the two delinquents. She did not, however, feel any better about being inside this mysterious cave.

Euthemio had seemed to tremble a little at merely mentioning it, and these two individuals, who didn't seem to be scared of anything else in the forest, refused to enter. Lillian couldn't possibly feel more worse about a situation.

But she took a deep breath, steadying her emotions; Euthemio had told her to just be quiet and to not touch anything and she should be fine. It would all be fine.

Repeating those two warnings in her mind, she took one last look at the forest and began her descent into darkness.

CHAPTER 16

Lillian could hardly see a thing as she made her way through the vast shadowy abyss.

The sun had still been up when she'd entered but that didn't seem to matter inside the jagged rocky walls; it was as if the inside was a black hole that swallowed any light it found. She could see enough to know where she was going but was unable to make out anything else. However, luckily for her, it shouldn't be too much of an issue as Euthemio had said it was a fairly straight shot through the cave.

As Lillian proceeded on her path, she could see areas lining the walls where instead of fuzzy images of solid surface, black gaping holes appeared to be. She assumed those hollow spaces must be pathways that connected farther into the cave which made Lillian all the more curious as to how deep this cavern's system truly went. She wasn't stupid enough to actually venture off and see but that didn't stop her from wondering.

Euthemio had mentioned that the rock formation wasn't only

massive on the outside but also had trails that went below the ground, winding in a never-ending pattern. Apparently if you knew how to navigate the maze, it could connect you to anywhere, but only few dared enter the deadly labyrinth.

Lillian couldn't even begin to imagine what manner of terrifying creatures lurked in the eternal darkness below.

But she decided to shift her mind to different things, not wanting thoughts of menacing beasts to lure whatever creature had every being so afraid of the eerie chasm. Lillian was in no mood to encounter the horrifying thing that prowled the darkness—especially considering all she knew about it so far was that it was utterly terrifying. She wondered what it had done or looked like to strike such an intense fear in everyone it had faced. Had anyone truly seen this petrifying creature or was it all built on rumors of whoever entered these unsettling caves?

More questions continued to breeze past her as she walked, but the one that was of most interest to her was if the vile beast only lived inside the cavern or if it left its dark home once night fell. Surely it had to leave at some point and hunt for food. Or did it perhaps wait for foolish individuals like herself to provide for its nourishment?

Her gaze shot out into the lightless atmosphere; the sun had seemed like it was getting ready to set by the time Lillian had managed to somewhat sneak in. If the creatures truly did go out and hunt at night, then she might end up crossing paths with something she'd much rather avoid.

Lillian walked a bit faster now, needing to be out of the cave before day disappeared completely. She wanted to break into a run and make her time in the cave as brief as possible but found herself unable to, fearful that her pounding steps would alert the horrible monsters of her presence. The only helpful warning she had gotten was to be as quiet as possible and to not touch anything. Only a fool would ignore such a caution.

Trying her best to stay true to the river being's words, Lillian kept far away from the chamber's walls and her hurried footsteps light. Taking small steps was slowing her down, but she could gauge her pace and keep track of time from the cracks high up above that allowed slivers of sun to seep through. She was grateful for the small trickle of light or else she would have been stuck walking aimlessly in the pitch-black labyrinth.

As she continued on her unsettling stroll, the thoughts of caves and darkness brought her mind back to the last time she had ever set foot into any cavern of sorts; it had been ages since she had wandered off to the rocky tunnels near her home.

When she had been much younger, her and Maxith used to be quite the adventurous pair. They would have this ongoing game where they would pretend to be grand explorers off discovering unmarked areas around the world.

Their mother would always get mad and tell them that the caves were far too dangerous to play around in but that never stopped them. They would wait until their mother busied herself with making a meal or occupied her time with whatever it was she usually did and then snuck off towards the supposedly unsafe caves.

Thinking back on it now, it probably had been rather reckless of them to be playing inside a mysterious cavern when they were only mere children, but nothing too bad ever did happen—to her at least.

Lillian had to suppress a chuckle as an image of Maxith running and screaming from the caves entered her mind. Her brother had brought in a stick and began whacking the cave walls, for a most certainly idiotic reason, and a dozen of startled bats went flying out in his direction. It was quite the spectacle watching Maxith run in terror with a swarm of black on his tail. Lillian had tried being a good sister and asked him if he was okay, but it had come out in wheezes as she instead fell over in laughter, tears streaming down her face.

Not trusting herself to keep her composure at the humorous memory, she switched her musings to her current task. So far, Lillian seemed to be doing alright, but she still scanned her surroundings as far as the dim lighting allowed, not willing to get caught by surprise. With each step she placed on the caverns floor, she grew more confident and eventually had to hold back snickers at how those two idiots had been too afraid to even *consider* setting foot in the dark chasm.

She shook her head at the thought of them.

Those fools had been distracted with that game when they should have been keeping an eye out for her. Clearly, they either underestimated her or they were just simply that stupid. They probably assumed she would have made an obscene noise or wouldn't have been intelligent enough to know how to sneak past them. But to their great dismay, Lillian had almost made it to the cave's entrance without them even batting an eye in her direction. And she would have made it too if she hadn't made the idiotic mistake of stepping on a branch that let out a huge crackling as it split in two.

If the gods were on her side, then she would be long gone by the time those two managed to get around the entire mountain. They were, however, unnaturally fast and she wasn't sure how that speed held up in the long run. She might have to pick up her pace if she didn't want to cut it too close.

It felt like she had been at least walking for a good half an hour if not more, so hopefully that meant she was more than halfway through this eerie gloom and could return to the slightly less horrifying woods soon enough. But she wouldn't be surprised to find out time worked differently in this part of the forest; it would make entirely too much sense if this already frightening cave also messed with the way time passed.

Lillian closed her eyes and took in a deep breath; there was no point in worrying about things that might not even be true. The main thing that should be consuming all her thoughts and energy was the mysterious beast that prowled this dreary atmosphere. The wrong thoughts regarding that, however, greeted her too curious brain.

A small part of her was itching to see the monster that could strike such terror. A very stupid thought for her to have, but her more curious side was always hard to subdue. She wouldn't be torn up about not seeing it—in fact, she would be thrilled if she avoided the horrendous beast—but that inquisitive part inside of her still yearned to know.

An image of an enormous, scaly beast with massive wings and razor-sharp teeth came to mind. There wasn't anything too specific brewing in her head, but it felt right for a creature dwelling inside a dark cave to have wings. Lillian *always* pictured the most terrifying and ferocious creatures with a pair of huge leathery wings.

She chastised herself at her rampant thoughts; if she kept thinking of the monster inside the cave, she would certainly manifest it into existence. But she was finding it impossible to think of anything else; it was a rather hard task to think of other things when inside the lair of a monster.

Lillian tried shifting her headspace, but her mind kept coming up empty. Her life as of recent hadn't necessarily been the most cheery as it solely consisted of running away, hiding, or fighting the chilling Ilaidae. It felt like years since she'd last had a civil conversation with a living being that hadn't tried to kill her at some point in their brief interaction. A journey that had been merely a few days long felt like it had been dragging on forever—but she supposed being in a constant state of terror and running for her life would alter anyone's view on time.

Ever since hearing of this ominous cave, she had assumed she would be bolting yet again, but was glad to have been proven wrong. She still, however, didn't allow herself to get too comfortable as there was still plenty of time for things to go horribly awry. A usual occurrence in Lillian's life but running seemed to be a solution to her atrocious luck.

A wave of embarrassment coursed through her as she again recognized that all she'd done so far was flee when she came across any trouble.

No, she said in her head, interrupting those belittling thoughts. Lillian was a damn good fighter and could do some serious damage if she wanted to. She just chose to be smarter and liked her chances of survival far away from the creatures attacking her. Her father had always told her that fighting should be a last resort and never be used unless absolutely necessary—and boy, had she been living by those words.

Remembering the mantra her father always lived by, she felt more at ease. She wasn't being a spineless coward by bolting at the first sign of danger, she was just being clever and conserving her life as much as possible.

But Lillian didn't feel very brave and clever as her feet ached from having to alter her steps on the cavern's gravely floor. Taking a brief glance at her dim surroundings, feeling satisfied that nothing too menacing was near her—at least from what she could see—she lowered herself down onto the cold floor to take a brief rest.

Careful not to make even a whisper of noise, she pulled out her water and unscrewed the cap as she gulped down the refreshing liquid. After taking a few sips, she set the canteen onto the floor next to her, sitting in silence as she let her feet relax. But she didn't linger too long. The more she stayed in one spot, the higher her chances of getting caught by those two idiots at the exit became.

Her muscles twitched in protest as she reached for her canteen, and she cocked her head to the side as her fingers came up empty. Continuing to pat the dirt and still not finding it, she slung her pack across her shoulders and got on her hands and knees, crawling as she blindly searched the darkness.

After fumbling around for a few minutes, her left hand finally was able to grasp the elusive water—but she paused as her right hand brushed past a cylindrical object. She let out a relived sigh as she stuffed her only source of water back into her bag and fitted the straps back onto her shoulders.

Lillian took one step forward, ready to be on her way, but stopped as curiosity possessed her. Kneeling down, she reached out her hand, examining what that odd item had been.

The object was rather light and long as she held it up in her hand and had a few rough ridges and grooves. She fiddled with the item and wasn't sure what it could be other than some strange looking stick that someone had brought in.

Standing back up and sticking out her leg, she felt around the area, noticing more of the peculiar articles littering the cavern's floor. She picked up another that was a little shorter than the one she was already holding and ran her hands all over it.

Lillian had no idea what these things were and tried holding up the two objects to the slivers of sun up above in the cracks, seeing if she could make out any semblance of what they were. She twisted one of them next to a bright ray, examining it all over with squinted eyes.

The light glistened off the white shapes, and she became paralyzed as terror swept through her. Her hands instinctively opened, and she couldn't stop herself as she dropped the two objects with a loud clanking.

Lillian walked backwards in a mixture of fear and disgust, but only went a few steps until her back hit the cavern's wall. Her hands trembled as she tried cleaning the evidence of what she had held off onto her clothes.

Bones—she had been holding bones.

All she could do was stand there as she thought on the multitude she had felt with her feet. There was a very good chance the bones she had been holding were from an animal, but something deep inside her told her they were human.

Fear continued to nauseate her, but her mind was jolted away from that powerful emotion as she remembered the raucous noise she'd made when the bones had dropped to the stone floor. A rumbling vibrated her skin and Lillian knew that even though she'd realized her slip up rather fast, it didn't matter as the wall she was leaning up against began to move.

Heart dropping to her stomach, Lillian turned around as the dark figure she had foolishly mistaken for the cave wall, opened up an enormous glowing eye.

CHAPTER 17

Lillian stared into the massive orange eye—the glow radiating off it vaguely illuminating the cavern around her.

It was now easy for her make out all the bones littering the floor, but Lillian didn't look at them too much as her full attention remained on the monster before her.

The giant eye appeared opaque and blurry as it darted its pupil in all directions, likely trying to pinpoint where she was. From what the low lighting allowed, she could see the creature was a large black circular mass, and the single eye took up most of its body. She didn't see if the thing had any other limbs but knew they could very well be folded up against its round form.

As if roots had grown and wrapped around her legs, she stood frozen, not wanting to alert the creature to her whereabouts. This whole time she had been walking slowly throughout the cave without an issue but that had been before the monster was aware of her being there—now it was searching for her.

Lillian fought every part of her as her nerves demanded they tremble. Everything she had encountered before had been terrifying, but the thing before her was an otherworldly nightmare.

And for once, Lillian had no idea what to do.

Her usual method of survival was to turn and run but that wasn't a feasible option at the moment. But she also couldn't very well stay here until the monster eventually gave up on looking for her—for all she knew it would hunt her down for days until finally surrendering. She had to think of something, and it had to be *now*.

The beast continued darting its eye as Lillian scoured her surroundings. All she knew of this beast was that it used sound to find its prey—once again, she cursed Euthemio for being so vague as to what creature lied inside the dark cavern.

With a panic growing inside her, Lillian looked for something of use, but the only thing around were the stupid bones strewn about the cave's bottom.

Bones.

Bones, Lillian repeated in her head as if finding a new meaning to the word. If this creature wanted noise to hunt her down, then that's exactly what she would give it.

Careful not to make a sound, Lillian bent down, keeping her balance as she picked up a bone lying by her foot. With the object held tightly in her fist, she stood back up, muttering a quick prayer before heaving it towards the cave's entrance.

The enormous beast's eye flashed towards the small item and two seconds later it began gliding over to where it had landed.

The creature now distracted, Lillian took the gifted opportunity and began tip toeing away. She'd been walking in this cave for at least an hour, so she *had* to be nearing the exit. All she had to do now was place one foot in front of the other. and not think about how the beast even the Ilaidae were terrified of was currently searching for her in the near distance.

Minutes passed as she smiled through her fear, the impromptu plan seeming to work as she inched farther and farther away from the creature. Light glowed in her peripheral, the shine letting her know the eye from hell was still searching the area where she'd caused the clamorous diversion.

Slowly, she continued, a faint beaming appearing out ahead causing Lillian to get the smallest bit excited as she realized that it must be the exit. She was so close—but she knew it would take forever for her to make those numerous steps to the end. She had been walking at a slow pace before but now had to relax her strides even more to keep that nightmarish creature from doing the gods knew what with her.

Just the mere thought of that thing catching her made her skin crawl, and Lillian tried ignoring her rampant imagination as she ambled towards the exit. She didn't know what the gigantic, freaky eye would do to her, and it wasn't her intention to ever find out. She was sure there was something more to the monster than just a shimmering eyeball; likely razor sharp teeth and wings for all she knew.

Attempting to soothe herself, she took in a few breaths—the last thing she needed was to break out in panicked tears and have the creature glide over to where she was. If she got killed by any sort of beast due to her sobbing, she would never forgive herself for being such an idiot.

Keeping to her quiet, slow steps, she was in utter disbelief that her plan was actually working; a simple distraction had been enough to evade the terrifying monster.

But gods it was taking forever. It felt like years were being taken off her life as she crept closer and closer, and she couldn't believe her eyes as she finally stared at the exit; a mere fifteen feet stood between her and the forest ahead. The sun had just begun to set, but the rays were still shining bright as she tip toed to the woods in front of her.

Lillian couldn't believe her luck as she looked behind her and still found the creature to be far into the distance. Every fiber of her wanted to make a run for it, but she knew better than to make such a foolish mistake.

So close—she was so close now that she could almost smell the lush trees lying up ahead. Smiling with excitement, she kept moving, eager to leave this wretched lair, when her foot slipped on a gravelly patch beneath her.

Lillian caught herself and slid to the side. It had only been a small crumbling sound of rocks, but she froze as she looked out behind her.

Mercifully, the creature was nowhere near her and hadn't seemed to have reacted to the minor noise—perhaps it hadn't been loud enough since the distance between them now was rather vast.

Convinced that she was still safe, she turned back around, about to take another step when a spiked tentacle struck down at the floor directly to her side.

Her heart had felt like it had shot out of her chest as she lurched back in surprise. The tentacle began retracting itself, and her eyes followed the lengthy black limb as she saw it leading to the monster now barreling after her.

Her lids flew open wide as she stared at the creature; it was still an enormous glowing eye but now had dozens of spiked tentacles coming out from all around it.

Lillian stood paralyzed as she realized that the spike would have gone right through her and ended her life right then and there. But she snapped out of her stupor as she saw another tentacle aimed right for her, eager to impale. She had managed to sneak past the beast before but that was no longer an option as four of the barbed appendages came rushing after her.

Lillian broke out into a run towards the forest, tremors shaking the ground as two limbs landed where she had been standing.

Her blood felt like it was on fire from how fast she moved, the exit so close now that she could feel the slight breeze coming in from the woods kissing her face as she neared. She was a mere three feet away from the opening—now two.

She was going to make it. She was going t—

One foot stepped out of the cavern, but her motions were stopped as something pulled her back and slammed her down onto the floor. Half a second passed before something began dragging her backwards across the cave.

A small lift of the head revealed a thick tentacle piercing the bag on her back. With a desperate need, Lillian clawed at the ground before her, fingers bleeding from vicious effort, but found nothing to give her leverage against the thing drawing her deeper into the cave.

Looking behind her for anything of use, she saw a stalagmite jutting out from the ground coming up on her right. She braced herself as she readied her arms to grab onto the rock with all her might.

The stalagmite emerged on her right, just as she had seen, and she lunged for it, wrapping her arms around it and holding onto it with all her strength as the tentacle yanked her with a fierce hunger.

Her legs flailed behind her with wild panic as she kicked the beast a few times, but still it didn't loosen its hold as she continued being jerked in the air. Each blow she landed on the tentacle seemed to irritate the creature even more, causing it to use more force as it tried hauling her towards it. Lillian heard her pack beginning to tear as it tugged on her with a maddened fury.

Arms burning as she held onto the rock for dear life, an idea came to mind. The creature wasn't holding her—it was holding onto the pack. All she needed to do was let the creature take her bag and while it was occupied with it, she could make a speedy exit. The bag had her food and water, but she was well past caring about that.

Taking in a courageous breath, she let go of the rock and began being dragged once more, wincing as she felt the rocks blanketing the floor cut into her skin.

It was now; she had to do it now.

She slipped the straps off her shoulders and heard her bag being hauled across the cave floor as she hoisted herself up and broke into a run.

Thirty seconds of sprinting had passed when the creature let out an ear-piercing shriek, the beast realizing she was no longer attached to the torn sack. It hadn't bought her a lot of time, but it was enough.

She heard the creature coming after her, its tentacles striking down at the dust she left behind. Only a few feet from the exit, she put all her remaining strength into her legs.

The spindly limbs came after her, leaving cracks and tremors where she passed, but this time they didn't catch her as she crossed into the forest.

The sun beat down on her face as she saw a black tentacle land beside her. Steam came off from where the spiked limb had touched down, and the creature howled in pain as it withdrew its limb back into the darkness of the cave.

She didn't dare stop running, and Lillian didn't know how long she went for, only risking skidding to a halt when she no longer heard or felt anything coming after her. She scanned the area all around her for anything amiss and slumped down against a tree, lungs burning as she processed everything.

Too much—this had all become too much.

Lillian buried her face into her palms, sobbing to herself.

Everything just kept getting progressively worse the longer she stayed in this wretched forest. She longed to be in the comforts of her bed where she had been oblivious to all the horribly unnatural creatures living alongside her. She had known the Ilaidae were unlike the humans and horrific, but she never could have imagined this, never could have imagined *anything* similar to the kinds of monsters she had encountered so far.

The thought of the beast from the cave and how close it had come to skewering her made her want to hurl. Nothing about this place was right. A sobbing chuckle tumbled out of her. A flower. She couldn't even trust a simple flower.

More despair flooded her as she remembered how she had been forced to leave her pack to the monster in the darkness. That bag had contained all her food and water that she needed to make the trip there and back.

She had lost *everything.*

She had no food, no water, and the one thing she had used for shelter had also been lost.

Her breathing hastened, and she felt as if she were in the beginnings of a panic attack. Feelings of worthlessness crashed into her as her chest tightened, and she continued to hyperventilate. Gods, she couldn't believe this. She was *actually* having a panic attack.

How could she expect to show her face in Iavothae in these pitiful conditions? They would laugh in her face and execute her if she broke down while trying to be the so-called Champion of the Flame.

Wanting to stop her growing feelings of terror, Lillian held herself as she tried to settle her racing heartbeat—surely everything wasn't as horrible as she thought. She just needed to readjust herself and figure out where to go from here.

Having no food or water wasn't the ideal situation, but she could work around it. She still had all her weapons, so hunting for food was a very viable option. She might have to go without water for a portion of the day, but she would make time to stop by a stream even if it slowed down her journey.

Her breaths came in more even as she thought everything through. Now calmer, she stood and wiped her damp cheeks, feeling a little embarrassed for having that mental break down.

Pretending that she was fine like she always did, she dusted off her clothes. She wasn't sure how much time she had until dark so finding shelter was her most important task at the moment—hunting for food and finding water would have to wait until tomorrow.

Ready to be on her way and look for a safe place to lie low for the night, she started walking but paused when she spotted a rabbit out in the distance. She had decided to hunt for food tomorrow, but it would be rather stupid of her to waste any chance she got.

Slowly, she slipped the bow off her shoulder and pulled an arrow from her quiver, stilling her mind as she recalled everything her father had taught her. She had done this a thousand times and knew what she was doing, but she'd never hunted in these conditions before—one where her life depended on it.

Thinking on all the times she'd gone hunting with her father and Maxith, she willed away the jitteriness from her arms, telling herself that there was nothing different between then and now as she drew back her arrow.

She stared at the innocent rabbit one last time and let go of the string as she let the arrow sail through the open forest.

CHAPTER 18

Lillian watched as her arrow flew through the air, struck true, and pierced the unsuspecting rabbit's head.

Eager to collect her kill, she started walking over, but stopped short as she stared at the animal in shock. The force of the arrow going through its skull had knocked over the rabbit, but it had gotten right back up and now hopped in her direction, unfazed by the arrow impaling the side of its head.

Baffled couldn't even began to explain what she felt.

A direct shot to the head should have been a fatal injury to any animal—at least that's what she had gathered from all her years hunting.

Still startled with the current predicament, she notched another arrow as she aimed for the bunny again. The sharp edge hit its mark once more, puncturing the rabbit's neck.

She was unsettled to say the least as she watched the rabbit get back up and hop along with now *two* arrows protruding from its body.

Lillian was feeling *very* disturbed as she stared at the animal that now had two fatal shafts sticking out from its body.

Beginning to draw back another arrow to see if three would do the trick, she saw the rabbit begin hopping faster in her direction. Lillian let loose the third arrow as it came closer, but, this time, the rabbit evaded the piercing blow and stood completely still as it stared at her from a few feet away.

Really starting to lose her patience, she pulled out her dagger, ready to gut the unnatural creature. She marched over to the paralyzed rabbit, blade in hand, and was mere moments from ending it when the thing she had thought to be a rabbit began to change.

The creature's skin turned inside out as it grew into a humanoid shape so tall that it towered over her; she imagined that if a human body were to be skinned, it would share a striking resemblance to the thing before her. Its hands and feet now ended in deadly claws, and it had a mouth full of pointed teeth that she knew could easily tear through her soft, supple skin.

Lillian turned a ghostly shade of pale as she held out her dagger, backing away from the horrifying Ilaidae.

The creature must have been aware enough to know just how afraid she truly was as it lifted its blood red eyes and smiled, a forked tongue coming out and passing over its lips.

Was nothing what it seemed in these gods forsaken woods? Why couldn't a simple rabbit *be* just a simple rabbit?

It was through a force of will she stopped the dagger in her hand from quivering, Lillian doing her best to pretend the beast didn't frighten her.

The Ilaidae only looked at her as if waiting to see what she'd do.

Her eyes darted in both directions, and she glanced at the beast one last time before choosing her favorite action and dashed to the side.

Not even three seconds had passed before the creature appeared in front of her, causing her to come to an abrupt halt to stop herself from crashing into the wretched beast.

Of course, the thing was unnaturally fast. Her preferred method of running seemed to be out of question now. She had known sooner or later she was going to have to fight one of these creatures, but she was hoping the whole running thing would have lasted just a little while longer.

Stilling her mind, she unsheathed her remaining dagger and readied her stance.

The creature smiled at her once more as if pleased she would put up a fight. A predator hunting its prey. That's all she was to this Ilaidae.

Her face showed no emotion as she glared back at the ghoulish being before her.

Not a half second sooner, the beast lunged towards her, whispers of its taloned hand slicing by her ear as she narrowly dodged its attack.

Right as she had evaded its claws, she swiped her dagger at its side, but the creature was far too fast and more than capable of avoiding the point of her blade.

The creature ambushed her with slashes of its claws, and she found herself on the defensive, scarcely able to get in a strike as she was too preoccupied with keeping her face from being split open.

Lillian ducked to the side, slicing her dagger into the creature's leg as a needle-sharp claw came at her.

The beast staggered back as it looked at its wounded leg, blackness oozing out from its deep gash.

She took the opportunity to pounce, coming at it with one of her daggers, but the creature had been anticipating the move as it caught her by the wrist.

Lillian smiled; she would have been surprised if the creature hadn't predicted her obvious attack, but she was hoping that it would assume her too stupid to think ahead.

She feigned struggling at the creature's grasp as she struck the monster with the blade in her free hand, dragging it up its abdomen.

The beast removed its steel clasp and glared at her with crimson eyes as it rushed after her in a crazed rampage.

With quick feet, she rolled to the side, but she hadn't been fast enough as those sharpened nails tore through the skin of her upper arm. A whelp escaped her as she clutched the gash on her arm, but she didn't slow as she rose to face the cursed Ilaidae.

Those red eyes gleamed as it brought blood-soaked nails to its mouth and began swirling its tongue over them, licking them clean.

Horror clouded her vision as each drop of her blood that entered its system caused its wounds to knit shut.

Oh, she was in *serious* trouble. She really needed to start doing some damage if she wanted this beast to stay down.

Sheathing both of her daggers, she pulled out her father's sword, holding it upright and steady just as he had taught her. She brandished it before the creature, imagining how the steel would lop its head clean off.

The creature bared its teeth in a feral grin, letting its tongue glide over its lips as if imagining what the rest of her would taste like before storming straight for her.

She cleaved her sword straight at its neck, more than ready to end its miserable existence. The blow had been aimed perfectly, about to slice through its revolting skin, but the creature stopped the blade as it grasped it with its bare hands.

Black liquid dripped off its palms as it used the momentum of her swing to flip her to the ground. The ghoulish beast pinned her to the dirt with an abnormal swiftness and began salivating as it stared at the open gash on her arm.

Lillian fought with all her strength, trembling with fear and effort, as the creature began bringing its face closer to the gushing wound on her arm. She watched in horror as the creature bared its mouth open wide and latched onto her bloodied skin. Intense pain lanced through her as she felt its teeth sink deep into her.

Vain were her attempts in fighting against ,the creature's immense power as it held her down, its forked tongue swirling all over her skin.

Lillian no longer cared who heard her as she began screaming in a mixture of agony and terror at the monster sinking its teeth into her already damaged skin.

Staring upwards at the sky, the monster still latched on, she realized that this was it. This was how she would die. There was no way she was getting out of this one. She had made it so close to reaching Iavothae just to be killed by something she had believed to be a harmless little rabbit. Lillian knew her luck had finally run out as she watched the creature gorge itself on her blood, unable to do a damned thing to stop it.

Her voice had begun to falter from her continuous shrieks of pain, but still she fought against the creature's vast force, even knowing that all her efforts were futile. Only out of sheer stubbornness did she still manage to fight.

But Lillian could feel herself gradually weakening as she thrashed against the creature's iron grip, her limbs beginning to fail as they slowly lost their strength. She felt so powerless knowing that she would soon have to surrender to the horrid beast.

But she never had to submit as she heard a squelching sound and saw the end of a blade jut out from where the monster's heart should be.

The beast looked down in shock and didn't even have a second to register what had occurred as another blade whisked through the air, slicing the ghoulish creature's head clean off its shoulders.

The sword piercing its chest disappeared as the now lifeless husk fell down on top of her.

Lillian struggled to shimmy out from underneath the immense weight of the, hopefully very dead, creature but used her remaining slivers of strength to get to her feet. Her arms trembled as she held out her sword to the unknown being that had brought down the ghoulish beast.

She almost dropped her sword at what she found. He had to have been the most magnificently handsome man she had ever laid eyes on.

Her gaze landed on a lightly tanned man with raven black hair standing in front of her. His hair wasn't cropped by any means but was still short as it hugged his head. Her eyes wandered lower, and she saw that he was wearing leather armor of all black that did little to conceal his strikingly strong physique. Dark liquid, oozed out from the ghoulish beast's body, coated his two swords as he stood tall, carefully watching her.

She gave a quick glance at the grime covered blades but couldn't help herself as her attention was drawn back up to his face, to a pair of mesmerizing eyes that were the deepest of blues. She had never seen the ocean, but she imagined that even the farthest parts of the seas were no match to the unfamiliar man's stunningly dark eyes.

Lillian stumbled back as she continued to struggle holding herself up.

A strange look of concern washed over the man's features as he took a small step towards her.

Her arms trembled wildly as she attempted to raise her sword. Sure, he had just saved her life, but she had no clue as to what this stranger's motives were—for all she knew he had only saved her to kill her himself.

Her gaze caught on the sides of his head as he continued to watch her. She had come to realize that all the Ilaidae had pointed ears, but this man had rounded ones much like herself; however not being an Ilaidae did *not* mean Lillian trusted him.

The man, noticing her obvious distrust, lowered his blades to the ground and lifted his hands to show that he meant her no harm.

Lillian couldn't help but stare at the muscles on his arms that flexed as he laid down his weapons, but she continued to hold her ground, even knowing she must look pathetically weak.

Realizing that she wasn't going to budge, the man spoke.

"Please, let me help you. I'm not here to hurt you."

Never again would she trust a single thing that set foot in this unforgiving forest—this was all probably another clever trick, and the now gorgeous man would turn into another ghoulish being. "*Stay back*," she spat. Lillian tried to sound as intimidating as possible, but it was rather hard when the sword in her hands quivered like a leaf caught in the wind.

The man tried taking another step forward in turn causing Lillian to raise her sword even higher. But her body, not being able to handle any more strain, failed her as the blade fell straight to the forest floor. She looked at the man in horror as she realized how she had just made herself weaponless.

Well, great, Lillian thought to herself. This man could now easily kill her, and she barely had the strength to put up a good fight.

Thinking she had sealed her fate, she expected to see the tall man pick up his sword and finish her off, but upon looking at him, she found him struggling to suppress a laugh.

Her cheeks burned red in embarrassment as she realized he was laughing at her.

Doing his best to hide his grin, he coughed while trying to get his bearings. "You're clearly wounded. Don't make this any harder on yourself."

Lillian glared back at the man. She still had her stubborn pride, and she wasn't very known for making things easy. "No," she replied.

The man blinked at her in disbelief. "Really? *No*? That's your answer?"

"You think just because you saved my life that I'm immediately supposed to trust you?"

He grinned at her as he pondered her words. "Well, generally yes. Usually if I save someone, they do tend to be eternally grateful."

Lillian hated that this man thought this was humorous. "And am I just supposed to assume you want to help me for no reason?"

"So you think I need to have a reason to help you, is that it?" The man looked her up and down as if assessing her state and smiled. "Well, you seem rather nice looking underneath all the dirt and blood. Is helping a pretty face a good enough motive for you?"

Looking at the man with obvious ire, she didn't say a thing; he was making fun of her right to her face.

The man chuckled at her seething rage. "Listen, I heard you screaming, and I thought I'd do the gentlemanly thing and help a dying girl out. If I had known you'd be this difficult, I would've left you to die in your own stubbornness. But seeing as it's too late for all that, you really would make me have a terrible night's sleep if I left you all alone like this."

She loathed this man and how he had the audacity to speak to her like a mere child. "Screw you and your *sleep.* Thanks for saving me, I *guess*, but feel free to leave. Don't stay on my account—I'm perfectly fine."

A smirk leaking with doubt surfaced on his face as he glanced at her and then at her blade lying on the floor. "Now we *both* know that's not true. You could barely hold up that sword, let alone yourself. Your legs look like they're going to give out on you at any second."

Clenching her teeth, she took in the man's words—abhorring that he was right. But she wasn't going to admit that. No longer wanting to chat with this *infuriating* individual, she turned to walk away. However, unfortunately for her, the man had been right. She made it a few steps in the opposite direction before her legs folded in on themselves, and she fell down hard onto her face.

The sounds of footsteps rushing over and a series of curses came closer.

Lillian had no clue why this stranger was so concerned for her, but she couldn't do a thing to stop him as she felt him scoop her up into his arms; she loathed how comforting it felt to be in the man's strong embrace.

His tone turned more serious, and she could've sworn she saw worry glaze over his features. "I'm not going to hurt you. I wouldn't have saved you if I was going to just turn around and kill you."

Whether it was because she was too weak or too prideful, she didn't respond as the man began walking. He had the most delicious aroma, but she only caught a small whiff of it as the world began turning black, her body finally giving in to an overwhelming wave of exhaustion.

And as the man carried her away, her eyes closing shut, she couldn't help but feel that something about him was familiar.

CHAPTER 19

Lillian awoke to find herself lying on a cool, hard surface. Everything around her was lined with shadows, and she assumed it had to be some point in the night.

She let her eyes get adjusted to the sudden darkness and started to make out being in a small cave. She scanned the empty cavern, her gaze landing on the silhouette of a man facing away from her.

"Someone's finally awake. I was beginning to think you wouldn't stir the whole night."

Instantly, she recognized the man's infuriating voice. "Where am I?" she demanded.

"Straight to the point I see. No, *thank you for not leaving me to die in the woods my oh-so-handsome savior*?"

Lillian took in a deep breath, not wanting to lose her head, and repeated her words. "Where. Am. I."

The man chuckled at her seriousness as he turned to face her.

"*We* are in a nice little abandoned cave I found. This was where I was hiding out for the night when I heard you causing a ruckus."

"I'm leaving," she said as she got up and stomped towards the exit.

He let out a loud exhale, and she swore she could hear his eyes rolling. "Sit down. You're not going anywhere."

Glaring at the man, she put her hand on the hilt of her dagger. "Is that a threat?"

"Such a violent woman," he drawled with an upturned lip, the lowered voice with which he used seeming oddly tantalizing. "But no, I'm not threatening you. It would just be rather idiotic of you to go out in these woods in the middle of the night, especially in your…weakened state."

Gods, Lillian hated that he was right. "For all I know, *you're* the most dangerous thing in these woods."

The man was grinning from what she knew he undoubtedly took as a compliment. "I'm truly flattered, but why must you assume everything is out to get you?"

"Because everything in these gods forsaken woods is!" she shouted back.

"Well," he said, holding up his hand in a mock vow. "You can rest assured that I'm not one of them and will do you no harm."

Lillian scoffed at his unconvincing statement. "And I'm just supposed to take your word for it?"

"By the gods, woman, why must you think I only want to kill you? If I wanted you dead, I, firstly, wouldn't have gone through the trouble of saving you, and, secondly, it would have been much easier to do so while you slept."

It was hard to claim that what he said wasn't rational, and it *would* be mindless of her to go out in the middle of the night when the gods knew what creatures were lurking about—but it didn't stop her from hating the words that came from her mouth. "Fine. I'll stay. But only for tonight and then I never want to see you again."

Smiling, the man gestured for her to come sit by him, but Lillian strode right past him, going as far away from him as she possibly could. "And stop calling me *woman*."

The man switched his tone to a lighter one. "Well, that can *easily* be remedied. Allow me to introduce myself. I'm Nolan—and you are?"

Lillian was quite fond of the name Nolan, but it was a shame it was attached to such an irritating individual. She refused to play into his tantalizing voice and kept her answer short. "Lillian Echethier."

"Lillian," he repeated, dragging out the syllables as if feeling how the name sounded on his tongue. "I think I rather like that name, Lil. But I do, however, find it humorous as to how such a violent and stubborn girl is named after a lovely flower."

She glared at him. "No. Not Lil. Lillian."

A devilish grin appeared on his lips. "Yeah. Lil. That's what I said."

She was starting to lose her patience. "No. Stop it. It's Lillian."

The man feigned confusion as he kept the same teasing tone. "Sure thing, Lil. No problem."

Groaning loudly, she stood. "Screw this. I'd rather take my chances with whatever's out there than spend another second here with you." She marched right past him towards the exit and almost made it out when she felt Nolan grab her from behind and cover her mouth with his hand.

Seconds from starting to thrash, he whispered in her ear. "Be quiet. There's something out there."

Turning her attention to the woods, she heard muffled footsteps rustling in the grass.

Nolan backed them away from the opening and sat her down between his legs while they watched the cave's exit in silence. He carefully took his hand off her mouth and brought both to rest on his legs, his thumbs grazing the sides of her outer thighs.

A feeling of warmth bloomed in her cheeks at the slight touch; she couldn't help liking the feel of someone, even if it was from someone as frustrating as Nolan. But she blamed those strange emotions on the fact that she hadn't seen another human or been so close to one for what had now felt like an eternity.

Small puffs of his breath caressed her neck as she breathed in his pleasant scent—he had the faintest smell of a combination of mahogany and sandalwood. She had no clue how he managed to still smell so divine after fighting a ghoul and lugging her all the way to this cave, but she wasn't too torn up about it as she continued inhaling his scent.

When the sound finally vanished, they sat there for a few more minutes, just to be sure that whatever creature was no longer around. Lillian knew she should probably get up, now that the threat was long gone, but she couldn't help but like the feeling of someone wrapped around her.

Her heart skipped a beat as she felt Nolan shift and bring his mouth up to her ear. His finger brushed a strand of hair behind the crook as he spoke softly. "While I'm glad you enjoy the feeling of me pressed up against you, I am going to have to ask you to kindly move because that stench of yours is starting to rub off on me."

Gritting her teeth together to the point of shattering, she let her elbow fly back into his chest and shot up to her feet. She left Nolan on his side clutching his stomach in pain as she went back to the spot farthest away from him.

He held his ribs, coughing and laughing as he tried to form words. "I was only kidding—well, mostly anyway. That Xefta did bleed all over you, leaving you with a not entirely *delightful* aroma, but we'll find somewhere for you to wash up tomorrow."

Her voice came out deadly low. "I already told you—I won't *be* with you tomorrow."

Nolan brushed off what she said as if he were speaking to a toddler that had missed their nap. "Yeah, okay sure. Just try and get some sleep. I'll take first watch."

She hated being dismissed as if what she said didn't matter and perhaps she was acting like a stubborn child, but she would be damned if she'd let this infernally aggravating man order her around. "No, I'm not tired. You can sleep first."

Nolan cut her a pointed glance. "You're obviously tired. Or did you already forget how you passed out in my arms earlier? You need to rest and get your strength back."

Lillian didn't care that he was right; he didn't know a damned thing about her. "I said I'm not tired. I guess we can both be up."

He shook his head at her as he exhaled. "You're impossible."

She couldn't make out too much in the dark, but it looked like his eyes were narrowing at her. "Fine, you can take first watch," he ground out. "But if you even start to feel the *smallest* bit tired, wake me up."

Nolan curled onto his side and slipped something under his head as he turned his back to her. He shifted a bit and Lillian knew he had a grin plastered on his face as he whispered, "Goodnight, Lil."

Not thinking he deserved a response, she instead rolled her eyes, a faint chuckle coming out of Nolan as if somehow knowing exactly what she'd done.

The cave went back to its usual silence, the only sounds Nolan's breaths as they slowly turned more even. He really had to have been tired if he could slip into a slumber so swiftly. He must have been up most of the night since Lillian had likely slept through a large portion of the evening. She found it rather chivalrous that he had offered to take first watch even though he was clearly exhausted, but the polite image she'd had in mind vanished as she remembered how infuriating he was.

A sigh escaped her lips. Lillian didn't quite know what to make of him yet and shifted so she didn't have to look or think of him any longer. But the slight movement, coupled with the adrenaline of the day having finally worn off, caused a painful throb to develop in her right arm.

Suddenly recalling the injury the ghoulish creature had given her, she dared a glance at her ravished arm. From what she could see—with the light the stars and moon provided—was a cloth bandage wrapped and covering her arm.

How had she not noticed it before?

Unraveling the soiled bandage from her wound, she cringed at what she saw. She imagined the gash had to have looked much worse before, but it still looked fairly gruesome. She had two overlapping wounds from where the monster had slashed her with its claws and then bit down on the same area. Surrounding her sliced up flesh, her skin was an intense puffy red and oozed a liquid that wasn't blood. It appeared that Nolan had tried to clean it up as best he could, but the mere sight of it still made Lillian's stomach churn.

Not able to gaze at it for another second, she covered up her wound with a dry part of the wrapping. Tomorrow she would find a stream and try to clean it out as much as she could—Lillian glanced down at herself—and a wash wouldn't hurt as well.

To her great dismay, Nolan had once again been right. She was indeed covered in that black gunk that had leaked out from the disgusting monster.

She shivered as she thought back to the wretched beast, remembering how it had pinned her down and feasted on her torn flesh. She had wounded the creature multiple times and still that hadn't been enough to put the beast down; never before in her life had she felt so helpless.

Shooting up to her feet, she ran to a corner as she heaved up the contents of her stomach.

She—she had almost died. She *would* have died if it weren't for……

Her gaze wandered to his sleeping figure as she exhaled. Even though he did save her and had given her no reason not to like him—other than his irritating personality—she still couldn't bring herself to let her guard down. She could tolerate him for the time being, *maybe*, but after tonight she would make sure they went their separate ways.

Regardless of what he'd done for her, she still had to be careful around him. Because even though he was human…he was deadly powerful. Lillian recalled how easily he had felled the beast that had almost ended her existence.

What had he called that thing?

Xefta, she remembered, saying the strange word again and twisting it on her tongue. She had glossed over him knowing the creature's specific name, not wanting to engage in any more conversation than she had to. Perhaps she would inquire tomorrow, before they split paths, on how he had come to be so familiar with the beast.

Standing in the dark, mulling over everything that had transpired, an overwhelming sense of thirst hit her all at once. She looked around for her pack and sighed, remembering she had lost it in those caves.

Her eyes roamed the area, and she found a shape that could be a canteen lying next to where she had first awoken. With soft steps, she walked over to inspect the small shape.

Lillian picked up the container, shook it around, and began looking for a cap as she realized liquid sloshed inside. Unscrewing the lid, she sniffed the unknown liquid first and concluded it was safe to drink as she gulped down mouthfuls of the water.

Once she had thoroughly quenched her thirst, she sat back down, resting her head against the cavern wall. Lillian really needed to come up with a new plan and relying on Nolan to help wasn't one of them. She couldn't trust a stranger—not one from these woods anyway.

A pang of despair and hopelessness coursed through her at her current circumstances. She still had no food or water and hunting had proven to be way more dangerous than she had originally anticipated; she didn't think she could ever shoot a rabbit again without going into a full-blown panic. A decent walk separated her and Iavothae, and after she crossed, she still had to find wherever the ruler of the lands dwelled; stopping every few hours and looking for a source of water would definitely set her back on her journey.

Lillian didn't want to think right now, especially since her mind was coming up empty on what she would do. She hoped once morning hit some ingenious plan would come to mind and drive all her troubles away.

A yawn slipped past her lips as her lids began feeling heavy—surely, she could keep watch just as well with her eyes closed for a few minutes. Just a quick five minutes. Nothing more.

And with her strength depleted, Lillian lacked the energy to stop herself as she fell into a much-needed slumber.

CHAPTER 20

Dreams of being back home in the comforts of her family's cottage careened through her mind.

Lillian stood at her bedroom door, looking out at her family gathered for dinner. How she wished she were truly there.

There was nothing special going on—just another one of their dinners they'd had a thousand times—but she longed for the loving embrace that was her family.

Smiling, she watched from her doorway as they laughed and ate whatever delicious meal her mother had prepared for everyone that night.

She hoped this was real—that they were truly happy. She didn't want her goings to have left them in a perpetual state of sorrow. The last thing she wanted was for anyone to grieve over her leaving.

At the head of the table sat her father, like usual, and the space where Lillian had always sat to his right now looked barren. Her father's gaze landed on the empty chair and then shot to her bedroom door, a pang of agony washing over his features as he stared to where Lillian was standing.

Her mother, sitting to her father's left, reached out and took his hand as they both cast a saddened look towards Lillian's door.

Was this a real vision she was seeing? And if it were, could they see her?

Lillian had no idea how it would be possible for her to be seeing a vision of her family, and she shifted a few steps to the right to see if her family was staring at the door to her chambers…. or something else.

Disappointment crept into her face as she found her father's gaze to be unmoving. It was clear now that they couldn't see her. But maybe there was a way to make herself known...

She walked back over to her bedroom door and hovered her hand over the handle. She had no clue if this was real or a dream, but she wouldn't pass up the chance to be with her family, even if it did turn out to all be an illusion.

Lillian reached out and grasped the knob with her hand, eyes going wide as she realized she could actually touch it. She hadn't been sure if this was going to be similar to the illusion in the forest where her hands had gone right through the ornate white railing.

Elated, she turned the knob and let the door fly open.

She turned to her father, a look of concern and confusion flooding him as he called towards her room. "Lillian?"

The sound of her name on her father's lips threatened to crush her. "Father," she said in a choked voice, tears already streaming down her face.

His eyes darted around at her chambers, and he ran into her room as if he'd actually heard her. Lillian watched as he dashed past her and repeated her name as he looked in every corner of her room. She was about to sprint towards him and call out his name a second time when her mother burst in and cut her off.

A maddened look clouded her father's eyes as he took apart her room, but he briefly stopped his rummaging as he glanced at his wife. "She was here, Halline. I heard her—my little girl was here."

Despair shrouded her mother's face as she shook her head. "She's gone, Grayson."

They both locked eyes and her father moved his head to the sides in a slow pace. "No… I know what I heard. She was *here*. I heard my Lily."

Guilt overwhelmed Lillian as she stood paralyzed; she hadn't ever seen her father in any state other than calm and collected.

Choking down her sobs, she stared at her father, crying out that she was here.

He seemed to be the only one who could vaguely hear her as he yelled out, "Did you hear that? I can hear her voice!" He began looking around in a frenzied manner as he spoke again. "Where are you, my sweet Lily. Speak to me!"

Halline walked over and stepped in front of her husband as she took his face in her hands. "*Grayson*," she croaked. "She's not here."

He shook his head, tears sliding down his cheeks. "She has to be—*she has to be*. Where else could she be?"

Her mother's eyes turned glossy. "I wish I knew, my love."

He laid his head against his wife's chest as they both sunk to the floor holding each other tight.

Oh gods, what had she done?

She *never* imagined that her leaving would have caused *this*. If she had known yelling out her father's name would've sent him into a pit of despair, she would have stood in silence, content with watching them eat their dinner.

Feeling like an outsider, she sat down, stifling her cries as she watched her father break down in tears—she had never seen this side of him. He had always been the one to comfort her and her family and was the only one who was able to maintain their cool in times of trouble.

An intense shame veiled her as she watched her mother caress his hair from the distress that *she* had caused him. So stupid. She was so stupid. Why had she spoken?

A minute later Kynra, Maxith, and Nimreth walked in, and Lillian shoved down her sobs as they surrounded their parents in a huge embrace. They all sat there huddled up against one another, sorrow leaking from their eyes.

Gods, she was the worst person in the world. She had done this—*she* had caused this pain and anguish.

Standing up, she wiped the tears from her eyes. She needed to fix this—*had* to make this right. She'd be damned if she was the cause of her family's pain. Her leaving and all she had done was to protect them. She wasn't going to let herself die and leave her family—not like this. Lillian was determined to live and come back to her family, no matter what she had to do or face.

A fiery passion gleamed in her eyes as she gazed at her family, vowing to do whatever she had to in order to see them again.

Lillian watched as they held each other, but the vision in her mind became interrupted as she felt something cold fall all over her head.

Waking with a start, she felt icy water coating her hair as her eyes flew open to find Nolan holding a canteen over her head.

Shooting up, she shrieked, "*What* is wrong with you?"

Nolan looked unbothered as if he didn't care what he'd just done. "I told you to wake me up if you wanted to sleep."

"I obviously didn't mean to fall asleep! It was an accident!"

"Accident or not, it was still reckless. *Maybe* if you hadn't been acting like a stubborn baby and allowed me to take first watch this wouldn't have happened."

Lillian clenched her jaw as her vision became shrouded in red. Who did this *idiot* think he was to speak to her in such a way?

He turned around to walk away, and Lillian couldn't control her anger as she let a hand fly towards his head.

Whipping around, he stopped her blow that was mere inches away from slamming into his stupid face. Nolan's eyes went wide as he gaped at her. "Did you just try to hit me?"

Lillian didn't say a thing, seething, as he held her by the wrist.

There was a tug at the corner of his lips. "You're going to have to do *much* better than that if you actually mean to do me some damage."

Staring at him in a silent fury, she balled up her other fist.

His eyes glanced down at the hand not in his grasp as he spoke in a lethally low voice. "Now don't you *dare* try to hit me again."

Ignoring whatever warning he had just uttered, she let her remaining fist sail towards him. But just as easily as the first, he grabbed her by the wrist. Her blow had been foolishly obvious, but she couldn't help defying whatever order her gave.

Nolan—now holding both of her wrists—held them above her head as he backed her up against the cavern wall. He had a smug look on his face as he hissed, "You really are a vicious one, aren't you?"

Lillian thrashed against him, kicking out her legs to make him let go, but he kept his grip firm as he held her pinned.

Whispering, he leaned in close to her ear. "I think you're starting to grow on me, Lil. I can feel a true friendship starting to blossom." His whisper turned lower, coming out more as a growl. "Or maybe something else if you wish—I *am* rather intrigued by your violent nature."

Lillian couldn't hear anything over the roaring in her head. Who did this bastard think he was to even *insinuate* that she would ever want anything to do with him in that way? But that wasn't even what bothered her the most. What she especially loathed is how he had been able to subdue her without barely even batting an eye.

Grinding her teeth together, she writhed under his iron grip. "Let me go, you prick!"

"As you wish," he said, chuckling at her rage as he obliged.

His hands no longer on her wrists, she shoved him from out in front of her, storming past him. Lillian grabbed all the belongings she had left—which weren't many—and marched out of the cave.

She squinted her eyes as she was greeted by the bright sun. Thank the gods it was morning. Now she didn't have to spend another second with that impossible man.

Taking a quick glance around, she began planning out where she would go first. She needed to get this disgusting black ooze off her and clean out her nasty wound, so finding a river would be her number one priority for the day. Figuring out food would be a problem for later, seeing as she had no clue what to do there. She had thought hunting to be the answer but now that wasn't looking like a viable option.

Crunching footsteps sounded on the grass behind her as she heard Nolan's voice call out. "So where are we headed to first, Lil?"

Lillian whirled around, glaring at him as she clamped her teeth together. "*We* aren't going anywhere. You are going back to whatever it was you were doing in these woods, and *I* will go back to what I was doing." She put on a saccharine smile and spoke in a voice leaking of false kindness. "Sound good?"

Pretending to consider her words, Nolan bounced his head from side to side. "Well.... seeing as what you were doing before was *dying,* I think I should probably stick around for at *least* a little bit longer."

Her poor attempt at a smile fell apart as she groaned in disbelief. "Were you not held enough as a baby? Is that why you crave attention so much?"

"Now that you mention it, I'm not sure. My mother, however, did always tell me it would take someone with an iron will to put up with me."

Lillian scoffed; boy was his mother right about that. She pitied whoever had to be around such a frustrating individual at all hours of the day.

Narrowing her eyes and shaking her head one last time, she turned around and began walking away.

His steps crumpled the leaves on the forest floor as she saw him jog up beside her.

Her pace quickened. "What do you think you're doing?"

"What do you mean?"

"I told you to leave. I don't want you following me around."

"I'm technically not following you if I'm walking alongside you."

Coming to a halt, she put her hands on her hips. "What do I have to do to get you to stop trailing me like a lost dog? Do I have to throw a stick and run away when you go fetch it?"

He snorted. "Now *that* would be a cruel trick."

Lillian didn't smile. "I'm being serious. Why are you *so* unwilling to leave me alone? I guarantee we aren't going in the same direction."

Intrigued, he cocked his head to the side. "Where are you going?"

A smiled formed on her lips as she realized he would finally let her go; no mortal would ever dare venture off to where she was going. "Iavothae," she said, batting her eyelashes.

Nolan's eyes went wide.

With a smugness dancing on her face, she began waltzing away. Why hadn't she thought to say that sooner?

But as she sauntered off, feeling satisfied and relieved that he would no longer be a nuisance to her, she heard him run up after her. "That's where I'm going too!" he exclaimed.

Stopping herself mid-step, she turned to look at him. "You're lying."

"Now why would I lie about that?" he countered.

"I don't know, you probably find it funny to toy with me or something like that. You have to be lying, only a foolish human would go to Iavothae."

He arched a brow, looking at her as if she were being ridiculous. "Strange words coming from a human going to Iavothae. What's your grand reason for going then?"

She cut a glare in his direction as she realized that it *was* rather hypocritical of her to say such a thing. "I'm not telling someone I just met everything I'm doing. Why are you even going?"

"So you expect me to tell you why *I'm* going when you won't tell me?" Nolan chuckled as he shook his head. "I don't think so."

What he said made sense, but it didn't make it any less annoying. "Fine. I didn't even care much to begin with."

"Good. Same here."

Lillian began walking away and to no one's surprise, he trotted right alongside her. She sighed but continued on without uttering a word.

After minutes of only hearing their steps and the chittering of animals, he was the first to break the uncomfortable silence. "Well, seeing as we *are* going to the same place, it would make a great deal of sense to stick together."

She said nothing as she stared on ahead, letting him say whatever stupid things he wanted.

"And I hope you've realized by now that I'm not here to kill you or torture you in horrific ways like you originally thought."

It was impossible to ignore that going to Iavothae together made a lot more sense than going by herself—and he *was* rather skillful with a sword. Having some extra protection wouldn't hurt, but was all that really worth putting up with such an obnoxious individual? Continuing to pad down the path, she pondered over his words in silence.

"I did also happen to notice you don't have any food or water with you." He patted the bag across his back. "As you can see, I happen to have *plenty* of both with me."

Nolan was very right. She didn't have any food or water and it would make her trip a lot harder without them—especially since she wouldn't dare hunting anytime soon. But she didn't want to have to rely on him—on a potentially dangerous stranger—to get to Iavothae; she wanted to get there of her own account.

The vow she had made in her dream—the one promising that she would do whatever it took to survive and get back to her family—popped into her head as she contemplated what he proposed.

Stopping her tracks, she turned to look at him, narrowing her eyes at him as she considered all he put forth.

He grinned at her as she stood there watching him; she hated how ridiculously handsome he looked smiling at her like that.

"Fine," she mumbled while rolling her eyes.

The bastard had the audacity to look surprised. "Really? Is that a yes?"

"Do you *want* me to change my mind?"

"No, no, of course not," he said holding up his hands. "I'm just glad you came to the smart decision." Lillian began to walk away, and he continued to stroll alongside her. "This is going to be *so* much fun, Lil, you'll see."

She groaned at his statement. "I *suppose* I can somewhat trust you not to do me any harm, but I can't make the same promise to you."

Nolan huffed out a deep laugh that warmed her bones. "Well, my dear Lillian, that's just a risk I'll have to take then, isn't it?"

Staring out ahead as they eased on by, she couldn't stop herself as the corners of her mouth twitched upwards—perhaps this wouldn't be so bad after all.

CHAPTER 21

The sun's rays beamed down hard as Lillian made her way through the dangerous Forest of Brittelia. But for the first time in this wretched place, she wasn't alone.

She cast a glimpse to the man trotting beside her on her right; it still felt so strange to have someone along with her. She had gotten so used to being alone, but it would have been mindless of her to decline his company. He could have killed her plenty of times and had chosen not to, and she also couldn't ignore the small detail that he had risked his life to save her from that nasty beast.

His motives for helping her were still unknown but that didn't matter for the time being. She wasn't trying to find someone who would be eternally loyal to her; she just needed a mercenary to act as an extra protection. She was only using him for his particular skillset in fighting off monsters *and* the nice plus that he had food and water. Lillian snuck another glance at the man walking next to her; she also didn't mind that he was rather easy on the eyes.

But her quick glance turned into a glare of annoyance—he was, however, an increasingly frustrating person to be around. She supposed it made sense that someone with so many positives had to have a negative somewhere and that just so happened to land on his obnoxious personality.

Her musings were stopped as she heard a faint sound of running water in the distance, and she halted her steps as she tried pinpointing where the noise originated from.

Nolan raised a brow, his eyes wandering around the forest before he opened his mouth. "So what—"

Lillian held up a finger, interrupting whatever useless thing he was going to utter. Nolan quickly got the message as he sealed his lips and nodded.

Closing her eyes, she concentrated on the sounds alone and could make out the flowings of a stream coming from the east. She then opened her lids and pointed in the direction she'd heard the noise. "This way." Lillian didn't give him a second to argue as she began going off to where she'd gestured.

He quickened his pace to catch up. "What's this way?"

"A stream, a river, some body of water I hope."

"Oh. I hadn't realized that's what you were listening for. I could have told you it was this way."

Lillian rolled her eyes. "Of course you could have."

Nolan let out a low chuckle. "Are you always this snarky? Or is it only around me?"

She plastered on a smile and batted her lashes at him. "Just for you."

A devilish grin formed on his face. "Just for me?" His blue eyes glistened with mischief. "I think I like the sound of that."

Glaring at him in disgust, she stormed off, flashing him a vulgar gesture with her hand as she went.

Her obscene motion caused him to roar in laughter as he made his strides longer to keep up with her hurried pace.

Lillian groaned internally; even his chuckling was enthralling. He did it in such a carefree manner that made her want to laugh along with him and leave all her troubles behind. She could see how it would be difficult for anyone to stay mad at him when he laughed in that charming way, but she'd be damned if she let that insinuating comment go unpunished.

"Oh, come on, Lil. Have you no sense of humor? I was only kidding."

"Believe me, I *have* a sense of humor. I just don't happen to think you're very funny."

Nolan held a hand up to his chest as he feigned offense. "You wound me. I had thought it to be one of my better qualities."

Scoffing she said, "You must have pretty terrible qualities if your humor was one of the better things about you."

He guffawed at her statement, eyes open wide. "My mother would certainly have hated to be witness to the slandering of her perfect little boy."

The mere mention of his family made her heart ache for her own. She didn't want to think about that awful dream, so she steered away from that thought in her mind. "Well, if I ever have the misfortune of knowing you long enough to meet whoever raised you, I'll be sure to tell them just how awful you turned out to be."

His face twinged with a flicker of sadness before reverting back to his normal smug demeanor. "That might be a little hard to do—unless you plan on conducting a seance of sorts."

Taken aback by his statement, she felt like an idiot for what she'd said before. She erased the anger from her tongue, replacing it with soft kindness. "I'm sorry. I—I didn't mean to make you bring her up."

Nolan put on a wan smile as he stared ahead. "No, don't feel bad. If anything, I was the one who mentioned her first. It happened a long time ago. I don't really talk about it much, but it doesn't bother me to bring it up anymore."

He didn't seem much older than her, so he must have been rather young when she died—but Lillian still felt horrible that she had caused him to relive such a terrible memory. Something inside her—or perhaps the way he had phrased that statement—made her ask him the question. "Do you *want* to talk about it? That must have not been easy for you and your family to go through."

She watched him as he stared out ahead—his deep blue eyes shimmering in the bright sun. Lillian was about to open her mouth and apologize for what he must have construed as prying when the corners of his mouth tilted upwards. He let out a dry chuckle that didn't hold its usual warmth. "Yeah, it was a little hard—especially when you lost half your family in one go."

Her heart sunk. She couldn't imagine what kind of pain losing a single family member would do to a person. But multiple? She would be in shambles.

Walking alongside her in silence, he let out a long breath. "There's not much to tell other than I wasn't there when I should've been."

Lillian looked at him and something inside of her yearned to make that saddened expression disappear. She didn't know what he was talking about but found herself trying to comfort him. "You can't blame yourself for not being there. Whatever happened couldn't have been your fault."

A cold scoff spurted out of him. "You don't know that."

"No—I guess I don't. But from what I've gathered about you is that you wouldn't have left someone you cared about if they were in danger. So, no—I don't think whatever happened was your fault."

A muscle twitched in his jaw and his eyes looked glossier than before. "I'm not looking for forgiveness from a stranger."

"Good, because I'm not here to give it to you. Only you can do that. I'm simply telling you what I think."

Nolan's tone turned harsher than she had ever heard before. "Well, let me tell you what happened, and you can tell me what you *think.* I was supposed to have been at home with my family, but I had gotten into some dumb argument with them and left to go wallow in my anger." He took in a deep breath and looked upwards as if replaying the memory in his mind. "To put it in more concise words—a wicked Ilaidae struck while I was gone and killed my mother, father, and younger sister." He turned his glare that was twisted with anger and grief to her. "Does that not sound like something I could've prevented, Lillian?"

She was at a loss for words as he stopped and stared at her with a fiery pain in his eyes. She had grown so used to him annoyingly calling her Lil that Lillian sounded foreign on his tongue. Opening her mouth to think of something to say, the words turned to ash as they crumbled on her lips.

Shaking his head once, he turned to walk away. "Yeah… I thought so."

Lillian grabbed him by the shoulder and made him face her, those eyes flickering with shadows. She refused to let him be tortured by something he so wrongly assumed was his fault. "You couldn't have predicted something so awful would happen. And even if you were there, do you really think you could have done anything to stop it?"

"I could have at least tried."

"What good would that have done? You could have died along with them."

Pain lanced through his face as he looked away from her. His tone lowered, and she could barely hear him as he muttered out a phrase. "Sometimes I wish that's what would've happened."

Her face dropped as she stood there, shocked that he would even say such a thing. It hurt her to know that his pain was so deep that he might rather be dead. She hardly knew this man, but it physically pained her that someone could feel that way. "Don't *ever* say that—don't even *think* such a thing."

Nolan looked into her eyes, furrowing his brows as if her concern surprised him. "I didn't actually mean that. I could never put that kind of grief on someone."

Lillian still didn't like that he insinuated he was only living for other people, but she let it slide, not thinking it was her place to comment.

Stretching out his arms, he awkwardly coughed. "Well.... that was more intense than I had ever thought to get with a stranger."

His usual demeanor returned once more, and she gave him a soft smile "Thank you—for sharing."

Nolan gazed at her, a twinkle in his eyes as he returned her smile. "It looks good on you."

Not sure as to what he was referring to, Lillian cocked her head to the side. "What does?"

His eyes danced with promise as his grin widened. "That gorgeous smile of yours."

Lillian rolled her eyes at what she knew was his way of defusing the tension but found herself blushing at the simple compliment. "Yeah, whatever."

They began walking on the set path once more—and she found herself secretly glad that he was back to his annoyingly flirtatious self.

"Now I don't want you to go on thinking my life is something to be pitied. It's not all so bad."

Lillian raised her eyebrow at him, motioning for him to continue.

"I've got a nice group of friends and a younger brother I happen to love dearly."

She held a hand up to her open mouth. "You have *friends*? Who would've thought such a thing possible."

Chuckling, he shook his head. "Believe it or not, smart ass, some people find me to be rather..." He leaned in close to her ear as the next word rolled off his tongue. "...*charming*."

Lillian batted his face away with her hands as she laughed out loud, that playful voice of his rumbling out once more at the sight of it. "Has anyone ever told you that you look beautiful when you laugh?"

A bright scarlet stained her cheeks as she averted his gaze. "Has anyone ever told *you* that you're an impossible flirt."

"Maybe once or twice but that doesn't make what I said any less true."

Not used to having so much attention on her, Lillian changed the subject. "T—Tell me about your remaining family," she said, trying to brush past that embarrassingly nervous stutter. "If you don't mind that is."

Nolan paused as he mulled over it, and Lillian instantly regretted her line of questioning. Of course, he didn't want to talk to a complete stranger about these things. She was about to tell him to forget what she said when he began. "Well, that depends on what you mean. My biological family consists of an older sister and my younger brother that I mentioned earlier—but I've grown to consider my friends to be my own little family of sorts."

Lillian noticed how he had failed to mention that he had another sibling earlier. "Do you not get along with your older sister?"

His face turned to one of disgust and she could've sworn a twinge of shame flickered in his eyes. "That's one way of putting it. She thinks we get along just great, but she's not exactly my favorite person to be around."

Lillian felt a little bit sad at the fact he felt that way about one of his only remaining family members. Surely, she couldn't be that bad that they couldn't be close once more. "Do you still speak with her?" she asked.

"Oh yeah—all the time, though I'd prefer not to."

It confused her as to why he would associate with someone he didn't like. "Why do you still put up with her then?"

A muscle feathered in his jaw as he looked out ahead. "I have my reasons."

Able to tell that he wasn't going to budge on the topic any further, she took the subtle hint and moved on to other things. "Tell me about your friends then."

Nolan's bitter mood subsided as a grin eased onto his face. "Oh, they're something special alright, but it looks like we'll have to leave that for another time." He pointed out in front of her. "We're here."

Looking to where he pointed, she noticed a stream out in the distance. They had been so caught up in conversation that she hadn't even noticed they'd gotten so close to the running water up ahead.

She marched up to the stream and stopped before it as she stared at her reflection a dozen times. She knew Nolan must have thought she'd gone insane as she moved her hands wildly in the air, but she wasn't willing to take her chances near bodies of water anymore.

Once she felt safe enough, she got to her knees, cupping her hands as she filled them and drank her fair share. She hadn't realized just how parched she'd become until the stream had appeared right in front of her.

Nolan dashed after her and took out his canteen, laughter rumbling out of him. "I see someone had an unfortunate encounter with a river nymph."

This man really did seem to have an extensive knowledge of the creatures in the forest. Lillian would definitely have to question him over everything he knew soon enough. But she didn't stop inhaling the water, needing to quench her thirst and just nodded as she continued to drink.

He knelt down next to her and filled up his canteen as he talked. "I'm glad we made this little stop. I was growing a little thirsty after having used the last of my reserves earlier today."

Lillian dropped her hands and glared at him, suddenly remembering what he had done this morning. "Well, maybe if you hadn't dumped the rest of your water on my *head,* you wouldn't have had to be so thirsty."

That irritating smirk of his greeted her. "And miss seeing you jolt awake in anger like that? I think it was worth the small discomfort a dry throat provided."

Lillian splashed water in his stupid face at what he'd uttered.

Wiping the dripping stream off himself, Nolan fixed his eyes on her with a diabolical grin. "Oh, you are *so* going to regret that, Lillian Echethier."

CHAPTER 22

Grinning ear to ear, Nolan leaned over and stuck his whole hand into the stream, splashing a giant wave of water straight at her face.

Lillian closed her eyes and spit out a portion of the stream as she used both hands to send water right back in his direction.

It wasn't a very fair match they had going on between the two of them. His hands, being much wider than hers, could produce larger torrents of water giving him an obvious advantage. Lillian needed a new strategy because he was clearly the superior at this current game of theirs. She was doused in water from head to toe, and she had gotten him decently wet as well, but was not *nearly* as soaked as she was.

Getting up from the bank, she let out a giggling shriek as she dashed away from his next wave—she couldn't remember the last time a noise like that had ever escaped her.

Nolan didn't waste a single second as he got up and sprinted after her. "You're not getting away that easily," he bellowed.

Usually, she wasn't a big fan of anything chasing her in these horrible woods... but she supposed she could make an exception this once.

He was right on her tail as she ran around the stream. She could feel him closing in on her and saw that she had two options—let him catch her and surrender or cross the shallow part of the water to the other side. Lillian was a rather stubborn individual and wasn't necessarily known for giving up so easily, so she darted towards the stream on her right.

She heard Nolan's voice calling out to her, but it had been too late. Lillian had forgotten the small detail that the stream had a rather slippery bottom. As soon as she stuck one foot onto the slimy base, she immediately lost her balance, falling flat onto her backside.

Nolan ran after her but stood on the bank as he tried to contain his laughter. "I did try warning you."

Her ego felt bruised, and she knew her bottom would be as well as she felt a dull pain beginning to emerge. She lifted her ankle to stand herself up but let out a wince at the smallest bit of pressure.

Erasing the grin on his face, he looked at her, concern tracing his voice. "Are you okay? Did you break something?"

So odd that someone she hardly knew acted like he cared so much. "I think I might have torn something. Could you help me up?"

Looking confused that she would even have to ask such a thing, he held out his hand.

As soon as she stuck out her good arm, Nolan reached farther out with his to haul her up. And once she felt like she had a good grip on him, she dug her heels into the mossy floor and pulled on him with all her strength. And Nolan, not having been expecting to brace himself against her extra force, fell down into the stream with a loud splash.

He wiped the water from his eyes and stared at her in disbelief as she fell into a laughing fit.

Shaking his head, a faint smile emerged onto his lips. "That was a dirty play. You really had me worried there for a second."

Lillian stopped her chuckling and looked at him—his wet mop of hair sticking to his head as droplets slid down his temples; there should be laws set in place making it impossible for someone to look that good drenched. "I couldn't let you win that easily. Where would the fun in that be?"

His gaze bore into her as he cocked his head to the side.

Lillian pursed her lips and made her eyes wander. "What?"

"You just keep on surprising me is all."

"Well, there *is* a lot about me that you don't know."

Standing, he extended his hand a second time. "And I can't wait to learn every bit of it—*especially* all your dirty little secrets."

Rolling her eyes at his last statement, she accepted his hand, hauling herself onto her feet. "I guess we'll have to see about that. But right now, we have more important things to be doing."

Nolan raised a brow as if he couldn't think of anything more important than this. "Such as….?"

"I don't know. Maybe like getting to Iavothae or not getting killed by awful creatures."

He nodded his head as if now recalling what she referred to. "Ah. That. You make it sound like those things are hard."

"Well, for some of us, who aren't chiseled like a god or are an expert in sword fighting, it is *a little bit hard*."

Nolan looked at her with that stupid cocky smile. "You think I'm chiseled like a god?"

"Of course that's the part you chose to focus on," she sighed shaking her head. "It just means you're strong." But her cheeks did start to burn as she realized what she'd admitted to him. "Turn around," she blurted out, changing the conversation.

"If you wanted to look at me from behind you could just say so."

Lillian knew her cheeks were bright red now. "No, you prick. I need to get washed up, and I'm *definitely* not letting you watch."

Nolan pouted as he batted his lashes. "Not even if I say pretty please?"

Glaring at him, unamused, she repeated herself. "Turn. Around."

Noticing that she was in no mood to play, he held up his hands in defeat. "Alright *fine*. But if a river nymph comes and drowns you, I hope you die happy knowing that at least your modesty was respected."

Lillian yelled an obscenity at him, and he laughed while finally whirling and trotting away.

Now with some privacy, she focused her attention on the stream and fiddled with the straps of her leather corset as she slid it off and laid it down on the forest floor.

As she looked at her wounded arm, she noticed that the small bandage covering it must have fallen off at some point during their travels, leaving her shirt directly over it. And the cloth having stuck to her wound as it dried, was now plastered tight onto her damaged skin.

Lillian tried lifting up a corner of her ruined shirt and dropped it as she felt a rush of pain go through her. She tried tugging the shirt again and had the same results as she winced out in pain. Something about that creature's saliva and her blood really caused the sleeve to be glued onto her skin.

The best course of action would be to rip off the cloth and suffer the consequences later, but she noticed it was in a rather difficult spot for her to yank off as fast as she would like. Lillian's expression changed to one of annoyance as she realized what she had to do. Taking in a long breath, she dreaded the words that came next as she opened her mouth. "Can you come over here for a second?"

Slowly, Nolan turned around, hands covering his eyes. "Is it safe to look?" His fingers were splayed over his face, allowing her to see it was obvious he was peeking.

"Yeah, you can look," she exhaled, shaking her head.

Nolan strode over to her and spoke in a sultry voice. "How can I be of service to you?"

Ignoring his teasing tone, she gestured to the wound on her arm. "This got stuck. Can you just rip it off?"

His eyes widened as he looked at her with pretend shock. "You want me to *undress* you? How scandalous of you to ask." He brushed an invisible speck of dirt off his shoulders as he sighed. "But I can't say I didn't see this coming—women find it impossible to resist my charms."

Lillian turned to walk away. "You know what, never mind. I'll just figure it out myself."

Grabbing her by the wrist, he didn't say a thing as he began surveying the gash on her arm. His eyes roved over it as a pained expression surfaced on his face. "If I'm being completely honest, this is going to hurt… a lot." He took a pause assessing the wound one more time before looking at her. "You ready?"

Lillian put her back to him as he started to slip the shirt off and held it firm as it clung to her bloodied arm. She hadn't worn any undergarment, as her corset provided enough support, and did her best to cover her exposed breasts with her one arm as she watched him grip her shirt.

Towering over her, he pressed her up close to him and reached his arm across her abdomen as he grabbed her free hand. "Squeeze on this," he offered. His gaze stayed focused on her wound until finally he looked down at her face.

No point in waiting, she nodded her head once, signaling that she was ready.

He ripped the cloth from her arm.

Screams threatened to burst out of her, but she reined them in as she clenched onto his fingers with all her strength. That stupid shirt of hers had gotten stuck to the scabs where her wounds had begun to heal, and the tearing of it had reopened her gashes as a considerable amount of blood now poured down her arm.

A series of curses mumbled out of her as her arm throbbed in pain.

Nolan grabbed the ruined shirt and held it out in front of her, a sleeve in each hand, as he still stood pressed up to her back. "Raise your arms."

Lillian didn't want to raise them, considering they were the only thing keeping her covered—but she didn't answer as Nolan again spoke. "Just trust me. I promise I'll close my eyes."

Even though she was reluctant to do what he said, she found

herself letting go of her breasts and putting her arms up like he'd ordered; following directions was the least she could do considering she had likely shattered his poor hand.

Her heartbeat quickened as Nolan's warm fingers brushed against her too tight skin. He placed the body of the ruined shirt onto her bare chest and brought the sleeves behind her as he tied them into a knot across her back. He then grabbed both of her wrists, lowering them back down to her sides, and grasped her by the hand as he led her towards the small stream. "I don't think you should be cleaning this thing out by yourself."

Sitting her down by the water, he pulled his bag towards him as he brought out a few strips of cloths. He then plopped down next to her and dunked one of the cloths into the water as he brought it up next to her arm. Holding it up, inches away from her skin, he stopped and looked at her, his face asking a silent permission.

Lillian gave an incline of her head and looked away as she braced herself for the excruciating pain. The cloth touched her raw skin and she jolted and winced from the stinging.

Nolan froze.

"No, keep going," she insisted.

He remained still as if her hurting bothered him, but she eventually felt him begin again and was surprised by how gentle his rough, calloused hands could be. Carefully, he washed out her gash, having to stop every few strokes to dunk the cloth before beginning once more.

After a few minutes, Lillian turned her head to look at him—the pain no longer quite as unbearable. She had never seen him look so—so....

She couldn't find the right word to describe it. His brows were furrowed in concentration, and his features were mixed with what she could've sworn was troubled.

Was he upset that she was in so much pain? He barely knew her. Why would he care? Most likely, he just didn't like to be the cause of someone's discomfort—that would make more sense.

The forest around them was so calm, the only sounds surrounding them the submerging of the cloth and the trickles of water as it got wrung out. She liked that they could sit in silence and not have an uncomfortable air suffocating them. But even though she appreciated the tranquility, she found herself wanting to hear his voice. "Won't the stream's water cause it to become infected?" she asked.

Nolan didn't look up from his diligent task as he continued the cleansing. "No, actually, the waters that run through the Forest of Brittelia are surprisingly sterile. If you compared this water to one that was freshly boiled, this stream would be purer."

"How does that work?"

A chuckle came out of him at her questioning. "How does anything in this forest work?"

He did have a point there—nothing in this wretched forest seemed to follow the normal laws of nature.

Nolan threw the soiled cloth onto the ground. "All done. I'll wrap it once you get the rest of yourself cleaned up."

Lillian nodded and locked her gaze with his—she could sit there all day looking into those deep-sea eyes. "Thank you," she managed to say.

Reaching up his hand, he ruffled his hair as a soft smile surfaced. "Anytime, Lil."

Recalling what they had come here for, she blinked a few times and looked down at her shirt, noticing that it was basically ruined. "Do you *maybe* have anything I could borrow?" She gestured to her shirt before continuing. "Because I don't think this is going to work anymore."

"I figured you might need something to wear. I have an extra set of clothes I can lend you."

Lillian glanced at his physique and noticed that he was a lot taller than she was.

Realizing where her gaze had landed, he smiled. "Don't worry I'll make a few adjustments while you finish washing up. Between your corset and belt, it'll fit you just fine." He grabbed his pack while getting to his feet and began walking away, giving her some privacy.

Lillian got up and grabbed her corset—thankfully there wasn't too much of that Xefta's blood on it, and she could easily wash it off the leather. However, she suspected her pants were ruined and wasn't the smallest bit confident that she could scrub out the blackness that had seeped into the cloth.

After turning in Nolan's direction once more to make sure he wasn't looking, she shimmied out of her pants and makeshift top. She walked into a somewhat deeper part of the stream but stayed close enough to the edge where she could touch the bottom with ease.

The water was ice cold as she let the current flow over her, and she found her body covered in goose bumps and felt the peaks of her breast harden as she submerged herself into the freezing stream.

Oh, how she missed her relaxing baths in the piping hot water—she would never get used to this ridiculous cold.

As accustomed to the water as she was ever going to be, she let down her hair and dunked her head underneath. Her teeth chattered as she scrubbed at her body, and she stopped once there was no longer a trace of that creature coating her skin.

Just about done, she heard Nolan call out her name. "Is it okay if I come put the clothes near you?"

Making sure she was submerged in the stream enough to cover any indecent areas, she cupped her chest before answering. "You can come over."

She watched as Nolan glided towards her and laid down the clothes near her. He had been about to turn around and leave but paused as his eyes wandered over her figure in the stream. She knew he was about to say something stupid as that roguish expression appeared on his face. "You sure you don't need any help getting dressed?" he purred.

Lillian opened her mouth to respond but wasn't quick enough as more idiocy flowed out.

"I must warn you though that if you do accept my assistance, I can't help it if my gaze isn't the only thing that roams."

Lillian grabbed a rock by her foot and threw it in his direction. "You're a real pig, you know that?"

Without hardly moving a muscle, he caught the rock in his hand, winking at her as he turned and sauntered off.

Scowling, she got out of the stream and threw the tunic and pants over herself; they weren't anything special as he had just given her a tan shirt and brown pants that had been cut off a few inches on the ends. She tightened the pants around her waist with her belt and adjusted the leather corset over her chest.

Pleasantly surprised to find that the clothes didn't fit her too bad, she finished off by rolling the long sleeves to her elbows. They were a little looser than she would have preferred but they would do just fine.

Once making sure everything was in place, she strolled over to Nolan who already had a fresh bandage in hand. With her permission he rolled the loose sleeve up to her shoulder and frowned at her damaged skin.

"What's wrong?" she asked.

Nolan furrowed his brows as he began wrapping the cloth. "Nothing really. It just looks like it might be starting to get infected."

Lillian's face paled—that was the last thing she needed on her way to Iavothae. Her eyes darted to his pack. "Do you have something in there that'll help?"

"No, unfortunately—but I know where we can get something that will." He finished bandaging her arm and lowered her shirt. "Looks like we're going to have to make a *small* detour."

"Where are we going?" she probed, her voice dripping with curiosity.

Nolan didn't answer her until he squinted his eyes in one direction as if deciding that was the way to go. "We, my dear Lillian, are going to pay Breoslies a quick visit."

CHAPTER 23

Lillian struggled to keep up with Nolan's hurried pace. "Slow down. Why are we rushing? And who's Breoslies?"

He didn't relax his steps, causing Lillian to jog to keep up with his long strides. "Have you ever heard of a siren?"

"Like the fish women who lure you to your death?"

"Think of her as a much more terrifying and deadlier version."

She already didn't like the sound of that. "And she's the only person who has whatever healing tonic or thing we need?"

"Unfortunately… yes."

Lillian dreaded having to meet yet another unfriendly creature that would probably much rather see her dead than alive. "And she'll just willingly hand it over?"

Stopping to take a quick drink, he sipped from his canteen. He held the water out to her, and Lillian—being far more winded than he was—grabbed it and took a big swig. "Well… not exactly," he said.

"We're going to steal it from her."

Lillian choked on her water as she struggled swallowing. "We're going to *what*?"

Packing the canteen in his bag, he began to walk once more in a hastened fashion. "It's not *technically* stealing if you think about it. She just happens to live near where this special flower grows."

Memories of another *special* flower she had encountered came to mind. "What's this flower look like?" she asked, voice coming out nervous.

Nolan arched an eyebrow at her in suspicion. "Does it matter?"

Twirling a strand of hair, she stared out ahead, trying her best to be inconspicuous. "Just thought it would be better if two sets of eyes were looking."

Not believing her entirely, he narrowed his eyes at her, but chose not to question her any further. "It's purple with yellow specks."

A weight lifted off her shoulders as she concluded that it was most definitely *not* the same flower. "Purple with yellow specks," she repeated. "And it only grows there? Not somewhere nice with perhaps fewer deadly monsters?"

Smiling, he chuckled at her statement. "No, the stubborn thing decided it *likes* growing near the deadly monsters."

Her legs started to ache at having to keep up with Nolan. "Can we slow down some?"

He looked at her and relaxed his strides as he noticed she couldn't match his speed with ease. "Sorry. But we really do need to hurry. I want to be long gone from there before dark."

Lillian looked at him waiting for him to provide her with an explanation.

"Breoslies is usually in a deep slumber throughout the day and likes to come out and play at night—much like a lot of the creatures roaming these woods. So—"

Lillian interrupted him not needing him to tell her the rest. "So, you want to steal the flower without waking the terrifying beast."

Nodding he said, "Precisely, and in order *to do that*—we have to make it there as soon as possible."

Trying to ignore her sore limbs, she picked up her speed. "You really know a lot about the things in these woods."

"Yeah, I guess you could say that."

"Why?"

Nolan let out a soft titter. "Someone's feeling rather inquisitive today."

Shrugging her shoulders she said, "I don't know, I guess I'm just curious about that part of you."

A smirk surfaced on his face as he raised his brows. "Oh yeah? What other *parts of me* are you curious about?"

Red burned on her cheeks as she shoved him in the shoulder. "That's *not* what I meant."

Nolan laughed as she pushed him to the side, but he quickly regained his composure as he began to ponder her question seriously. His smile faltered as he tried to hold on to his usual arrogant demeanor. "Well, after the *incident* with my family. I—uh." He coughed clearing his throat. "I found myself wanting to be in as much danger as possible." Nolan paused, thinking on his words. "I guess I felt like I wanted to punish myself for not being there…. If that makes sense."

Her eyes blurred as she continued to listen; she was amazed on how Nolan could be so easy going when he had all this he held onto so tightly. Lillian spoke her words low and soft. "It makes sense."

"I'm not proud of it, but I remember getting more *inebriated* than I should have and just coming into these woods, screaming at the top of my lungs for someone to fight me. I wanted to feel something—anything other than the constant pain."

Swallowing, she blinked back the tears in her eyes. She had thought Nolan to be rather young when he lost his family since he spoke of it like it happened so long ago. But she pushed that thought away—now was not the time to inquire. She walked alongside him in silence as she waited for him to go on.

"I know this sounds bad, but I don't really remember caring if I lived or died out here. I—I think a part of me was hoping, praying, that some beast would come along and finally put me out of my misery."

Lillian couldn't help herself as she instinctively reached out to grab his hand.

A look of surprise veiled his eyes as they wandered down to their intertwined fingers—but he didn't reject her gesture as he held it, brushing his thumb over her skin.

Something in what she did seemed to snap him out of his temporary gloom as she heard him speak with that teasing tone she found herself growing to enjoy. "But as you've seen for yourself. I'm *much* too skilled, not to mention handsome, to be felled by some measly forest monster."

A snort escaped her. "Yes, I'm sure whatever creature spotted you in the forest took one look at you and said, 'Hmm yes, he is *much* too good looking to be killed. Let us spare him.'"

Nolan laughed at Lillian's deep voice. "*That*—was awful."

A wide smile covered half her face. "What? You didn't like my impression?"

He shook his head as he chuckled. "It was something alright."

A surprisingly comfortable silence settled over them as they continued, but she found herself breaking it as Nolan's gaze kept flicking to hers. "What?" she finally turned and said.

Sparks danced in his eyes as he looked at her in what she thought was awe. "How do you do that?"

"Do what?"

"Make it so easy to talk about things. You don't even force it out of me. I just find myself actually *wanting* to tell you."

Heat bloomed on her face at the small compliment. "I don't know. I guess I'm just really easy to talk to."

"Must be something like that," he muttered, but his eyes hinted that he thought there was more.

Nolan stopped and let go of her hand as he looked around, his eyes casting serious glances as he made sure they were heading the right way.

A coldness swept over her palm as it felt strangely empty, and she found herself missing the feel of his fingers brushing up against her skin. Lillian flexed her hand, unsure of what to do with that odd feeling.

Glancing around and up at the trees, he veered their direction slightly to the right as he decided on the best path to follow. Lillian had no clue as to how he knew his way around this forest with every tree they passed looking just like the previous. She had only been able to make her way to Iavothae this far due to it being a straight shot and Euthemio's helpful directions.

They began moving again, and Lillian tried breaking whatever odd tension had started brewing between them. "Since you seem to have such a *superior* knowledge of this forest, what should I be expecting?"

Nolan smiled at her somewhat mocking tone. "You are correct in that I'm superior."

Lillian rolled her eyes. "I only said you were knowledgeable."

Pretending he hadn't heard her comment, he continued to speak. "The slightly terrifying Breoslies" —he made a motion with his fingers to show a small amount— "lives in a large lake, and the flower that we're looking for grows on a grove in the middle."

The color leeched from her face. "So we have to swim to get there?"

"Seeing as it would be strange for any boats to be lying around—yeah, we'll have to swim."

It was truly stupid that she was more afraid of the act of swimming than the creature that lurked in the waters.

Arching a brow he asked, "Are you feeling okay? You look a little… ghostly."

Lillian tried playing off her fear and plastered on a smile that didn't quite meet her eyes. "Yeah, just felt a little lightheaded. But getting back to the lake thing. We *both* have to sw-swi—" She cleared her throat trying to draw attention away from her stutter and tried her sentence again. "We both have to swim?"

Nolan seemed to have bought her excuse as he replied, "Now that you mention it, only one of us really has to swim across and your arm will only slow us down. I'll just go across and get it."

Air entered her lungs as she felt she could breathe again; never would she have thought she'd be thankful to have her arm torn up by a monster.

Looking off into the distance, his expression hardened, and she could tell he was serious about what he spoke next. "You see that mossy tree up ahead?"

Lillian followed where he pointed and nodded as she saw a tall oak tree suffocating from the amount of moss coating its bark.

"Once we pass that tree, we have to be completely quiet. I don't want to risk our chances of waking up that demon."

Glancing down, she took steadying breaths in, feeling entirely unprepared to face another beast—especially considering her last encounter with one hadn't exactly ended well.

Nolan seemed to have picked up on her grim mood and placed a finger under her chin, tilting it up. Those deep blues, filled with worry, bared into her soul as his voice came out laced with warmth. "We are going to be fine."

She hadn't been expecting this man to be able pick up on her emotions so easily but found herself oddly liking it along with the touch of his fingers on her skin. "Yeah, I know," she murmured.

"Say it with me then."

Groaning, she turned around, getting out of his grasp. "Do I have to?"

He walked back around to face her. "It's nonnegotiable."

She sighed as Nolan slowed down his syllables, and they both repeated the phrase.

"See, was that so hard?"

Gesturing to the forest around her, she said, "*This* isn't the part I'm worried about."

Nolan went a few steps ahead before turning to extend his hand. "Well, lucky for you, you have an expert warrior to protect you from all the nasty monsters."

Tentatively accepting his open palm, she snorted. "Are you always this arrogant? Or is it only in a poor attempt to impress me?"

He looked offended as he exclaimed, "Poor attempt? You should be on your *knees* worshiping me for how incredible I am."

A smirk crept onto her lips. "Hmmm, I bet you'd like that."

He brought her hand up to his lips, grinning as he gave it a soft kiss. "You have *no* idea."

Lillian yanked her hand back as she glared at him. "You're disgusting."

Laughter boomed out of him. "You just bring out the best in me."

She feigned distaste at his statement, but riotous thoughts flooded her as she realized that she liked that he thought of her in that way. He was still a pig—but a rather *nice-looking* pig.

However, whatever cheery mood she'd been in was chased away as they reached the moss-covered tree.

With a face more somber than before, he looked at her. "You ready?"

Lillian took one last glance behind her and turned her attention back to him as she spoke in an exhale. "As I'll ever be."

He gave her a half smile as he grabbed her by the hand, squeezing it tight.

And holding her breath.... they crossed into the home of Breos-lies.

The forest wasn't vastly different as they walked in utter silence, but as they went on, she could tell the area was turning into one that resembled a swamp.

The air became suffocating—a smell of rotten eggs assaulting her senses—and strands of moss hung down from the decaying trees as they walked over a thin layer of muck. The trees that surrounded them curved inwards, forming a tunnel, and she could vaguely make out an opening to a body of water covered by a thick layer of the hanging moss in the distance.

An annoying sensation pricked her leg, and she gently brushed away the nuisance. The deeper they ventured into the boggy atmosphere, the more relentless the mosquitoes had grown, causing her to constantly have to battle the urge to slap them dead on her skin.

Her feelings of unease intensified as they continued and not even the reassuring chatter of the insects could soothe her growing anxiety.

It was all so scarily silent, the only noise, other than the buzzing mosquitoes, the squelching of their feet on the damp soil. But their sloshing steps came to a halt as they made it to the massive curtain of moss.

Nolan looked at her, raising a brow as he mouthed, 'You okay?'

All Lillian could do was nod.

Seeming satisfied enough with her answer, he turned towards

the hanging plants and brushed aside part of the moss as it unveiled an enormous lake lying behind it. She could clearly see the water in most areas, but some parts were covered with a thin sheen of floating green that looked like freshly cropped grass.

Nolan tapped her on the shoulder, and she whirled her head as he proceeded to point to a floating bush in the middle of the lake. Just like he had claimed, before her in the distance, laid a small cluster of purple flowers with yellow specks. He let go of the moss, letting it fall back down, once again hiding the lake from sight.

Sauntering towards a tree, he began to unsheathe the two blades across his back and leaned them up against the thick bark. He then proceeded to undo the top parts of his armor and laid them propped up next to the rest of his belongings.

A shade of crimson painted her cheeks as she failed in averting her eyes. One by one, he took off every piece until his chest lay completely bare. She felt a deep pooling in her core as she watched the muscles covering him ripple as he disrobed. Lillian had suspected he had a striking physique—but knowing and seeing were two *very* different things.

With his back facing her, she caught a glimpse of words inked in black running down his back. She squinted her eyes at the strange lettering and realized it was in a language she didn't recognize. But she didn't get to see much as he twisted to face her.

Instantly realizing that she had been staring, she whirled and attempted to busy herself with anything else.

He kept his pants on and a dagger strapped to his waist as he slinked past her back towards the curtain of moss, Lillian struggling to keep her eyes focused on his face.

Nolan raised a brow as he saw her fail to keep her eyes from wandering and a small grin appeared as he shook his head and mouthed, 'Naughty girl.'

Glaring at the smug bastard, she mouthed back a retort. 'Prick.'

She knew he had caught what she'd said as his grin grew even wider. It was so peculiar that she was able to perfectly picture the chuckle he would have rumbled out.

He pulled the hanging greenery back and winked at her one last time as he mouthed, 'Be right back,' and then submerged himself into the murky waters.

Lillian held her jaw shut, needing to stop herself from drooling as she watched his strong arms glide him across the still lake.

With the swamp utterly silent, the only sounds were Nolan's strokes that caused ripples in the stagnant water. A glance around the perimeter revealed nothing to be out of place, but she couldn't ignore the sinking feeling in her gut as she watched him swim closer to the small grove.

The flowers were about thirty feet away from where she stood at the edge, and he was already halfway there. Now closer.

Breathing was lost to her as she watched him make it to the cluster of flowers ahead. He yanked a handful of the plants and stuffed them in a small pouch that hung low around his waist and then started swimming anew, Lillian feeling infinitely more at ease as he made his way back to her.

Nolan had gotten to the mid-point separating the grove and where she stood when a ripple far off in the water caught her attention.

She watched in horror as the rippling glided to where Nolan was swimming.

Flailing her arms out in a craze, she jumped up and down in a desperate attempt to catch his attention and after a torturous few seconds, Nolan finally took notice of her as she pointed behind him like a deranged person.

But with barely a moment to react, Lillian watched as he got pulled under, disappearing into the muddy lake below.

CHAPTER 24

Disbelief and shock coursed through her as she watched the water return to its usual stillness. If she hadn't seen it with her own two eyes, she would never have guessed something had gone amiss in the now tranquil lake.

Panic shrouded her eyes as she stared at the water; she had absolutely no idea what to do.

Would her diving in after him do any good? She had a ridiculous fear of the water and couldn't swim.

The best-case scenario of her jumping in would be that maybe—just maybe if she were lucky—she could rip Nolan out of the creature's grasp. But then that would either leave her drowning and sinking to the bottom, or Nolan would have to save her and bring her to the surface; *and* he'd have to do all that while fighting or fleeing Breoslies. Nolan was a skilled fighter from the sounds of it, but she didn't know if he was *that* skilled.

It seemed like diving into the lake would do more bad than good, but what did that leave her? She couldn't just stand here and do nothing. Sure, she barely knew the guy, but she couldn't leave him to the mercy of that wretched monster.

A minute passed and still there was no sign of anything in the water.

Swallowing hard, she looked at the murky lake, a bead of sweat dripping down her temple. Was this really her only choice?

Closing her eyes, she took a deep breath as she thought of Peter and that little boy in the woods. She could not in good conscience leave someone to the claws of an Ilaidae, even if it meant putting her own life in danger.

Thirty more seconds passed, and she was running out of time. She had no clue how long he could hold his breath for. She had to act now.

Lillian stuck a foot into the water, and her heart felt like it was going to burst out of her chest as she was finding it hard to breathe; now was *not* the time to be having an anxiety attack.

She could do this. People swam all the time. She just had to get past whatever stupid mental block was in her head.

Lifting her foot to take another trembling step, Nolan burst through the surface, a bloodied dagger in his hand as he gasped for air and got hauled underneath the lake once more.

Not even two seconds passed when he emerged again. The water rippled a few feet away from him, and she suspected that's where the monster must be.

Nolan hurtled towards her, coughing up half of the disgusting swamp as the waves began to near him, catching up to where he floated.

Assuming it was pointless being quiet anymore—now that the Breoslies was *very* aware of their presence—she yelled out, "Behind you!"

With inhuman speed, he turned, swiping his dagger at the ripple behind him as he called out to her. "A little *help* here would be ni—"

The rest of his sentence got swallowed by the lake as he was dragged under for the third time.

What did he want her to do? Did that mean he wanted her to jump in?

His head popped out once more, and she could've have sworn his eyes glowed a bright red as he thrashed in the water. "Sword—*now*."

Lillian didn't even ponder his command as she flew towards the tree that had his two blades lying against it. She picked one and ran back to the lake, chucking it with all her strength to where she last saw his figure in the water. The sword slowly began to sink, and she prayed it would reach him.

She wanted to use her bow, but they were far too close together underneath the waves, and there would be no way of knowing who was who. The *last* thing Nolan needed right now was to be shot through the chest as he fought for his life. But still, she took out her weapon and notched an arrow for when Nolan hopefully managed to get away.

The jerking in the lake came to an immediate stop, and she saw a wave dashing towards her. Anxiousness coiled in her gut, and she pulled back the string on her bow as she kept her aim trained on the unknown moving figure.

An intense wave of relief crashed through her as she saw Nolan's familiar face shoot out from the muddy lake. Lillian swung her bow across her back and reached out her palm to help him up.

He launched his hand upwards to meet hers, hauling himself out of the water. Still grasping her fingers, he led her towards his stuff by the tree. "We have to go. *Now*."

He skipped putting on his leather armor and only stopped to strap the two blades to his back as he kept glancing back at the curtain of plants. A gash raked down his back, she noticed as he stuffed as many of his things into the bag as he could, and, whatever belongings he couldn't fit, he gathered in his arms as he rushed them back out towards the forest.

They passed the moss-covered tree, and Nolan seemed to relax some, but still walked in a hastened pace. After a few minutes longer, he scanned the area around them and deemed it safe enough as he stopped to put on his black leathers.

Lillian couldn't possibly wait anymore and asked the burning question in her mind. "What happened out there?"

Nolan finished tightening the straps of his leathers and walked past her. "That *bitch* was awake is what happened."

Jogging a bit to catch up, she said, "I gathered that much. But I don't get it. We did everything right."

"I've fought her before, but it was obvious when she had awoken because I wasn't exactly trying to be stealthy." A twinge of sadness consumed her as she recalled how he had wanted his life to end, but Nolan didn't seem to notice as he shook his head and went on. "But something about today was *different*."

Arching a brow she asked, "What makes you say that?"

"This time she had been awake, and it was almost like…"

Lillian was never one for suspense, so she pressed. "Almost like what?"

"It was almost like she knew we were coming.... like she was waiting for us."

A shiver went through her entire body. "How could she have possibly known that?"

"*That*, I have no clue."

Strolling next to him in an eerie silence, she thought over what he'd said. Was someone watching them? She scanned the trees and felt disturbed at the thought of someone tracking their every move. Lillian chased that thought from her head—she was already paranoid enough as it was and didn't need to add another thing to her never-ending list of things that made her skin crawl. "I take it she still lives?"

Nolan scoffed coldly. "It would take a lot to put that thing down. But I managed to slow her down some."

Lillian paled at the thought of that. This man who had *easily* felled the ghoulish beast that had almost taken her life had only been able to slightly deter this creature. Her laugh held no emotion as she spoke. "Why do all the most powerful creatures *have* to be inherently bad? Do no good ones exist?"

He looked like he wanted to say something but kept his mouth shut.

"What? What is it?".

"Well... according to what I've *heard,* Breoslies didn't used to be so bad."

"Really?" she questioned. "Then what in the gods' names happened to her?"

Nolan pinched his lips into a thin line as he debated on how to word his sentence. "Apparently she used to be a god of some sort to the Ilaidae."

It would, she supposed, make sense that a god would be hard to kill. "How does one simply stop *being* a god?"

His brows furrowed as he contemplated her question. "I think it's when people no longer believe in you."

Lillian could agree that that did make a decent bit of sense, but what did that leave her as? Just an immortal being of power? Looking at him, she urged for him to continue.

"Legend says that the swamp used to be a beautiful garden, and the murky waters were crystal clear and blue. But as people slowly stopped seeing her as a god to be worshipped, her home started dying and so did all the goodness inside her."

She couldn't blame the old god—she too would turn increasingly bitter if her once stunning home started to wither and decay. "Can't she just leave?"

He shook his head. "She's somehow tethered to the lake she lives in and is forced to stay there for an eternity."

Feelings of lament for the creature filled her soul. "That—that sounds *horrible*."

"It does," he said, shaking his head in agreement.

No one, not even someone as bad as Breoslies deserved to live like that. Lillian wished she had the strength to one day go back there and put the poor creature out of its misery, but that would be a highly unlikely scenario considering she was only a mere mortal that would have to fight *and* defeat a living god. And she also couldn't forget the whole living in water part either. She just felt bad that the creature would never be able to find peace.

With a somberness in her gaze, she glanced up at the sky through the canopy of trees, watching the sun begin to set as the forest around her got dusted in beautiful shades of tangerine and periwinkle.

Taking notice of the sky as well, Nolan said, “We need to find a place to rest and get that wound cleaned up before dark. I know a place not too far from here.”

She followed him as he led the way—he really did seem to know these woods. Another pang of sadness struck her heart as she thought on why he had spent so much time here.

They walked for a little while longer until they reached a rock wall with a large shrub covering it.

He pulled out his sword and pushed the bush to the side, revealing an entrance. “Just need to make sure nothing decided to make this thing its home.” He winked at her. “Be right back.”

Unease crept inside her as she waited for him outside, the sun lazily setting around her. Her unease magnified as she remembered those were the last words he had uttered before going into the lake and being pulled under. But thankfully her discomfort only lasted half a minute as he popped back out, giving the all clear to go in.

The cave looked similar to the one they’d been in previously save for it being a smidgen smaller. As she walked in deeper, she could make out algae and moss growing in the jagged rocks on the cave wall and a glance upwards revealed a hole decorating the top.

She didn’t like that there was a small opening on the cavern’s ceiling as she recalled having had some bad experience with creatures drooling on her from above, but she supposed it would have to do. At least now they could take watch in turns and be sure nothing had the opportunity to sneak up on them. Lillian, however, wasn't sure Nolan would be too keen on her taking watch after having fallen asleep the last time.

Lillian's mind drifted to earlier at the simple thought—was that really only this morning when he had dumped that canteen of water on her head? She remembered how angry she had been at how infuriating Nolan was, but she found that the longer she spent with him, the more he had started to grow on her. She rolled her eyes internally as she recognized that she could never admit that to him or he would become relentless as his absurdly large ego would inflate even more.

Turning her attention to the male in question, she watched as he sat down on the cave floor and produced the handful of flowers he had picked, separating eight of the violet, gold specked flowers into groups of two. He kept the two piles divided as he began to grind one of the groups with a small rock and then proceeded to do the same with the other. She was beginning to wonder the importance in separating the two piles until he pulled out a canteen of water, poured a splash onto one group and continued to ground it into a paste. Once both mounds were pulverized, Nolan motioned for her to sit by him.

Curiously, she plopped down at his side.

He scooped up the dry pile, dumping it into her hands as he handed her the canteen. "Drink that."

Lillian looked at the crushed flowers in her hand. "All of it?"

"Yes, all of it. I know it seems weird but just trust me on this."

Shrugging her shoulders, she shoveled the pieces of flower

into her mouth and washed them down her throat with water. A chuckle escaped him as Lillian cringed at the bitter taste on her tongue.

After she finished swallowing the clumps, he took her arm in his hand and glanced up at her face. “May I?” Lillian nodded, and he began rolling up her sleeve, undoing the bandage and exposing the gruesome gash on her arm.

Nolan flinched.

“What’s wrong?” she said, panic lacing her voice.

In an attempt to ease her growing nerves, he said, “No. Nothing. It’s just a little redder than I’d expected.” He paused and looked at her. “But you’re feeling okay?”

Her heart started to race at the simple question. “Should I not be?”

Grabbing the paste in his hand, he began smearing it on her wound. “Calm down, Lil. You’re fine. But if you start feeling off, even if it’s just a little, let me know.”

Calm wasn’t exactly easy to maintain with what he was suggesting. “I mean, I feel a little chilled but other than that I feel relatively normal,” she sputtered.

Nodding, he said, “Good, then nothing to worry about. But if you do start feeling colder, also let me know.”

Nolan grabbed a new piece of cloth and began wrapping it around the paste covered gash. Once he finished with that, he lowered her sleeve back down from her shoulder.

He wasn’t very good at picking his words because Lillian stared at the ground, *panicking* over everything he had just said.

Likely noticing the worried expression clouding her, he leaned in and lifted her chin to look at him. "You will be *fine*. Stop worrying that pretty little head of yours."

She must either be *really* bad at hiding her emotions or he was oddly good at knowing how she always felt. "Yeah, yeah. Whatever."

Nolan smirked as he let go of her chin and turned to rifle through his pack. "Here, eat this," he said, handing her a small bundle of bread. "You need to keep your strength."

Her stomach rumbled as she realized how long it had been since she'd eaten.

She shoveled the food down her throat, and Nolan raised an eyebrow at how fast she'd inhaled the simple grain. "Hungry?"

Covering her stuffed mouth, she tried to say 'a little' in a muffled voice, causing him to snicker at her poor attempt at forming words.

She swallowed the enormous amount of bread and cocked her head at him. "Are you laughing at me?"

Bringing a hand to his chest, he gasped. "How could I possibly even *think* of doing such a thing?" Mischief danced in those dark eyes as he continued. "*Especially* to such a breathtaking girl."

Lillian rolled her eyes and went to shove him in the shoulder but noticed he had started to sway. No wait…... that was *her* swaying.

The ground suddenly came crashing to meet her face, but she never did feel it, and instead felt warmth against her skin as she saw Nolan's hands underneath her head. Lillian looked up at him and could barely make out his face as the world started to spin. She could hear his voice, but it sounded strangely foggy as her mind struggled to register it.

"*Lillian*," he called out, saying her name with a desperate urgency. "*Come on, Lil.* Talk to me."

An intense wave of cold passed over her as she began to tremble from the freezing temperature. She focused on the figure in front of her and saw those eyes overflowing with concern. Feelings of weakness crashed into her, and she could hardly say any words as she shivered. "It's so cold."

Nolan put a hand to her forehead as muttered a curse. "You're freezing, Lillian."

Gently, he lowered her head to the floor as he shuffled to sit beside her; she didn't have the strength to stop him as he laid down next to her and put his arm underneath her head. Grabbing her by the hips, he pulled her flush against him as she felt his warm breath caress her ear. "You can argue all you want later about how 'I'm a no-good heathen and would take any opportunity to have you next to me' but for now… just accept my help."

He said those last few words with such a deep need. Had she really been so awful that he would assume she would think all his intentions were inherently bad?

Her teeth chattered as she formed a single word. "Okay."

Holding her tight, he draped his arm around her side as he brushed his thumb against her hand. His warmth was seeping into every inch of her skin, and she felt drastically less cold but continued to shake in his arms.

Drained—she felt so drained. She had been fighting for what felt like forever. Rest, that's what she needed—all she wanted to do was close her eyes and rest.

As the sickness continued eating away at her, a dark part of her mind wished she could just fall asleep and not wake to see the morning.

But as the thought wrapped itself around her, she felt Nolan's warm breath tickle her ears. "Fight, Lillian. It's the Xefta's poison making you feel this way, not you. You're stronger than this."

She didn't feel very strong. She could feel herself slipping away but what scared her most about it all....is that the feeling didn't bother her. Done. She just wanted to be done.

A voice, Nolan's voice she recognized, interrupted those dreary thoughts that threatened to suck away her life. "While I know you're not feeling your best, I have to admit you do feel *delicious* pressed up against me."

Lillian could perfectly imagine the stupid smirk across his face. Her skin felt tight as his hand danced down her sides, his fingers tracing circles on her thighs. "What do you think you're doing?" she asked.

Nolan lazily answered. "Hmmm? Just warming you up."

"And you need to be touching my thigh because...."

"I need to be sure I get every part of you warm, *obviously*," he purred.

Rolling her eyes, she continued to quiver. "*Sure*."

Lillian didn't have the energy to care at the moment—didn't feel like playing. She just wanted to rest—drift away from all the constant horror going on around her. If he wanted to keep messing with her, then that was fine. It didn't matter. Her heart felt heavy as venomous claws kept sinking deeper and de—

She felt Nolan lean in closer, his teeth grazing her ear in a gentle caress. "One of these nights..." A pooling in her core began to emerge as he spoke in a deep voice she swore was full of wanting. "...you'll be trembling like that against me, and it won't be from that horrible gash on your arm."

Her face heated as she took in what he said. He said those words with such an intensity, such rawness that she almost believed him—almost thought him to be sincere. But she knew he didn't mean it—knew he was only saying it to get a rise out of her. "You really are a disgusting pig, you know that?" she spat back at him.

He let out a low chuckle from that mouth she knew was sporting a wide grin. "It *is* my specialty." His fingers stopped and once again went up to drape over her arm. "But we should probably get some sleep now."

Lillian hadn't realized how dark it had gotten as she took a look at the empty cavern.

But as she stared, something felt different, she felt more—*alive.*

Whether he had planned it or not, he—and his *particular* choice of words—had made her forget about that pit of despair building up inside of her, filling her with a powerful vigor instead. A smile bloomed on her face as she recognized the small shred of life he had given her. "Goodnight, Nolan."

"Goodnight, Lil," he whispered as he leaned in and laid a soft kiss on her temple.

No sooner did sleep find her as she began drifting off to a dream of large leathery wings keeping her warm throughout the night.

CHAPTER 25

A faint warmth crept onto her face as sunlight filtered in through the uneven opening of the cavern's ceiling. Bright rays burned into her sensitive eyes, causing her to blink to keep the newfound light from singeing her corneas.

Lillian yawned, groggy at first awakening, but clamped her mouth shut as she noticed a person pressed up against her. Not just any person—Nolan.

Every inch of her stiffened as she took in the person wrapped around her. His breaths were even, and she could feel his chest slowly expanding against her back, indicating he must still be asleep.

A low sigh escaped her as his warmth leaked into her; she was surprised that someone so muscular could be so cozy and welcoming. Lillian relished the feeling of being in someone's arms—but she didn't exactly know how she felt about that someone being Nolan.

Confused is what she felt when it came to him. How could

someone so absolutely infuriating be so charming? Charming might not be the right word, but she couldn't think of another one to describe him at the moment. Something about the way he spoke—about the way he acted made her feel… *alive*.

Surely it was just her going insane because of the circumstances she was currently in. But for some strange reason, she felt drawn to him.

Regardless of those complicated emotions, it wasn't something she wished to delve into now and instead nestled up against him, enjoying the small shrivel of closeness he offered.

His mahogany scent enveloped her as he shifted, his arms unconciously tightening as he pulled her in closer. Gods, this was nice. She hadn't felt this relaxed—hadn't even been in someone's arms since...

Lillian's lips pinched into a tight line as she struggled to recall the last time she'd been curled up in someone—it couldn't have been that long? But her brain seemed to be failing to remember such a time. She knew she'd been with a few men in the past, but she usually never lingered long enough afterwards.

Her face dropped as she paled.

Oh gods—it couldn't be.

All at once, she remembered the last man she had been this close with… Peter. Of course it was Peter. Who else would it have been?

A pit grew in her stomach as a wave of guilt overwhelmed her. The nights of him holding her close and staring up at the stars came flooding back into her all at once.

She felt like she was going to be sick.

Lillian knew it was wrong to think that way—that Peter wouldn't have wanted her to swear off the feeling of another person—

but she couldn't stop the powerful emotions that consumed her.

It's not that she had sworn off men completely, she'd had a little rendezvous here and there, but something about this was different. This level of intimacy—no matter how minuscule it was—she had only ever experienced with Peter. And she knew it was stupid, *knew* it was unfair to herself, but she felt like she was betraying him by simply lying here in Nolan's arms. She felt even worse that she found herself *enjoying* the feeling of another man around her.

A heaviness now weighed in her side as she glanced down at her hip. Lillian's hand drifted towards the pocket of her pants, and she reached in, producing a small wooden ring. She had made sure to switch her ring out of her old pair before discarding them; she would be utterly devastated if it were ever lost.

Bringing the ring up to her face, she examined the simple design. There was nothing inherently special about the band she twisted in between her fingers, but that didn't stop it from meaning the world to her.

It was the only part of Peter she had left.

She did have her bow, but that was more of a gift from her father than anything else. The plain wooden band was solely Peter.

A faint smile bloomed on her lips as she fondly recalled the day he'd given it to her. It was the first time he had told her he loved her. No one had ever spoken those words to her before—not in that way. She had always thought she was bland looking and nothing to look twice about, but Peter had made her feel like the most beautiful girl to ever grace the earth.

A tear slid down her cheek as she remembered what he'd said. 'Promise me you'll always have it so long as you love me.' Without having to think for even a second, she'd made that vow, kissing him deeply and keeping it with her ever since.

Lillian blinked back her watery eyes as she tried to hold back the flood threatening to burst past her lids. She didn't need to be sobbing in front of Nolan—and she especially didn't feel like explaining who Peter was.

Now feeling completely uncomfortable in Nolan's arms, she shuffled out of his embrace and sat before him.

Looking at Nolan's figure as he slept, she found it hard to believe such a frustrating individual could look so peaceful while they slumbered, but she supposed the common saying was indeed true—looks *could* be deceiving.

Lillian furrowed her brows as she stared at him, her thoughts drifting back to that strange dream she'd had. She didn't remember much, but it had felt so *real*.

All she could recall was the feeling of enormous wings wrapped around her. She cast a subtle glance at his torso; it had been as if they were a part of Nolan and sprouted out from his back. But she knew it was all a figment of her imagination because as she looked at him now, she obviously saw no wings attached to his defined back.

So odd that she had dreamed such a thing, seeing as she'd always associated leathery wings with creatures of horror, but she remembered being pleasantly surprised at how much she liked the soft, smooth texture caressing her skin. She had never felt so—so *safe*. At least not for a long while and something about being there…had felt right.

Lillian shook her head as she got her bearings; there was no use in analyzing weird dreams when there was work to be done. They had wasted enough time on detours, and she needed to get to Iavothae as soon as possible. If all went according to plan, they should cross into its borders today.

Needing to get moving, she poked Nolan in the face.

No response.

She shook him lightly and still got no response.

Sitting back, she debated on how he would wake her if presented with the same dilemma. Her eyes drifted to the canteen sitting nearby, but she vetoed that idea; unlike him, she didn't feel like wasting their water.

So, she settled for the next best thing and plugged his nose with her fingers.

It only took a few seconds, and Nolan jolted awake as he clamped down on her wrist, eyes open wide before he pressed them shut at the beaming sun.

The light really must be playing tricks on her because his irises had looked a shade of crimson when they'd first opened.

After a few moments he finally squinted his eyes, that usual deep blue of his greeting her.

Lillian's lips twisted into a pout. "Oh, I'm sorry. Did I wake you?"

Nolan ran a hand through his hair as he let out a lazy yawn. "Glad to see someone's in better spirits today."

"Yeah, actually. I am feeling a lot better."

"Must have been my excellent care." Sitting up, he stretched out his arms and Lillian hid her gaze as she tried not to watch—but she knew Nolan had spotted her as the corner of his lips twitched upwards.

Internally, she sighed, knowing something stupid was about to flow from those lips.

"You sure you're feeling your best? I wouldn't mind warming you up again."

Doing her best to convey distaste, Lillian looked him up and down with a sneer. "No thanks. I think I'd rather not."

That amused grin of his made its way onto him. "Didn't seem that way last night. I seem to remember someone rubbing themselves up against me."

Lillian pretended to gag. "In your dreams. Me letting you be so close was an obvious momentary lack of judgement on my part. I blame it on my illness."

Bobbing his head up and down, he said, "Sure thing, Lil. Blame it on that all you want, but that won't change how you really feel."

"I don't feel a thing towards you," she spat.

"Yeah, yeah of course. You keep telling yourself that."

Her blood started heating. "Do you just wake up with a reservoir of obnoxious things or does it just flow out of you naturally?"

He pretended to contemplate her question. "Probably a little bit of both."

Lillian dragged a hand down her face as she got up to walk away. "Gods, I'd probably be better off on my own."

"And yet for some reason I'm still here. Seems like there's something about me that *intrigues* you."

"The only thing *intriguing* about you is that you haven't been killed for the nuisance you are."

Nolan smirked as he made a big scene of bowing. "Many

have tried, and *all* have failed." He grabbed his pack and strolled past her. "And let's not lie to ourselves, Lil. I see the way you're constantly undressing me with your eyes. You'd think one would be less obvious about it."

Boiling—her blood was boiling now. Bending down, she picked up the first thing she found and hurled a rock at him.

Without even blinking, he turned and caught it, barely even lifting a finger. He stared at the rock and then at her, a look of shock coating him before a small smile crept up onto his face. "There's that violent girl I've missed." He let the rock slip from his fingers and fall to the floor. "But like I said before, you're going to have to do *much* better than that."

Lillian glared at him, sending an obscene gesture in his direction.

He huffed a laugh as he motioned for her to come. "We need to get a move on if we want to reach Iavothae by tonight."

Grabbing her few things, she held her head high as she walked past him; she was in no mood to talk to such an idiotic man.

They began walking alongside each other in the woods with only the sounds of their crunching footsteps and the buzzing of insects around them.

Nolan cast a quick glance at her, noting her silence. "Not feeling chatty today?"

Lillian didn't dare respond.

"Don't feel like talking? That's alright I suppose. It is rather nice to hear the sounds of nature without any bothersome noises."

Calming herself, she took in a slow breath. He just wanted to get a reaction out of her, and she would be damned if she gave him what he wanted.

Another look in her direction.

She ignored him, keeping her face expressionless and devoid of any emotion. Calm and collected. That's what she was and would remain.

"While the silent treatment *is* a very effective method to display anger," he said with a lecturing tone. "It is a little childish I have to admit."

The building rage inside her burst out of her all at once. "*You* want to talk about being childish? You are the most immature man I've ever had the misfortune of meeting!"

Nolan stopped his walking, but Lillian didn't feel inclined to wait for him as she went on by.

He didn't respond and she couldn't stop the fury bubbling inside her as she yelled out in a snarky tone. "Oh, look who's being *so* mature now ignoring me. You really are a hypocri—"

She never finished her sentence as she felt Nolan's hand cover her mouth. "Can you cease your yelling for just one second, woman," he whispered in a harsh voice.

Lillian bit down on his hand—*hard*—and he muttered a curse as he yanked his hand back. She turned to face him, matching his hushed tone. "Quit covering my mouth, you imbecile. A simple 'stop talking' would suffice."

"Fine then—*stop talking*." He clutched his hand as he added, "And gods, woman, you bite hard."

Lillian flashed him a smile that contained pure attitude—but she immediately dropped it as they both turned their heads to a cracking sound not too far off.

They crouched in silence as she heard a man call out in the distance. "She has to be her somewhere—I *know* it."

No… it couldn't be. Lillian let out a small groan and rolled her eyes—would those two idiots ever leave her alone?

Turning to Nolan, she found his expression to be similar to hers. "Do you know those guys?" she asked.

"Yeah," he sighed. "I've run into them a few times. How do *you* know them?"

"We've just been playing a little game for a while." She smiled as she recalled how those two idiots were messing with their daggers when they were supposed to be on the lookout. "And I've been winning."

The two men started to come into view, the forest a little darker than before, and they kept low to the ground as Nolan surveyed the area. "Well, we do have a little problem. See where they're standing," he said, pointing at Killian and Malik. "That's where we have to go."

Of course it was. Those two men could never make her life easy.

"So what's the plan then?" she asked in a whisper.

"I'm thinking I distract, and you run."

Running away *had* become her specialty, so she could easily manage that. "Wait—but what are you going to do? How will I find you again?"

A feline grin took up most of his face as he looked at her. "Worried about me, are you?"

Lillian glared at him. "Don't be an ass. I'm being serious."

"I'll worry about distracting them. You just concern yourself with running as fast as you can when you see them go after me. Sound good?"

Good was not the word she would use to describe his plan. She didn't feel too keen on it, but knew he wasn't going to change his mind. "*Fine*," she grumbled.

"The border between Grigaros' half and Iavothae's should be coming up. Stop there, and I'll catch up to you."

"But wait. How will I know when I reached it?"

Nolan got up and readied himself. "You'll know it when you see it," he said with a wink before dashing through the woods.

Lillian rolled her eyes—she hated when people didn't explain things. 'You'll know it when you see it.' Gods, she loathed when people said things like that. Why couldn't they just explain things? Noooo, they just had to be ominous and vague.

But she didn't dwell on his phrasing too long as she saw Killian and Malik dart off in the direction Nolan went.

She hoped he'd be okay. She knew that he could handle himself considering he'd been in this forest thousands of times and even fought off an old god while *drowning*, but still she couldn't help herself as she muttered a small prayer for him.

Half a minute passed since Killian and Malik had gone, and she burst into a full-on run. Trees whisked by the corners of her vision as she flew, the wind's icy caress kissing her cheek as she went.

No idea—she had *no idea* what she was looking for, but she trusted herself to know it when she stumbled across it. But after jogging for an eternity and seeing the forest look utterly the same, she wasn't so sure on that.

Was there something she was missing? Did she already pass it or make a wrong turn? That seemed impossible since she hadn't veered her path in any way.

Lillian's legs couldn't bear the run any longer, and she slowed her pace, settling for a light jog. Her eyes roamed the perimeter as she looked around for any sign of the border, but only the same cursed trees she'd seen a thousand times carpeted the forest's floors.

As she kept searching for anything, *any* sign that she was nearing the gate, she was beginning to think the term—you'll know it when you see it—didn't apply to her. How quickly she was proven wrong as something out in the distance caught her gaze.

Squinting her eyes, she looked at some sort of... archway? Lillian hurtled in the direction of it and stopped, amazed at what she saw.

Thick roots had sprouted out from the ground and twirled around themselves, creating a massive gate. Sparse white flowers grew on it, the pattern in which they lay impressively symmetrical, but it was mostly made up of the brown gnarled roots that twisted into a perfect curve. As she got nearer, she could see what looked to be dust hanging inside the gate, but, upon closer examination, she noticed it wasn't dust but small specks of light that hung suspended in the giant arch.

Her jaw hung loose as she stared at the breath-taking sight. She had never seen something so—so *magical* before in her entire life. The gate was simply enchanting without even trying.

She eased closer to the gate until she stood directly before it, curiosity lining her features. What was even the purpose of the giant arch if one could simply just go around? Unless....

Lillian sauntered over to an area to the side of the gate and tried to stick her hand through. But just as she had suspected, her hand came in contact with an invisible wall. It had to be some sort of barrier spell to control which areas you could enter Iavothae.

Backing away from the mystical gate, she sat down on a nearby boulder. She didn't know what awaited on the other side and knew she needed to wait for Nolan before crossing over. If there were guards or Ilaidae on the other side, it would be in her best interests for him to be present.

Picking up a stick, Lillian prodded the dirt floor as she sat on her rock, patiently awaiting his arrival.

A quick fifteen minutes turned into thirty and then into forty-five.

Legs refusing to stay still, she got up and began pacing back and forth. Where was he? Surely nothing could have happened to him.

But Lillian's mind thought otherwise as it began wandering over all the dark possibilities.

Had Killian and Malik actually caught him? They *were* Ilaidae and had to be extremely powerful, but Nolan had seemed confident that he could take care of them. Her thoughts began turning over every conceivable outcome. Had Breoslies caught up to him and finally finished him off? Or had he gotten stuck in a trance from one of those wretched flowers.

It was nearing an hour since she'd last seen him, and Lillian was going into a full-blown panic. He had told her to wait but hadn't specified how long. Ten more minutes—she would wait ten more minutes before going after him. But what if when she left, he finally emerged, and they missed each other completely.

A groan escaped her; she didn't know what to do. She couldn't just sit here when the gods knew what was happening to him.

Grabbing her bow, she swung it across her back. She was done waiting.

She would go out and find him not only because it was the right thing to do, but because she knew—knew for some odd reason that he would do the same for her.

Praying that she wasn't too late, she started to venture off when a voice came out from the far left. "And where do you think *you're* going?"

Sheer shock flooded through her at that sound. Slowly—so slowly—she turned to face that voice. Relief slammed into her as she saw that stupidly handsome face staring right back at her.

She stood, gaping at him like an idiot, before dropping her bow and hurtling towards him. He had to catch his balance as she came up tackling him with a powerful fierceness. Lillian held onto him tight, and he took a second before returning the gesture.

"Miss me?"

Tears pricked the edges of her eyes as she heard that voice. Gradually, she loosened her grip and tilted her chin upwards.

There they were—those dark eyes that always seemed to glisten. She didn't know what came over her in that very moment but one second she was gazing at those punishing blues and the next her mouth was on his as she leaned in to kiss him.

All the emotions—everything she had been feeling—she put into that kiss. Her worry, the panic of not knowing where he had been, and that hunger—the hunger she had felt for him the moment she'd laid eyes on him.

Nolan was still for an instant before he met her lips with an equal ferocious desire.

She hadn't realized how badly she had wanted this—*needed* this. She wanted to forget everything around her; her constant state of fear, the horrible monsters, everything—absolutely everything—in these gods damned woods.

Lillian let her tongue slip into his mouth, and he let out a growl of approval as he devoured her whole. Her hands wandered towards the hem of his shirt, and she cursed at his tight armor. She wanted to run her hands down that perfect abdomen—the one she had caught a glimpse of at the swamp and hadn't gotten out of her mind since.

Her skin felt as if a thousand sparks were alighting inside her. Her body *burned* with the need to feel him against her.

Nolan's hands slid down to her waist as he pulled her in closer. Like she weighed nothing, he picked her up and backed her up into a tree as he continued to consume her entirely.

Lillian hadn't known when the switch had happened in her mind. She didn't know when he went from being that infuriating man—to the one she couldn't get enough of.

A gasp slipped out of her as his tongue trailed down her neck causing her to arch against him; he let out a deep snarl at the sounds of her moans.

Relishing his touch, she tipped her head back, giving him full access to her as she ran fingers through his dark silky hair.

His hands went up the bottom of her shirt as he caressed the sensitive skin on her waist—just the touch of him made her feel undone and she gripped his hair as she cried out. She wanted more—needed more.

But instead, Nolan pulled away and brought his forehead to rest against hers as they stared at each other, breathing heavy.

He pinned her with a look full of wanting. "Gods, you're magnificent," he said in an exhale.

Red stained her cheeks as he carefully put her down, the throbbing in her core slowly beginning to subside.

As their gazes remained intertwined, she could have sworn a pained expression flashed in his eyes as he looked at her. "Close your eyes," he whispered.

Confused, she cocked her head to the side. "For what?"

"Just—just trust me."

Biting her lip, she closed her eyes, nervous as she didn't know what to expect after what had just occurred. Was he going to continue what they'd started?

A twinge of desire flared up inside her as she stood with her lids shut—but she was left with surprise when he leaned in and planted a soft kiss on her forehead.

He grabbed her hand, his voice coming out choked and full of agony. "Please… please forgive me."

Lillian barely even had a second to register his words as something smashed into her head, and the world around her faded into darkness.

CHAPTER 26

Pangs of nausea razed her senses as the hard thumping of her temple blurred her surroundings. Drawn towards the pain, she winced as her fingers grazed that tender spot on her head.

Gradually, she concentrated her vision, willing herself to take in all that was around her. A twinge of discomfort coursed through her as she jerked her brows back—no longer was she in those treacherous woods.

She rubbed that aching bump on her scalp as she struggled to recall how she'd gotten here. Bits of hay, plastered to her cheek, fell to the ground as she eased herself into a sitting position, ice leaking into her bones from the mere touch of the stony wall.

Now fully aware that she was far from the forest, her eyes began to wander. The room she sat in was small and dimly lit from the few torches lining the walls, and she blinked, trying to refocus her eyes as the painful throbbing made her vision go foggy. She could see shackles bolted into the ground, and she let out a relieved sigh as she examined her limbs, noticing that none of the iron cuffs were attached to her.

But her alleviated state was cut short as she soon realized where she was. The color leeched from her skin as it all clicked together.

She was in a dungeon.

The blood rushed to her head as she shot to her feet, and she had to catch herself as she started to sway. She ignored that faint feeling as she ran to the barred door and violently shook it in what she knew was a fool's attempt to open it.

Her memory came crashing back as she recalled what had occurred. She channeled all her rage, all her frustration into her voice as she yelled into the darkness. "Show yourself, you bastard!"

The moments leading up to where she was flashed into her mind. Where had things gone wrong? Her thoughts went a million miles a second as she tried to recall everything. She… she had been with Nolan? Yes—she had been with him.

Her head pounded as it roved over everything.

She had been so relieved to find him alive… that she had allowed her emotions to get the best of her. And then he—he had…

Her lip began to violently quiver as she couldn't even bear to think of the words; tears began welling up in her eyes.

He had betrayed her.

Lillian's hand instinctively went to where he had landed the blow to her head.

He had *hurt* her.

How could she have not seen it coming? He had saved her from that beast and had even risked his life in that swamp for her. It didn't make any sense.

She didn't know why he had done it or what his grand plan was. All she knew was that she had been so stupid to have ever trusted him in the first place. This whole time—the entire time they had been together—he had been slowly gaining her trust until he could get her to let down her guard.

A droplet slid down her face.

And let down her guard she did.

Waves of nausea reverberated through her that she had even allowed him to touch her in such an intimate way. The feeling of his lips against hers and how he had matched her same fiery passion—it had all felt so right.

But it had all gone so wrong. She had been so naïve to think he had reciprocated what she'd felt.

Lillian's stomach swirled as she thought of what she had done with him—how he had made her *feel*. She felt sick as she thought of those words he had said—that simple phrase that had flowed off his tongue. 'Just trust me,' he had said. And like the fool she was, she had.

The worst part of it all was that she truly had. She had *allowed* herself to completely trust him. And that had been the biggest mistake of her life.

Her voice cracked as she continued to yell obscenities through the steel bars, tears streaming down her face. She rested her back against the metal door and slid down them as she held herself sobbing.

What would she do now? She had no clue where she was. She still had a trial to complete—a family to get back to. A deep pit of despair formed inside her as she thought of being stuck here, rotting away.

No—she couldn't allow that to happen.

A sudden rage chased away her pathetic sadness. She refused to cry over an idiotic man she had just met—that wasn't her. She came here to compete in that bizarre Trial of the Flame, and that's exactly what she would do. She had a family to protect, and she would be damned if they got massacred while she sat in this cage doing *nothing*.

She hadn't come all this way to be stopped by a stupid man that she barely even knew; she had come to fight for her people and die for them if it came down to it.

A steely resolve came over her as she wiped her sleeve over her damp cheeks. She had dealt with much worse than being stuck in a measly little cell. And if she really took her time to think about it—this was the easiest problem she had encountered so far. Definitely much preferable to any of the horrifying monsters she had come across in her brief time in the woods.

Taking in a deep breath, she assessed her current predicament. Her bow, sword, and dagger she kept sheathed at her side were taken away. Zero belongings. She now had zero belongings. She wiggled her foot at the thought—perhaps she still had one trick left.

Bringing her foot near, she reached a hand into her boot. Relief—it was relief she felt at the touch of that familiar steel still tucked away. Whoever searched her clearly didn't do a good job or simply hadn't cared enough as they had missed the dagger she kept hidden in her boot.

Lillian felt the slightest bit better. She had one dagger and the clothes on her back. Not great—but not terrible either. She could very well have been stripped naked and been left with absolutely nothing—she could at least be thankful for that small mercy.

The cell didn't look like it had anything of use—all she could see were the shackles and bits of hay littering the ground—but as she kept looking, her eyes stopped at a dark corner where she saw something round tucked away.

Lillian approached the object, but, as she neared it, she realized she shouldn't be asking herself what it was—but instead who.

Her entire body tensed as she stared at the person she had mistaken for an object. They laid facing away from her, curled up into a ball, and she would've thought them dead could she not see their chest rising and falling as they took in frantic breaths.

Bending down, she grabbed her dagger, gripping it tight as she nudged the person with her foot.

A girl who looked to be in her late twenties turned to face her. She couldn't see much in the faintly illuminated cell, but she could make out a thin frame with disheveled black hair. Fear shone in her face as the girl's eyes darted to her dagger. "Ple—please, don't hurt me," she said in a trembling voice. Tears slid down the stranger's face. "I can't take it anymore."

A wave of empathy consumed her as she stared at the broken girl before her. Lillian shoved her blade back into her boot, cursing herself as she could obviously see it was frightening her. Crouching down, she spoke in a soft, soothing tone. "I'm not here to hurt you."

The girl's voice still shook. "You—you're not?"

"No—I'm not." She wanted to reach out and comfort her but refrained from touching her, not knowing how she would react.

The girl gradually turned towards her, fiddling with her fingers as she was still nervous. "Then what are you doing here?"

Lillian huffed a sigh. "Well… it looks like I'm being held prisoner—like you I assume?"

The girl hung her head low, looking at the ground as she nodded.

It seemed like she had been here for a while, so maybe she could be of some help. Lillian felt a twinge of guilt about using this clearly terrified girl for information—but she needed to find a way out of here. "Do you know where we are?" she asked.

"In the dungeons."

Well, she had already gathered that much, but she kept her tone level, trying to hide her slight annoyance since she knew the girl meant well. "Yes, but *where* exactly?"

The girl blushed. "Oh, sorry. We're in the castle." She said that like it was blatantly obvious where they were. "In Iavothae."

Her heart quickened at the last word.

Iavothae.

She had made it. She was *in* Iavothae.

This was where she had been so desperately trying to go. This was where she had almost *died* trying to get to. And here she was, actually standing on Iavothaen soil. She couldn't believe it—couldn't believe she had actually managed to do what so few had ever done.

Lillian stood up and began to pace. Her journey was over. She was *here*.

All she had left to do was get out of this wretched dungeon and get an audience with the queen. But Lillian knew better than to think the hard part of her task was over. If anything, the most grueling part had just begun.

She recalled what Killian and Malik had spoken of their *beloved* queen. If she was anywhere near as horrible as they'd described… then Lillian had a world of trouble coming for her.

Somehow, she had to convince the queen to not kill her on sight—and if she had plans to massacre all the humans, she doubted she would hesitate in murdering one that came right to her door. And if that wasn't already enough, she still had other issues to deal with.

Her breathing hastened as she thought about the Trial of the Flame—the trial she hadn't an inkling of what it would entail. All she knew was that it was an arduous task that barely anyone—if even anyone at all—had ever survived.

A dry chuckle came out of her; how lovely for her. Beads of cold sweat dripped down her temple as she paced faster and faster.

"Are you okay?"

Lillian stopped her walking and turned to the startled girl. "Yeah… just thinking."

"About what?"

It was peculiar that a girl who had been quaking in terror minutes prior, was now so inquisitive. But she considered telling the girl her thoughts regardless—perhaps airing out her mission and talking it through would help her come up with some sort of plan.

Lillian glided over to the girl and crouched back down to her level. "Have you ever heard of the Trial of the Flame?"

She cocked her head to the side. "Yes. Why do you ask?"

"I need to know what it is."

The girl bit her lip as she contemplated her request. "All I know is that you have to complete a task that very few have ever survived."

Curses careened through her head.

Did no one know what this damned trial was? She knew there was a law not to speak about it, but was it really *that* strict?

A solemn expression shrouded the girl's face as Lillian knew she had failed to hide her disappointment. "I'm sorry if that's not much help," she said in hardly more than a whisper.

Looking into the scared girl's eyes, Lillian spoke to her in a kind voice. "It was. Thank you. I appreciate any help you can give me."

A gentle smile tugged on the corner of her cheeks. "Why do you even want to know about the Trial of the Flame?"

Chewing on her words, she debated telling this stranger her plans. But she supposed it didn't really matter keeping it a secret anymore seeing as she was already in the castle. "I'm going to compete in the trial," she declared.

Her jaw hung loose as she took in her statement. "You came *all* this way—just for that?"

Lillian nodded as she opened her mouth, but she kept her tongue still as she looked at her with confusion.

The girl had rolled over in laughter—actually fell onto her back and *rolled* on the dungeons floor.

She didn't think it was *that* absurd to assume she would want to compete. Lillian was so baffled by the girl's response that she didn't even think to be mad at her evident mocking. The frail thing had been so frightened and jittery a moment ago but now laughed like she had told the world's funniest jibe.

After a few more seconds of chuckling and snorting, the girl finally stood.

With an agonizing slowness, she stalked towards Lillian until standing directly over her. A menacing grin crept onto her face as she spoke with a bone chilling voice. "You really are a fool, Lillian Echethier."

CHAPTER 27

Clambering away from the woman, Lillian slammed into the cell wall as she hurried onto her feet.

A curtain of crimson mist began to envelop the woman, spiraling around her like a tornado tinged with blood. And slowly, from the bottom up, the scarlet tinted fog began to disappear as it unveiled someone else entirely.

The new woman looked ready for battle as the mist revealed tight black armor, cinched at her waist, that was somehow rather elegant as the bottom half of her ensemble flowed out into a gown. Her skin was a stark white that made the contrast of her ruby lips stand out even more than they already did. And as the red sheen evaporated into nothing, it revealed pin straight black hair that held a glass crown atop it.

Lillian had always imagined kings and queens to have luxurious crowns that stunned others with its beauty—but this crown was not that.

The glass crown sat atop her head with multiple jagged shards decorating the headpiece, the uneven ends of it sharp enough to slice her with even the smallest touch. Brushing a strand of that dark hair behind her ear, the woman showed that they came to a pointed end.

Lillian hadn't needed to see her ears to know that she was no mere mortal. The woman before her radiated a power and fear that made her want to curl up in the corner and hide.

The Ilaidae's lips curved into a wicked smile as she stared at her with icy blue eyes.

Despite her cowardly instincts, Lillian held her ground, but she didn't dare pull out her dagger—she knew it would do her no good here. "Who are you?" she asked, even though Lillian was fairly certain she knew the answer.

The woman took a step forward, ebony booted heels clicking against the stone floor. "Oh, don't tell me you don't know. I thought you to be smarter than that."

Not wanting to be any closer to her, Lillian backed up a step as she willed her voice to come out confident. "Allania."

Her mouth parted into a grin. "So she isn't as dumb as she looks. And that's Queen Allania to you, but I can let it slide just this once. You poor humans don't know any better." She pouted at the last part, as if humans were pathetic creatures to be pitied.

Lillian clenched her jaw as she gazed at the *queen* in front of her. This was the woman who would be the demise of her family—of all Grigaros. And for what—just because they were a bothersome pest in comparison to her infinite power? Her blood began to heat as she looked upon the all-powerful ruler of Iavothae.

Anger needing to stay in check, she smoothed her features into a steady calm. She needed to be smart about this and choose her words wisely if she wanted a chance of getting out of here alive.

Seeing as there was no point in dancing around the obvious since Lillian had already declared her intentions loud and clear, she said, "I wish to be the Champion of the Flame."

Allania didn't even bother to contain her chuckle. "Of course. How could I ever forget? Do you even know what you speak of, girl?"

Lillian seethed. "I know enough."

That wicked smile resurfaced onto her cruel face. "Oh… I seriously doubt that."

Keeping the snarky tone out of her voice was a feat in itself as she addressed the vicious ruler. "Then please, enlighten me, your *maj-esty*."

The queen glared, her face veiled with an icy terror that made Lillian remember who she was talking to. "Do not *test* me, Lillian Echethier. You will soon find out I am not the type to forgive."

Bile stung her throat as she swallowed down the panic manifesting inside of her. She was smarter than this. She had to keep her emotions in place or they would be her doom.

Lillian refocused herself onto the conversation and noticed that was the second time she had referred to her by her full name. The queen was familiar with her, but she didn't think much of it as she assumed that bastard had told Allania everything when he had dumped her in this horrid place.

Speaking through clenched teeth, she tried feigning politeness to this tyrant. "I meant no disrespect, Queen Allania. Please continue."

The woman smiled at her submissiveness, clearly used to getting her way. Lillian hated that she was only adding on to the pile of people who didn't defy her out of pure fear. "That's more like it. Now where were we—the trial, yes." Allania snickered at the simple word. "What fool told you that you could be champion? I really must thank them for bringing me such a treat."

Lillian took another step back. Did these Ilaidae eat humans? She could picture some of the monsters partaking in mortal flesh, but Allania seemed too humanoid-like that the thought seemed appalling.

Allania seemed to have noticed her choice of words as she rolled her eyes. "I'm not going to eat you, stupid girl. I only meant it was a nice gift."

"A gift?"

Pacing, Allania spoke in an excited tone more to herself than to Lillian. "Yes, we haven't had a champion in ages! It was getting a tad mundane around these parts. This is *exactly* what we needed to liven things up."

Liven things up? Lillian felt all the more nervous that her being champion made the queen ecstatic. She rifled her mind as she tried to think of reasons as to why the trial would make her so elated and cursed in her head for not knowing more. She didn't care anymore if it made her look stupid at this point. She needed to know exactly what she was getting into. "Tell me about the trial," she demanded.

That caught her attention. "You still don't know what it is, do you?" With a menacing slowness, she stalked towards her—a predator sizing up its prey—until the bars dug into Lillian's back. "Tell me what you do know," she purred.

Not much, she thought to herself, but that wouldn't be an answer she'd like. "I know that if I win you have to grant me one wish."

"That would be correct," she said as she whirled and walked in the other direction, her frighteningly beautiful features dulling out in the darkness. "Allow me to fill in some of the gaps. You will participate in one challenge of my choosing, whatever that may be, and *if* you die… no wish. Sound simple enough?"

It didn't sound difficult the way she phrased it, but she knew better. Nothing was easy here.

"Then why is it so funny that I chose to participate?" she countered.

Allania laughed, a venomous sound curling off her tongue. "Well, that would be the nature of being a Champion of the Flame. My ancestors created it as a form of… how can I put this nicely? *Entertainment.*"

Lillian's face paled as she saw Allania's white grin perfectly illuminated in the dark corner of the room. This whole elaborate trial was just to entertain a few stuck up royals? Her potentially dying a horrible death was meant to provide… *amusement*?

Her stomach felt like it was turning inside out as Allania began to speak. "You see. The humans were never meant to actually succeed in whatever task we gave them—which is what makes it *infinitely* more fun."

Red began to swarm her vision as she thought of all the humans who had died at the price of this perverted game. "So this was all a ruse then—set up by a bunch of your twisted relatives?"

The queen's steps pounded towards her as she came up in front of her and grabbed her chin in between her thumb and index finger.

"Make no mistake, Lillian. I have not lied. If you succeed, you will get your wish. But if not…" She let go of the grip on her jaw to make a motion of her finger gliding against Lillian's throat. "Now does that sound like something you want to do, my darling?"

Her tongue felt thick and heavy as Allania stared at her, waiting for an answer. She didn't know what to say—didn't know how to *feel* at this moment.

Allania let out a cruel chuckle. "I figured as much." She turned towards the cell's door, waving Lillian to the side as she unlocked it and pushed it open.

Slamming it shut, she began to walk away, but before she made it too far, she turned around to address Lillian one last time. "I'll give you a bit of time to think about it." The corners of her lips twitched into a grin as she continued. "I'm *dying* to know your decision." The sounds of heels clinking against the hard floor echoed as the queen held up a hand and wiggled her fingers behind her. "Until next time, Lillian."

Turning a corner, she vanished out of sight, leaving Lillian utterly alone in her cell.

Huffing a sigh, she sat down, leaning her head against the wall. She savored the feeling of the cold stone seeping into her skin as she sat in the suffocatingly hot cell. Her eyes stared aimlessly out in front of her as she tried processing what had just transpired.

She still couldn't believe it. The queen—that was *the* queen. Her mind felt numb, still in shock, that she had actually spoken to the ruler of Iavothae.

Lillian groaned. What a mess everything had become. A part of her wished for the straight forwardness of the forest.

Oh gods. Things had gotten really bad if she thought her time in the woods was less complicated than this. What was she supposed to do? What even were her options?

According to Allania, this whole Champion of the Flame deal was engineered to kill her. The Ilaidae didn't even want her to have a fighting chance at completing whatever task she was forced to do. And that—already as bad as it was—wasn't even the worst part.

The queen got to choose.

With that information alone, she knew she was dead. Anything and everything she had heard about Allania was that she was a vicious and cold-hearted monster. They had only spent a small amount of time together but already she could tell that she was *more than* capable of committing unspeakable acts.

Was Lillian's fate simply to die? She had known before embarking on this journey that death was a *very* viable possibility, but she had assumed that she would have at least had a chance of making it out alive.

Her breaths became faster, and her heart began to gallop as she thought on what Allania had claimed.

No one had ever survived.

Her skin became devoid of color as her mind raced, thinking of anything to calm her down.

Maybe all those things she had said were only to scare her. But why would she even bother? She *wanted* Lillian to participate and be made a spectacle. It made no sense for Allania to want to deter her.

Lillian had to assume she spoke the truth, meaning… this really could kill her.

But what choice did she have? Lillian had known being the champion might be the death of her but somehow hearing it finally made it sink in. It felt *real* now that she was in the castle's dungeons.

It was far too late to get cold feet now. She had traveled all this way and almost been brutally killed more times than she would've liked. It would be silly of her to turn back now. And she knew that she couldn't either. It would be absurd for any Ilaidae to just let a mortal go on their way in peace. Leaving was off the table.

Not that she would ever choose to anyway. She wouldn't leave Grigaros at the mercy of these wretched creatures. She'd seen firsthand what they could do—what they were capable of. Grigaros wouldn't stand a chance. She would not be responsible for the decimation of her family—of all her people.

If she thought that being champion would give them even the *smallest* chance of survival, then that was it. There was no use in turning the matter over in her head. She would choose them over herself a million times if she had to.

Thoughts of her family made tears slide down Lillian's cheek, and she sniffled as she struggled to keep her soft cries from turning into sobs. She hadn't even been gone that long, but it had felt like a lifetime since she had last been in their comforting embrace.

A chuckle flitted off her lips as she thought of Maxith and his stupid jokes that always made her burst out in laughter. She would even settle for her mother's nagging of marriage and her horrible hobbies. Good or bad, it didn't matter—she just wanted *them*.

Lillian wiped her damp cheeks as a determination settled over her. If no one had been able to survive the trial in the past, then she would have to be the first. She had made a promise to her family—a vow that she would see them again. Lillian had never been one to break her word, and now was not the time to start.

Things couldn't be too bad, could they?

Lillian had a knack for making things seem worse than they actually were, but she had a feeling that this time she wasn't being overly dramatic. She had managed to get away from *many* deadly monsters—truly, a surprising amount—while getting away pretty unscathed. Sure, she had danced naked amongst colorful flowers and lost her pack to that monster in that cave, but all her previous interactions had been pretty decent.

Lillian knew she was forgetting one very important event, but she was trying hard not to let her thoughts drift there—to that Xefta that had almost taken her life. It would have too if it hadn't been for…

Her throat tightened as the image of that moment and all that followed came cascading back. Tears threatened to leak out of her eyes as she pressed her jaw tight.

That bastard—that *stupid* bastard. She hated him—she hated everything about him. The way he looked—the way he made her feel. She loathed the mere thought of him.

But the sobs that desperately tried to escape her begged otherwise. If she hated him so much, then why did she feel so broken. So… shattered.

It was ridiculous for her to be feeling this way. She had known the man for barely three days. But something about him… It was almost like she had known him her entire life. He had a way about him that had made her feel so… so complete—like she had found the missing piece she had been searching for all her life.

She knew she sounded insane because that was utterly impossible. He had just deceived her, and like the fool she was—she had fallen for his cruel tricks. Her blood began to boil as she thought of what he had done. How he had touched her. How he had *allowed* her to kiss him.

And *kiss* was putting it lightly. A blazing passion had consumed her at the mere touch of him. So stupid—she had been so stupid to think he had reciprocated her fierce desire.

Lillian's cheeks burned as she thought of that moment by the gate. She'd be lying to herself if she said she wouldn't have let him do more if he hadn't stopped her. But instead of continuing like she had wanted, he had indeed stopped her, and said those awful words that made her let her guard down.

She clenched her jaw and balled her fists as a feeling began to overwhelm her.

Anger. She felt an intense *anger* inside her as she thought of the part that followed. How he had smashed her head in with the hilt of his dagger and then dumped her here. Rage coursed through her veins as thoughts of him continued to plague her mind. If she ever saw him—ever saw that appalling man again—she would make him pay.

Feelings of wrath grew inside her as she shot up. She couldn't sit here anymore—she had to get out of here.

Lillian ran up to the bars, ready to violently shake them as she yelled at the top of her lungs for someone to let her out of this wretched place—but when she laid her hands against the many rungs, the door swayed open.

It was unlocked.

CHAPTER 28

The door was open.

Giving the heavy iron bars a shove, she watched as they groaned open. Her body went completely still as she stared at the empty hallway.

Had Allania forgotten to lock it after she had left?

No. She had to have done it on purpose.

Did she want her to try and escape? Or was it just to show how little of a threat Lillian posed to her? Knowing Allania it was the latter. The queen seemed cruel and devious but not stupid. Everything she did seemed to serve a purpose, and this one was to show her how weak she truly thought her to be.

Lillian's face heated at the obvious insult Allania had left for her to find.

Bitch.

Eyeing the vacant hall, she weighed her options. She could stay here in the cell where it was relatively safe and wait for Allania to return. Her chances of survival would rise drastically if she stayed put and didn't wander the unknown castle with who knows what kinds of horrible creatures.

But that would be doing exactly what Allania wanted.

It would prove that Lillian *was* just a scared mortal girl who hadn't known what she signed up for. Granted, those things were true, but that wasn't all she was. She was strong and courageous and wouldn't let a glorified Ilaidae get in the way of what she had set out to do.

With those thoughts fresh in her mind, she took a few steps forward until she stood in the darkness of the hall. The temperature instantly dropped a few degrees as an eerie chill emerged, the icy feel snaking past her neck.

She narrowed her eyes to examine what laid out in the distance, but she couldn't see much other than a string of cells that went on endlessly in the dark.

However, what she couldn't see very well, she more than made up for in smell. A putrid combination of decay and rancidness assaulted her nose. The smell wasn't too bad for now, but she wasn't looking forward to learning where it seeped out from.

But out of everything, the thing she found most horrifying was what she heard.

Muffled screams rang out all around her. Inside her cell, everything had been utterly silent, but, as soon as she took a single step out, faint shrieks billowed past her ears.

She hoped—no, she *prayed*—that hers was the only cell she would find unlocked, because if not… she would be in *serious* trouble.

Her heart started beating faster as thoughts of Ilaidae and death swarmed her mind. Shaking her head, she groaned, mentally scolding herself for thinking such things. She really needed to stop doing that.

Lillian tried her best to keep happy thoughts as she began ambling in the direction Allania had gone. She wanted to get as far away from the dungeons as she could—but she didn't presume the other areas of this place would be any safer, it would just hopefully be preferable to the gloomy prison.

As she began to walk forward, the faint smell of rot started to become a more prominent stench—and the farther she went, the stronger the scent became as it began to burn in her nostrils. Her eyes stung as the smell of decay began to overwhelm her senses.

Lillian plugged her nose in an attempt to alleviate the powerful smell, but she immediately gagged and let go of her nose as the smell made it to her tongue, causing her to taste the horrid aroma. She settled for bringing her sleeve up to her face and did her best to ignore the stench.

What is that? she thought to herself.

Lillian wasn't too keen on finding out, but she knew that with her chances, she would certainly figure it out soon enough. But the smell… there was something about it that made her think she had encountered it before.

The blood drained from her face as she realized what the stench reminded her of.

Death.

Did Allania keep dead people down here? She supposed it would make sense that carcasses would be kept in a dungeon, but Lillian didn't care about what made the most sense. She did *not* want to see all the people Allania had tortured and killed—not only because it sounded horrifying, but also because that could very easily be her.

Lillian bit the insides of her cheeks as she pictured what was giving off the appalling scent.

If things didn't go well out there… she would be just another lifeless corpse added to the pile. Lillian didn't need to see the bodies to know that they were all horribly disfigured in ways that pleased Allania. The mere thought of what she was capable of doing to Lillian made her stomach want to twist itself inside out.

A mercy or not, her thoughts were interrupted as the intense aroma became overbearing—not allowing her to think of anything else. Still struggling to breathe, she spotted a door a few feet ahead. Lillian quieted her steps as she stopped in front of what appeared to be a heavy iron door. The door was unmarked, but she was positive that the stench lay beyond it.

Her eyes glanced towards its knob as she debated turning it. If there were people, other humans trapped in an endless torture, she couldn't just leave them there—couldn't leave them to the will of the Ilaidae. She could already picture—already knew what she would find in there, but her hands still trembled as she reached out to grasp the knob. She clutched the cold iron and began to turn the handle but was met with a stiffness.

Locked.

Lillian exhaled. She didn't know whether to feel disappointed or relieved in finding herself unable to open it. If she had walked in through that door and saw what Allania had done—she wouldn't know how she would've reacted. What scared Lillian the most was finding them, not only horribly tortured, but still alive and slowly fading away in pain.

Shaking her head, she tried erasing those images from her mind. She could very well be making all of this up in her head. Nothing—she knew nothing of this queen or of these lands. Perhaps all that was behind the door was rotten meat and nothing more—but something deep inside her told her that it was more than just old animal carcasses that lingered past.

A shudder crept through her as she willed herself to carry on. She couldn't afford to waste time standing in front of every ominous door she came across; she had to get out of these dungeons.

And do what? She had no idea. But she decided to take things one issue at a time.

Finally, she reached the far corner that Allania had rounded, and she peeked her head over the side of it. A groan fell from her mouth at what she beheld—more cells. How big *was* this damned dungeon? It seemed to go on forever.

Lillian took a long breath in as she forced her legs to move through the massive prison.

The only good thing so far was that at least the awful smell seemed to be subsiding as she walked farther and farther from those mysterious doors.

The suspense of not knowing what was in that room would eat at her, but it had probably been for the best that she was unable to enter; she didn't need to be having a mental breakdown from whatever she would have seen in that room. She would have to save the breaking down for later when her life wasn't in any imminent danger.

She chuckled coldly at that thought. If that time ever came.

Happy thoughts, she reminded herself. She needed to keep her wits about her lest she go insane before she even had the chance to participate in this cruel game of being champion.

But even though Lillian was trying, she struggled to keep those light thoughts in mind as her entire self stiffened. She had thought the murmurs of faint screams to be unsettling before but found these noises to be *far* worse.

Echoes of whispers and low laughter rang out all around her. That alone was making her feel uneasy, but that wasn't the part that had her most worried.

A low, guttural growl rumbled the cells.

The constant mumbles and snickers were making it impossible for her to pinpoint the noise as she heard a horrible scratching on the stone floor and the growling becoming louder.

Her eyes whirled in every direction, desperately trying to figure out where the noise was coming from, as they landed on a cell a few feet in front of her to her right. She stalked towards the cell, the scratching and unearthly noises becoming louder, and had to refrain from shrieking when she saw the beast.

A creature from a nightmare she knew all too well stood behind the bars. It had long spindly limbs and pale skin that was stretched taut against its wiry frame. Stringy black hair decorated its scalp as her eyes roved towards those familiar hands that ended in lengthy talons. Its pointed teeth glinted in the light, and she didn't need to look into the monster's eyes to know what she would find—black gaping holes.

She had fought this monster before.

Painful memories threatened to come crashing back as she took in shaky breaths. It was the very same creature that had killed Peter in the woods so long ago.

She wasn't sure what she felt, if it was fear… or anger as she looked at the beast in the cell.

The monster's mouth flicked upwards as it licked its lips with that long black tongue. Just looking at it reminded her of how it had felt against her damp tear-stricken cheeks. The disgust she had felt in that moment rushed through her and she settled on rage being the emotion she felt.

Peter was *murdered* by this thing.

Before, she had been too scared and nowhere *near* skilled enough to end this creature's awful existence. But she could do it now. She *had* to. It was her fault Peter had gotten attacked—it was her fault he had *died*. Lillian owed it to him to get revenge on the monster that had felled him.

She knew she was being an idiot—knew she should just leave—but she couldn't stop herself as wrath took over, and she bent down, pulling out her dagger from her boot.

A savage energy flowed through her veins as she glared at the monster in glee. Her skin felt hot as she bared her teeth at the monster—eager to end its existence.

Blinking a few times, she stood before the barred door.

Never had she felt such an intense feeling before. Was this… bloodlust? She shook her head a couple times trying to control herself. Was she *excited* to kill this thing? The thought of her being thrilled—*actually thrilled*—to end something's life, whether it be good or bad unnerved her. It scared her enough to snap her out of whatever anger had overpowered her for a second.

What was wrong with her? She backed away from the cell and slipped her dagger back in her boot. This wasn't her. She didn't *like* killing—she did it when she absolutely had to.

Lillian shuddered as she thought on the way she had felt seconds ago about ending the monster's life. She had felt giddy. For gods sakes, she had even *smiled.*

Lillian stumbled back. She needed to get out of this place. Something here must be affecting her, and she didn't like it one bit.

But still there was a glimmer of hatred in her eyes as she looked at the monster one more time. She grinded her teeth. It wasn't right. Peter died, and this monster got to live. How did that make *any* sense?

She sighed as the answer came to her. It didn't.

This creature *deserved* to die, but she wasn't a god, and it wasn't her call to make. She didn't get to decide who lived and died.

Defeat poured through her as she stood before the cell, a frustrated tear sliding down her cheek. Reluctantly, she tore her gaze from the beast and turned to continue walking down the lengthy hallway.

Ten feet stood between her and the cell when a loud clashing blared behind her.

Whirling, she saw the beast pressed up to the bar, a snarl rolling out of its mouth. Her toes curled as she watched the creature lick the metal with that familiar black tongue as it bore its gaze into her soul.

She began backing away, and the monster kept its eyes—if she could even call them that—glued on her as it began to look at the door separating the cell from the hallway.

Her mouth slackened as her eyes widened at what they beheld. It began using its limbs to pry open the bars.

What kind of a dungeon was this? What was the point if it couldn't even keep its prisoners inside?

Lillian stayed for a total of three seconds before she took off into a run. She rounded corner after corner, running in whatever direction took her as far away from that thing as possible.

Her chances against that beast wouldn't be great. She had managed to get away all those years ago, but that was with Peter already having severely injured it. Here, it seemed to be as fresh as ever; that didn't necessarily bode too well for her and her small dagger. And she also couldn't forget the tiny detail that she hadn't even killed it the last time; it had chosen to leave after being so hurt.

She scoffed as she continued to dash past dozens of cells—things always had a way of being so *perfect* for her.

More corners whisked by her as she rounded each one, but the next one she passed seemed to be gloomier than the rest. Regardless of the sudden change, she didn't stop. She wasn't sure how far back the monster was or even if it was following her for that matter, but she didn't want to make the wrong choice and have it catch up to her.

As she made it farther down the long hall, it had gotten so dark to the point where she was squinting to see whatever the small slivers of light allowed.

An uneasiness grew inside her as she ran in the darkness of the dungeon, and she slowed her pace down to a leisurely jog as she tried to survey her surroundings.

Why was it so pitch black?

Her eyes darted in the glim dungeon as she fiddled with her hands, her thoughts rifling through the multitude of reasons for keeping it almost pitch black. The theory that made her the most nervous was that this area was used for the most horrifying creatures, that even to bear a single glance at them would make you go insane with fear.

She didn't know whether she should keep going or turn back. All the dungeon's corridors seemed to be the same, and she should reach another one soon enough… but would they all continue in darkness?

Marching on, she considered her options. Turning back might be the smarter choice. She was already at a huge disadvantage being a human in the land of the all-powerful Ilaidae, so she *needed* her sight to make her chances of survival at least possible. But on the other hand… that monster was probably back there looking for her and so far, there were no monsters here that she could detect. Maybe they kept this area dark because no one was here? It wasn't likely, but it could be possible.

Her pulse raced in panic, making all her attempts of being logical rendered useless. There was no point in trying to convince herself of anything. Her brain would settle on the most horrifying option and go with that until proven otherwise. So it seemed like going through the dark—no matter how terrifying—was the choice she would stick with.

There was just no one here—that's why it's so dark, she repeated to herself a thousand times in hopes that it would make it true.

Everything seemed to be going fine as she continued to jog through, but all her wishes and prayers proved to be futile as she ran into something in front of her. The force of her running caused her to fall flat on her backside onto the dungeon floor.

Two glowing yellow eyes illuminated in the darkness as the

thing she had run into turned around. The corners of its mouth curved upwards as an unfamiliar voice spoke out. “Well, what do we have here?”

CHAPTER 29

Lillian shuffled backwards, letting those yellow eyes survey her as she stood up and held her hand out in front of her. "Don't come any closer," she barked. She tried to make herself sound as threatening as possible but found it hard to do once having embarrassingly fallen down.

The man ignored her as he took a single step and cocked his head to the side. The only way she could tell was by the way his eyes shifted to the side in the darkness. "And why would I want to do that?" he said, voice slithering out low and raspy.

She took a step back to match the one he took. "I *said* stay back."

He glanced down at her extended hand. "Are those pretty little fingers meant to stop me?"

Red burned across her face as she muttered a low curse; she probably did look pretty stupid right now holding out absolutely nothing.

But she moved past that, deciding to try and bluff her way out of here. She didn't know who this Ilaidae was, and he most likely didn't know her either. Maybe she could get him to believe she was just as dangerous as all the other horrifying creatures in this prison. "You don't want to find out what I'm capable of," she said in a low growl.

His glowing eyes narrowed as he pondered on her words, but he seemed unfazed as that unsettling smirk returned. "I think I would rather like to find out what you're capable of," he crooned.

Flashing her teeth, she scoffed as she tried to continue her ruse. "That would be a mistake."

The man's gaze traveled her up and down as he examined the validity of what she spat. He looked unsure of what his next move would be, and her heart skipped a beat at the suspense.

Was her plan working? That would be a first.

She thought for a split second that things had finally started going her way but was reminded of her awful luck when he started chuckling.

Her vision flooded with red as the man continued to laugh at her. Lillian *hated* when people made fun of her. Who did this bastard think he was? Was it so hard to believe she could be a threatening person? Was it *that* obvious how utterly helpless she was?

The man cleared his throat as he settled his snickering. "They had told me you were *complex*, but they failed to mention how feisty you were—*Lillian*."

Her heart leapt into her throat at the sound of her name. The anger she had felt was replaced with a rush of fear as her plans of convincing him that she was deadly crumbled to pieces.

What did that leave her? Her fists, a small dagger, running

again? Her muscles started itching for movement as she thought of the last option. She couldn't go the way she came because that creature might still be back there. She could try and run past him, but that would leave her incredibly vulnerable and exposed for an attack. Her best course of action would be to distract him or somehow get past without him noticing—so for now, talking seemed like her best chance at survival. "So you've heard of me," she said.

The stranger nodded. "Only vaguely. I was told a woman by the name Lillian would eventually come by." His tongue passed over his lips as he let his eyes roam her body. "But I hadn't been expecting someone as delicious as you."

Her arms slackened at her sides, and she felt the sudden urge to hide behind something as those glowing eyes seemed to undress her.

Uncomfortably, she took a step back as she tried to get his attention away from her. "Who told you about me?"

His eyes stayed glued to her as he took a lazy stride forward. "The queen, of course."

Lillian moved back a step for every one he took—and her insides began to quiver as the man continued to creep closer. She tried saying something, anything, to get his eyes off her. Questions began rolling off her tongue as she spoke in a hastened fashion. "What did she say? What did she want? What do you even look like?"

He smiled as he noticed the bead of sweat sliding down her temple. "Do I make you nervous?"

Wanting to hide the shakiness in her voice, she willed her tone to come off as relaxed. "No, and you didn't answer my question."

Another step forward. "So *demanding*." He brought his hand up to his chin as he rubbed it. "Hmm, I didn't know I liked that."

His hungry eyes turned to her figure once more, causing Lillian to blurt out more nervous words. "Well, are you going to answer?" she sputtered.

The man let out an exhale, becoming annoyed with her pestering. "Very well."

A glowing orb appeared next to him, illuminating him completely. He was rather... *interesting* looking. She still saw those yellow eyes, but she could now see the entire face and body attached to them.

His skin was a pale green that was accompanied by dark green hair to match. He was lean and tall and wore a kind of intricate armor that made her assume he was a guard of sorts. She peeked a glance at his back and thought the armor must have had to have been specially fitted because behind him sprouted out huge purple, tattered wings. Her eyes wandered back up to his face and as expected—his ears came to pointed tips.

Uneasiness floated through her as he flashed his teeth in a grin, revealing them to be razor sharp.

He inched closer. "Does that answer one question?"

Lillian shook her head in a quick nod as she tried concealing her growing anxiety—but she knew she was failing as a smile that filled her with dread appeared on his face once more.

"And as for the other question about Allania…" he murmured in a low voice.

Too fast for her to ever register, he glided across the floor and pinned her up against the stone wall.

Lillian thrashed against his forceful grip as he leaned in close to her ear.

His teeth grazed her soft skin as his breath came out icy on her cheek. "*She told me to do whatever I want with you.*"

CHAPTER 30

Lillian's eyes went wide as she wrestled against his steely grasp, her words coming out in choppy breaths as she struggled against him. "Let *go* of me."

His lips curved upwards revealing those pointed teeth once more. "I'll let you go—*eventually*." He chuckled to himself before leaning in to nibble at her ear. "But first… *we're going to have some fun*."

A weight dropped in her stomach at those words. She wasn't naïve—she knew exactly what *fun* he was referring to. And she wanted no part in it.

His tongue slid down her jaw, and the mere *touch of him* made her writhe in disgust. This couldn't be happening—this couldn't be real. But it felt real as his hands slid down to cup her hips.

Oh gods, this was really happening.

Lillian flailed every part of her body to try and get away—anything to get him to stop touching her. She tried ramming her head into his, but he avoided her blow with ease, keeping her securely pinned. The air struggled to get into her lungs as she wrestled against him, her movements growing increasingly more hysteric.

His hand slipped down her thigh as he slowly began to creep towards her most intimate parts.

Fear and disgust began to overwhelm her, and she wasn't sure if she was talking or shrieking as she called out. "Get *off* me." Panicked tears started sliding down her cheeks as he continued to glide his fingers over her body. Her voice came out choked as she struggled to speak. "Stop—*please*."

The last word made him pause and look up at her tearstained eyes. He made a show of groaning as those yellow eyes glared at her. His fingers dug into her skin as he grabbed her chin. "Why must you woman all be *so* dramatic?"

Weak—she was so weak as droplets kept sliding down her face—but she could do nothing to stop the ongoing flood pouring down her face.

He clenched his teeth together and had the audacity to look annoyed. "*Stop* crying," he ground out.

Something snapped in Lillian at his harsh words.

Who did this *scum* think he was?

A savage fury began enveloping her as she stared at this man. She was *Lillian Echethier*, and she would *not* be weak and submit to the horrors he wanted to do her. She had survived far too much to be shattered by an Ilaidae prick who didn't know the meaning of the word stop. She was strong and she was *powerful*—and she would *not* go down without a fight.

She didn't know what possessed her in that moment as she spit in his face and bared her teeth in a newfound ferocity. "I said, *Let. Me. Go.*"

His eyes went wide as he blinked a few times, trying to register what had just occurred. He brought a hand up, wiping her show of defiance off his face as he dragged his eyes up to meet hers. Anger clouded his vision as he stared at her.

Good. That made two of them.

A menacing cold settled over his features as he spoke through clenched teeth. "I'm going to make you regret that, you nasty *bitch*."

Still possessed with that savage energy, Lillian matched his steely gaze. "Screw. *You*."

He must've not been used to people standing up to him because that sentence seemed to snap something in him as he turned her around and slammed her hard against the stone wall.

The jagged rocks brushed up against her skin, and she knew she would have a nice-looking scrape there later. The buckle on his pants rattled as she stood facing away from him, and Lillian thrashed as she yelled obscenity after obscenity at the top of her lungs.

The Ilaidae shoved her hard against the wall once more. "*Be* quie—"

He didn't finish the rest of his sentence as it was replaced by a gurgling noise, and the pressure pressing her up against the wall disappeared.

Lillian turned and saw his figure crumple to the floor as blood began to leak out of his mouth. Three arrows now protruded from his back as he lay bleeding out.

Normally she would turn and run from whatever had shot those arrows, but a fire exploded inside her as she bent down and reached into her boot, pulling out her dagger.

She stalked towards him, flashes of red in her vision, as she clenched the blade.

She was fury unleashed.

Lillian launched herself on him as she began to stab him again and again. Multiple wounds gushed blood, and she had lost track of how many times she pulled out the blade just to jam it back in.

If anyone walked in on her, she knew they would think her insane.

Tears slid down her cheeks as her voice turned hoarse from the vulgarities she yelled. A slick green blood drenched her entire body as she kept violently piercing his skin even long after he had stopped writhing in pain.

After a few more minutes of uncontrollable sobbing and blood spraying her, she finally dropped the dagger, letting it clatter to the ground. Her hands shook as she sat back, struggling to breathe, and she brought her knees tightly into her chest as she began to profusely sob into her bloodied palms.

She stayed like that for a few minutes, silently crying to herself, before finally bringing her eyes up once more. The Ilaidae's blood spattered and lifeless corpse laid in pieces before her.

She had done that. She had killed him.

Technically he might have died with just the arrows, but she most definitely delivered the final blow.

As if struck with a jolt of static, Lillian jumped up and clutched her dagger. *Arrows.* She had forgotten about that part.

She twisted her head all around but didn't see anything as she scanned the lengthy hall. She had to get out of here.

Lillian looked up at the glowing orb that illuminated the room. How she wished she could bring it with her; wandering around in the dark was growing tiresome.

Her eyes darted from the dead body to the glowing orb. Maybe she *could* take it. If he was dead and the orb remained, did that mean it was a permanent light?

Jumping for the floating light, she swung her hand at it but felt nothing as she landed back on the ground—but when she looked down at her hand… it was glowing. It wasn't exactly what she had wanted, but it would have to do for now.

Before she began walking down the dark hall, she walked towards the lifeless husk. Her throat felt tight as she looked at his broken corpse.

Nausea tickled her senses as she bent down to grab the Ilaidae's sword. It would be the smart thing to take it with her, and there was no sense in leaving it behind since he clearly wouldn't have use for it any longer.

She wasted no time in leaving as she rushed down the gloomy corridors, holding her hand out in front of her and doing her best to light the path ahead as she continued rounding a few more of the same looking corners.

The dungeon was beginning to look like it was never ending when suddenly a wide staircase came into view. Walking up the numerous and tiresome steps, she realized they opened up into a large chamber.

After catching her breath, she took a few cautious strides into the room when the light in her hand vanished.

Great, she thought to herself. The glowing orb had to *of course* have a time limit—because why wouldn't it?

She walked deeper into the chamber but didn't have to suffer the darkness any longer as the lights turned on all at once.

Spots floated in her vision as her eyes burned, blinded from the brightness—but she didn't need her eyes to know who spoke next.

"How nice of you to finally join us, *Lillian*."

CHAPTER 31

Her jaw clenched as she recognized who spoke.

Allania.

Turning to the far end of the room, her gaze landed on the queen atop a throne—but Lillian's eyes strayed as they darted around the massive throne room.

Giant columns jutted out from the sleek marble floor leading to where Allania sat across the vast chamber. A deep ebony painted the entire room save for the white, slithering streaks on the marble floor that made it appear cracked. Looking up, she saw a few rectangular windows high above, but they did little to eliminate the perpetual state of gloominess that enveloped the chambers. The room was completely still, and, if it weren't for her eyes, she would have never known there was an enormous crowd of people littering the grand hall.

She looked at the crowd again.

No, not people—Ilaidae.

Her gaze roamed over the multitude of Ilaidae, a combination of wings, horns, and other strange features just standing there, watching her with leering faces. She had never seen so many pointed ears all gathered in one place, and she had *especially* never had all their attention solely on her.

Lillian tried to ignore the mass of Ilaidae as her eyes wandered back to the end of the hall. Back to… *her*.

A face of steel masked Lillian's features as she held her head high and began walking down the vast length of the room. She didn't have to look around to know all eyes were on her.

She wondered what they thought upon looking at her; Lillian knew she must look unhinged. That disgusting ooze coated her entire body, and she had gashes on her cheek that had caused blood to drip down her jaw, making a beautiful canvas of red and green cover her skin.

Needless to say—she knew she looked bad. But she chose to disregard that detail as she eased down the silent chamber, her eyes instead catching on a grandiose fountain on the far wall to her left.

The fountain was colored the same sable as the rest of the room, but was impossible to ignore as it stood out, just begging to be admired. It was so enormous that it went halfway up the wall that separated the marble floor from the intricate ceiling. Her gaze drifted to its top where a black figure with large batlike wings kneeled on a small base. Shimmering water trickled down the levels of jagged rock before eventually emptying into a huge basin at the bottom.

The enchanting fountain captivated her, and she found herself struggling to tear her gaze from it, but forced herself as she made her way closer to Allania.

A sneer decorated the queen's face as her frosty gaze pierced into Lillian.

Her eyes moved lower from the cruel queen down to where she sat. High up above on a dais, Allania sat perched upon a dark throne, the impressive seat made of numerous black rocks. Lillian blinked at the strange throne of rocks. No—they weren't rocks. Horror thudded in her as she realized what the throne was made of.

Skulls.

Skulls that were painted with the darkest of colors and fashioned into a massive throne.

It was a concentrated effort to maintain her composure as she looked at the dozens of bones the queen casually sat strewn atop as if it were any ordinary chair.

Her stomach churned as she thought of all the poor souls Allania had condemned to be the furniture she sat upon. This had to only be a small fraction of the terror she had inflicted, and the mere thought of all she had done only made her insides toss even more.

Eventually, she made it to the throne and stopped a few feet back from the steps of the dais. She looked up at Allania, trying to keep her confident demeanor and wondering how obvious it was that it was all a façade.

Allania sat motionless as she watched her from above, but, after a few seconds, she sat up straighter and raised a brow as if waiting for her to do something.

A muscle flexed in Lillian's jaw, and she bit the inside of her cheek as she realized what she was waiting for. She wanted her to bow. Lillian glared up at the queen with what she hoped wasn't too obvious of distaste.

A thousand thoughts swarmed her mind as she looked up at Allania. This wasn't her queen; she didn't answer to her. This was a cruel and vicious monster that didn't deserve Lillian's respect.

But she knew she had to give it.

Whether she liked it or not, she was no longer in Grigaros. This was Iavothae, and this was her castle. And if she wanted to live past this evening, then she had to follow her rules—no matter how sick and twisted they might be.

Lillian huffed an internal sigh before looking up at Allania one last time. She put one leg behind the other and did her best attempt at a curtsy, not entirely sure the correct way to execute one. She held the position, her head turned down, as she spoke words that didn't feel right. "My queen."

She stayed like that for longer than she would've liked, and it was enough for her legs to start to burn before she heard Allania speak. "Rise," she commanded.

Getting up from the uncomfortable pose, Lillian raised her head to gaze upon the ruler. A small smirk formed across her blood red lips as she looked down on her, pleased on how obedient she had turned out to be.

Lillian's nails dug into her palms as she balled her fists, struggling to keep her emotions in check. Now was not the time to lose her temper—especially not with this audience. Any disrespect she showed in front of her subjects would be *severely* punished. She shoved down that growing rage and stared at the ruler as she waited for her to speak.

The queen's eyes roamed her filthy state a few times before she finally opened her mouth. "You look a little… different than I remember. Last I saw you, you looked less… " She gestured at her with her hands. "Let's just leave it at *less*."

Blood roared in her ears as she thought of what happened down in those dungeons. How that guard had...

She stopped herself, not wanting to recall what he had planned to do with her. Bile stung in the back of her throat as the feelings of fear and panic she had felt threatened to overpower her.

Glancing downwards, she kept her breaths even, doing everything within her to remain calm. Her eyes caught on the bloodied dagger in her hand.

A sick feeling of pleasure consumed her as she thought of what she had done to him—of how many times that blade had pierced his disgusting flesh. And how she had… *repaid* him for his kindness.

She looked back up at the queen and smiled in a way she never had before. "I did have a little run in with one of your guards." She flipped the dagger in her hand causing the queen's eyes to dart towards the blade. "But I don't think you'll be hearing from him any time soon."

Allania's eyes went wide.

She didn't know if the queen was angry, shocked, or a combination of both. But what Lillian hadn't been expecting was for her to start laughing.

"My, my. I seemed to have judged you too quickly—perhaps there might be something interesting about you yet."

A feeling of dread overcame her. Lillian didn't like that response. She didn't like that she had *pleased* Allania—that the twisted queen had actually *approved* of what she had done.

The devious grin Lillian wore dropped as she wrestled to a get a grip on herself. If she had managed to make the queen like her more, she really had to evaluate her past choices—the queen was not someone she wanted to please. What she had done to that man was not something she should be proud of—no matter how much a person like him deserved it. If she gloated in his death, it made her no better than someone like Allania—and that was not someone she wished to be.

The tyrant's words interrupted Lillian's dark thoughts from consuming her whole. "Poor, poor Theo. I rather liked him as a guard. I told him to go off and find you—but to have a little… *fun* with you first. After all, I do have to keep my subjects happy." The queen's smirk turned into a vicious grin as she looked at Lillian. "But it looks like you were the one who had all the fun, darling."

Lillian's vision swarmed with red. This wretched bitch had sent him to—

Her mind faltered. To do—*that*. Wrath coursed through every part of her.

She was going to kill her.

She had no idea how or when, but she wouldn't rest until she saw her lifeless corpse lying on the floor. Lillian's breathing turned heavy as she failed to maintain her calmness of before.

A glance up revealed her to find a corner of Allania's lips tilted upwards. She wanted this—she wanted Lillian to snap so she could just kill her now and be done with it. But she wouldn't let that hag get to her; she was here for a reason, and she would see that reason through. But after that… Lillian had a date with the devil.

Maybe. Lillian sighed as some semblance of logic began to

seep into her enraged mind. She couldn't go making promises that would get her killed—not when she had a family to think about. She settled on dealing with what she would do later and just focused on the task at hand—completing this damned trial.

As if reading her mind, Allania began to speak once more. "Now enough pleasantries. Let's talk about why you're *really* here." The queen smiled as if it was the most exciting news she'd ever heard.

Bracing herself for what came next, Lillian opened her mouth but halted, noticing how utterly silent the room had become. Her mouth felt dry as she looked at all the eyes on her, and she swallowed once more as she uttered those cursed words. "I wish to be the Champion of the Flame."

The crowd stayed quiet, taking in what she had proclaimed—but gasps and murmurs quickly invaded the eerily silent atmosphere. She could pick up bits and pieces all around her as they all spoke of the trial.

Allania stood and clapped her hands twice in irritation and the room went back to its normal state, vacant of sound. Sitting down, she smiled, pleased at the soundless ambience. "So *you*—Lillian Echethier—wish to be the Champion of the Flame?"

Lillian was unsure if the question was meant to be rhetorical, but she responded anyway with a simple yes.

"And why is that?" she pressed.

She blinked a few times. No one had ever asked her why. She wasn't sure if she wanted to tell her in fear that she wouldn't be allowed to participate. Mulling over her words, she decided to go with the obvious answer. "For the wish, of course."

"Don't toy with me, Lillian. *I know that.* What do you want the wish for?"

Opening her mouth to spout out something random, she was immediately interrupted.

"And no lying," she spat. "I'll know if you're being untruthful—and I don't take kindly to those who try to deceive me."

Lillian huffed a loud exhale. Great. She would be *furious* if she came all this way for nothing. But it didn't look like she had any other choice than to tell the truth.

Wanting to get it over with and have the bad news told to her, she sputtered out her answer. "I know about the impending attack on my kind. I wish to stop it and save my family."

The queen nodded while considering what she'd said. "How very noble of you. We haven't ever had a champion who used their wish for something so... *righteous*." She paused and crossed one leg over the other, reclining back in her throne. "I see why you wanted to keep this to yourself. I assume you think I won't let you participate now that I know?"

Her heart pounded as Lillian panicked over what she would say next—say those words that would deny her of the trial. All of it would be for nothing. All the danger and strife had been worthless. Her head hung low as she waited for those dreaded words.

Allania sat up straight in her throne. "But you would be mistaken. I won't stand in your way of risking your life for a foolish wish."

Her head shot up, not sure if she was hearing correctly. It was happening—it was really happening. She was going to be the champion.

"Now don't get too excited, Lillian. Before you accept, I have something to offer you first—*a choice*."

Not sure what choice she was alluding to, Lillian arched a brow. The room went silent as they all waited with eager ears to hear what she had to say.

"I'm going to give you a choice. I'll spare you… and your family from my imminent plans." Allania bared her teeth in a malicious grin. "*But no one else*."

Lillian's eyes went wide as she considered what had been so plainly uttered. Her family would be safe. She would be safe. But everyone else… everyone else would suffer the Ilaidae's wrath.

Her mind swirled with what that could mean as she glanced at Allania, her smug face satisfied with the inner turmoil she had just caused.

She didn't know what to do.

On the one hand, she could take her offer and save her family. She wouldn't have to do the dangerous Trial of the Flame, and she could go back to her family. But if she did that… she would be condemning everyone else.

What would life even look like? Everyone around her being murdered and torn to pieces while they sat back, safe in the comforts of their home. She knew her father wouldn't stand for that, knew *she* wouldn't be able to stand for that—doing nothing while the world around her fell to pieces.

Lillian groaned in her mind at how morally conscious she had to be. She should just take the offer—should just accept it and leave while she still could. Because if she turned it down and failed… her family would die along with her. At least with the offer, they would have a fighting chance.

Her head pounded as it battled back and forth on what to do. She wanted to take the deal—she really did—but she couldn't. She wouldn't be able to live with herself if she gave up the chance to save everyone, wouldn't be able to live with herself if she were that *selfish*.

It was so clear what she had to do—had always been.

Allania stared at her, impatiently awaiting a response. "Well? What's it going to be?" she demanded. "I'm afraid I don't have all day for your mortal brain to process and decide."

Calming her nerves, she took in one last deep breath. Her voice came out firm and louder than she intended as it echoed in the large chamber. "I want to be the champion. I don't want your offer."

Allania rose from her throne, a satisfied grin appearing on her face. "Very well." She tore her gaze from Lillian and addressed the crowd. "It looks like we have ourselves *a Champion of the Flame*." A power reverberated in her words and the room hummed with energy as if she had just awoken something. The Ilaidae queen closed her eyes and when she opened them, a red orange danced inside them.

Those eyes were curling fire come to life, but she didn't stare at them for too long as her attention was caught by a glowing behind her. When she turned to face it, she realized it wasn't a light that emitted the intense glow—but *flames*.

The beautifully ornate fountain from before that had been trickling water now spewed bright flames down its many levels. It should have been impossible, but she knew impossible didn't exist here.

A fountain of flames.

Mesmerized by the burning fountain—gazing at it in awe and watching the flames grow brighter—an intense pain consumed her, causing her to double over in anguish. A searing on her chest made her cry out in agony. It felt like something was being burned into her—like hot coals were being forced onto her chest, and she could do nothing to escape the fiery torment.

She laid on the floor twitching and thinking the scorching would be never-ending when it suddenly vanished, leaving only a tender ache behind.

Lillian sat up, peering down her shirt to see what the cause of the intense searing had been and could only make out the beginnings of something branded into her flesh.

Loud, thundering footsteps caught her attention as she looked up from her newly marred skin, and the masses turned their leering to the throne where a figure walked from out behind it.

Her heart threatened to shatter as she recognized the man who emerged.

Nolan.

He sauntered in without a care in the world and stopped to stand next to the throne.

Glancing up at his face, she saw an icy mask as his eyes wandered over her lying on the floor. It looked like Nolan but...

No—this wasn't Nolan. This was someone else entirely. Or perhaps this is who he had been all along, and she had just been too foolish to see it.

His eyes locked with hers as they started to destroy her with that unfeeling face he wore. They both stayed like that for what felt like far too long before he plastered on a grin she knew all too well.

"Let the games begin," he announced to the crowd.

CHAPTER 32

The crowd burst into cheers at the statement, but her eyes stayed focused on the man before her.

He now wore a sable tunic adorned with swirls and brocaded with glittering silvers. Mostly, he looked the same except for those cold features that felt completely foreign on him. She had been so used to the annoying, easy-going Nolan that she barely recognized the man standing in front of her.

Something else was different.

Her gaze snagged on his ears, and she felt her jaw drop as she took in what she saw.

They were pointed.

How could she have not noticed? No, she would have seen that—she wasn't blind. Somehow, he had managed to hide that.

She felt sick as everything in her mind clicked into place.

That voice—she *knew* that voice. Not just because of Nolan, before that—before she had ever met him. It was that night in the tree when Killian and Malik had almost found her. There had been a third figure who she hadn't been able to identify.

It had been him.

She hadn't been able to connect the two until now because of the way he had just spoken. When he spoke to her back in the woods, he had seemed so relaxed—infuriating—but relaxed. And now when he spoke… his voice was laced with a malice she hadn't heard except on that night.

Lillian felt like she was going to explode. He had been following her from the beginning. It hadn't been by chance that he had found her—he had *planned* that. He made her let down her guard enough for her to trust him, enough for her to…

Her cheeks burned scarlet as she thought on what they had done—what *she* had done. Her lip curled as a bitterness coated her tongue—and with an Ilaidae no less.

A fire began to fuel her veins as her eyes bore into him. She didn't know what to say—what to do. Her voice became deadly calm as she spoke. "*You.*"

A small smirk formed on his lips as he narrowed his eyes at her. "I'm sorry, do I know you?"

Oh, she was going to murder him.

But before Lillian could say a thing, he gasped as if feigning remembrance. "That's right. Aren't you that desperate girl I met in the woods?"

Lillian clenched her teeth so tight she feared they might shatter. Her words felt like venom as they dripped off her tongue. "*Desperate.*

You—"

He didn't let her continue as he swiftly cut her off. "Well, you *did* seem rather desperate when you all but threw yourself at me. I think I recall you even whimpering when I pulled away?" He looked at the crowd chuckling before continuing. "But please—Lillith, was it?—enlighten me if you call that something else." He grinned, and the Ilaidae laughed at his mocking.

Done—she was *so* done playing nice. Being polite to Allania was one thing, but this prick didn't deserve *any* of her respect. "It's Lillian, you pretentious bastard!" she barked through gritted teeth. "Come down here and say that to my face you—"

Allania stopped her before another nasty slur slipped off her tongue. "Now, now. Why don't you both be kind. We have more important things to discuss other than your little *run in*." She said those last two words with a pinched expression as if the thought of them together visibly appalled her. "But I see I don't need to introduce you to my beloved brother."

That one word snapped Lillian out of her growing rage. *Brother*. This was the vicious queen's twisted brother—this was the Ilaidae those two men in the forest were scared of?

And she had thrown herself at him in a fit of lust. She was going to be physically ill.

Oh gods—when had her life gotten so complicated? Not only had she had a passionate encounter with an Ilaidae—that right there was bad enough—but the queen's *brother*. This was all beginning to get ridiculous.

Nolan winked at her one last time, causing a wave of fury to cascade through her before he turned to his sister. "I apologize for being late. I seem to have lost track of time."

The queen slinked down the steps of her throne to stand next to her brother, smiling before greeting him with a soft kiss on the cheek. "No apology necessary." They both turned to look at Lillian and the queen's voice reverted back to its venomous tone. "You're *just* in time for the fun to begin."

Everyone's gaze laid upon Lillian.

She did *not* like the sound of that. She felt completely helpless as she stood there like a rabbit caught in a snare just waiting for someone to come snap its neck.

Allania started to walk over to her, and the crowd turned mute as they watched their queen. The clinking of her heels on the marble floor echoed as she came to a stop two feet in front of her. "Now, Lillian, there are customs we must follow since you've been named champion. The trial won't take place right away. First, we must have a feast that you will be attending." A smile crept onto her face that caused the hairs on the back of Lillian's neck to rise. "In your honor, of course." Lillian must have looked perturbed as Allania addressed her once more. "But don't be nervous. Iavothae has an *excellent* reputation of hosting the most wondrous feasts—you'll see."

Lillian gave a numb nod, knowing that the feast would not be as wondrous as she claimed. Not for her at least.

The queen rubbed her hands together. "But that won't be until later. For now, I have something else for you to do."

Waiting for her to explain, Lillian raised a brow.

Allania laughed. "Well, you didn't expect to just spend your days in your cell, did you? I know how fickle you little human things are, needing attention lest that adorable brain go mad with boredom."

Lillian paled, already not liking where this was going.

"Oh, don't worry. I'm sure it's nothing you can't handle. I wouldn't put the champion in harm's way, now, would I?"

Indeed, she likely would put the champion in harm's way, but Lillian knew better than to voice that.

"I just want you to do three simple things. Right now, all you have to do is feed my pet. Does that sound simple enough?"

There was no denying that it did sound rather easy, but she wasn't fooled; she knew how these things went. It wouldn't be anything like it seemed.

But she had no say in the matter as Allania clapped her hands, causing two guards to emerge from the crowd. "Please show our lovely guest the way to go."

The guards bowed in schooled silence before turning to whisk her away from the throne room, and, as she went, she couldn't stop her eyes as they landed on Nolan.

Lillian stared at the man she thought she'd known as he gazed back at her with the intensity she had mistaken for passion in those woods.

Gods, it felt like so long ago.

Their eyes remained locked as she disappeared in the passage-way behind the throne.

Recalling her last encounter with an Ilaidae guard, she kept a hand on the hilt of her stolen sword and her eyes glued to the backs of their heads as they walked her through the winding corridors. They led her down so many hallways and staircases that she had already lost track. She did her best to try and map out what the castle looked like in case she needed to make a speedy escape—but she knew she would inevitably get disoriented in the confusing palace.

As they strolled the castle's halls, her mind wandered back to the grand throne room. There was no denying now that she was the champion. She still had no idea what was on her chest, but she imagined it was some elaborate branding of sorts to signify she was the Champion of the Flame.

But her marred skin wasn't what stood out to her the most of the day's events. Her thoughts landed on that smug bastard who had waltzed in as if nothing were the matter. Fire hummed beneath her skin as she thought on how he'd had the audacity to even *insinuate* he didn't remember who she was.

Lillian bit the inside of her cheek. Oh, she'd make sure he'd remember her.

She still couldn't believe him. How he had lied to her—how he had *betrayed* her. But it was herself she was most mad at for being able to trust him so easily.

Never again—never again would she make that same mistake.

An aching sensation started spreading in her legs as they continued to go down dozens of stairs. And after they went down enough to make her limbs beg for mercy, they finally reached the bottom, stopping before a pair of large wooden double doors.

They looked rather plain, but she knew something horrible

must lie behind them. Her stare landed on the handle as she noticed the doors were lined with an absurd number of locks, and she began to fear whatever manner of beast laid inside that made them take so many precautions.

The guard pulled out a ring filled with keys, and she watched as he fiddled with the numerous locks on the door.

Standing there waiting as the man undid each latch one by one, she thought on the chore Allania had given her. She scoffed as she remembered what she'd said—*needing to keep her entertained.* She wanted to strangle her.

But her mind moved on as it thought on the queen's task—*feed my pet.* A chill went through her bones as she thought of what that Ilaidae queen would deign to keep as a pet. Maybe she would get lucky, and it would be a large wolf, but she knew better than that. She didn't even know what classified as a pet in Iavothae.

The guard finished unlocking the last clasp and pushed the doors open with a shove. The two men looked back at her and gestured for her to go first as one of them said, "After you."

Lillian looked down the dimly lit hall as she steadied her nerves. *Just a pet*, she said to herself as she began to walk down with one of the guards following closely behind.

"Stop at the end by that pen," he ordered.

Not saying a word, she continued to pad down the hall. A faint light glowed at the end, and she assumed that must be the pen.

Time slowed as a tightness settled in her chest. She braced herself for whatever horrible creature lay at the end and found herself unconsciously holding her breath and needing to remind herself to breathe.

Nearing the enclosure, she squinted her eyes as the supposed creature of nightmares came into view. She had prepared herself for the worst and couldn't stop herself this time as she held her breath and saw the horrifying creature turn out to be…

Dogs.

Lillian blinked a few times. That couldn't be right. She took a closer look at what was inside the pen and realized her eyes had not been mistaken. It was just a couple of regular dogs. There were six in total—all the same shade of black—and they looked up at her as they nervously wagged their tails.

A sigh of relief escaped her as she looked down at the sweet things. This was the grand monster she was meant to feed? This was what she had been so scared to meet?

Despite their adorable furry faces, she still didn't feel completely at ease as she remembered that innocent looking rabbit from the woods. She looked back at the guard and asked, "Are these just regular dogs?"

The guard nodded. "Yep."

Lillian felt the smallest bit better to hear that they weren't going to turn into another one of those ghoulish monsters, but that relief was extremely short lived as the man continued to speak. "Now stop messing around with the food and get on with it."

Her stomach dropped as she turned to look at the guard. "What did you just say?"

The man noticed the utter shock on her face and broke out into laughter. "No… don't tell me you thought *these* were her pets? You really are a stupid girl, aren't you?" He chuckled as he pointed to an enormous cage down the hall. "*That's* her pet."

Choosing to ignore the snide remark on her intellect, she creeped to where the man had gestured and stopped before a heavily barred door with rungs that were close together.

Nothing stood out to her in the large cell except for what looked like an absurdly thick rope stacked up in the corner. This was unlike any rope she had ever seen, having to at least be fifteen inches wide and covered in dark scales.

No, she knew better. This wasn't rope. She just didn't want to believe it.

Paralyzed, she stared at the lengthy scaled skin, her eyes landing on the creature's face as it opened up its enormous purple lids that revealed black slits.

It was a snake.

CHAPTER 33

A snake. And not just any ordinary snake—a ridiculously massive beast of a snake.

Lillian turned to face the guard, shock washing all over her features.

The man sneered at her evident discomfort. "Not a fan of Solrac?"

Her face turned stern at his mocking tone. "So what, I'm supposed to feed *Solrac* a dog's carcass?"

The man shook his head. "Who said anything about the dog being dead?"

Her eyes went wide, causing the guard to burst out in more laughter. But she didn't care—not right now. She loathed this twisted place. A live dog—she had to feed this monster a *live* dog? No, she wouldn't do that—she couldn't.

A feeling of dread overcame her. But what choice did she have?

The guard cleared his throat, wiping away his tears of glee. "Do you know nothing of snakes, girl?" His next words came out quieter, more vicious. "Of how they like to *kill* their food."

Lillian didn't know much about snakes, only ever hearing to avoid them because some were known to be venomous, but she didn't like how this guard was talking down to her like she was some common idiot. "I know that some are venomous."

The man nodded his head. "Indeed, some are. But Solrac here is special." He looked back at the snake, awe glinting in his eyes. "Not only does he have venom, but he's also known as a constrictor."

Lillian thought she knew where this was going and braced herself for him to continue.

"Solrac here has two options when it comes to killing. He can either bite them and inject whatever prey with his venom or" —a wild grin surfaced on his face that made a shiver crawl down her spine— "he can choose to throw his coils around his prey and slowly suffocate them while cutting off their blood supply and eventually snapping their bones."

The guard smiled at her, amused with how ghostly she had turned. "Do you want to guess which method is Solrac's favorite?"

She didn't need to guess. She knew. Oh, this was bad—this was *really* bad. Just imagining what she had to do made her insides threaten to claw out through her mouth.

Lillian felt ill as the guard looked at her with a perverted glee. "Ready?" he asked.

No. She wasn't and she would never be. Not for this. But she had to be. She knew these little chores weren't a choice—they were an order. And if she disobeyed… She didn't want to know what happened to people who defied Allania's commands.

Lillian took slow steps towards the pen holding the six dogs, stalling as long as possible. The too thin dogs looked up at her with sad eyes while she waited for a command.

"Pick," he grunted.

Lillian blinked a few times and turned to him. "*What*?"

"I said *pick*. Don't make me ask you again."

Oh gods. *Oh gods.*

Her eyes roved over all the frail looking dogs. They were all black as night and had blue colored eyes save for one in the corner.

Her eyes were drawn to the thin wolf-looking dog. He had pointed ears and did have one blue eye, but the other one was a bright orange. Something was different about this dog—it looked like the others—but something about it stood out. It seemed stronger, more *deadly,* and not nearly as weak as the others.

The guard saw where her gaze had landed and smiled. "That one it is. He's a good choice." He wrangled the dog onto a chain and handed the end of it to her. "Go put it in."

The chain trembled in her hand as an uncontrollable shudder swept through her. She looked down at the dog beside her; he didn't so much as tug in an attempt to run away—almost like he knew what his fate was and didn't bother fighting it.

Lillian took a shaky step forward towards the cage and had to swallow down bile as it made its way up her throat. Her mind felt numb as she closed her eyes and spoke in her head. *It's okay, all you're doing is opening a door and putting a dog in a cage—nothing else.*

She repeated the last phrase in her mind, attempting to trick herself into believing it as she halted in front of the cage doors. The animal sat calmly at her feet as the guard walked up and handed her a key. Her fingers quaked as she grasped the thin metal in one hand and the chain in the other.

Is this really what her life had come to?

A tear slid down her cheek as she looked at the innocent black dog. Her lips quivered as she closed her damp eyes and shoved the key in the lock, turning it and causing the door to fling open.

The guard didn't skip a beat as he unchained the dog and kicked him inside as if he were a toy and not a living being. He rubbed his hands together in an excited anticipation that made Lillian feel sick. "*Now* comes the fun part."

Body entirely too stiff, she watched the snake take notice of the canine and begin to slither its way closer to him. The snake had to at least be forty feet long; this dog didn't stand a chance.

The serpent prowled its way over, and the frail animal didn't move a muscle. Why wasn't the dog doing anything? *Do something*, she wanted to cry out.

Lillian couldn't watch and her body betrayed her as she bent over to the side and heaved the contents of her stomach all over the floor.

The guard came up and grabbed her by a fistful of hair as he shoved her face into the bars hard enough to make her wince. "*Watch*," he ordered through clenched teeth.

Doing as she was told, she watched as the snake glided closer, the serpent still causing no reaction from the canine. What was it waiting for? Was it just going to accept its death?

She squinted her eyes, not wanting to see the dog be squeezed of its life in a torturous slowness, but, right when she thought the snake was going to open its massive maw and pounce, the dog sprang into action.

He stood tall baring his teeth as his hackles rose, making him appear larger than he was. A quiet snarl roared out of him as he snapped his pointed teeth at the snake.

The snake only observed with its piercing purple eyes as its forked tongue flicked out of its mouth. It opened its jaw wide, revealing its long white fangs as it hissed, the sound terrifying enough to make a chill course through Lillian.

But despite that, the dog stood its ground as he growled and snapped its teeth with his pointed ears pulled back.

The guard chuckled at the sight as he loosened his grip on her hair. "Looks like we've got ourselves a fighter."

The snake lunged its massive head at the canine with its mouth open wide, eager to stab him with its fangs—but the dog matched its speed as it avoided its blow and jumped away, using the opportunity to latch onto the monster's body. He shook his head a few times before letting go and backing away seconds before the monster whipped back at him.

The snake bared its fangs, hissing as it coiled up and readied itself to strike once more.

The dog remained unfazed as it growled and snarled, showing the serpent its flesh-shredding teeth.

Lillian couldn't bear to watch any longer. This was all her fault. She did this—she had put this poor animal in this position where it had to fight for its life. What hurt the most is that she knew that this dog—no matter how much it fought—would inevitably lose to this monstrous creature. And it was all because of her.

She stared at the brave dog that desperately grasped onto its life when something dawned on her. This dog—this *valiant* dog—knew that the odds were against him, but still he fought. Still, he had the courage to not go down without giving this beast every piece of himself he had to offer. She knew how that dog felt. Too many times had she been put in the same situation when she had decided to go through the Forest of Brittelia and become the Champion of the Flame.

Whether it was courage or sheer idiocy, she didn't know what came over her as Lillian let her elbow fly up high behind her, the pointed edge of her arm connecting with the guard's face. Not a single second was wasted as she opened the cage door, ran inside, and pulled out her sword as she yelled at the creature Solrac.

Lillian held her blade up as the snake turned its attention to her. She clenched her teeth as she stared down the creature with a fierce gaze. "*Come and get me*," she growled, the words a lethal calm rolling of her lips.

The snake bounded towards her as if obeying her command, and Lillian raised her sword, waiting to slash it down on the creature's scaled skin.

But right before she brought it down, the guard ran in through the door, a sword already in hand. "You idiot! All you had to do was stand still and *watch*!"

The creature fixed its attention on the guard.

Oh, she would've died.

As she watched the snake lunge, she realized it had been holding back with the dog, simply toying with it. Now it was *mad.* And it was only getting madder as the guard dodged the attack and slashed his blade at its shimmering skin.

Using the gifted opportunity, she ran towards the dog. She didn't know if it would come or if it would lash out at her as well, but, as she made her way over, it stopped its snarling and loosened its ears back to their normal pointed state.

Lillian gestured at the door, beckoning for it to follow, and the dog cocked its head to the side before beginning to trot over with cautious steps. She couldn't believe it; this dog was smarter than most people she knew.

They both made their way towards the door as she kept an eye on the snake and guard; she could see him start to slow down as the beast continued to strike with its jaw hung open wide.

As they got closer to the exit, she was shocked at what the dog did next. It snarled as it moved to shield her from the snake, herding her closer to the wall. This little dog, who had been condemned to being food, had so much bravery that it put itself closer to the snake, not allowing her to near it.

Tears pricked the edges of her eyes as she walked towards the door, faster now, wanting to get both of them out as quickly as possible while the snake was still occupied at the far end of the cage. A few second later, they both crossed the cage's rungs, and she slammed the door shut and locked it.

The loud clanging noise caused the guard to turn towards her and his eyes went wide with fury as he yelled, "You little *bitch.* I'll have your head for thi—"

His sentence was halted as he had made the fatal mistake of taking his eyes off the snake. The serpent opened its mouth wide and clamped down on the guard's torso—but it didn't stop there. It threw its black coils around the guard as it began to squeeze him, and the Ilaidae writhed in agony from the creature's considerable strength.

The man stopped squirming and his eyes glossed over, but she still couldn't peel her eyes from the sight.

The only thing that broke her from her trance was the second guard running up from his post at the wooden double doors. His face paled as he looked inside the cage. "What did you *do*?"

Shadows churned inside her as she dragged her gaze towards the other guard. Her voice came out cold and she knew her face held no feeling as she spoke. "You said feed the snake." She paused as she gritted her teeth together and spoke once more in that strangely wicked tone. "*And I did.*"

The remaining guard didn't utter a single word as they went up the silent steps.

She hadn't wanted to leave the dog down there in that pen, but she hadn't been presented another option. She would come back for them—she made a promise to herself that she would.

As they continued, Lillian was the first to break the uncomfortable quiet. "Where are you taking me?" she asked.

He didn't turn to look at her as he kept climbing up the stairs. "To get ready."

"Ready—ready for what?"

"For the feast, of course."

Lillian had forgotten about that; the queen had briefly mentioned a feast would be taking place in her honor. *Her honor*. She didn't like the sound of that.

They stopped clambering up the numerous steps and went down a long corridor before halting at a door. The man produced a key as he unlocked it and swung it open. "In you go. I'll be waiting here until you're ready."

The guard put his back to the door, staring forward and Lillian took that as her cue to enter. She walked into the room and as she set foot inside, she realized she was in a grand bathing chamber.

Dull lights floated all around her, illuminating the large room. Her gaze began wandering the chamber, and she noticed it was rather empty save for the immense golden tub and a vanity on a far wall. She'd never been in this room, but it looked similar to the throne room with its shiny marble floors and ebony-colored walls.

Her eyes turned towards the center as she spotted puffs off steam coming out of the huge basin in the middle and a strange looking woman tending it. She would have looked normal had her skin not been grey and covered in cracks that reminded her of a rocky wall.

The odd-looking woman stood up and straightened her aproned dress as she looked at her with wide eyes. "Oh my. It looks like I've got my work cut out for me."

A blush peeked onto her cheeks as she remembered what she must have looked like to this woman, the dried green blood caked all over her skin and the gashes on her cheek.

The woman held out her hands and gestured for her to come

forward. “Come, child. Let’s get you cleaned up.”

CHAPTER 34

Lillian could stay like this forever.

In the large tub, she sat content, soaking in the scorching heat as the woman scrubbed at her feet with a sponge. Lillian had been a lot dirtier than she'd remembered but she didn't care much as that only meant she got to linger longer in the deliciously warmed water.

It had felt a little weird getting undressed in front of this stranger, but she had waved off that thought once she'd submerged herself in the welcoming heat. Her body was so relaxed that she hadn't even minded when the woman had waxed and plucked her. She had been forced to take dips in those freezing streams that she had almost forgotten how good it felt to lounge in a tub—even if it was inside this treacherous castle.

The woman's hand started drifting up her thighs as she finished cleaning her legs, and Lillian sat up a little straighter, holding out her hand—she wasn't too keen on allowing this person to touch her more *sensitive* areas. "I can do the rest," she said.

The Ilaidae looked up from her task and handed Lillian the sponge. "If that would please you."

Lillian took the saturated sponge and continued to wash herself while the woman moved to work on her hair. As she scrubbed herself, she found it odd that she didn't even know this woman's name. A pot of water was poured onto her head as Lillian began to speak. "My name's Lillian."

The unfamiliar maid dutifully continued her task as she dumped a vial that smelled of citrus onto her hair. "I know." Usually someone responded with their name when one told theirs, so Lillian patiently waited for her to introduce herself. A gentle voice came out seconds later. "You can call me Nillipa."

Nillipa. She had never heard such a name before. "Well, thank you for helping me wash up, Nillipa." Lillian chuckled to herself. "I know it must not be the *easiest* chore."

Her comment got a snort out of the woman. "You did do a rather good job of dirtying yourself up, but I've dealt with much worse throughout the many years."

She wondered how many years that was. The woman didn't look too old. If she had to wager a guess, she would place her a few years younger than her mother—but she knew age worked differently for the Ilaidae.

Nillipa grabbed another big pot of water and picked it up in her arms. "Close your eyes."

Doing as she was bid, Lillian shut her eyes as she felt the warm water start to trickle over her head, rinsing out the citrus smelling vial from her hair. Rubbing at her eyes, she watched as Nillipa brought over a large towel.

Lillian brought the sponge up to her chest to finish up but winced as she touched a piece of tender skin. The searing—she had forgotten about that pain she'd felt when named champion.

Daring a look down, she stared in awe at what she saw. It looked as if a design of sorts had been branded into her skin, but she wasn't able to examine it for too long as Nillipa held out the towel, beckoning for her to get out.

Reluctantly, she eased herself out of the now tepid water and wrung out her drenched hair. She stepped out of the tub and wrapped the soft towel around her as Nillipa led her to sit in front of the vanity.

The woman brushed through her wet hair and then held a hand up to Lillian's head. "Now this might seem a bit strange but don't worry."

A heated air began radiating out from her stony hands as she glided them over her thick strands. Lillian had never seen anything like it. Usually, she had to wait *at least* an hour if not more for her long hair to dry, but, here, she was doing it in mere minutes.

A glance in the mirror revealed her hair to be pin straight as opposed to its usual slight waves. Her hair wasn't curly by any means, but it had never been *this* straight.

Gathering a clump of her mane, Nillipa began fashioning a horn on one side of her head and then proceeded to do the same on the other. Once she seemed satisfied with that, she moved on to her lips, painting them a deep red that looked closer to black than anything else. She then finished by lining her eyes with kohl, and Nillipa nodded to herself, content with her work. "Up you go now. Let's get you dressed."

Nillipa ushered her over to a small table that held a dark green fabric on it, but, as she grabbed it and held it up to the light, Lillian noticed that the fabric was completely sheer. Her face dropped. "You can't be serious. *That's* a dress?"

The Ilaidae gave her a soft nod.

"Where's the rest of the damned thing?" she said with a sharp tone.

Nillipa let out a low laugh. "I'm afraid this is all I was given."

With a sigh, she dropped the towel as she let Nillipa help her slide the dress on.

A dress.

Lillian scoffed; she could hardly even call it that. It looked more like a transparent piece of cloth that was somehow fashioned to cover only a few choice areas. Two gauzy strands of fabric went down her front as they struggled to conceal her breasts. But it's not like it mattered as the cloth didn't do much of anything. The second she hit even the smallest bit of light, she would be entirely bare for the world to see.

She turned her attention back to the dress as Nillipa fitted a tight silver belt, the only thing keeping the strands together, low at her hips. The shiny metal looked like a series of claws or talons as they dug into her sides at the waist. Dark green continued down her skin, the bottom half of the dress a long single piece of cloth that hardly managed to cover her front and back below the waist.

Goose bumps tickled her skin as the gown left her upper back and the whole sides of her exposed. She really hoped this feast was inside because if there was any sudden gust of wind, she feared this sorry excuse for clothing would come flying off of her.

Nillipa finished the ensemble by adding silver chains to her horns and placing a long necklace that dropped to her breasts around her neck. The pendant was rather simple, having only a small silver talon at the end.

Taking a step back, Nillipa admired her work. "There. All done."

Lillian glided over to the large mirror, her jaw almost dropping as she scarcely recognized the person who gazed back. Her eyes roved over the reflection, once again catching on the sensitive white skin on her sternum. Now she was able to see what it was.

Flames.

Beautiful flames that were somehow magically burned into her skin. The design was surprisingly tasteful. The swirls of fire were larger between her breasts and curled out to the sides to cup them, making it a rather large piece. Even though the dress was nothing more than a sheer cloth, she had to admit that it did accent her new flames nicely.

Her eyes drifted to the soiled bandage on her right arm, and she reached up a hand, unraveling it as she let the strip of cloth fall to the floor. A huge bite and slash took up most of her upper arm, but the deep wound was no longer bleeding, and she was glad to see that it was healing nicely. Whatever that flower was supposed to have done seemed to be working properly, and she was surprised there was no residue of the paste left on it.

A clap of Nillipa's hands caught her attention before she could dive back into that memory. "Off you go. We can't have the guest of honor being late."

Before the woman rushed her out of the room, Lillian dashed

over to the pile of her dirty clothes. She reached into the pocket of her pants, pulled out the wooden ring Peter had made her, and slipped it onto her finger. She wouldn't *dare* leave that behind.

Lillian didn't even have a chance to thank her again as she shimmied her out to the Ilaidae waiting outside. The guard looked her up and down once before turning to leave, not even bothering a single word.

Clutching onto her gossamer dress, she hurried after him as he led her to the feast.

Lillian had never felt so naked before in her life. Never was she one to be accustomed to wearing frilly gowns or scandalous attire. Not once in her life had she ever worn something so—she rifled her mind for that right word—so *revealing*.

And it wasn't that Lillian was self-conscious, she knew she had sinful curves that could drive any man to madness, but this was just being excessive.

Doing everything possible to ignore the transparent dress, she continued down the silent corridor, a tall ornate door coming into view. A force emitted from it, beckoning her to go through the nearer she got, and she was certain the feast would be behind the grand entrance.

Muffled music brayed out from behind the closed doors and, as they made their way closer, she could make out two guards standing still, each grasping a handle. They didn't so much as stop to look at her as they swung the door open—likely having done it a thousand times already that night.

With one last deep breath, she glanced down at her sheer dress once more. It was far too late to start being insecure now.

The music came to a halt, and the silver heeled sandals snaking up to her thighs echoed on the marble floors as she walked into what she assumed was the dining hall.

The ongoing chatter of the room vanished as all eyes turned to her.

Lillian willed the panic out of her mind as she drank in her surroundings. Gods, this room was magnificent.

The walls around the room were painted with the most devastating of murals—all depicting different scenarios of hardships in battles. The room had a strange octagonal shape to it and had numerous tables lining the various walls. The tables looked simple but were tastefully adorned to all look the same save for one. There wasn't a doubt in her mind as to where Allania was sitting.

Directly across from the grand entrance stood a beautiful table colored the deepest of onyxes. Behind the dark wood lay a large ornate chair—too grand to be for anyone other than a ruler—and two smaller chairs that looked just as intricate but not nearly as elegant as the one in the middle. Her gaze roved over the miniature thrones, and she was forced to remember her unfortunate encounter with Solrac this morning as she noticed carved serpents coiling up the chair's armrests.

Lillian began crossing the large expanse of the room towards the queen sitting atop her serpentine chair.

Her pupils darted to the sides as she looked at the Ilaidae around her. There was no mistaking this crowd for ordinary humans. Series of wings and strange colors of skin continuously caught her gaze, each creature more terrifying than the last.

That screen of false confidence stayed plastered on her face as she made her way across the room, silently commanding all eyes on her.

But she didn't care about them. There was only one person's attention she had wanted—and he was staring right at her as she maddingly swayed her hips.

Nolan's eyes wandered over her figure, halting as they caught on the sheer fabric covering her breasts.

A smirk danced on her lips as a feeling of satisfaction washed over her. She *knew* she looked damned good, and she would do everything in her power to make him regret what he'd done to her in those woods.

But as she thought on those words, she allowed herself to get lost in those dark eyes as their gazes locked.

There was a twinge in his expression, and she swore the Nolan she'd known in the woods had broken through that icy demeanor, but it only lasted for half a second before that unforgiving mask returned.

Making it all the way to the table, she held her head low, curtsying like she had done before.

Allania motioned for her to rise, a smile on her face. "Don't you look radiant."

Lillian bowed her head. "Thank you, my queen." She hated how good she was getting at this whole meek act.

Gesturing to the chair on her right she purred, "Come sit, my darling." Lillian did as she was asked and sat in the chair beside her as Allania turned to her brother standing in front of them. "Doesn't she look ravishing, Nolan? I know of a few males who would *die* to be with someone as devastating as her."

The idea of any Ilaidae male coming near her made her insides twist. And apparently, she wasn't the only one who hated the thought.

Nolan turned his attention to her, a muscle twitching in his jaw. A pinched expression veiled his face as he looked at her with what appeared to be a silent fury.

Was he.... *jealous*? That couldn't be right. It would be insane of him to be protective after all he had done to her. They had one moment—one stupid, unimportant moment—where Lillian's lust had gotten the best of her. That gave him *no* right over her or what she could do. But who knew, maybe Ilaidae men were strange and once you *interact* with one, they feel a certain level of... entitlement.

Lillian arched a brow in question as she shot a glance at his clenched jaw.

Dropping and relaxing his features, he strode up beside her and picked up one of her hands as he began lifting it to his lips.

Just the feel of him made sparks fly through her body. She hated the way her body betrayed her when he was near. It was only because he was the queen's brother that she wasn't at his throat with a knife.

But she wasn't so confident in that as his soft lips brushed against her sensitive hand, each touch a butterfly fluttering across her skin.

The memories of them by the gate came crashing into her as the mouth on her hand forced her to recall how good it had felt devouring her neck.

Blue eyes, laced with shadows, pierced into her as he murmured into her skin. "*Ravishing indeed.*"

Gods, she loathed the man.

But it was herself that she loathed more. She hated that two words—*two words*—could make her crave the man.

Lillian rolled her eyes, causing a chuckle to rumble out of him.

More memories flooded back in. Her heart couldn't take much more.

Some god must have taken mercy on her as he glided over to the queen's left and sat down in his designated chair; she wouldn't have been able to take much more of that.

Her mind throbbed as it battled itself. She didn't know what she wanted more—to murder the man who had caused her so much anguish or pounce on him and give herself over to what her body so desperately yearned. Definitely the former.

Mercifully she didn't have to analyze those confusing emotions as Allania got her attention. "Did you have fun with that first task?" Lillian swallowed hard at the question but didn't speak as the queen continued. "I couldn't help but notice that all the dogs are accounted for. Whatever did my poor Solrac eat?"

With all the preparation of the evening, she had almost forgotten how she had *accidentally* fed the giant snake one of her guards. Her heart flinched as she wasn't sure if that would get her punished. But she had made her choice when she'd locked that guard in. There was no point in hiding from it now. "Oh, Solrac looked like he needed *much* more nourishment than what that small dog could provide. Ilaidae seemed to be his preference." Her eyes glinted with something dark as she went on. "I'd be careful next time you visit. Never know when someone might push you in."

Sounds of someone coughing caught her attention. Turning to

Nolan, she saw him setting down his glass, his brows raised as a corner of his lip twitched upwards.

The queen glared at her brother who now stared at his plate as if were the most fascinating thing in the world. Allania looked at her through narrowed eyes, tongue poking the inside of her cheek. "Interesting."

Interesting? She didn't know what to make of that.

Seemingly bored with the conversation, the queen clapped her hands.

Seconds later, the doors burst open as Ilaidae with trays of food came bounding in. They made their way across the room, depositing a meal in front of every person they came to.

Her stomach growled as the delicious aroma enveloped the chamber, tendrils of foods drifting past her nose. When was the last time she had eaten?

Lillian watched with eager eyes as the trays made their way closer, and she was practically drooling by the time the food made its way over. It looked to be some simple assortment of meats and vegetables but, gods, did it smell heavenly.

Allania looked over at her with a saccharine smile. "Hungry, are we?"

That tone snapped her out of her trance. She didn't like the way she had said that. Lillian squinted at her food. Would she be bold enough to poison it?

It was obvious that she hadn't hid her suspicions as Allania let out a laugh. "You really think that after all this, poisoning your food is how I'm going to kill you?" Lillian could agree that it *would* be rather stupid to waste all this time to end her in such a plain manner. "Eat. You can rest assured that it won't kill you."

It had been ages since she'd had a real meal, and that was all her stomach had needed to hear to grab a fork and dig in. She stabbed an unfamiliar slab of meat and shoved it in her mouth. The food melted as she chewed; it was heaven on her tongue. She stuffed her face with the various foods decorating her plate, each one more savory than the last. But she halted herself from wolfing down another too large bite as she remembered that she should be eating at a slow pace, her stomach not being used to having such full meals. It would be wholly too embarrassing for her to throw up in the middle of the feast, especially being the guest of honor.

Throat feeling tight, Lillian grabbed her glass and took a sip as she looked over to Allania. Her vision was going fuzzy, and she blinked a few times to clear her sight.

A cruel grin was spread wide across Allania's face. The queen parted her lips to speak, but it came out all slow and distorted.

No—it wasn't her.

Lillian whipped her head around as time suddenly began to slow. Panicking, she opened her mouth to speak, but her tongue didn't cooperate as her words came out all slurred. Her head turned towards the queen, body gliding as if it were moving through honey.

Allania brushed a strand of Lillian's rust-colored hair behind her ear. "Now this… this is going to be fun."

Terror coiled around her gut at those few words as the feast around her faded into nothing.

CHAPTER 35

Ice grazed her senses as the chilled marble touched every inch of her body, the blanket wrapped around her doing nothing as the freezing floors seeped into her flesh.

There was a dull pounding in her head as she began to open her eyes, rubbing at them without entirely knowing where she was.

A glimpse of that familiar throne made of skulls was enough to jolt her awake completely, and she clutched on to the wool blanket as she made the horrible realization that it was the only thing concealing her unclothed body.

Where had her dress gone? She looked up at the window above the throne, light streaming in. Where had the *time* gone?

Her mind began running through the events of the previous night. It had been dark, and they had been at the feast. The servants had just brought the food. *The food.*

It all came rushing back to her.

That *lying* demon had told her the food wasn't poisoned.

Her face turned a ghostly shade of white.

No—she hadn't. She had only said that it wouldn't kill her.

Lillian gritted her teeth. At what? She hadn't the faintest clue. At Allania, at these stupid games, or at herself for being so stupid.

Eating the food likely wouldn't have been a choice, so she felt better knowing that if she'd refused, she would have been forced to consume it regardless. But that didn't matter, she should have at least been *expecting* a trick to have been played on her.

Lillian brought her gaze up to Allania who sat strewn across her throne as relaxed as a cat taking one of its numerous slumbers of the day.

"Is there a problem, Lillian?" A devious look glistened in her eyes. "Did you not enjoy yourself last night?"

Not a single syllable did she utter as she kept the blanket hugged around her and watched the vile queen rise.

Allania perused her disheveled state. "Well, at least if *you* didn't, I know of some other people who" —a snicker escaped her as her voice dropped wickedly low— "*enjoyed* you."

Lillian's eyes went wide as that stony face she'd been wearing vanished.

No—she couldn't be referring to that.

She looked down at the blanket in her hands. That *couldn't* be it—her breathing became faster—that couldn't be what happened.

Allania wore a smug satisfaction as she spoke. "What's the matter, Lillian? Would you like me to refresh your memory?"

No—she wouldn't. Because if what she insinuated was true…

Panic invaded her mind as she wrestled to control her breathing.

"Well," the queen began, "after you had finished eating that *delicious* meal, we had a chat for a little while but then it dawned on me—I was being far too selfish keeping you all to myself."

Lillian didn't even know if she was processing her words as she continued to watch her lips move, each phrase chipping off a piece of her.

Allania's grin turned wild, knowing she had gotten to her. "So I did what any good host would do. I shared you with rest of them." Lillian's stomach roiled as a nausea rushed her—but the queen went on, not caring how her words affected her. "That dress really must have caused quite the commotion, seeing as they all ran to tear it off."

Lillian didn't know if her heart could beat any faster without exploding out of her chest. The color had drained from her body as her stomach threatened to empty itself all over the marble floor.

This couldn't be real. This couldn't be happening. They couldn't have done—*that*.

Tears welled up in her eyes as Allania continued to tear her down word by word, but the torment paused as everything went silent and Nolan sauntered in.

A proud fierceness overtook the queen's features at his entrance. "But they were all fools to think they could beat my brother. You should have seen how he fought."

The world stopped. She didn't know if she was breathing. Her face dropped as she lifted her gaze to Nolan, the whole room turning to look at him at once.

A smirk formed on his lips, a complement to that vile mask. Nolan feigned offense as he spoke. "Don't tell me you don't remember,

Lil?"

Her heart stumbled, threatening to shatter into a million pieces at the sound of her name on his tongue.

Not him. *Anyone* but him.

She prayed that his was all a horrible nightmare, that she would awake in the dungeon in mere moments. But this was real—this was happening. Her lungs struggled to draw in air as she waited for him to confirm what she already knew to be true.

"I thought you were having a rather fun time when I whisked you away to my chambers. You even screamed my name." He pinched his lips as he looked upwards, pretending to ponder his words until an amused smile appeared. "But now that I'm thinking about it… it was only the first two letters."

Lillian ran to a corner as she heaved up her insides. She didn't care if she was embarrassing herself anymore—didn't care about what they thought as she wiped her mouth. Lillian looked down at herself. She didn't feel any different, but she knew everything was. He—he had…

She threw up once more, not wanting to process what he claimed to have done to her. After all that had happened, she hated that she was still shocked he could have done something so horrible. Th—that he was capable of doing that to her.

Tears streamed down her face as she clutched her stomach. How pathetic she must look. For some twisted reason, a part of her deep down had still trusted him—had *yearned* for him. She had wanted to believe that the man from the forest was in there somewhere, but now she knew for certain it had all been a fabricated illusion only to gain her trust.

She'd never make that same mistake again.

Standing tall, she wiped her mouth and the drops on her cheeks. She was done getting her feelings hurt over someone so insignificant. She came here for one thing and nothing else.

Willing her face into a frosty indifference, she squared her shoulders as she strode over to the throne—not bothering to spare a glance in Nolan's direction as she stared at the queen. A lethal calm shadowed her voice. "I came here for one reason, my queen. Let me compete in the Trial of the Flame."

Allania nodded her head in what she deduced was her more *impressed* look. "All in good time, darling. The trial will take place when I so choose, but I do have another chore in mind to keep you busy." Lillian didn't dare let any emotion show as she let the queen speak. "The hedges need to be clipped. My guards will take you there as soon as you get dressed," she said, pointing to a pile of clothes in the corner.

Walking over to where she had gestured, she was glad to see they were a simple tunic and pants. Modesty was useless at this point, seeing as the whole room had already seen her, and she forced herself not to think on how they had stripped her bare as Lillian dropped the blanket to the floor and clothed herself.

The guards began leading her away, and she heard Allania's voice call out in the distance. "Be sure not to get *too* tangled up in the vines."

Lillian didn't care to give the queen a response as her legs dragged her out of the throne room.

The Ilaidae men led her through a series of halls—all colored the same deep onyx—as she compelled herself not to think of what had occurred in that chamber. She couldn't afford to break down—not now. She needed her strength for right now and for whenever that queen decided to have the trial, but after that… she would let herself wallow in her misery as much as her heart wanted.

If she even got that far.

It was unnerving that the thought of no longer living didn't bother her as much as it had before. She felt broken. A hole had already been growing inside her but now that hole was threatening to swallow her entirely.

Bringing her hands up, Lillian rubbed at her eyes, trying anything to distract herself from bursting into tears yet again. As she wiped her face, her vision snagged on that wooden band around her finger, the one that had been given to her so long ago.

Lillian's heart swelled as thoughts of Peter whirled in her mind. She wished he was here by her side. A part of him always would be, she realized as she continued to stare at the simple ring, letting a warmth fill her. He would have been *much* better suited to be champion. He wouldn't have let these awful creatures wound him like they had so easily done her.

Her mood darkened as thoughts of him forced her to recall the day he had been so wrongfully taken away—when he had been murdered by that Ilaidae. A renewed sense of determination settled over her at that memory.

That was why she was here.

She wouldn't let what happened to Peter be the fate of her family—or anyone for that matter. No one deserved this. To be around these wretched monsters—to be subject to all the horrors they could inflict. If she had to be the one to take all their cruelty to save them, then so be it. Lillian wouldn't let anyone go through what she had. She would do that stupid trial, and she would *win*. Failure wasn't an option.

Not wanting to risk losing it in whatever chore Allania had given her now, Lillian slipped the ring off her finger and slid it into her pocket.

Clip the hedges. It sounded simple enough, but, if she had taken anything away from the last chore, she knew it was anything but.

The guards took her through a door that led out into a large courtyard, and her eyes landed on a simple fountain in its center, not nearly as intricate as the one in the throne room. Her eyes turned towards the walls and lining them were series of tall rose bushes, each with various vines and leaves running rampant.

As she looked closer at the roses, she noted their coloring. In Grigaros, she had only ever seen white or red roses, but the ones surrounding the courtyard were the deepest of blacks. Lillian rolled her eyes as she sensed a rather obvious theme going on in the castle.

She followed the guards as they walked on a stone path, both men making cautious efforts to avoid the grass. They strolled towards the fountain, and she noticed a pair of shears and crimson boots leaning against it.

One of the guards bent over, picking both items up and handed her the boots. "You're going to want to put these on. The grass has a tendency of wanting to wrap around you. The boots will stop that."

Great, she thought to herself. Magical grass that had attachment issues—why would she have been expecting anything else?

Lillian looked at the thorny bushes. "Do the hedges do that too?"

The guard nodded. "Just don't get too close to them, and you should be fine. Let the shears be the extra reach you need." Lillian gave an incline in understanding as he handed her the shears. "We'll be waiting for you inside when you're done."

The Ilaidae males went back the way they came, leaving her completely alone to deal with the magical thornery.

Slipping the boots on, she stood and took the shears in her hand as she looked at the grass in front of her. It *looked* normal, but she knew by now nothing here ever was.

Using the utmost caution, she put a foot down on the cropped lawn.

Nothing happened.

A small part of her had been expecting the guards to have lied and that the grass would swallow her whole, but she was glad that hadn't been the case. Now feeling slightly more sure that it wouldn't tangle her up, she placed both feet on the ground.

Glancing up from her new shoes to the hedges around her, she noticed that they thankfully didn't look too bad. They were decently trimmed save for a few loose vines here and there. If they had been any worse, it would have taken her the entire day to clean up the whole courtyard.

With one last sigh, she walked over to the first rose bush and got to work.

For someone who hated gardening so much, she was damn good at cleaning one up.

Several hours had passed, and only a few more hedges remained. Granted all she was doing was snapping a few wild vines, but it still wasn't an easy task as she felt aches in her already sore arms.

The discomfort was only magnified as the sun blared down on her, causing sweat to bead down her forehead. She would need a nice long bath after this, but she frowned as she realized that it had most likely been a one-time occurrence.

She moved on to the next shrub as the wind picked up, the tendrils of air kissing her sweat-stained face and providing some much-needed relief from the sweltering heat.

Lillian breathed in the sudden gust of freshness as she sighed. This was *exactly* what she had needed. But she refocused her attention on the chore and kept snipping the shrubs as the wind continued to grow more intense.

The breeze still strangely strong, she stopped her cutting and peered up at the sky. It *looked* like a clear day, but the winds seemed to disagree as they were indicating a storm was coming.

Brushing past the odd change of weather, she decided not to think much of it and went back to her chore a little faster now, trying to finish in case a storm did come.

The winds continued to get wilder, and her hair began flying around her face as she tried to keep on clipping the hedges, the task infinitely harder now as her long strands blinded her.

Lillian grabbed the shears with one hand as she wrestled her lengthy locks, but she found her chaotic mane to be the least of her problems as the shears flew out of her hand and shot across the courtyard.

This couldn't be natural.

Now having two free hands, she put her hair up into a crazed bun as she surveyed the area around her. The vicious winds were slamming the bushes into one another as the water from the fountain sloshed out, soaking into the grassy lawn. The winds had turned so powerful that even the hedges had started being dragged across the yard.

Lillian glanced back towards the hedges. That couldn't be right. She looked down at her feet and was left horror stricken as she realized that it was *herself* that was being dragged.

Clawing at the air around her, she flailed her arms, fighting against the wind, but it was of no use as she continued being shoved through the courtyard.

The entire garden glided past her until she stopped, something prickly touching her arm. She didn't think on whatever brushed against her as the strong breeze vanished almost as quickly as it had appeared, and the day resumed to its previously sultry temperature.

Her hair was still as wild as ever, and she went to fix her unruly locks but felt resistance when she tried bringing her left arm up. On instinct, she yanked again but stopped as an intense sharp pain lanced through her limb. Her skin blanched at what she beheld.

Her arm was touching the rose bush.

Fear coursed through her as the thorny vines began creeping up her hand at a leisurely place. *No, no, no*. This was the one thing she had been warned against. Of course, she had managed to do the *one thing* she had been cautioned against.

The prickly plant continued crawling up her limb, and she knew that she had to think fast. Lillian tried pulling her arm back for the third time but stopped as she felt the barbs sink into her delicate skin. If she did that, she would end up tearing her arm open.

Lillian desperately looked around for anything that would help and cursed as she saw the shears lying across the garden. Her voice turned hoarse as she yelled for the guards, but she knew no one would come. She was utterly alone as the spiked plant continued pulling her in.

What options did she have left? Do nothing and let the plant wrap around her completely… or yank her arm out now. Time was running out as the vine was already almost to her elbow. Her breaths turned quicker as her eyes darted down at her arm. It looked like the latter was her only choice.

She couldn't wait too much longer or else she would be marring more skin than she had to. Lillian took in a shuddering breath, feeling faint as she prepared herself for the excruciating sensation. Only slightly tugging her arm had caused her such an intense pain, so she could only *imagine* what tearing herself free would feel like.

The vine was about to cross her elbow—she had to do it now.

Clenching her teeth to the point they might break, she pulled on her arm with all her strength.

Screams of agony roared out of her as the thorns dug into her arm, shredding her muscle and skin. Ripping flesh would forever haunt her ears, each tear sounding like leathery fabric being forced apart.

After an excruciating few seconds, she opened her eyes and stared at her forearm as blood poured out from the numerous deep wounds. Oh, this wasn't good. She needed to stop the bleeding *now,* or she might lose too much.

The guards came rushing in at her screams, their eyes going wide as they took in her arm. One of them yelled something about getting the healer, but she couldn't hear it very well as her vision started going in and out.

Her lids blinked once, and she was confused as to how she had gotten to be lying on the floor in the hallway.

The two guards—and what she assumed was the healer—were kneeling next to her as one of them plucked out thorns and another started securing a bandage around her arm. They were speaking amongst themselves, and she heard the one with the bandages utter that she would be fine as he pulled out a vial from his belt and shoved it down her throat.

A new feeling of invigoration flowed in her as she swallowed down the liquid. She looked at the vial in the man's hand as he continued wrapping her arm. "What was that?" she asked.

"Just something to ease the pain and liven you up a little."

Testing what he claimed, she flexed her arm and was shocked that no pain radiated from it.

The Ilaidae finished with the bandages and stood up, reaching out his arm to her. "The queen is waiting for you."

Lillian took the man's hand and eased herself onto her feet.

The guards didn't skip a beat as one of them grabbed her by her uninjured arm and began leading her away.

Yanked so forcefully that she was stumbling over her feet, she was led down another ebony hallway towards what she now recognized was the path to the throne room. They opened the doors and shoved her inside, slamming the grand double doors shut behind her.

The throne room looked exactly like it usually did save for one thing. An X-shaped cross stood in the center of the room with a man shackled to it.

Lillian approached the man with cautious steps and narrowed eyes.

He was battered and bruised, his clothes stained with blood, and she could see gashes covering his body as well as an ankle bent in the wrong direction.

Her nose wrinkled as a wave of empathy crashed through her for the poor man.

As she stared at the individual and his black, gray streaked hair, she couldn't help but feel a familiar air surrounding him. She came to a stop before him and watched as he struggled to raise his head.

A jolt shattered through her as she stumbled back a step. Air failed to reach her as her voice quivered and shook. "Father?"

CHAPTER 36

Her heart thrashed in her chest as the man who raised her hung strewn upon a wooden X. Every inch of him was bruised, a nasty shade of blue and purple tinging his skin.

He squinted his painfully colored eyes as his voice came out far too faint. "Lillian? Is that you?"

Tears streamed down her face as she ran towards him and put a hand up to his face. "It's me. I'm here."

He smiled despite whatever agony he was in. "My sweet Lily. I found you."

Her body trembled as if lightning crackled under her skin. "Why would you come here?" Lillian looked over his ruined state as her voice began collapsing. "Look what they've done to you."

Her father winced as his expression hardened. "It doesn't matter what they did. I couldn't let you be out here alone. I couldn't fail you again."

More tears poured down her face as she laid her head on his chest. "You never *failed* me. Don't say that."

Someone's voice came from the far end of the room. No, not someone—*Allania*. "How sweet," she crooned.

Rage replaced her sorrow as she looked at the wretched queen. Lillian's eyes held only malice as she turned her attention to her. "*You*." Allania raised a brow as she parted her lips, but Lillian didn't let her speak. "*You did this*."

The corners of her mouth flicked upwards. "And what if I did? Tell me, Lillian, what would you do if I did?"

Her head roared in anger as she looked at the queen with nothing but fury.

Her father. *Her father* who had come looking for her—who had thought he had failed her—had come all this way through the treacherous woods for *her*. All for her and that stupid fight they'd gotten in when she had gone looking for that boy in the woods. *And this*—this is what he got?

No. She wouldn't accept that. Someone would pay for this. Someone *had* to.

Lillian balled her hands into fists, nails digging into her palms as she thought of all the horrible things she would do to this woman—how she would revel in her death. She didn't care what kind of person that made her as she let those venomous thoughts consume her whole, a warped sense of darkness slowly erupting inside her.

Her ire must have been obvious as Allania shook her head. "Careful, Lillian," she tsked. "It would be unwise for you to lose your temper, *especially* with your poor father here. What would he say of your bad manners?"

It took everything in her to battle the growing shadows as she tried to remain calm. Her nostrils flared as her whole body shook, her limbs wishing they could tear this heinous queen's head clean off.

But she wrestled against herself, forcing her anger to go from a boil to a simmer. It would do her father no good if she lost it. Her biggest concern right now was getting him out of here in one piece.

A heartless façade smothered her frenzy of rage, and she stared up at the queen.

Allania smirked in amusement at her obedient little toy. "That's *much* better, my darling. After all, this was supposed to be a nice surprise." She clapped her hands together in a twisted glee. "Isn't this family reunion fun? He was rather easy to find screaming your name out in the woods."

Lillian looked up at the perverted queen. She was done being a part of whatever sick game this was. "What do you want with him? I'm your champion. There was no need to bring him into this."

The queen stood from her throne and took slow, lazy steps to where she stood. "On the contrary my… what did he call you again?" —she feigned realization— "There was *much* need to bring him into this—*my sweet Lily*."

Lillian seethed; this sadistic monster was *really* testing her limits.

Allania strutted up to where her father hung strung up.

A surge of protectiveness flooded her the closer she got, but there was absolutely nothing Lillian could do as she walked right up to his limp form.

"Let's play a little game, shall we?" Allania grabbed her father's chin and spoke to him as if he were a child. "But you don't talk or else it makes this no fun."

Letting go of him, she turned her savage gaze to Lillian. "It's a rather simple game really. You just answer one question honestly—and I mean *honestly*—and your father gets to live. Seem easy enough?"

Already, she didn't like where this was going. There had to be some twisted catch, and she didn't want her father to be any part of it. "Please, just let him go," she begged. "I'll tell you whatever it is you want but just let him go."

Allania's gaze flicked upwards as she exaggerated a sigh. Turning to look at her father, the queen spoke to him as if Lillian weren't standing right there in front of them. "It seems this *one* child of yours didn't turn out to be the brightest. I suppose you can always try aga—" She sucked on her teeth, wincing as if her words had somehow cut deeper than she had intended. Allania cringed as she cast a glance down at her father's groin. "How insensitive of me. I forgot that after our previous encounter—that's not really an option anymore, is it?"

Shame glistened in her father's eyes as he looked downwards, chin dropping to his chest.

Red—she saw red.

So clearly could she picture herself holding a knife to that bitch's throat, laughing as she felt the spray of blood coat her. She vowed that the vision would turn into a reality.

The queen clapped her hands together, moving on as if the previous conversation hadn't just occurred. "Now to the game."

Lillian clenched her teeth together, barely managing to rein in her wrath.

Everyone's attention turned to the door as it slammed shut with a boom. It felt strange that she had already grown accustomed to the crowd of Ilaidae watching her every move. They all waited in excited anticipation as Nolan stepped out from behind the throne.

She didn't give him a reaction. She didn't have time to think about what had happened this morning. He wasn't worth her time. Her father was more important than anything he'd ever done to her.

Allania had the nerve to look giddy as he walked up next to her. "Perfect timing brother! We were just about to start."

With his brows pressed together, his head jolted back a centimeter as he took in her father strapped to the wooden X. Whatever initial emotion had been his instinctual response, it got drowned by the cruelty he wore so well. "And this is…?" he asked, gesturing to her father's chained figure.

The Ilaidae queen smiled wildly. "Lillian's father has so *kindly* decided to be a part of this fun game of mine."

Lillian observed Nolan's face, looking for any inkling of a reaction, but his face remained its usual harsh self, except for something in his eyes. Shadows flecked them as if holding fragments of something. But she brushed past that observation; she didn't care how he felt, if he even felt anything at all.

As Allania went on explaining the rules to Nolan, she noticed his gaze snagged on her bandaged forearm for a brief moment before he went back to ignoring her. She looked down at her arm and was shocked that she had almost forgotten about it completely—whatever had been in that little vial seemed to still be working.

She was snapped out of the depths of her mind as Allania used the endearing name her father always preferred. "Sweet Lily, here, is to answer my question honestly or her father dies." She then explained that it was necessary for her father to remain silent for the game to be fair, so no answers were swayed. "Now before we begin, there's a few things we need to clear up. I take it no one has explained the nature of the trials, correct?"

Lillian gave a singular nod.

"Good, it was made that way on purpose. But I suppose it's time you knew."

A flutter bloomed in her chest as her pulse quickened. This was it. This was the burning question she'd been waiting for an eternity to be answered. Everyone she had ever asked knew nothing or had refused to tell her. But now—now she would finally know.

"The trial is different for each champion, each tailored specifically for them. But do you know why that is?"

Lillian shook her head, not sure if she wanted a real answer.

A knowing smile decorated her. "I didn't think so. The trial each champion must face…" This was it—this was the moment she'd been waiting for. "… is that of their greatest fear."

Her stomach sank as her face dropped.

"Now are you ready to hear my question?" Lillian didn't need to hear it to know what she was going to ask. Allania's face turned ruthless as her tone lowered. "What is your greatest fear, Lillian?"

Lillian did little to hide the look of shock and terror on her face.

That was what the trial was? She didn't know whether she felt relieved or worse now that she finally knew. At least she could find solace in that it wasn't going to be some horribly awful task where she would have to fight to the death with some absurdly strong Ilaidae.

But that meant…

Processing the part about it being her greatest fear hadn't yet happened as she had been too focused on it not being some terrifying task—but now it was setting in. The color leeched from her skin as she remembered what her fear was.

Gods, she was an idiot. Her fear was so pathetic that it made complete sense that it would be the thing to kill her. It would be the perfect end to her perfectly miserable existence. Laughing roared in her head at how ridiculous this all was, and Allania looked at her strangely making her think it might have been out loud. She didn't know—she didn't *care*. Not when her big fear was this stupid.

Swimming—*swimming* was her greatest fear.

A wave of embarrassment settled over her. Would Allania even accept that? Or would she just deem it too pitiful and force her to pick something else. Lillian didn't know if that would be better or worse, at least if it were something else, she might have a fighting chance.

Years she'd been trying to swim—*years*. But anytime she hit the water, something happened in her body where her legs stiffened, and she sunk to the bottom like a brick. Every time, without fail, when her father would make her try, he would have to inevitably dive in to save her from drowning.

Allania gave her a pointed glance as she tilted her head. "Well? What's it going to be, Lillian?"

Panic started coursing through her. She couldn't swim—she just couldn't. There had to be another option—another version of the trial where she could *at least* have a chance. Lillian blanched and opened her too dry mouth to speak, but words didn't seem to want to form.

Allania was seriously irritated now. "Did I mention this game is *timed,* Lillian? I don't have all day for you to decide on a choice. But you do surprise me, I thought saving your father would be the obvious option but perhaps I've misjudged you yet."

Lillian abhorred what this vile witch was insinuating. Of course she would choose her father over anything—even herself. She was just trying to stall as she thought of a way out of this. But nothing was coming to mind, and she was running out of time.

She parted her lips. To say what? She had no idea. But whatever had been about to roll off her tongue got interrupted as her father's frail voice filled the room. "Don't listen to them, Lily—don't play their wretched games. I'm an old man, I've lived my life, but you can still live yours."

Tears began to blur her vision as she stared at her father—her father, who was so willing to give up his life for hers. Lillian's heart swelled as she looked at him. She wouldn't let him die for her. Not now—not *ever*. She knew what she had to do.

Lillian turned her eyes to Allania who had begun shaking her head as she wore a half-clenched smile. Her voice dripped of false sympathy as she spoke. "Now what was my *one* rule? I see where your daughter gets her inability to follow simple directions from. I thought I said no talking." Allania pouted and turned to her brother. "Didn't I say no talking?"

Nolan pressed his lips together and gave a nod. "I do recall that being said."

The Ilaidae queen groaned as if she wasn't enjoying every second of this. "Now what am I to do? I very well can't let that go unpunished. How would that look if it was known that my orders don't have to be followed?" That sinister smile appeared on her as she looked at her brother. "What do you think—are two fingers enough?"

Lillian's face turned ghostly white as her breathing turned more frantic.

Her attention turned to Nolan as he bobbed his head back and forth in consideration. How she loathed his wicked voice. "*Technically,* he broke two rules if we count the speaking *and* swaying her decision. So really an entire hand would be more appropriate."

Allania let out a depraved laugh. "I love the way that mind of yours works, but since Lillian has been such a kind guest—I'm feeling merciful."

Lillian prayed that they would leave him unharmed—he didn't deserve this. It should be *her* strung up there—not him. But none of what she thought mattered as Allania said the words she hadn't wanted to hear. "Two fingers should suffice."

A guard came up to the queen and handed her a sharpened axe as she ordered another one of them to hold her father's arm out steady. Allania began bringing the axe to his fingers and her father didn't so much as react as he continued to hang his head low, already defeated and no longer wanting to fight.

Fear for her father began to rush through her veins as she began yelling hysterically. "Stop, please! I'll tell you whatever you want—anything! Just please, *please,* don't hurt him."

The Ilaidae tyrant stopped the axe mere inches away from his finger as she raised an eyebrow in waiting. "What is it, Lillian? Out with it."

Taking one last shuddering breath, she readied herself. It wouldn't be so bad—would it? Her heart galloped at a crazed pace, and she hadn't even uttered a word. There was no more stalling, no more thinking of a way out; she had to spit it out now. "Swimming—my greatest fear is swimming."

Allania's eyes widened as an uncomfortable air settled across the room. "You can't be serious?" she finally said.

Red began to stain Lillian's cheeks at the obvious mocking.

"By the gods, it is."

The queen doubled over in laughter and the entire audience joined in as dozens of Ilaidae all ridiculed her at once. Allania wheezed as she struggled to catch her breath, chuckles continuing to escape her. "Swimming—*swimming* is your greatest fear? I can't decide if that makes you incredibly brave or downright pitiful."

Lillian didn't care if they made fun of her—all she cared about was that Allania had dropped the axe and stepped away from her father.

The queen gestured to his figure strung up. "Unchain the poor man. He's been through enough."

They unshackled him, letting him drop to the floor, and she ran up to him as she took him into her arms. Not even a second passed before her face turned damp. "I'm here—your Lily's here."

He felt so weak as he struggled to hold her tight, his eyes leaking into her shoulder. She had never seen him so broken. "I'm so sorry.

I'm so sorry I failed you, Lily."

More tears poured down her cheeks. "You didn't—you never have."

Allania clapped once in the distance. "That's enough of that," she barked.

Two guards came up and pried her father out of her arms as Lillian's eyes darted back and forth from Allania and her father. "What's going on? Where are you taking him?"

Terror razed her senses as one of the Ilaidae holding her father pulled out a small dagger. She went to lunge after him but couldn't as two strong arms wrapped around her, pinning her in place. Whipping her head around, she saw Nolan holding her tightly.

She thrashed as the queen grinned at her. "I'm sorry, Lily, but what did you expect? I don't particularly like people who make me wait. You really should've answered faster."

Lillian's eyes went wide as she watched the queen nod to the guard holding the blade. The color drained from her as she began to flail in Nolan's arms, doing anything to get him to let her go. Sobs spilled down her face as she bit, kicked, and screamed, but he held on strong, and all she could do was watch as the guard raised the blade to her father's neck.

A pained voice whispered in her ear as she continued to thrash. "I'm so sorry."

But she didn't register it as she watched the metal slice clean across her father's throat.

Time stopped as waves of blood spurted from his gash. Her shrieks vibrated the throne room as her father collapsed to the floor, choking on the blood spewing from his mouth. She didn't stop screaming—not even after her throat burned her to continue.

Nolan let her go, and she sprinted to her father lying on the floor. She ripped off part of her shirt and held it up to his neck, desperately trying to stop his bleeding.

No, no, no… Gods, she prayed this wasn't actually happening.

A flood of tears tried escaping her eyes as her voice felt tight. "Please don't leave me. Please just stay." Her lips quivered as he struggled to raise his hand up to her face, and she picked it up, bringing it the rest of the way up. She nuzzled her cheek against his warm palm and repeated her same words from earlier. "I'm here—your Lily's here." Her face trembled as she tried smiling at him. "You found me."

Her father looked at her, eyes so full of love before they blinked one last time and glossed over. Lillian choked on a sob as she felt his hand go limp in hers.

No, not yet—he couldn't leave her yet.

Lillian's low voice turned to screams as she called out, pleading for her father.

Allania's laughs echoed in the room as she continued to yell out in tears. "Guards, take this pathetic thing to her cell," ordered the queen.

Lillian screamed as the guards tore her away from her father. She had to stay with him—she couldn't leave him. Fighting with everything, she thrashed as they picked her up and began dragging her away towards the door.

The air felt too cold, and her chest felt like it would cave in from pressure as she was hauled away. She looked back at her father for what she knew was the last time, and her heart snapped in half as she saw his lifeless body, lying still on the cold marble floor.

CHAPTER 37

Lillian didn't bother fighting them as they tossed her in the dungeon cell—didn't care about the pain as her body skidded and scraped across the stony floor.

She was back where she started… but nothing felt the same. Gods, so much had happened in these past few days.

It was all too painful for her to think about, but her mind didn't give her a choice as it began to piece apart her time here, replaying those stupid chores and the feast that she could scarcely even remember.

It was a small blessing that she didn't have memories of that night—but it didn't make her feel any less tainted. She still hadn't processed what Nolan claimed to have done to her, hadn't had a moments peace to fully take in what he'd boasted.

A part of her was thankful that she'd been forced to push it in the back of her mind and forget about it for a while—because if she took even a minute to pick apart all that he had done, she would shatter completely.

Tears continued falling down her cheeks as moments cascaded through her broken mind—she hadn't stopped crying since the throne room.

Strangled sobs crashed out of her as her thoughts betrayed her and made her relive it all. Lillian held herself as she wept, still being able picture it so clearly—still able to perfectly see the blade as it sliced across her father's already too damaged skin.

He was gone—he was really gone.

She had wanted to lunge after the guard who'd been holding the blade. Anything, she would have done absolutely anything in that moment to stop it from touching her father. But she hadn't been able to; she had been held back… by *him*.

Images of his arms wrapped around her poured into her head. Nolan had been holding her back, using all his force to keep her tightly in place. She wasn't sure how much strength Ilaidae had, but they must have a considerable amount for him to have been able to hold on to her with all the flailing she'd been doing.

A faint memory tugged at the back of her mind. He had said something. She struggled to remember the few words he had uttered when it all at once flashed into her.

Had he… had he said he was sorry?

How would that make any sense? Why would he be sorry for her father's death? He thrived on being a malevolent monster just like his sister.

The insides of her skull pounded as she tried to decipher what those words meant. Hurting already too much, she went back to replaying the horrible moment.

He had been holding her back when it all happened. Lillian knew she should be grateful that someone had been keeping her back because, if he hadn't been, she would've certainly done something that would have gotten her killed. Her family didn't need two people to mourn.

More sobs poured out at that notion.

Gods, what would she tell them? How could she even *begin* to explain what had occurred?

Thoughts of the trial ahead swarmed her. The grief her family would go through if they lost her father *and* her in one swift go. Her dying wasn't an option. She needed to live, needed to ease her family's pain at what had so wrongfully taken place.

Swim. All she had to do was swim. Sounded simple enough, but she knew it wasn't as her heart began to race, panic coursing through her veins. Gods, she was so weak—it was just a *little* water.

Her chest hitched as she took in shuddering, shallow breaths, attempting to steady herself. She had to get back to her family, had to live even if it was out of sheer stubbornness.

A droplet slid down her cheek as a dark thought seeped into her mind. Would they even want her back? It had been her fault that her father had come all this way.

Bringing a hand up to her mouth, she muffled a sob. S*he* was the sole reason he had been out here; he had been calling out *her* name when he had been captured. Lillian laid her head down on the floor, lacking the strength to hold herself up.

If only she had answered the question faster, he might still be here.

The darkness continued to envelop her as she went deeper into a pit of despair. Her family wouldn't want her back. She was far too damaged and had already caused them enough grief. They didn't need any more problems.

The image of her father's lifeless corpse kept flashing in her mind as the words, *my fault*, repeated in a horrific loop.

With that phrase strong in her head, she cried herself to sleep, nightmares of her father plaguing her throughout the night.

CHAPTER 38

Everything was dark. Everything was broken. Her skin, her heart, her. Nothing felt right anymore.

She hoped this darkness was the end, that somehow she had slipped into the afterlife in her sleep—but the feel of the cold stone told her otherwise.

Pain and defeat. That's what it felt like to be in this wretched cell.

She wasn't sure how long she'd been in here, the pitch black being unending. Perhaps they had forgotten about her—perhaps this was another cruel trick, and they would keep her here until she went mad. Minutes, hours, days, it didn't really matter at this point. It had all gone so horribly wrong.

Her already shattered heart fractured even more at the thought of what had happened in that throne room.

It was all her fault.

Tears streamed down her face as she shut her eyes, a broken part of her praying that it would all swiftly end.

CHAPTER 39

Light flickered through her closed lids, and she squinted as the flames of the torches lining the walls burned into her sensitive eyes.

The cell door rattled open, and she blinked her sight into focus, one of Allania's guards motioning for her to come. "Get up," he ordered.

Lillian stood and glanced down at the blade sheathed at his side—all the guards wore similar uniforms, and the dagger resembled the one that had glided across her father's neck.

Anger began to cloud her vision as she took in the guard before her. He wasn't the same one, but he might as well have been. They all followed *her* orders. It could've just as easily been him who had executed the sentence.

Her nostrils flared as she wrestled her growing fury. It wasn't the guards she was mad at—all they had been doing was following their queen's commands—it was *Allania* she wanted to make suffer.

Lillian willed air to fill her lungs. The trial—she just had to get through the trial. After that everything would be over, whether it ended for the better or worse, it would at least be *over*.

Something about knowing that caused a calm to settle in her bones, and she walked over towards the guard, letting him lead her out to where she assumed was Allania. They made their way through the halls, and the usual ornate onyx doors greeted her as she waltzed into the throne room. The large chambers were back to how they usually looked, making it seem like nothing had ever occurred.

She looked over to where she had last seen her father's lifeless body—where she had last felt the warm touch of his hand before she had been torn away. But when her eyes landed on the spot where his blood had poured out and pooled on the floor, all she saw was the polished marble floor glossed and shiny.

She didn't even bother curtsying as the queen's lips curled into a malicious grin. "Sleep well?"

Lillian was done playing her stupid game. "Just tell me what you want me to do."

Allania tilted her head as she brought a finger up to her parted lip. "Where are your manners today, Lillian? Oh, how I cherished your lovely demeanor."

Silence was all she gave her as Lillian waited for whatever chore she would delegate to her today.

The Ilaidae ruler's smile dropped as a look of ire surfaced onto her face. "Fine, no more playing nice today, I see. But before I give you a new chore, let's go over the last one."

Lillian stared, not allowing any emotion to show. She was done giving Allania the reactions she so badly craved.

The queen clenched her teeth at her, but a sneer soon emerged as her gaze drifted down to Lillian's bandaged arm. Malice glinted in her eyes as she pursed her lips together and created a faint wind that blew Lillian's hair behind her shoulders. "It was a little windy that day, wasn't it?"

Her nails dug into her skin from the force Lillian used in holding them tight. Hate—so much hate. That wretched witch had caused her arm to snag in the bush—*she* was the sole reason that she'd had to tear her arm open to get out. The gashes had been so severe that she might've bled to death had the healer not been so quick. Her skin would be scarred for the rest of her life and all because of what—because it amused her?

The queen's mouth tugged upwards, pleased that she had gotten the reaction she wanted. That Lillian had given it only fueled her fury even more.

"Now, moving on to today. I need you to clean up a room." Guards emerged as she clapped her hands, the Ilaidae whisking Lillian away by the arms. "Don't leave me waiting too long, Lillian." There was no need to even see her to know that she had an evil grin plastered onto her as she added the last few words. "You *know* how I hate it."

She was sick of being dragged around this wretched castle.

Very easily could she walk on her own, but she wasn't given the option as they hauled her along the many winding halls. They went up a vast number of steps as they brought her up a spiraling tower and stopped at a wooden door at the top.

A mop and a bucket filled with soapy water leaned against the wall as one of the guards pointed to them. "All you have to do is clean the moldy areas."

Lillian looked at the mop and then back at the guards. "That's it?"

The guard nodded. "That's it."

They let go of her arms, depositing her at the door, and began their descent down the spiraling staircase, leaving her alone with the bucket and mop.

She picked up her long hair, throwing it up, and then grabbed the mop and pail as she stood before the door, speaking out loud to herself. "Clean a room. I can clean a room."

Turning the doorknob, she swung open the door—almost dropping the supplies at what she beheld.

The layout of the room resembled one of any ordinary bedroom, but the part that made her jerk a step back was the layer of thick black mold that covered the entire room. Walls, floor, and ceiling alike were all covered with patchy patterns of the dark growth.

One whiff of the room made her nostrils burn with how strong it smelled. Lillian groaned and muttered a curse to herself as she held a sleeve up to her face.

"And so it begins," she murmured as she shoved the mop into the water-filled pail and got to work.

Lillian wiped at her sweat drenched forehead as she picked up her black stained mop and dunked it in the bucket for the thousandth time.

She had been at this for at least an hour and had barely made a dent. Her nose had gotten used to breathing in the powerful stench, and her eyes only stung a little as she ventured deeper into the room.

Submerging the filthy mop into the soapy water once more, she paused as she noticed a large welt on her hand. Had something bit her—a bug that she maybe hadn't noticed? She went to touch the angry red skin and winced as a throbbing pain radiated from it. What in the hell was that?

Her eyes drifted towards the ceiling, noting more of the disgusting mold. She couldn't afford to be distracted; there was so much more of the room left to clean and she still hadn't the faintest idea how she would get anything up there.

Sighing, she grabbed the mop anew, trying to ignore the welt as she scrubbed at the muck-covered floors.

Half an hour had passed, and she wiped her damp forehead again; gods, it was getting hot in this room.

She began rolling up one of her sleeves and noticed another piece of blotched skin peeking out. Lillian yanked the rest of her sleeve up, revealing more of those throbbing welts covering her soft skin. With hurried hands she tore up her other sleeve to see more of the swollen lumps coating her body.

Growing frantic, she searched the rest of her body, more and more welts beginning to appear everywhere she looked.

What was happening to her? This all couldn't be some bug that she hadn't noticed.

Her throat tightened as she coughed from breathing in the foul mold.

The mold.

Her eyes went wide as realization crashed into her. Something about the air had to have been causing all these blemishes. This room was poisoning her. The longer she had stayed in the room, the more welts that had begun to appear.

Lillian looked at the mold-infested room around her. She couldn't just leave—she still had to finish cleaning.

Her eyes stung as they opened wide, staring at another burning welt forming on her skin. That was enough to send Lillian running out of the room, slamming the door behind her.

The fresh air rushed into her lungs like a river breaking through a dam. The crisp atmosphere jolted her senses, feeling as if she'd chewed a thousand mint leaves all at once. It shocked her that she hadn't noticed how used to the toxic aroma she'd grown.

Hurtling down the stairs, she found the guards waiting at the bottom.

"All done?" one of them asked.

Lillian was nowhere *near* done. She turned her attention to the men as words began to stumble from her mouth. "Well, not *exactly*…"

One guard began shoving her up the stairs. "No excuses, you don't come back down here until you're done." Lillian tried pleading with the man as he kept dragging her up the stairs, but he only shook his head. "I don't make the rules. If you have a problem, take it up with the queen."

Lillian seethed at that statement; she had a lot she wanted to take up with the queen.

After battling her to the top, he opened the door, ready to throw her in, but the man loosened his grip on her as he peered into the room.

"So you are done. Why didn't you just say that?"

Lillian shoved past the guard as she tried to see what he was talking about. She hadn't been anywhere close to done when she'd left.

Her head jerked back as she took in the room—it was spotless, not a speck of mold in sight. The surfaces that had previously been overrun actually shined with how pristine they looked. No way—there was absolutely no way—she could have ever made it look this good even if she had somehow survived the intoxicating smell.

The room sparkled as her jaw hung loose in awe. She hadn't done this. But that only left one question—who did?

CHAPTER 40

The burning question was left unanswered as the guards led her back through the halls.

Why would anyone want to help her? All the Ilaidae were the same, each one just as debased as their queen. The only person she could even fathom for a second didn't carry the same darkness was Nillipa, but she had only known the maid for mere moments and couldn't be certain. Nillipa also had no reason to help her, and she doubted the maid would endanger her life for someone she hardly knew.

Thoughts continued to swirl in her mind as massive regal wooden doors appeared in the distance. She squinted her eyes and could make out a design of swirling flames glowing brightly off the onyx doors. Steady beatings of drums came from the other side as a leeching cold slithered past her nape the nearer she got.

She knew what laid across them.

With an excruciating slowness, the guards pulled open the doors, revealing what appeared to be an enormous arena. Shadows adorned the chamber as there were no windows, the area only illuminated by hanging pots of flames that littered the ampitheater. Crowds of Ilaidae howled in the stands above at her entrance, their feral roars all blending into one.

But the audience with their vicious grins and cruel faces was the least of her concerns as her attention was drawn to the center of the room.

The color was sucked out of her face as she noticed a large rectangular pool carved into the floor of the pit. As if swimming wasn't a death sentence enough, the pool was massive, stretching sixty feet long.

Her insides started to contort as Lillian walked the vast expanse of the arena to the queen that sat upon an elevated platform across the room. Lillian kept her face neutral as she made her way to the queen and her brother, the rows of Ilaidae screeching and hollering as she passed. She did what she could to rein in her growing anxiety, but deep inside she knew that no matter what happened, this wouldn't end well.

Lillian didn't bother with any pleasantries as she stood before Allania, the queen looking her up and down. Sitting up taller—the dull lighting making her a thousand times more frightening—a sneer surfaced across the queen's face. "Ready for a dip, my darling?"

A jab of pain struck her insides as bile began scraping its way up her throat. She swallowed down that fear as she tried to keep herself from falling apart entirely.

Her mind went numb as she kept her eyes focused on the queen, not even bothering a glance over at Nolan. But it didn't matter whether she looked at him or not, she knew what she would find there. The mere thought of him made her violently ill; she wanted nothing to do with him.

Forcing her attention onto the queen, she nodded, her voice coming out more shaken than she'd intended. "Ye-yes."

Allania smiled. "Feeling a little nervous?"

Her face burned red as the queen ridiculed her, the mocking arising howls from the crowd.

Allania rose and slinked over to where Lillian stood, grabbing her by the forearm. With Lillian in her grasp, she turned to face the stands as she raised up both their arms and yelled to the audience around them. "Iavothae, do you accept this *meek*, *lowly* mortal to be your champion?"

The Ilaidae went wild as they all began to yell in incoherent phrases.

Ice brushed past her ear as Allania leaned in and whispered, "Looks like it's too late to back out now."

The queen turned back to address the mass of Ilaidae surrounding the room. "Who here thinks *poor*, *innocent* Miss Echethier will succumb to her fear? Let me hear you now, loud and clear!"

The crowd went feral, howling and roaring as Allania paraded her around in a circle, showing her how little they all thought of her. Not a single soul in the stands wasn't screaming and cheering for her demise.

On the verge of closing her eyes—not wanting to see another Ilaidae that craved her death with such a vicious ferocity—her eyes landed on the man standing on the elevated platform.

Nolan.

His face was stern as his gaze bore into hers with those haunting eyes. He just stood there, utterly silent, as the crowd around him went savage with glee.

Why wasn't he cheering?

Allania whisked her away from him as she faced her towards the pool of water. The tyrant's voice whispered past her ear, causing a chill to echo through her as it came out laced with venom. "See how little they think of you—see how they *thirst* for your failure."

The queen grabbed her, nails digging into her skin, as she dragged her before the pool.

Up close, she could see three descending ledges before it dropped down into an endless abyss. Allania shoved her down the first step before turning to address the audience once more. "Are you ready for your champion to complete her trial?"

The swarm of Ilaidae roared in anticipation as Allania whirled towards her, teeth bared in a vicious grin. "*Swim*, Lillian."

Ice leached into her bones as she gaped at her feet in the cold water.

Those two simple words made her breaths turn quick and shallow as she felt a pounding inside her chest. A sticky pale adorned her skin as her eyes began darting around the arena, her gaze noticing all the cruel faces chanting her name as laughter rang out all around her.

Lillian's stomach dropped as she took another step down, getting deeper into the pool. Cold sweat beaded down her temple as she felt the water reach her shins.

This couldn't be it; she needed more time. Lillian's head whirled around the room, desperate for a way out of this. This couldn't be the trial. There had to be something else—something she could actually *win*.

"*Now*, Lillian," commanded the queen. "You *know* I don't like waiting."

Another step down. The water rushed up to her knees. It was the last step separating her from the murky water. And when she went off the ledge, she knew there would be no bottom. It would simply be a matter of swimming or death—and her fate would be the latter.

Allania groaned from behind her. "Pathetic."

Wild trembles jolted through her body as she lifted her foot to step off into the depths. Her chest tightened as she began hyperventilating, air unable to reach her lungs.

Quaking violently, she set her foot back down as tears began streaming down her face. She tried to speak but only stutters came out as her mouth refused to cooperate. Shame coated her bones as she hung her head low in defeat. Allania had been right—she was pathetic.

A depraved laugh came out from behind her as she heard that awful voice. "You really are such a sad little girl. But don't worry—I'll give you a hand."

Lillian lifted up her head as her eyes went wide. That same rush of wind that had shoved her in the courtyard, came out from behind her as it thrust her into the watery abyss.

The murky liquid rose up all around her as she sank deeper and deeper.

In a desperate attempt, she flailed her arms out, but it was no use as she felt her legs stiffen, turning into dead weights that would drag her down into the depths. Holding her breath, she clawed at the water looking for anything to grab onto, but there was nothing.

Her eyes darted around, looking for something—*anything* that would help—but all she saw was the same muddy pool any direction she turned.

Her eyes welled up as the panic began to overwhelm her—could she even cry in the water? Lillian felt like she was sobbing as she continued to thrash her arms out.

This was it—this was the end. All her hard work—everything she went through, everything she had *suffered*—had been for nothing.

Her lungs began to tighten as she recognized her air was running out. Lillian stopped moving her arms. It was no use.

Accepting her fate, she clamped her eyes shut, letting herself drift farther into the water, ashamed that this was how it all would end.

CHAPTER 41

The pressure in her chest only intensified as she descended farther into the watery depths. She didn't feel like fighting anymore; there was no point. Her legs would refuse to budge no matter how much she wanted them to.

A venomous darkness began seeping into her veins. She had gone through all this suffering for *nothing*; she had survived all these awful things for *nothing*. All this to just be killed by her own stupid fear. She would have chuckled at the irony had her panic not been so severe.

It was absurd how much she deserved this, to die like this. If not just for the sheer stupidity of trying to be champion, then for what she had done to her father—for the torment she had forced him endure.

Lillian wanted to wail in agony, her heart hurting too much as the anguish burned inside her.

Sealing her eyes shut, she waited for the small amount of air she had left to finally give out—she was done with this life. Her chest tightened even more, and she knew it was almost time.

More bleak thoughts began churning around in her broken mind, but they all stopped as something small bounced off her cheek. Lillian opened her eyes, trying to see what had hit her, as her gaze landed on a small wooden band.

The ring Peter had made her was floating right beside her.

Lillian lunged out her hands as she reached out to grab it, and she twisted it around her fingers, a thousand memories rushing past her brain.

Anytime she saw the ring, anytime she thought of Peter really, she was forced to remember that awful night by the woods. The night of her birthday when that monster had murdered Peter, and she had been utterly useless as he lay there dying. Useless like she had been yesterday when her father had been tortured and killed right before her.

A switch flipped in her mind as she stared at the wooden band.

This wasn't about her. If she died right now, then she was condemning all of Grigaros to the same fate Peter and her father had been tormented with.

That couldn't happen.

Lillian looked up and saw the hanging pots of flames in the distance. She wasn't allowed to die yet, no matter how much she wanted to. She had to live first. That damned wish would be hers even if it was the last thing she ever did.

But after that…

She made a silent promise to herself that she would go back into those woods and let whatever creature she came across first tear her to shreds and put her out of this infernal misery.

But she couldn't leave this world yet. She wouldn't let her family or any other human go through what Peter and her father suffered—what *she* had suffered.

Something deep inside her rumbled to life, a key clicking into place. Power reverberated through her bones as a feeling of resolve settled inside her. She slipped the ring onto her finger and shoved that stupid fear out of her mind—there was no place for it here.

Lillian flailed her arms out to the side, straining as she compelled her legs to obey. Thoughts of Peter, her father, and all those who had been subject to the horrors of the Ilaidae flashed in her mind. She wasn't fighting for herself—she was fighting for *all of them.*

Her legs started to move.

All the horrible things the Ilaidae had done burned her soul as she reminded herself of her purpose. More energy soared into her blood.

The surface was getting closer.

She thought of Peter and her father until it hurt so much that she let out a muffled scream underneath the water. Her legs moved in tandem with her arms as the hanging flames got closer. She was doing it; she was swimming.

Her head broke the surface, and Lillian gasped for air as she continued to thrash her way across the pool.

She didn't even want to know what she looked like; she was swimming, but *barely*. Her head threatened to go under after each stroke as she constantly reminded her legs to keep kicking.

A newfound feeling of power ignited in her veins as she made her way closer to the ledge.

Lillian lunged out a hand and clawed onto the edge of the pool as she used her remaining bits of strength to haul herself out. Water spewed from her lungs as she lay on the floor coughing and struggling to catch her breath.

On shaking knees, she pulled herself up as she wiped the wet hair plastered to her face.

The crowd was no longer cheering as they went mute, everyone turning their attention to their queen. A look of wrath radiated off her as she glared at Lillian.

The ruler was a terrifying sight, but Lillian wasn't sure who to look at as she caught a glimpse of Nolan in her gaze.

As if frozen in time, he went completely rigid, those dark irises locking on to hers. His eyes had gone wide with shock, and his nostrils flared as the tanned face he usually wore paled. He took a stumbling step back as if something about her had stunned him.

Lillian was taken aback at how plainly he was showing his emotions, but her head jerked back to Allania as the queen began to roar. "LIAR! Admit that you cheated!"

Cheated? How could she have possibly cheated?

The queen continued to ramble in rage. "You said swimming was your greatest fear, but that was all a clever deception, wasn't it." The Ilaidae ruler barked a crazed laugh as she continued. "You were rather cunning for a mortal, but you weren't devious enough to fool me."

Lillian had no idea what the deranged maniac was going on about—did she think she had *lied* about swimming being her greatest fear?

Allania didn't give Lillian a chance to speak or deny any of her claims as she yelled out for her guards. "I want her brought to me. *Now*."

Lillian's face dropped at all she had said. Her head whipped all around the arena as she looked for a way to escape—but everywhere she looked there were more guards. If she bolted in any direction, they would catch her. She was stuck. There wasn't a thing she could do as two guards picked her up and dragged her to the queen.

Screams of how she hadn't lied or cheated burst out of her, but the Ilaidae ruler ignored her shrieks as she walked up to her and looked her in the eyes. "I don't know how you did it, but I will *not* be made to look a fool."

Her entire body thrashed as she stared at the queen. "I *won.*" Lillian had to have had a death wish as she bared her teeth at Allania and spit in her face. "Give me my *wish,* you wretched bitch."

The queen's eyes went wide as she staggered back a step—Lillian gathered no one had ever treated her with such blatant disrespect.

Specks of saliva glistened on Allania's face as she began to walk away, but she made it only ten feet before she whipped around, wrath flashing across her face as she addressed her guards. "*Tear out her throat.*"

CHAPTER 42

Pure unending panic rushed through her as she tried to process the ruler's command. The guard's grasps were unflinching as she flailed against their strength.

Oh gods—she was going to die.

One of the Ilaidae men unsheathed his weapon, and her face blanched as she noticed how sharp it was. Time began to slow as she watched the small dagger, her entire self thrashing as the blade inched closer and closer to her neck.

She hadn't *lied.* She *won*—she had actually won. And this, this was her prize?

Every part of her contorted as she tried anything to get away, but no matter how much she bit, kicked, or slashed, they stayed their ground like mountains weathering a hurricane.

Lillian fought back frustrated tears as she screamed. This wasn't fair. It couldn't end this way. Shrieks filled with fury and anguish filled the chambers. Her raw voice, laced with rage carried through the arena, so powerful that it vibrated the castle's walls.

No—that should be impossible. She wasn't the only one screaming.

Her lids pulled back as she watched the dagger nearing her neck go flying as the Ilaidae's wrist holding it snapped. More sounds of bone cracking came from behind her as the man grabbing her let go all at once. She leaped out of his grasp and looked back to see both of the guards' necks broken, their lifeless bodies lying still on the floor.

The cruel faces in the stands, chanting for her demise, disappeared as a fear bled into the Ilaidae's features. Rumbles shook the entire arena as the flames lining the room flickered, a darkness dancing around them that threatened to swallow everything whole.

"No one—*touches* her."

Lillian whirled to look at that voice. At… Nolan.

Power, pure unleashed power reverberated through the chamber as he spoke. There was an intensity to his words, to his vicious command, that if she hadn't known him, she would've thought he cared, would've thought she mattered.

His jaw was clenched to the point of shattering as his knuckles turned white from how hard they were clamped at his sides.

Allania's fury grew even wilder as she stared at her brother with gritted teeth. "Care to explain why you say that, *brother*."

He locked eyes with Lillian for a mere moment, a fervor glowing inside them as they blazed a deep red. But both the emotion and color disappeared as he willed his features to relax. He slid his hands into his pockets and sauntered over to his sister as his voice reverted to normal.

"We can't sentence her to death quite yet. If it turns out she had been telling the truth and we denied her the wish…"

Allania's brows knitted tight in thought.

Did something bad happen if they broke a rule?

With an uncharacteristic gentleness, she brought a hand up and caressed her brother's cheek. "You're right. It seems I let my anger cloud my judgement." Looking up at her brother, she batted her eyelashes. "Thank you for looking out for me," she said with a delicate smile that looked all wrong on her face.

The gentle demeanor crumbled to pieces as the queen tore her gaze away from her brother. "We'll throw her back in her cell for now while I figure out what to do with her."

Guards began to walk her way, ready to drag her back into that prison.

Allania glared at her with malicious eyes as a demonic grin washed away any trace of that kind facade. "But there's no sense in not letting her suffer just a little bit."

The tyrant glanced past her, and Lillian spun to see a fist flying right at her face. She fell to the floor, a foot colliding with her rib as she screamed out in agony. A boot crashed into her face, and a loud crack echoed through her body as she felt her nose give way to the pressure. Another foot came shooting at her side, and she cried out as she heard her ribs fracture.

Sharp pains undulated through her as she struggled to breathe, blow after blow landing somewhere new on her already battered body. Blood leaked from her mouth as she felt another kick go straight to her stomach.

Lillian wailed in pain, but she was silenced as another punch slammed into her face. She remembered tasting metal as the room around her disappeared.

CHAPTER 43

Lillian awoke back in her dungeon cell with only the dull flame of the torch lighting the room. Spots danced in her vision as she lay propped up against the stone wall, and she winced as she soon realized everything hurt. The feeling of the cool stone felt nice on her injured skin, and she tried shifting to her other side but stopped as a pang of nausea threatened to overtake her completely. She could only open one of her eyes as the other one was swollen shut.

With gentle fingers, she brought a hand to touch her face, trying to deduce where the damage was, but she regretted the attempt as she was instantly reminded how her nose had been fractured.

Yelps of pain filled the cell as she clenched her jaw tight, causing yet another wave of agony to go through her. Her head throbbed violently, and she wanted to double over each time she took in a breath through her shattered ribcage. She tried moving her legs and was surprised to find that neither one of them were broken, but she didn't let herself get too excited as she knew everywhere on her body was horribly bruised, every inch of her aching and purple.

A distraction, that's what she needed. She forced herself to try and think of the positives, something to get her mind off the searing pain, but instead tears began emerging in her eyes, causing her already torn up face to sting.

There were no positives. Lillian couldn't even wipe her damp eyes without crying out. All she could do was sit there and taste the coppery tang of blood coating her tongue.

Gods, she never should have come here.

Her bandaged forearm began to pulse with sharp pains. It seemed like the magical little vial had run out, just like her luck had so long ago.

She just wanted it to be over. She prayed she would get some sort of infection and let it take her away. She had lived through far enough; she just wanted peace.

Lillian sobbed as she replayed the trial in her mind. She won—she had conquered her fear and *won*.

But what good did that do her? All it got her was battered and bruised in a dungeon cell as she waited for a blood thirsty Ilaidae to decide her fate.

Familiar warped thoughts swarmed her mind as she wished she still had her dagger to just end it all now. She knew she could never actually do it, but that didn't stop the idea from poisoning her mind.

Death didn't sound too bad now. She *had* almost died back there. The queen had been so caught up in her rage that she had ordered her throat to be torn out right then and there.

Her brows furrowed, the simple motion causing her face to feel like it was in flames as she imagined what had followed next.

Nolan—*Nolan* had stopped them. She would never understand that man. How it seemed he cared for her one minute and then did unspeakable acts the next.

Lillian didn't have the energy to think of what happened at the feast, didn't feel like crying about that horrible night any longer.

She laid her head back against the cold wall and prayed that her death would come swiftly. It was time for her to go.

Closing her eyes, she tried to drift off but was unable to as she heard a jangling at her cell door. She lifted her head, trying her best to ignore the twinge of nausea and black spots as she opened her one good eye at the rungs.

A cloaked man crept in and held out his hand as he spoke in a deep and hushed tone. "It's time to leave, Lillian."

CHAPTER 44

The cloaked man took a step closer, and Lillian raised her fists in a poor attempt to defend herself. She mentally scolded herself as she failed to hide the wince the action caused her. "Who are you? Wh-What do you want?"

The man knelt down to her level and pulled back the hood of his cloak to reveal his face. The cell was rather dim, but she could make out a toned man with long black hair pulled into a bun before her. His voice came out low and commanding in a way that made her heart skip a beat. "I'm here to get you out."

He reached out to take her hand, but Lillian shimmied away. This could be another trick sent by Allania made to torture her mind even more. "And how am I supposed to know you're telling the truth?"

The stranger narrowed his eyes at her in an obvious annoyance that he hadn't even bothered trying to hide "I don't know; take my word for it?"

Lillian scoffed; she'd heard that one plenty of times. She began scooting away, each shuffle sending another wave of agony through her injured frame. "Yeah, I don't think so."

He stood and put his leg next to where she was dragging herself towards. "Listen here," he ground out, jaw clenched in irritation. "I'm not really supposed to be here, and you're not being very helpful. So let's just make this simple and get up and go."

A snap lined her voice as she began to scoot in the other direction. "Wow, does that line work on all the ladies or just the ones you find in cells?"

Grunting a low curse, he went to put his leg on the other side of her, stopping her motions once more. "He warned me you would be difficult," he muttered under his breath as he rolled his eyes.

Lillian looked up at him, wincing as she raised a brow. What, *he*, was the cloaked man referring to? Did someone send him to get her?

She was rifling her mind at who could possibly come searching for her as the man knelt down to look at her. "Look, I want this to be as easy as possible. What can I do to make you come with me?"

Tilting her head to the side, she pondered his words. What *could* he do to prove that he had good intentions? Lillian thought on it for a few seconds until the perfect thing came to mind. "I want the dog."

His eyebrows squished together. "You want me to get you a dog?"

"Dogs," she said, emphasizing the *s*. "Plural. And not just any dogs. I want you to release the six dogs that are meant to be fed to the snake."

The stranger looked at her as if she had told him to carve out his own heart. "You want me to go *all* the way down there and sneak back six dogs through this castle? I don't know if I mentioned this part already—*but I'm not really supposed to be here*."

Lillian shook her head. "No, I only want you to bring back one. It's got pointed ears and black fur."

His head bobbed up and down, mocking her. "Yes, very specific. I'm sure all the dogs aren't black with pointed ears."

She cut a glare in his direction. "If you had let me *finish*, I would have told you that it has one blue eye and one orange. Bring me that one and let the rest of them go. They don't deserve to be snake food."

Standing up, he began pacing around the room as he brought his hands up to his face while muttering a string of curses in between phrases. "Gods, I should've let Fenric come."

Never had she heard of a Fenric. Could he be the one who sent for her or was it perhaps a codename that they had made up?

The unknown male turned back to look at her as he gritted his teeth. Lillian matched his stare with an equal level of defiance. They stayed like that for a few moments until he exhaled and groaned. "You are *so* lucky he said not to harm a hair on that pretty little head or you would already be knocked out and slung over my shoulder."

Lillian rolled her one eye. "My what a gentleman. You really broke out the manners just for me, didn't you?"

Shaking his head, he glared at her sarcastic tone. "I'll be back in half an hour. *Stay. Put*." The aggravated man stormed out of the cell, shutting the door behind him.

A million thoughts circled her brain as she sat alone in her quiet prison. Who was he? Who had sent for her? What did they even want with her?

Lillian shut her eyes as the thoughts began pounding in her head. She hadn't noticed how tired she was as the action of closing her lids caused her to start nodding off.

Wondering if the unfamiliar man would return, she let her drained body get some rest.

It had felt like mere seconds since she'd fallen asleep when she was awoken to a wet feeling on her arm. Opening her one decent eye, she saw a mass of black fur lying against her as it continued to lick her forearm. The dog lifted its face, those familiar blue and orange eyes staring back at her.

With a twinge of pain, she lifted her hand and gave the dog a nice scratch on the head, but her attention was drawn to her other side as she heard an impatient cough.

The cloaked man held out his palm. "I did what you wanted. Now, Let's. Go."

Lillian couldn't believe he had actually fulfilled her request—and seeing as she had no better option, she reached out her hand, letting the man haul her on to her feet.

What a huge mistake that had been.

An overwhelming surge of nausea coursed through her as her head began to pound with anger. Her knees began shaking as black spots started to invade her vision, growing larger until everything turned black. She felt her legs start to give in, causing her to collapse towards the floor.

But she never did collide with the harsh stone as she felt strong arms catch her, cradling her tightly. The cloaked man carried her as curses careened past his tongue. "I should've let you stand up. I *literally* should have just let you try and stand up."

She heard a whimper come from the dog, and those were the last things she registered as she felt herself pass out in the stranger's comforting arms.

Her eyes fluttered open as she regained consciousness. Immediately, she noticed that she wasn't lying on the floor of her cell anymore. Using her one good eye, she could see that she was lying on a lush cream-colored mattress that did wonders for her aching back.

Gods, she couldn't recall the last time she had slept on a bed.

Scanning the room, she noticed that it resembled a cabin, the walls made of series of wooden panels. A nightstand with two flower vases laid to her right along with a large candle that did plenty to illuminate the small room. Two more vases filled with pink lilies sat on her left, both lying atop another side table

Lillian lifted her hand to rub at her eye but stopped as she noticed bandages coating her. Looking at her entire body, she could see more pieces of gauze and cloth covering all the areas that had been bruised or bleeding. Another bandage covered her nose as she reached up to touch it.

What fascinated her the most of it all was that none of it hurt. Someone must have given her another one of those nifty little vials that took away all her pain—she really needed to figure out what was in those things.

Lillian sat herself up on the bed, amazed at how much better she felt, but noticed that something was new. Somehow, she felt stronger, more powerful. It was as if the blood in her veins teemed with energy. She didn't know if that made any sense—perhaps it was just those vials that had affected her in some way.

Deciding to move on from whatever that was, she looked down at the rest of herself. A white tunic and dark green pants clothed her body. She was glad that she was finally out of her filthy garments but wasn't too pleased knowing that someone had disrobed her.

She threw the sheets off of her and was about to get up and take a look around when she heard muffled voices coming from behind the door. Sounds of someone yelling leaked in from underneath the frame. It was the cloaked man's voice. Lillian had no idea how she was able to hear what he was saying so clearly from all the way across the room, but she continued to listen as he spoke in that aggravated tone she noticed he favored. "Gods, how many times do I have to tell you. *I didn't touch her*. She passed out on her own. I mean, for Ildara's sake, take a look at the girl. She was already bruised up enough. I even went and got that stupid dog for her. That wasn't easy considering someone got me *banished*."

Grumbles and a set of footsteps retreating from the door was all she heard in response.

Lillian's eyes darted to the doorknob as she saw it starting to turn. Her entire body cringed as the screeching hinges from the door creaked open, causing a sharpness to stab her newly sensitive ears.

A tall man with raven hair and a beautifully toned physique waltzed in through the door. She noticed he wore simpler clothes than she was used to as he glanced at her propped up on the bed. Those stunning ocean eyes locked onto hers as the smirk she knew all too well emerged onto that devastatingly handsome face.

Nolan parted his lips, that tantalizing deep voice rumbling out, “Did you miss me, Lil?”

ACKNOWLEDGMENTS

There are a few people in particular that I want to thank for making this book happen. It's all been so wondrous creating this, and I'd like to extend my infinite appreciation to the following:

To JT, my boyfriend, my partner, and my other half. I can't begin to say how much I love you. Besides meaning the world to me, I can't thank you enough for putting up with me these past few months. I know me slightly ignoring you when I'd get hyper focused on writing or editing (I can't multi-task) might be construed as annoying. Or perhaps some might see it as obnoxious when I'd shriek and burst your eardrums whenever you'd try and peek at what I was typing away at on my laptop. But you took all of that and more in stride and put up with all my quirks and when I'd scream that my book wasn't ready to be seen by your eyes yet. There will never be enough words to describe what you mean to me. Never forget how important you are.

To Rachel, my coffee and book club partner, my best friend, and my soul sister. I'll never be able to thank you enough. I can remember the day you inspired me so clearly. We were having dinner at our favorite sushi place, and for some strange but incredible reason you asked me if I had ever thought of writing a book. That night I came up with a thousand ideas and it was all because of you. I don't remember exactly what day, but I think it was the very next when we went to get coffee on a Saturday morning, like we usually do, and I told you all about my ideas. You were my first reader and the person who pushed and encouraged me. For that I will be eternally grateful to you.

To Isabella, my sister, my best friend since day one (yes, a person can have two), fantasy romance partner in crime, and number one fan. I couldn't have done this without you either. Even though Rachel technically read my beginning few chapters first, you were the first to finish it. I remember producing the rough drafts—and boy were they *very* rough—and you being so eager to read them that you'd start reading as soon as I'd finished typing the last word on a chapter. I can still picture you sitting across the couch from me giggling, laughing, and getting mad in all the right places. Thank you and I can't wait for you to read the next one.

To Fabian, the best dad and editor a girl could ever ask for. You were the person who introduced me to fantasy. I can recall sitting in the patio—I had to be around seven or nine—and you asking Isabella and I if RPG sounded interesting to us. After that moment, it was all history. Thank you for not only reading but editing my entire book (I knew having a geeky dad would come in handy one day). And thank you for helping me come up with ideas whenever I'd get stuck. Thank you for everything.

To my wonderful artists, Chris Stanzione, my map maker, and

Patricia Pria, my front cover artist. I can't thank you both enough for creating such incredible pieces of art for me. Simply being able to see what I had in mind come alive is amazing enough, and you both did that for me and more.

Lastly, I want to thank whoever is reading this. The fact that anyone could be reading this is bizarre to me. But whoever is reading this, I hope you enjoy it. It's been a dream come true being able to bring the story and the characters in my mind to life. I hope you love them as much as I do because there is so much more yet to come.

AN AUTHOR'S WORD OF ADVICE

If you are an aspiring author or already are one, then here is some of my advice. Don't ever get discouraged or think that your book is not enough. Writing is a feat, and even being able to create a single paragraph is incredible. Know that we all must start somewhere, and it all starts with a simple thought.

Here is the one that started it all for me:

You are either born into a magical bloodline or you can gain magic through an incredible/selfless feat(something intense).

ABOUT THE AUTHOR

Vanessa is a new—and I mean *very* new—author, and she is thrilled and honored that you even gave her book a chance. The fact that she even created this is absurd to her, and she is absolutely terrified that she actually went through with publishing it (but a good terrified).

After years of devouring and hoarding countless fantasy and romance books, she finally decided to go through with making one. She hopes that this book touches your heart in at least a fraction of the way it did hers.

And if you ever meet her in public, and you pry just enough, she might just end up spilling all the secrets of the books yet to come because she is terrible with spoilers.

But above all, she can't wait to share the next few stories.

Made in the USA
Columbia, SC
20 February 2024